The Great King

Also by Christian Cameron

The Great King

CHRISTIAN CAMERON

First published in Great Britain in 2014 by Orion Books,
an imprint of The Orion Publishing Group Ltd
Orion House, 5 Upper Saint Martin's Lane
London WC2H 9EA

An Hachette UK Company

1 3 5 7 9 10 8 6 4 2

A CIP catalogue record for this book
is available from the British Library.

ISBN (Hardback) 978 1 4091 1414 7
ISBN (Export Trade Paperback) 978 1 4091 1415 4
ISBN (Ebook) 978 1 4091 1416 1

Typeset by Deltatype Ltd, Birkenhead, Merseyside

Printed in Great Britain by CPI Group (UK) Ltd,
Croydon CRO 4YY

The Orion Publishing Group's policy is to use papers
that are natural, renewable and recyclable products and
made from wood grown in sustainable forests. The logging
and manufacturing processes are expected to conform to
the environmental regulations of the country of origin.

www.orionbooks.co.uk

For the Persians

Glossary

I am an *amateur* Greek scholar. My definitions are my own, but taken from the LSJ or Routeledge's *Handbook of Greek Mythology* or Smith's *Classical Dictionary*. On some military issues I have the temerity to disagree with the received wisdom on the subject. Also check my website at www.hippeis.com for more information and some helpful pictures

Akinakes A Scythian short sword or long knife, also sometimes carried by Medes and Persians.

Andron The 'men's room' of a proper Greek house – where men have symposia. Recent research has cast real doubt as to the sexual exclusivity of the room, but the name sticks.

Apobatai The Chariot Warriors. In many towns, towns that hadn't used chariots in warfare for centuries, the *Apobatai* were the elite three hundred or so. In Athens, they competed in special events; in Thebes, they may have been the forerunners of the Sacred Band.

Archon A city's senior official or, in some cases, one of three or four. A magnate.

Aspis The Greek hoplite's shield (which is not called a hoplon!).

The *aspis* is about a yard in diameter, is deeply dished (up to six inches deep) and should weigh between eight and sixteen pounds.

Basileus An aristocratic title from a bygone era (at least in 500 BC) that means 'king' or 'lord'.

Bireme A warship rowed by two tiers of oars, as opposed to a *trireme*, which has three tiers.

Chiton The standard tunic for most men, made by taking a single continuous piece of cloth and folding it in half, pinning the shoulders and open side. Can be made quite fitted by means of pleating. Often made of very fine quality material – usually wool, sometimes linen, especially in the upper classes. A full *chiton* was ankle length for men and women.

Chitoniskos A small *chiton*, usually just longer than modesty demanded – or not as long as modern modesty would demand! Worn by warriors and farmers, often heavily bloused and very full by warriors to pad their armour. Usually wool.

Chlamys A short cloak made from a rectangle of cloth roughly 60 by 90 inches – could also be worn as a *chiton* if folded and pinned a different way. Or slept under as a blanket.

Corslet / Thorax In 500 BC, the best *corslets* were made of bronze, mostly of the so-called 'bell' *thorax* variety. A few muscle *corslets* appear at the end of this period, gaining popularity into the 450s. Another style is the 'white' *corslet*, seen to appear just as the Persian Wars begin – re-enactors call this the 'Tube and Yoke' *corslet*, and some people call it (erroneously) the *linothorax*. Some of them may have been made of linen – we'll never know – but the likelier material is Athenian leather, which was often tanned and finished with alum, thus being bright white. Yet another style was a tube and yoke of scale, which you can see the author wearing on his website. A scale *corslet* would have been the most expensive of all, and probably provided the best protection.

Daidala Cithaeron, the mountain that towered over Plataea, was the site of a remarkable fire-festival, the *Daidala*, which was celebrated by the Plataeans on the summit of the mountain. In the usual ceremony, as mounted by the Plataeans in every seventh year, a wooden idol (*daidalon*) would be dressed in bridal robes and dragged on an ox-cart from Plataea to the top of the mountain, where it would be burned after appropriate rituals. Or, in the *Great Daidala*, which were celebrated every forty-nine years, fourteen *daidala* from different Boeotian towns would be burned on a large wooden pyre heaped with brushwood, together with a cow and a bull that were sacrificed to Zeus and Hera. This huge pyre on the mountain top must have provided a most impressive spectacle; Pausanias remarks that he knew of no other flame that rose as high or could be seen from so far.

The cultic legend that was offered to account for the festival ran as follows. When Hera had once quarrelled with Zeus, as she often did, she had withdrawn to her childhood home of Euboea and had refused every attempt at reconciliation. So Zeus sought the advice of the wisest man on earth, Cithaeron (the eponym of the mountain), who ruled at Plataea in the earliest times. Cithaeron advised him to make a wooden image of a woman, to veil it in the manner of a bride, and then to have it drawn along in an ox-cart after spreading the rumour that he was planning to marry the nymph Plataea, a daughter of the river god Asopus. When Hera rushed to the scene and tore away the veils, she was so relieved to find a wooden effigy rather than the expected bride that she at last consented to be reconciled with Zeus. (Routledge *Handbook of Greek Mythology*, pp. 137–8)

Daimon Literally a spirit, the *daimon* of combat might be adrenaline, and the *daimon* of philosophy might simply be native intelligence. Suffice it to say that very intelligent men – like Socrates – believed that god-sent spirits could infuse a man and influence his actions.

Daktyloi Literally digits or fingers, in common talk 'inches' in the system of measurement. Systems differed from city to city. I have taken the liberty of using just the Athenian units.

Despoina Lady. A term of formal address.

Diekplous A complex naval tactic about which some debate remains. In this book, the *Diekplous*, or through stroke, is commenced with an attack by the ramming ship's bow (picture the two ships approaching bow to bow or head on) and cathead on the enemy oars. Oars were the most vulnerable

part of a fighting ship, something very difficult to imagine unless you've rowed in a big boat and understand how lethal your own oars can be – to you! After the attacker crushes the enemy's oars, he passes, flank to flank, and then turns when astern, coming up easily (the defender is almost dead in the water) and ramming the enemy under the stern or counter as desired.

Doru A spear, about ten feet long, with a bronze butt-spike.

Eleutheria Freedom.

Ephebe A young, free man of property. A young man in training to be a *hoplite*. Usually performing service to his city and, in ancient terms, at one of the two peaks of male beauty.

Eromenos The 'beloved' in a same-sex pair in ancient Greece. Usually younger, about seventeen. This is a complex, almost dangerous subject in the modern world – were these pair-bonds about sex, or chivalric love, or just a 'brotherhood' of warriors? I suspect there were elements of all three. And to write about this period without discussing the *eromenos/erastes* bond would, I fear, be like putting all the warriors in steel armour instead of bronze . . .

Erastes The 'lover' in a same-sex pair bond – the older man, a tried warrior, twenty-five to thirty years old.

Eudaimonia Literally 'well-spirited'. A feeling of extreme joy.

Exhedra The porch of the women's quarters – in some cases, any porch over a farm's central courtyard.

Helots The 'race of slaves' of Ancient Sparta – the conquered peoples who lived with the Spartiates and did all of their work so that they could concentrate entirely on making war and more Spartans.

Hetaira Literally a 'female companion'. In ancient Athens, a *hetaira* was a courtesan, a highly skilled woman who provided sexual companionship as well as fashion, political advice and music.

Himation A very large piece of rich, often embroidered wool, worn as an outer garment by wealthy citizen women or as a sole garment by older men, especially those in authority.

Hoplite A Greek upper-class warrior. Possession of a heavy spear, a helmet and an *aspis* (see above) and income above the marginal lowest free class were all required to serve as a *hoplite*. Although much is made of the 'citizen soldier' of ancient Greece, it would be fairer to compare *hoplites* to medieval knights than to Roman legionnaires or modern National Guardsmen. Poorer citizens did serve, and sometimes as *hoplites* or marines, but in general, the front ranks were the preserve of upper-class men who could afford the best training and the essential armour.

Hoplitodromos The *hoplite* race, or race in armour. Two *stades* with an *aspis* on your shoulder, a helmet and greaves in the early runs. I've run this race in armour. It is no picnic.

Hoplomachia A *hoplite* contest, or sparring match. Again, there is enormous debate as to when *hoplomachia* came into existence and how much training Greek *hoplites* received. One thing that they didn't do is drill like modern soldiers – there's no mention of it in all of Greek literature. However, they had highly evolved martial arts (see *pankration*) and it is almost certain that *hoplomachia* was a term that referred to 'the martial art of fighting when fully equipped as a *hoplite*'.

Hoplomachos A participant in *hoplomachia*.

Hypaspist Literally 'under the shield'. A squire or military servant – by the time of Arimnestos, the *hypaspist* was usually a younger man of the same class as the *hoplite*.

Kithara A stringed instrument of some complexity, with a hollow body as a soundboard.

Kline A couch.

Kopis The heavy, back-curved sabre of the Greeks. Like a longer, heavier modern kukri or Gurkha knife.

Kore A maiden or daughter.

Kylix A wide, shallow, handled bowl for drinking wine.

Logos Literally 'word'. In pre-Socratic Greek philosophy the word is everything – the power beyond the gods.

Longche A six to seven foot throwing spear, also used for hunting. A *hoplite* might carry a pair of *longchai*, or a single, longer and heavier *doru*.

Machaira A heavy sword or long knife.

Maenads The 'raving ones' – ecstatic female followers of Dionysus.

Mastos A woman's breast. A *mastos* cup is shaped like a woman's breast with a rattle in the nipple – so when you drink, you lick the nipple and the rattle shows that you emptied the cup. I'll leave the rest to imagination . . .

Medimnos A grain measure. Very roughly – 35 to 100 pounds of grain.

Megaron A style of building with a roofed porch.

Navarch An admiral.

Oikia The household – all the family and all the slaves, and sometimes the animals and the farmland itself.

Opson Whatever spread, dip or accompaniment an ancient Greek had with bread.

Pais A child.

Palaestra The exercise sands of the gymnasium.

Pankration The military martial art of the ancient Greeks – an unarmed combat system that bears more than a passing resemblance to modern MMA techniques, with a series of carefully structured blows and domination holds that is, by modern standards, very advanced. Also the basis of the Greek sword and spear-based martial arts. Kicking, punching, wrestling, grappling, on the ground and standing, were all permitted.

Peplos A short over-fold of cloth that women could wear as a hood or to cover the breasts.

Phalanx The full military potential of a town; the actual, formed body of men before a battle (all of the smaller groups formed together made a *phalanx*). In this period, it would be a mistake to imagine a carefully drilled military machine.

Phylarch A file-leader – an officer commanding the four to sixteen men standing behind him in the *phalanx*.

Polemarch The war leader.

Polis The city. The basis of all Greek political thought and expression, the government that was held to be more important – a higher god – than any individual or even family. To this day, when we talk about politics, we're talking about the 'things of our city'.

Porne A prostitute.

Porpax The bronze or leather band that encloses the forearm on a Greek *aspis*.

Psiloi Light infantrymen – usually slaves or adolescent freemen who, in this period, were not organised and seldom had any weapon beyond some rocks to throw.

Pyrrhiche The 'War Dance'. A line dance in armour done by all of the warriors, often very complex. There's reason to believe that the *Pyrrhiche* was the method by which the young were trained in basic martial arts and by which 'drill' was inculcated.

Pyxis A box, often circular, turned from wood or made of metal.

Rhapsode A master-poet, often a performer who told epic works like the *Iliad* from memory.

Satrap A Persian ruler of a province of the Persian Empire.

Skeuophoros Literally a 'shield carrier', unlike the *hypaspist*, this is a slave or freed man who does camp work and carries the armour and baggage.

Sparabara The large wicker shield of the Persian and Mede elite infantry. Also the name of those soldiers.

Spolas Another name for a leather *corslet*, often used for the lion skin of Heracles.

Stade A measure of distance. An Athenian *stade* is about 185 metres.

Strategos In Athens, the commander of one of the ten military tribes. Elsewhere, any senior Greek officer – sometimes the commanding general.

Synaspismos The closest order that *hoplites* could form – so close that the shields overlap, hence 'shield on shield'.

Taxis Any group but, in military terms, a company; I use it for 60 to 300 men.

Thetes The lowest free class – citizens with limited rights.

Thorax See *corslet*.

Thugater Daughter. Look at the word carefully and you'll see the 'daughter' in it . . .

Triakonter A small rowed galley of thirty oars.

Trierarch The captain of a ship – sometimes just the owner or builder, sometimes the fighting captain.

Zone A belt, often just rope or finely wrought cord, but could be a heavy bronze kidney belt for war.

General Note on Names and Personages

This series is set in the very dawn of the so-called Classical Era, often measured from the Battle of Marathon (490 BC). Some, if not most, of the famous names of this era are characters in this series – and that's not happenstance. Athens of this period is as magical, in many ways, as Tolkien's Gondor, and even the quickest list of artists, poets, and soldiers of this era reads like a 'who's who' of western civilization. Nor is the author tossing them together by happenstance – these people were almost all aristocrats, men (and women) who knew each other well – and might be adversaries or friends in need. Names in bold are historical characters – yes, even Arimnestos – and you can get a glimpse into their lives by looking at Wikipedia or Britannia online. For more in-depth information, I recommend Plutarch and Herodotus, to whom I owe a great deal.

Arimnestos of Plataea may – just may – have been Herodotus's source for the events of the Persian Wars. The careful reader will note that Herodotus himself – a scribe from Halicarnassus – appears several times ...

Archilogos – Ephesian, son of Hipponax the poet; a typical Ionian aristocrat, who loves Persian culture and Greek culture too, who serves his city, not some cause of 'Greece' or 'Hellas', and who finds the rule of the Great King fairer and more 'democratic' than the rule of a Greek tyrant.

Arimnestos – Child of Chalkeotechnes and Euthalia.

Aristagoras – Son of Molpagoras, nephew of Histiaeus. Aristagoras led Miletus while Histiaeus was a virtual prisoner of the Great King Darius at Susa. Aristagoras seems to have initiated the Ionian Revolt – and later to have regretted it.

Aristides – Son of Lysimachus, lived roughly 525–468 BC, known later in life as 'The Just'. Perhaps best known as one of the commanders at Marathon. Usually sided with the Aristocratic party.

Artaphernes – Brother of Darius, Great King of Persia, and Satrap of Sardis. A senior Persian with powerful connections.

Behon – A Kelt from Alba; a fisherman and former slave.

Bion – A slave name, meaning 'life'. The most loyal family retainer of the Corvaxae.

Briseis – Daughter of Hipponax, sister of Archilogos.

Calchus – A former warrior, now the keeper of the shrine of the Plataean Hero of Troy, Leitus.

Chalkeotechnes – The Smith of Plataea; head of the family Corvaxae, who claim descent from Herakles.

Chalkidis – Brother of Arimnestos, son of Chalkeotechnes.

Cimon – Son of Miltiades, a professional soldier, sometime pirate, and Athenian aristocrat.

Cleisthenes – was a noble Athenian of the Alcmaeonid family. He is credited with reforming the constitution of ancient Athens and setting it on a democratic footing in 508/7 BC.

Collam – A Gallic lord in the Central Massif at the headwaters of the Seine.

Dano of Croton – Daughter of the philosopher and mathematician Pythagoras.

Darius – King of Kings, the lord of the Persian Empire, brother to Artaphernes.

Doola – Numidian ex-slave.

Draco – Wheelwright and wagon builder of Plataea, a leading man of the town.

Empedocles – A priest of Hephaestus, the Smith God.

Epaphroditos – A warrior, an aristocrat of Lesbos.

Eualcides – A Hero. Eualcidas is typical of a class of aristocratic men – professional warriors, adventurers, occasionally pirates or merchants by turns. From Euboeoa.

Heraclitus – c.535–475 BC. One of the ancient world's most famous philosophers. Born to an aristocratic family, he chose philosophy over political power. Perhaps most famous for his statement about time: 'You cannot step twice into the same river'. His belief that 'strife is justice' and other similar sayings which you'll find scattered through these pages made him a favourite with Nietzsche. His works, mostly now lost, probably established the later philosophy of Stoicism.

Herakleides – An Aeolian, a Greek of Asia Minor. With his brothers Nestor and Orestes, he becomes a retainer – a warrior – in service to Arimnestos. It is easy, when looking at the birth of Greek democracy, to see the whole form of modern government firmly established – but at the time of this book, democracy was less than skin deep and most armies were formed of semi-feudal war bands following an aristocrat.

Heraklides – Aristides' helmsman, a lower-class Athenian who has made a name for himself in war.

Hermogenes – Son of Bion, Arimnestos's slave.

Hesiod – A great poet (or a great tradition of poetry) from Boeotia in Greece, Hesiod's 'Works and Days' and 'Theogony' were widely read in the sixth century and remain fresh today – they are the chief source we have on Greek farming, and this book owes an enormous debt to them.

Hippias – Last tyrant of Athens, overthrown around 510 BC (that is, just around the beginning of this series), Hippias escaped into exile and became a pensioner of Darius of Persia.

Hipponax – 540–c.498 BC. A Greek poet and satirist, considered the inventor of parody. He is supposed to have said 'There are two days when a woman is a pleasure: the day one marries her and the day one buries her'.

Histiaeus – Tyrant of Miletus and ally of Darius of Persia, possible originator of the plan for the Ionian Revolt.

Homer – Another great poet, roughly Hesiod's contemporary (give or take fifty years!) and again, possibly more a poetic tradition than an individual man. Homer is reputed as the author of the *Iliad* and the *Odyssey*, two great epic poems which, between them, largely defined what heroism and aristocratic good behaviour should be in Greek society – and, you might say, to this very day.

Idomeneus – Cretan warrior, priest of Leitus.

Kylix – A boy, slave of Hipponax.

Leukas – Alban sailor, later deck master on *Lydia*. Kelt of the Dumnones of Briton.

Miltiades – Tyrant of the Thracian Chersonese. His son, Cimon or Kimon, rose to be a great man in Athenian politics. Probably the author of the Athenian victory of Marathon, Miltiades was a complex man, a pirate, a warlord, and a supporter of Athenian democracy.

Penelope – Daughter of Chalkeotechnes, sister of Arimnestos.

Polymarchos – ex-slave swordmaster of Syracusa.

Phrynicus – Ancient Athenian playwright and warrior.

Sappho – A Greek poetess from the island of Lesbos, born sometime around 630 BC and died between 570 and 550 BC. Her father was probably Lord of Eressos. Widely considered the greatest lyric poet of Ancient Greece.

Seckla – Numidian ex-slave.

Simonalkes – Head of the collateral branch of the Plataean Corvaxae, cousin to Arimnestos.

Simonides – Another great lyric poet, he lived *c.*556–468 BC, and his nephew, Bacchylides, was as famous as he. Perhaps best known for his epigrams, one of which is:

> Ω ξεῖν᾽, ἀγγέλλειν Λακεδαιμονίοις ὅτι τῇδε
> κείμεθα, τοῖς κείνων ῥήμασι πειθόμενοι.
> *Go tell the Spartans, thou who passest by,*
> *That here, obedient to their laws, we lie.*

Thales – *c.*624–*c.*546 BC The first philosopher of the Greek tradition, whose writings were still current in Arimnestos's time. Thales used geometry to solve problems such as calculating the height of the pyramids in Aegypt and the distance of ships from the shore. He made at least one trip to Aegypt. He is widely accepted as the founder of western mathematics.

Themistocles – Leader of the demos party in Athens, father of the Athenian Fleet. Political enemy of Aristides.

Theognis – Theognis of Megara was almost certainly not one man but a whole canon of aristocratic poetry under that name, much of it practical. There are maxims, many very wise, laments on the decline of man and the age, and the woes of old age and poverty, songs for symposia, etc. In later sections there are songs and poems about homosexual love and laments for failed romances. Despite widespread attributions, there was, at some point, a real Theognis who may have lived in the mid-6th century BC, or just before the events of this series. His poetry would have been central to the world of Arimnestos's mother.

Vasileos – master shipwright and helmsman.

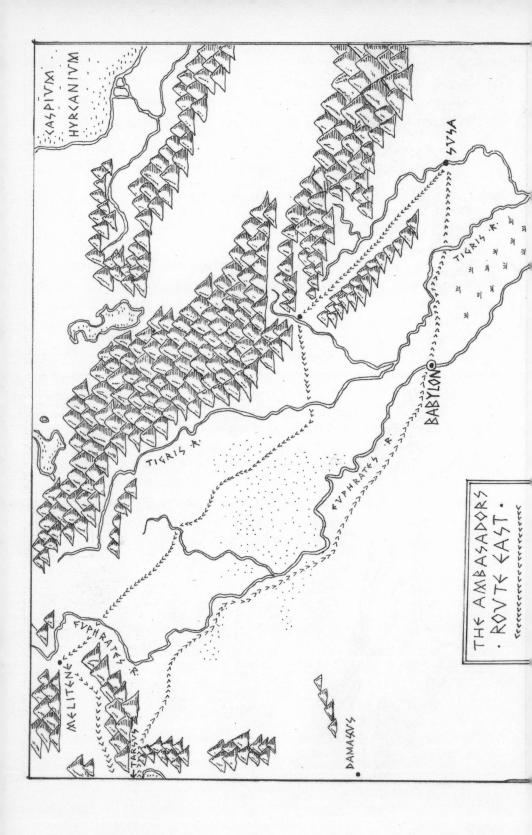

CASPIVM HYRCANIVM

TIGRIS R.

TIGRIS R.

SVSA

BABYLON

TIGRIS R.

EVPHRATES R.

EVPHRATES R.

MELITENE

EVPHRATES R.

TARSVS

DAMASVS

THE AMBASADORS ROVTE EAST.

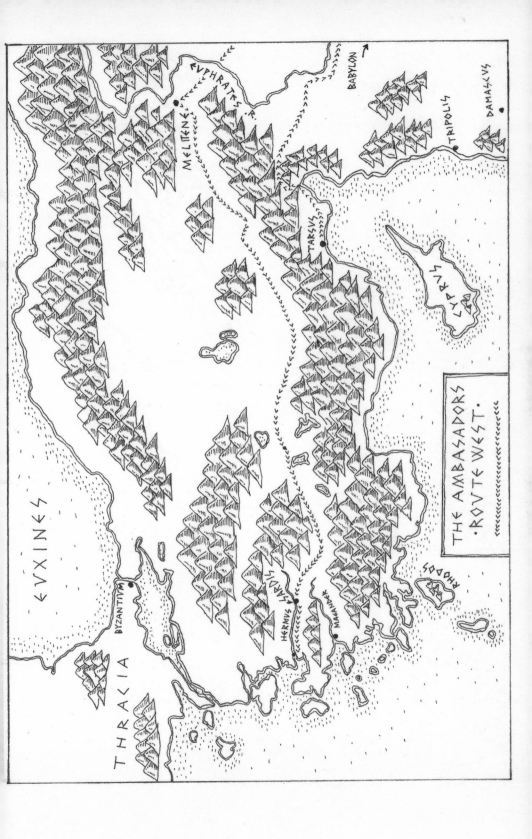

Prologue

If you all keep coming, night after night, my daughter will *have* the greatest wedding feast in the history of the Hellenes. Perhaps, should my sword-arm fail me, I can have an evening-star life as a rhapsode.

Heh. But the truth is, it's the story, not the teller. Who would not want to hear the greatest story of the greatest war ever fought by men? And you expect me to say 'since Troy' and I answer – any soldier knows Troy was just one city. We fought the *world*, and we triumphed.

The first night, I told you of my youth, and how I went to Calchas the priest to be educated as a gentleman, and instead learned to be a spear fighter. Because Calchas was no empty windbag, but a Killer of Men, who had stood his ground many times in the storm of bronze. And veterans came from all over Greece to hang their shields for a time at our shrine and talk to Calchas, and he sent them away whole, or better men, at least. Except that the worst of them the Hero called for, and the priest would kill them on the precinct walls and send their shades shrieking to feed the old Hero, or serve him in Hades.

Mind you, friends, Leithos wasn't some angry old god demanding blood sacrifice, but Plataea's hero from the Trojan War. And he was a particularly Boeotian hero, because he was no great man-slayer, no tent-sulker. His claim to fame is that he went to Troy and fought all ten years. That on the day that mighty Hector raged by the ships of the Greeks and Achilles skulked in his tent, Leithos rallied the lesser men and formed a tight shield wall and held Hector long enough for Ajax and the other Greek heroes to rally.

You might hear a different story in Thebes, or Athens, or Sparta. But that's the story of the Hero I grew to serve, and I spent years at his shrine, learning the war dances that we call the Pyricche. Oh, I learned to read old Theogonis and Hesiod and Homer, too. But it was the spear, the sword and the aspis that sang to me.

When my father found that I was learning to be a warrior and not a man of letters, he came and fetched me home, and old Calchas ... died. Killed himself, more like. But I've told all this – and how little Plataea, our farm town at the edge of Boeotia, sought to be free of cursed Thebes and made an alliance with distant Athens. I told you all how godlike Miltiades came to our town and treated my father, the bronzesmith – and Draco the wheelwright and old Epiktetus the farmer – like Athenian gentlemen, how he wooed them with fine words and paid hard silver for their products, so that he bound them to his own political ends and to the needs of Athens.

When I was still a gangly boy – tall and well muscled, as I remember, but too young to fight in the phalanx – Athens called for little Plataea's aid, and we marched over Kitharon, the ancient mountain that is also our glowering god, and we rallied to the Athenians at Oinoe. We stood beside them against Sparta and Corinth and all the Peloponnesian cities – and we beat them.

Well – Athens beat them. Plataea barely survived, and my older brother, who should have been my father's heir, died there with a Spartiate's spear in his belly.

Four days later, when we fought again – this time against Thebes – I was in the phalanx. Again, we triumphed. And I was a hoplite.

And two days later, when we faced the Euboeans, I saw my cousin Simon kill my father, stabbing him in the back under his bright bronze cuirass. When I fell over my father's corpse, I took a mighty blow, and when I awoke, I had no memory of Simon's treachery.

When I awoke, of course, I was a slave. Simon had sold me to Phoenician traders, and I went east with a cargo of Greek slaves.

I was a slave for some years – and in truth, it was not a bad life. I went to a fine house, ruled by rich, elegant, excellent people – Hipponax the poet and his wife and two children. Archilogos – the elder boy – was my real master, and yet my friend and ally, and we had many escapades together. And his sister, Briseis—

Ah, Briseis. Helen, returned to life.

We lived in far-off Ephesus, one of the most beautiful and powerful cities in the Greek world – yet located on the coast of Asia. Greeks have lived there since the Trojan War, and the temple of Artemis there is one of the wonders of the world. My master went to school each day at the temple for Artemis, and there the great philosopher,

Heraklitus, had his school, and he would shower us with questions every bit as painful as the blows of the old fighter who taught us pankration at the gymnasium.

Heraklitus. I have met men – and women – who saw him as a charlatan, a dreamer, a mouther of impieties. In fact, he was deeply religious – his family held the hereditary priesthood of Artemis – but he believed that fire was the only true element, and change the only constant. I can witness both.

It was a fine life. I got a rich lord's education for nothing. I learned to drive a chariot, and to ride a horse and to fight and to use my mind like a sword. I loved it all, but best of all—

Best of all, I loved Briseis.

And while I loved her – and half a dozen other young women – I grew to manhood listening to Greeks and Persians plotting various plots in my master's house, and one night all the plots burst forth into ugly blossoms and bore the fruit of red-handed war, and the Greek cities of Ionia revolted against the Persian overlords.

Now, as tonight's story will be about war with the Persians, let me take a moment to remind you of the roots of the conflict. Because they are ignoble, and the Greeks were no better than the Persians, and perhaps a great deal worse. The Ionians had money, power and freedom – freedom to worship, freedom to rule themselves – under the Great King, and all it cost them was taxes and the 'slavery' of having to obey the Great King in matters of foreign policy. The 'yoke' of the Persians was light and easy to wear, and no man alive knows that better than me, because I served – as a slave – as a herald between my master and the mighty Artaphernes, the satrap of all Phrygia. I knew him well – I ran his errands, dressed him at times, and one dark night, when my master Hipponax caught the Persian in his wife's bed, I saved his life when my master would have killed him. I saved my master's life, as well, holding the corridor against four Persian soldiers of high repute – Aryanam, Pharnakes, Cyrus and Darius. I know their names because they were my friends, in other times.

And you'll hear of them again. Except Pharnakes, who died in the Bosporus, fighting Carians.

At any rate, after that night of swords and fire and hate, my master went from being a loyal servant of Persia to a hate-filled Greek 'patriot'. And our city – Ephesus – roused itself to war. And amidst it all, my beloved Briseis lost her fiancé to rumour and innuendo,

3

and Archilogos and I beat him for his impudence. I had learned to kill, and to use violence to get what I wanted. And as a reward, I got Briseis – or to be more accurate, she had me. My master freed me, not knowing that I had just deflowered his daughter, and I sailed away with Archilogos to avoid the wrath of the suitor's relatives.

We joined the Greek revolt at Lesvos, and there, on the beach, I met Aristides – sometimes called the Just, one of the greatest heroes of Athens, and Miltiades' political foe.

That was the beginning of my true life. My life as a man of war. I won my first games on a beach in Chios and I earned my first suit of armour, and I went to war against the Persians.

But the God of War, Ares, was not so much in charge of my life as Aphrodite, and when we returned to Ephesus to plan the great war, I spent every hour that I could with Briseis, and the result – I think now – was never in doubt. But Heraklitus, the great sage, asked me to swear an oath to all the gods that I would protect Archilogos and his family – and I swore. Like the heroes in the old stories, I never thought about the consequence of swearing such a great oath and sleeping all the while with Briseis.

Ah, Briseis! She taunted me with cowardice when I stayed away from her and devoured me when I visited her, sneaking, night after night, past the slaves into the women's quarters, until in the end – we were caught. Of course we were caught.

And I was thrown from the house and ordered never to return, by the family I'd sworn to protect.

Three days later I was marching up-country with Aristides and the Athenians. We burned Sardis, but the Persians caught us in the midst of looting the market, and we lost the fight in the town and then again at the bridge, and the Persians beat us like a drum – but I stood my ground, fight after fight, and my reputation as a spear fighter grew. In a mountain pass, Eualcides the Euboean and I charged Artapherenes' bodyguard, and lived to tell the tale. Three days later, on the plains north of Ephesus, we tried to face a provincial Persian army with the whole might of the Ionian Revolt, and the Greeks folded and ran rather than face the Persian archery and the outraged Phrygians. Alone, on the far left, we the Athenians and the Euboeans held our ground and stopped the Carians. Our army was destroyed. Eualcides the hero died there, and I went back to save his corpse, and in the process found that Hipponax, my former master, lay mortally wounded. I gave him the mercy blow, again failing to think of the oath I'd sworn, and my once near-brother Archilogos thought I'd done it from hate, not love. And that blow stood between us and any hope of reconciliation. To Archilogos, I'd raped his sister and killed his father after swearing an oath to the gods to protect them. And that will have bearing on tonight's tale.

From the rout of Ephesus, I escaped with the Athenians, but the curse of my shattered oath lay on me and Poseidon harried our ship, and in every port I killed men who annoyed me until Hagios, my Athenian friend, put me ashore on Crete, with the King of Goryton, Achilles, and his son Neoptolymos, to whom I was war tutor. I tutored him so well that in the next great battle of the Ionian War, Neoptolymos and I were the heroes of the Greek fleet, and we helped my once-friend Archilogos to break the Persian centre. It was the first victory for the Greeks, but it was fleeting, and a few days later, I was a pirate on the great sea with my own ship for the first time. Fortune favoured me – perhaps, I think, because I had in part redeemed my oath to the gods by saving Archilogos at the sea battle. And when we weathered the worst storm I had ever seen, Poseidon had gifted me the African-Greek navigator Paramanos and a good crew in a heavy ship. I returned to Lesvos and joined Miltiades – he who had wooed the Plataeans at the dawn of this tale. And from him, I learned the facts of my father's murder and I determined to go home and avenge him.

I found Briseis had married one of the architects of the Ionian Revolt, and he was eager to kill me – the rumour was that she called my name when he was with her at night. And I determined to kill him.

After two seasons of piracy with Miltiades and further failures of the rebels to resist the Persians, I found him skulking around the edge of a great melee in Thrace and I killed him. I presented myself to Briseis to take her as my own – and she spurned me.

That's how it is, sometimes. I went back to Plataea, an empty vessel, and the Furies filled me with revenge. I found Simon and his sons sitting on my farm, Simon married to my mother, planning to marry his youngest son Simonalkes, to my sister Penelope.

I'll interrupt my own tale to say that I did not fall on Simon with fire and sword, because four years of living by the spear had taught me that things I had learned as a boy from Calchus and heard again from Heraklitus were coming to seem important and true – that justice was more important than might. I let the law of Plataea have

5

its way. Simon hanged himself from the rafters of my father's workshop, and the Furies left me alone with my mother and my sister.

That would make a fine tale, I think, by itself – but the gods were far from done with Plataea, and by the next spring, there were storm clouds brewing in all directions. An Athenian aristocrat died under my hypaspist's sword – Idomeneaus, who comes all too often into these stories, a mad Cretan – he had taken up the priesthood of the old shrine. I went off to see to the crisis, and that road took me over the mountains to Athens, and into the middle of Athenian politics – aye, you'll hear more of that tonight, too. There I fell afoul of the Alcmaeonidae and their scion Cleitus, because it was his brother who had died in our sanctuary and because my cowardly cousin Simon's sons were laying a trap for me. He stole my horse and my slave girl – that's another story. Because of him, I was tried for murder – and Aristides the Just got me off with a trick. But in the process, I committed hubris – the crime of treating a man like a slave – and Aristides ordered me to go to Delos, to the great temple of Apollo, to be cleansed.

Apollo, that scheming god, never meant me to be cleansed, but instead thrust me back into the service of Miltiades, whose fortunes were at an all-time low. With two ships, I reprovisioned Miletus – not once but twice – and made a small fortune on it, and on piracy. I took men's goods, and their women, and I killed for money, took ships, and thought too little of the gods. Apollo had warned me – in his own voice – to learn to use mercy, but I failed more often than I succeeded, and I left a red track behind me across the Ionian Sea. And in time, I was a captain at the greatest sea battle of the Ionian Revolt – at Lade. At Lade, the Great King put together an incredible fleet, of nearly six *hundred* ships, to face the Greeks and their allies with almost three hundred and fifty ships. It sounds one-sided, but we were well trained, we should have been ready. I sailed with the Athenians and the Cretans, and we beat the Phoenicians at one end of the line and emerged from the morning fog expecting the praise of our Navarch, the Phokaian Dionysus – alongside Miltiades, the greatest pirate and ship-handler in the Greek world. But when we punched through the Phoenicians, we found that the Samians – our fellow Greeks – had sold out to the Persians. The Great King triumphed, and the Ionian Revolt collapsed. Most of my friends – most of the men of my youth – died at Lades.

Briseis married Artaphernes, who had slept with her mother – and became the most powerful woman in Ionia, as she had always planned.

Datis, the architect of the Persian victory, raped and plundered his way across Lesvos and Chios, slaughtering men, taking women for the slave markets, and making true every slander that Greeks had falsely whispered about Persian atrocities.

Miletus, which I had helped to hold, fell. I saved what I could. And went home, with fifty families of Miletians to add to the citizen levy of Plataea. I spent my fortune on them, buying them land and oxen, and then – then I went back to smithing bronze. I gave up the spear.

How the gods must have laughed.

A season later, while my sister went to a finishing school to get her away from my mother's drunkenness, I went back to Athens because my friend Phrynicus, who had stood in the arrow storm at Lade with me, was producing his play, *The Fall of Miletus*. And Miltiades had been arrested for threatening the state – of which, let me say, friends, he was absolutely guilty, because Miltiades would have sold his own mother into slavery to achieve power in Athens.

At any rate, I used money and some of the talents I'd learned as a slave – and a lot of my friends – to see that Phrynicus's play was produced. And incidentally, to prise my stolen slave-girl free of her brothel and wreak some revenge on the Alcmaeonidae. In the process, I undermined their power with the demos – the people – and helped the new voice in Athenian politics – Themistocles the Orator. He had little love for me, but he managed to tolerate my success long enough to help me – and Aristides – to undermine the pro-Persian party and liberate Miltiades.

I went home to Plataea feeling that I'd done a lifetime of good service to Athens. My bronze smithing was getting better and better. I spent the winter training the Plataean phalanx in my spare time. War was going to be my hobby, the way some men learn the diaulos or the kithara to while away old age. I trained the young men and forged bronze. Life grew sweeter.

And when my sister Penelope – now married to a local Thespian aristocrat – decided that I was going to marry her friend Euphonia, I eventually agreed. I rode to Attica with a hunting party of aristocrats – Boeotian and Athenian – and won my bride in games that would not have disgraced the heroes of the past. And in the spring I wed her, at a wedding that included Themistocles and Aristides and Miltiades – and Harpagos and Agios and Moir and a dozen of my other friends from every class in Athens. I went back over the mountains with my bride, and settled down to make babies.

But the storm clouds on the horizon were coming on a great wind of change. And the first gusts of that wind brought us a raid out of Thebes, paid for by the Alcmaenoidae and led by my cousin Simon's son Simonides. The vain bastard named all his sons after himself – how weak can a man be?

I digress. We caught them – my new Plataean phalanx – and we crushed them. My friend Teucer, the archer, killed Simonides. And because of them, we were all together when the Athenians called for our help, because the Persians, having destroyed Euboea, were marching for Athens.

Well, I won't retell Marathon. Myron, our archon and always my friend, sent us without reservation, and all the Plataeans marched under my command, and we stood by the Athenians on the greatest day Greek men have ever known, and we were heroes. Hah! I'll tell it again if you don't watch yourselves. We defeated Datis and his Persians with the black ships. Agios died there on the stern of a Persian trireme, but we won the day. Here's to his shade. And to all the shades of all the men who died at Lade.

But when I led the victorious Plataeans back across the mountains, it was to find that my beautiful young wife had died in childbirth. The gods stole my wits clean away – I took her body to my house and burned it and all my trappings, and I went south over Kitharon, intending to destroy myself.

May you never know how black the world can be. Women know that darkness sometimes after the birth of a child, and men after battle. Any peak of spirit has its price, and when a man or woman stands with the gods, however briefly, they pay the price ten times. The exertion of Marathon and the loss of my wife unmanned me. I leapt from a cliff.

I fell, and struck, not rocks, but water. And when I surfaced, my body fought for life, and I swam until my feet dragged on the beach. Then I swooned, and when I awoke, I was once again a slave. Again taken by Phoenicians, but this time as an adult. My life was cruel and like to be short, and the irony of the whole thing was that now I soon craved life.

I lived a brutal life under a monster called Dagon, and you'll hear plenty of him tonight. But he tried to break me, body and soul, and nigh on succeeded. In the end, he crucified me on a mast, and left me to die. But Poseidon saved me – washed me over the side with the mast, and let me live. Set me on the deck of a little Sikel trading ship, where I pulled an oar as a near-slave for a few months. And then I was taken again, by the Phoenicians.

The degradations and the humiliations went on, until one day, in a sea fight, I took a sword and cut my way to freedom. The sword fell at my feet – literally. The gods have a hand in every man's life. Only impious fools believe otherwise.

As a slave, I had developed new friendships. Or rather, new alliances, which, when I was free, ripened into friendship. My new friends were a polyglot rabble – an Etruscan of Roma named Gaius, a couple of Kelts, Daud and Sittonax, a pair of Africans from south of Libya, Doola and Seckla, a Sikel named Demetrios and an Illyrian kinglet-turned-slave called Neoptolymos. We swore an oath to Poseidon to take a ship to Alba and buy tin, and we carried out our oath. As I told you last night, we went to Sicily, and while my friends became small traders on the coast, I worked as a bronzesmith, learning and teaching. I fell in love with Lydia, the bronzesmith's daughter, and betrayed her, and for that betrayal – let's call things by their proper names – I lost confidence in myself, and I lost the favour of the gods, and for years I wandered up and down the seas, until at last we redeemed our oaths, went to Alba for the tin, and came back rich men. I did my best to see Lydia well suited, and I met Pythagoras's daughter and was able to learn something of that great man's mathematics and his philosophy. I met Gelon the tyrant of Syracusa and declined to serve him, and sailed away, and there, on a beach near Taranto in the south of Italia, I found my friend Harpagos and Cimon, son of Miltiades, and others among the friends and allies of my youth. I confess, I had sent a message, hoping that they would come. We cruised north into the Adriatic, because I had promised Neoptolymos that we'd restore him to his throne, and we did, though we got a little blood on it. And then the Athenians and I parted company from my friends of Sicily days – they went back to Massalia to till their fields, and I left them to go back to being Arimnestos of Plataea. Because Cimon said that the Persians were coming. And whatever my failings as a man – and I had and still have many – I am the gods' own tool in the war of the Greeks against the Persians.

9

For all that I have always counted many Persians among my friends, and the best of men – the most excellent, the most brave, the most loyal. Persians are a race of truth-telling heroes. But they are not Greeks, and when it came to war ...

We parted company off Illyria, and coasted the western Peloponnesus. But Poseidon was not yet done with me, and a mighty storm blew up off Africa and it fell on us, scattering our little squadron and sending my ship far, far to the south and west, and when the storm blew itself out, we were a dismasted hulk riding the rollers, and there was another damaged ship under our lee. We could see she was a Carthaginian. We fell on that ship and took it, although in a strange, three-sided fight – the rowers were rising against the deck crew of Persians.

It was Artapharenes' own ship, and he was travelling from Tyre to Carthage to arrange for Carthaginian ships to help the Great King to make war on Athens. And I rescued him – I thought him a corpse.

So did his wife, my Briseis, who threw herself into my arms.

Blood dripped from my sword, and I stood with Helen in my arms on a ship I'd just taken by force of arms, and I thought myself the king of the world.

How the gods must have laughed.

Olympia – 484 BCE

'Water is best, and gold, like a blazing fire in the night, stands out supreme of all lordly wealth. But if, my heart, you wish to sing of contests, look no further for any star warmer than the sun, shining by day through the lonely sky, and let us not proclaim any contest greater than Olympia.'

Pindar. 476 BCE

I

Artapharenes stubbornly refused to die.

After an hour, it was plain to any man who'd known as much strife as I that, despite the six deep sword-cuts in his side, he was not mortally wounded. He had a contusion on his head where a pike haft had laid open his scalp, and he'd been hacked at by desperate men, but he was merely unconscious.

Don't imagine I hovered at his side like Hermes attending on Zeus. Despite the sea fight, my ship still needed repair, and we were uncomfortably close to Africa – a strong north wind and we'd have been wrecked. And the coast of Africa was the coast of Libya – Carthage's coast, and all hostile to me and mine. Megakles was between the steering oars. I had Sekla watch the coast – he knew Libya better than any man in my crew. Ka, my new African master bowman, had two men wounded, and he was doctoring them, and Leukas, my Alban oar-master, was with me in the water, patching the two man-lengths of riven wood where the storm had opened *Lydia*'s seams along the starboard side.

It was Brasidas – my former Spartan marine – who was left with the complex job of watching the vessel we'd taken. Complicated because, in truth, we hadn't taken her – we'd rescued her. The presence of Briseis, the love of my life, made everything complicated. But the Persians aboard – my three friends, Darius, Cyrus and Arayanam, and Artapherenes himself – complicated things still more. We were not at war with Persia, that summer. And the Persians were clearly an embassy, and embassies were sacred to all the gods. I'm a pious man, even when I'm a fool – I could see the boughs of ivy and laurel in the bow, and I wasn't going to betray my guest oaths and friend-ship oaths with these Persians, but I was hard put to decide just what to do with them. Or my love.

Had Artapharenes just died …

He wasn't going to die. And that being plain, I dived into the cold seawater to help repair my ship and to clear my head, despite a wounded hand and the stares of Briseis' women at my naked body, or perhaps because of them.

Leukas, bless him, had no worries beyond the ship, and he went down under the hull and back up, again and again, shaking his head until, with ten men hauling the sodden remains of the other ship's boat sail, we managed to get at our sprung timbers and bind the sail over it. It didn't stop the leak, but it reduced it.

We still had six oarsmen at the wooden pumps all day and all night.

The Carthaginian ship we'd taken was in even worse shape. The mast had been down when the storm hit, but my guess – all the officers were dead – was that the tackle hadn't been stowed properly and had blown loose in the night, rolling and pitching, driving the oarsmen mad and finally blowing over the side in the darkness, after swamping the ship and tearing a grisly hole in the side. The boat sail spar had smashed half the oars and stove a hole right through the side, and when dawn showed them calmer water and the coast of Africa under their lee, the oarsmen revolted.

That ship was finished. I thought perhaps I could get it on to the beach of Libya, but that was the last place I wanted to go myself. Good sense told me to take my own and row away. But Artapherenes held my guest oath and had given me my life, and I had worn his ring for years.

When we had the hole in our side patched, I rolled aboard and dried myself, and stood in the sun. Thirty feet away, Briseis smiled at me across the water.

Damn her.

I puffed out my chest, no doubt.

Why are men such simple creatures? Eh?

Sekla had the deck. The steering oars were inboard, waiting until there was way on the ship, but Sekla stood between them, the traditional command space, at least on my ships. He leaned forward.

'That's the famous Briseis,' he said. He had the temerity to laugh.

'Yes,' I said.

He shook his head. 'Beautiful,' he said. 'She never took her eyes off you, while you were in the water.' He shrugged.

I was watching Briseis.

He elbowed me. 'Are you the mighty pirate Arimnestos, or some spotty boy?' he asked.

I glared at him. I'd saved him from lovesickness – I thought, *How dare you*.

He laughed in my face.

I had to laugh with him. 'A spotty boy,' I agreed. 'That's what she always does to me.'

Leukas was drying himself on his chiton. The Alban shook his head but remained silent.

Megakles didn't. His broad Italiote accent added emphasis to his comic delivery. 'While we all drool at her, my lord, any Liby-Phoenician in these waters will snap us all up. And we'll all be slaves.'

Sittonax – my lazy Gallish friend – stretched like a cat. 'That is one well-formed woman,' he agreed. 'Not worth dying for, though.' He nodded at Megakles. 'You know he's right.'

'They're an embassy,' I said. 'Even the Carthaginians respect an embassy.'

I gathered that my friends didn't agree. Their intransigence made me angry, and I remember biting my lip and trying to keep my temper. I was thrice tired – awake all night at the helm, fighting a boarding action, and now I'd helped fother the hull – and it was all I could do to stay on my feet, and their teasing got under my skin far too easily.

I stood there, watching my oarsmen pump water out of my damaged hull. I couldn't see us making any of the southern Peloponnesian ports – too far, and too much chance of another spring storm.

Brasidas motioned with his usual economy of effort – a single flick of the hand.

I leaned over the port-side rail. 'What do you need?' I called.

'Nothing,' he said. 'But the woman wants you.'

In any other man's mouth, that might have sounded like ribaldry, but the Spartan was carefully spoken. We don't call them Laconic for nothing.

On any other day, I'd have ordered the oarsmen to use boarding pikes to pull the ships closer. But Briseis was watching, and so, despite fatigue, I seized a chiton and pulled it on, belted it with a corded zone, pulled my sword belt over my head, and leapt – leapt, I say – from one oar bank to the next. I noted as I landed that the other ship was lower in the water.

I managed to jump inboard over the terrified survivors among the slave oarsmen – what was left after the fight, watched like hawks by my own marines – and I tried not to swagger too much as I went aft to Briseis.

I bowed. She had a scarf over her head like a good matron and the only flesh on display was one ankle and one hand, but I knew her body.

I suppose that Sekla was right. I was a pimply boy, when it came to Briseis.

'Come,' she said, and led me aft, to where Cyrus – the best of my friends among the Persians – sat with Artapherenes' head in his lap.

The satrap's eyes were open. I knelt by him, and just for a moment, some dreadful fate tempted me to put a dagger in his eye and take the woman for my own. I am a man like other men – I think of awful things, even if I try to do the right ones.

He beckoned me closer.

I leaned over to hear him.

'Arimnestos,' he said softly.

'My lord,' I said.

'A mighty name,' he murmured. 'Carthage,' he said, and his eyes closed.

Briseis put a hand on my shoulder, and that contact was like the flash of lightning across the sky that heralds the storm. 'He is asking you to carry us into Carthage,' she said.

For once, I looked past her, and my eyes locked with the heavy black eyes of Cyrus, captain of Artapherenes' guard and his right hand.

I sat back on my heels. 'Cyrus,' I said. 'If – I say if – I take you into Carthage – can you guarantee my safety? I have no love for Carthage. Nor she for me.'

Cyrus scratched his beard – so much the old Cyrus, full of humour and Persian dignity, that he made me feel fifteen years old again. 'Who can guarantee anything that Phoenicians do?' he said. 'They lie like Greeks.' He grinned. 'I can't promise that the Carthaginians will treat you as part of our embassy.' He shrugged. 'I can only promise that if you take us there and they turn on you, I'll die beside you.'

That's a Persian. And he meant it.

If you have any honour in you, you know when another man is honourable. And when he makes a request – a certain kind of request ...

Artapherenes had spared my life, and other lives, the night I found

16

Hipponax dying on the lost battlefield north of Ephesus. I had saved his life, too. Cyrus and I had traded sword-cuts and guest pledges a few times, as well.

And it is not on a sunny day that your faith is pledged. The value of your oaths to the gods is tested when the storm comes. I sat on my heels, and within three heartbeats of Cyrus's affirmation that he'd die by my side if the Carthaginians betrayed the truce, I knew I had to do it.

I rose and sighed. 'Very well. I will tow you to the beach, and see if this ship can be saved. If it cannot, I'll row you around to Carthage. May Poseidon stand by me. May Athena give me good council.'

Cyrus smiled. 'You are a man,' he said.

What's that worth?

All of my friends glowered at me. I stood their displeasure easily enough, and crossed to the stricken Phoenician ship with half of my deck crew and two dozen of my best rowers and Leukas, who was – and is – a better sailor than I'll ever be. I left Megakles with the command. I also took young Hector, my new *pais*. He had been seasick since Croton, and not much use, but he was finally getting his sea legs.

Evening found us wallowing in the light surf, twenty horse-lengths off the coast of Africa. The beach was a ribbon of silver in the light of the new moon, and to say that my rowers were exhausted wouldn't do justice to their state. Remember that most of them were slaves who'd risen against their masters and been beaten.

But no one wants to drown.

Cyrus stood by me. I was between the steering oars, while Leukas led the bailing party and tried to keep the water out of the hull by willpower. Our rowers – tired and desperate – were also pulling a waterlogged hull that weighed three times what it should have.

Lydia went in first. I saw Brasidas lead his marines over her stern and jump into the shallow water – in case there was a welcoming party.

Cyrus grunted. 'Your men are very well trained,' he said.

I nodded. 'Piracy is a hard school,' I said.

He frowned.

The oarsmen poured over *Lydia*'s sides and up the beach, and the slick black hull was hauled ashore almost as if by the hands of the gods. It was splendid to watch, despite my worries about the ship I was in. Despite the presence of Briseis just a few feet away – so close that I swear that I could feel the warmth of her body.

Aye.

I tapped the steering oar and took us a few more yards down the beach. I wanted the damaged hulk to land well clear of my beautiful *Lydia*, just in case.

Leukas laid out pulling lines along the decks of the capture, and as soon as *Lydia* was lying on her side, well propped, the oarsmen ran down the beach to us, and it was time. I looked at Briseis, and as my eye met hers, she smiled.

It took long enough to turn the ship end for end that the moon began to peep over the rim of the world. We didn't 'spin', we wallowed, but eventually we were stern first to the beach and the surviving rowers had their cushions reversed.

Cyrus looked at me, eyes very white in the new darkness. 'I think the rowers are considering another rising,' he said.

Cyrus was no fool. Neither was Arayanam, who took his bow from its case and strung it.

There was a curious quality to the rowers' silence.

'Leukas!' I called, and he came back to me.

'Take the helm,' I ordered, and he did.

I ran forward to the space amidships where a good trierarch stands in battle – where his voice carries over the whole sweep of the benches.

'Listen up, oarsmen!' I called. 'When we have this ship on the beach, I will see to it you are fed. This ship won't last three more hours – stay with me and I'll see you ashore and alive. If you try me now – all I can promise is that every one of you will die.'

I looked down into the gloom.

'A lot of these men don't give a shit whether they live or die,' called a man bolder than the rest. His Greek was Ionian.

'I can only speak to the Greeks aboard,' I said. 'But I'll do better for them than the Phoenicians ever did. Or I'll kill them and land the ship anyway.' I stood above them, and I knew from my time toiling under the lash of Dagon how powerful the voice on the command deck could seem.

I walked back along the catwalk. I didn't hurry – I wanted to seem as confident as possible. The truth was that we were a hundred yards from shore and I was in no danger, but I had no idea whether Briseis could swim and I couldn't imagine that Artapherenes would survive the journey.

I heard some muttering.

Muttering is a good sign, usually.

I took the steering oars from Leukas and he began to give orders in his Keltoi-Greek. 'Pull!' he commanded.

He began to beat time.

Some oars stayed in. But my rowers dug in with a will, and enough of the others pulled that we made way sternwards, and the sternpost kissed the sand with a gentle thump. Immediately, the current and the waves began to push the head in towards the beach – the worst thing that could happen, and something that a helmsman feared on a stormy day on a windswept beach, but not on a nearly dead calm night on a broad belt of sand.

Luckily for me, Sekla and his oarsmen already had the lines that my borrowed deck crew flung them, and they dragged us with more will than the oarsmen pulled.

Leukas yelled, 'Over the side, you whoresons!'

Some went, and some didn't. I couldn't tell whether I was facing mutiny, desertion or utter, desperate exhaustion. So I walked down the catwalk, abandoning the steering oars – I think I pulled them inboard. I started to prick men lightly with a borrowed Persian spear. One man, with a long scar over his forehead, cursed me and crouched like an angry dog on his little bench, but he couldn't even reach me with spit, and when his spirit broke, all the men around him went, too. Men are odd animals – too intelligent, sometimes, for their own good.

Leukas and I started them, and the Persians helped – came and threatened – and we got them over the side and on to the beach. A dozen tried to run and were swatted down like errant children by Brasidas and his marines. The last thing we needed was a pack of runaway slaves giving away our positions.

My three Persians got their lord over the side and carried him between two spears to the fire that Sekla had already lit on the beach, and in an hour we had mutton cooking. Any plan to keep our presence secret was wrecked when a pair of cautious shepherds approached and offered to sell us sheep.

By the time the moon was high in the sky, we had the local head-man at our fire, and he knew we were Greeks.

★

19

I would love to say that I lay with Briseis that night. I desired her – I watched her at the fire the women had, and I sent her a joint of meat after I made the sacrifices to Poseidon and poured libations to all the gods for our safe arrival at land, and she sent me back a cup of sweet wine. But my feelings of the sacred – of what was owed to Artaphernes – kept me from her side. Instead, I introduced my Persian friends – the friends of my earliest youth – to the friends of my recent slavery.

Brasidas, as a Spartiate, took to the Persians immediately. They value most of the same things – indeed, Spartans and Persians have a great deal in common.

But Sekla had no love of the Persians, and they in turn treated him much like a slave – at least in part because the only black men they knew were slaves, I suspect. And the Persians, for their part, were amazed to hear that Megakles was from Gaul – still more amazed that Leukas was from Hyperborea.

'He looks just like any other man!' Darius laughed. 'Well – except for the odd eyes and the dead white skin.'

'And the size of his nose,' Aryanam said, but Leukas couldn't be offended, as it was all said in Persian. Still, they handed wine around to the others, and after an hour, even Sekla was less prickly.

I remember that I looked at the moon – Artemis's sign – and wondered again at the risk I was running. 'Cyrus – you are bound to Carthage to get allies there against the Greeks. Am I right?'

Cyrus narrowed his eyes. 'In effect – yes.' He shrugged. 'Really, it is far more complicated than that,' he continued.

'Why?' Brasidas asked. He rarely asked questions. It was fascinating to see how animated the Persians made him.

Cyrus made the Persian hand sign for 'a little of this, a little of that', rocking his hand back and forth. 'It is not that the Great King needs their ships, or their men,' he said. 'But there is a rumour at Sardis that Gelon of Syracusa might lead his fleet against the Great King.' He frowned. 'You might know more of that than I, eh? Arimnestos?'

I smiled grimly. 'I might,' I allowed.

Brasidas laughed when the silence lengthened. 'Perhaps you could become a Spartan,' he said.

Cyrus nodded. 'You don't wish to tell us what you know?'

I looked around the circle of firelight. The Persians had all taken one side of the fire, at least in part so that they could tend to their lord, who lay close to the fire, wrapped in three cloaks. On my side of the fire were Sekla and Brasidas – Ka stood alone by the wine, almost asleep, and Leukas was already gone, wrapped in his chiton. Megakles sat quietly, wrapping rope-ends in linen, and showing Hector – patiently – how to do it.

'Are we to have a war, then?' I asked. 'I have been gone from the world of Medes and Greeks for five years.'

Cyrus looked away, and Arayanam frowned, and Darius met my eye and smiled. 'Aye, little brother, it's war,' he said. 'And I'll guess you've been at this Syracusa about which we hear so much these days.'

I nodded. Persians are great ones for telling the truth, and truth-telling can be habit-forming. Yet even then, I was calculating some lies. I'm a Greek.

'I was a slave, not a trierarch,' I said. 'And pardon me, brothers, but I think that I have captured you, and not the other way around. It is my hospitality you enjoy here, and in this situation I may choose not to answer every question.'

Cyrus nodded. 'I, too, may decline to answer.'

I bowed slightly, in the Persian way. 'Elder brother, I respect your right to be silent. But I beg you to see this from my point of view – I am a Greek. I fought Datis at Marathon.'

All three of the Persians laughed. 'Ah, Datis,' they said.

We all knew Datis as an ambitious and somewhat power-mad man.

'I thought Marathon was the end of the Great King's ambitions in Greece,' I said.

'Ambitions!' Cyrus said, truly stung, I think. 'My lord is the right-ful ruler of all that is under heaven, and the resistance of a few petty states of pirates and terrorists on the fringes of the world will scarcely constitute the *end of ambition*. Athens encourages the Ionian rebels. Athenian ships prey on our shipping and disrupt our trade. Athenian soldiers burned the temple of Cybele in Sardis. Even last year, Athenians aided rebels against the Great King's authority in Aegypt. Greek mercenaries are serving against the Great King at Babylon! It is not my lord's ambition, but the foolish and militant posturing of the Greeks! A culture of hate and war, where no man respects his neighbour! Much less a lawful ruler!'

Brasidas chuckled. 'In Sparta, we say many of the same things about Athens,' he said.

Cyrus wasn't done. 'Sparta! A nest of godless vipers who executed one of the king's sacred messengers!' He leaned in to the fire. 'When I was a boy, no one in Persia had ever heard of these two cities – Athens and Sparta. But now the Great King knows both of these names, and he will erase them as if they had never been.'

I shook my head. 'Cyrus – Cyrus. You are letting unaccustomed anger cloud your thoughts. The Great King lacks the reach to take Athens – or Sparta. You have no idea how big the world is.'

I had been outside the pillars of Herakles. I had been to Alba in the Western Ocean, and my idea of the size of the world was profoundly affected. The world was *immense*.

Cyrus shrugged. 'In truth, the intransigence of Athens makes me angry, which is foolish.' He frowned, looked away, and smiled. 'And a poor return on your hospitality. But yes – the world is wide, and we should be conquering it together – Greeks and Persians side by side – not squandering our strength on each other.'

I poured a libation to the King of the Gods, Zeus. 'Cyrus – it pains me to say this, but if we stand at the edge of a great war of Greeks and Medes, perhaps it is not the wisest course for me to take you to Carthage.'

Darius sighed. 'And yet we are an embassy, and embassies are sacred to all the gods,' he said.

Brasidas nodded. 'So they are. I come from a family of heralds – I recognise the sign of the god upon you. And surely – leaving aside the differences in our opinions – surely this war is not so imminent?'

Darius looked at Cyrus. Arayanam simply drank another cup of wine, as was his wont. He seldom spoke, unless he had something vital to say, and might have been welcomed in any Lacedaemonian mess group.

Cyrus shrugged. 'The Great King has ordered a canal dug across the isthmus of Mount Athos,' he said. 'He gathers a fleet. Now that the revolt in Aegypt is broken, Athens will not take so long.'

'How long?' I asked.

'Two years?' he said. 'A year to defeat Babylon, anyway. See, I am honest.'

I laughed, my mood restored. 'Two years?' I said. 'By Poseidon, Cyrus, I imagined you were speaking of weeks or months. Two years? Pardon me, but in two years storms may wreck a fleet, the Great King may die – a year of famine might cripple your army, or the will of the gods might make itself manifest in a hundred ways.'

Cyrus spread his hands. 'Perhaps. But Athens can count its days.'

He looked at me. 'What do you care? You are not an Athenian or a Spartan. You could be one of us. Your former master, Archilogos, is one of the Great King's most trusted officers. You could be the same, or even greater.'

I frowned. 'Cyrus, my elder brother,' I said. 'I no longer know what I want from life.' I looked across the fire to the women's fire, but Briseis' slim, deep-breasted figure was gone. 'But I know that service to the Great King is *not* what I want. And my city is Athens' closest friend.'

Cyrus shrugged. 'Athens is doomed,' he said.

In the morning, we bought every scrap of wood that the Berbers could bring us – herdsmen and villagers from a fishing port a few stades farther west. In the end, after two days attempting to effect repairs with too little wood, I gave up on the Phoenician ship and broke it up. It seemed like a defeat, and a waste, but there simply wasn't enough good wood to repair the two great gashes in its side. And then there were the rowers. They were mutinous, and the more I fed them, and the more they recovered their strength, the more mutinous I found them. So after two days, I ordered the Phoenician broken up, and her good timbers were immediately pressed into the repairs of my lovely *Lydia*. With the worked pine and cedar of the other ship, we had our own repaired in a day, and we had enough pitch in our own ballast to caulk her tight.

My rowers were all free men, and professionals – a mixture of the very best of all the fishermen, herdsmen and freed slave rowers I'd had for the last few years. Every man of them had arms, and I lined them up on the soft sand and formed them four deep, like a small phalanx, with my marines on the right and my archers on the left, and I took them to the other rowers before they could consider flight or resistance. We had weapons and training and numbers. They had nothing but sullen ferocity.

Men who are ill used become evil men themselves. Ill use is like a disease that robs men of their worth and leaves them broken, empty vessels capable of filling with ire and hate and inflicting only harm. They stood like a sullen pack, and I eyed them with something like loathing.

The fact is, I couldn't take them, and I couldn't leave them behind. If I left them on the beach, they'd rape and murder among the local Berbers until one of the lords raised an army and massacred them.

And even though these were not Sekla's people, they were close enough that I couldn't inflict so much suffering on them.

I'm a soft-hearted pirate.

If I took them, I'd be selling them as slaves in Carthage, and I had *been* a slave rower in Carthage. Carthage, unlike Persia, is truly evil. She lives on the backs of her slaves. And orders parents to kill their children.

Bah. You can smell their children roasting on their foul altars when you land a ship in the harbour. Think of that, and tell me that Carthage is a state like the others.

The answer was obvious – to massacre them myself. At thirty, I might not have hesitated, but I was older, and I had finally begun to appreciate the wisdom of Apollo and practise mercy.

So I looked at the sullen men as they cringed at the edge of the hard sand.

I made a sign to Brasidas. 'I am going to let the gods decide which of them lives and which dies,' I said. 'Watch me – but not too closely.'

The Spartan nodded. He wore a small smile.

Ka put an arrow to his Persian bow.

'All the Greeks, form on the right,' I called out to them.

'Phoenicians!' I called, but there were none.

'Aegyptians!' I called, and there were a few, and a pair of Jews, and a single Babylonian and a dozen Keltoi and two Illyrians. I divided them by nation, and I moved among them, talking to those who could, or would, talk.

And as I expected, as I walked among the Greeks, further dividing them into Ionians and Dorians, the angry dog – that's how I thought of him, the man with the scar on his forehead – came at me. I saw him early, moving among his friends, if such a man has friends, and I didn't let him know I had seen him. But I never quite gave him my back.

He had a knife. And some idea how to use it. And his friends – or his followers or his flunkies or what have you – seized stones and clubs they'd made themselves and came at me. Most of them were Greeks, I'm saddened to say.

There were four of them close enough to me to do me immediate harm. But the youngest Greek, who was closest to me, gave them away with an odd noise – the angry dog gave a great shout, and the boy struck me with an ineffectual blow and cringed, rather than, say, grappling my arms, or legs.

24

I drew my long xiphos from its scabbard and killed the boy on the draw, the rising blade opening his naked belly and the edge of the upper leaf cutting through the bone of his chin and spraying teeth as it exited his face. Then I pivoted slightly on my right foot and cut down with the other edge, and the next man died, too.

Ka shot one who was at my back.

The fourth man stumbled back, but the gods had played their role, and I killed him with a cut across his eyes and a merciful thrust.

Brasidas didn't fence with the angry dog, either, but put a spear in his throat with brutal economy.

'Kill only those who are armed, or resist!' I shouted.

The two Jews and the Babylonian, who all seemed to know each other, lay flat. The Keltoi gathered in a huddle.

I confess that some innocent men probably died on our spears, and perhaps some who were merely foolish, but in a minute I was rid of the most vicious.

While their blood was still soaking into the sand, I rounded up the rest, had them searched, and called them forth by nation.

'Are any of you worth a ransom?' I asked. Several of the Greeks claimed that they were. I sent them to Brasidas. Trust a Spartan to be able to spot an aristocrat.

The two Jews and the Babylonian all claimed to be worth ransom. And many other men had stories – some scarcely believable, some patent lies, and a few truly horrible.

I spent an hour listening, and then I had them distributed among my own rowers. They'd been bled of their most dangerous men, twice – there were fewer than forty of them left, and I was almost twenty rowers short. They brought me to full complement. In fact, with Briseis and her women, with Artaphernes and his soldiers and his four servants, we were as crowded as a trireme can possibly be, but on the positive side, with twenty extra rowers, I had reliefs, and because my *Lydia* was a hemiola and not a true trireme, I had the deck space to ship them all – aye, and sleep at sea if required. So we coasted to a small inlet and took on water, and then we started west, into the afternoon sun, for Carthage.

Carthage, on whom I had made war for years.

Dagon's home.

The masters of the tin trade.

Laugh if you like. Sometimes, when you make a decision, you know it is right before you feel the consequence.

2

Carthage enjoys one of the finest natural harbours in all the great aspis of the world, improved by the genius of man. The breakwater is longer and stronger than that of Syracusa, and the two beaches that flank the promontory like the guard on a xiphos's hilt each have berthing for a hundred ships, and there are ship-sheds – the largest and best in all the Middle Sea – all along the promontory coast, an incredible fortune in quarried stone, and every shed holds a hull, dry, well stored, ready for sea.

The last time I entered that harbour, I'd been a half-dead victim of a month of the most extreme humiliations and tortures at the hands of Dagon, the mad or cursed helmsman. This was the first time I'd entered the magnificent harbour in command of my own vessel, and the view was better.

On the other hand, I could smell the roast-pork smell of human sacrifice rising to the gods. Down in the urine-soaked hull of a slave-rowed trireme, I'd never smelled it.

Listen, friends. The Greeks have been known to sacrifice men. I watched Themistocles do it once, and frankly, it sickened me, like a lot of the other crap that half-mad demagogue did. But it is scarcely the norm, for all that power-mad Agamemnon sacrificed his own daughter for a fair wind to Troy. I say again – Greeks can do such things, but most Greeks think them barbarous.

The whole trip to Carthage, I had Briseis on my deck. She would walk the catwalk like a queen, or settle on the short bench by the helm. We talked as we had not talked in many years.

At any rate, she sniffed the air and looked at me. 'What is that, love?' she said. 'Pigs instead of sheep?'

I shook my head. 'The Great King's allies sacrifice children to Ba'al for fair weather and good sailing,' I said.

In the face she made, I read the utter disgust of the mother. I seldom thought of Briseis in those days as anything but a lover, but in that moment I had to see that she had children whom she loved – perhaps loved far more than she loved Artaphernes. Or me.

'How are your own children?' I asked. 'And dare I ask how you come to be here?'

She leaned back and let the fold of her shawl fall away from her face. 'My children are wonderful,' she said. 'My two sons are tall and strong, and will be fine men.'

I laughed to see her pleasure in thinking of her sons. 'Better men than their father, I hope?' I asked. Her first husband had been, in my eyes, a coward and a fool – for all that he was, for a while, one of the most powerful men in the Greek world. I'd killed him, of course.

'I hope that Heraklitus, at least, will not be the fool his father is,' she said. 'And Dionysus will be a scholar.'

'You called your first after the teacher?' I asked. 'My teacher?'

She looked at the growing crescent of the Carthaginian harbour. 'You have never asked his name before,' she said. 'You know that he is fourteen years old? He goes to the gymnasium of Sardis with the Greek boys, and throws his spears. He wishes to compete in the boys' pankration.' She raised her eyes and met mine. 'He looks like you.'

That struck me like a sword-blow – like being hit with another man's shield, right in the face, or like the blow of another ship hitting your own ship, so that you are knocked flat.

'He's . . . what?' I asked.

Briseis shook her head. 'Why do I love you so?' she asked. 'You are sometimes the merest brute.'

Megakles was beginning the landing routine. A pair of pilot boats were pulling out from the main wharf, and two warships were being put into the water.

Someone had recognised my ship.

Sekla came to stand by me. Brasidas was fully armed, and so were all of his marines, and Ka had all his non-wounded archers in the bow, bows strung. Cyrus and his two friends were amidships, fully dressed in rather formal Persian robes over trousers and tucked into their beautiful red-leather boots, and Artaphernes reclined on a pallet of their cloaks, his beard neatly trimmed.

Sekla bowed to Briseis and turned to me. 'Time to pay the ferryman,' he said. 'Or whatever you Greeks say when you are about to

27

die. May I just say …' he pointed at the onrushing shapes of the two Carthaginian warships '… that I told you so? I'd like you to accept that I told you this would happen before we died.'

I was still looking open mouthed at Briseis. She pulled a fold of her shawl over her face.

In the time it took the rowers to pull five strokes, everything about my life had changed.

Because I had a son. By Briseis. Named Heraklitus.

The pilot boats put an elder on my deck, and the two Carthaginians lay off, with burning fire pots prepared on their marine decks and bows strung. As soon as the old man came aboard, he faced me without a bow.

'I am old and have grown sons,' he announced. 'No one will ransom me, and if I raise my right hand, this ship will be rammed and sunk with all hands, and no one will account me a loss. Understand, pirate?'

I nodded. 'Sir, I am merely the tool of the gods, in this instance. My ship bears the tokens of an embassy, and I carry the Lord Artapherenes, who comes from the Great King of Persia to speak to the council of Carthage.'

I think his face must have worn the look I had when Briseis told me that her son was also mine.

I motioned to him, and led him forward to where Artapherenes lay among his attendants.

'This is the Lord Artapherenes, Satrap of Phrygia, relative of the Great King,' I said. 'And his wife Briseis and men of his bodyguard.'

I suppose it might have been possible to impersonate such rank, but not in such numbers. The Carthaginian bowed deeply. 'I'm sure that the tale of your presence here will bear some telling,' he snapped at me. 'But I will see to it your tokens of embassy are respected, at least until you clear the harbour.'

I nodded. I had my own plan, now that my duty was done. I went and knelt by Artapherenes, and I motioned Cyrus to attend. He knelt by my side.

'My lord,' I said.

His eyes were open and his face was stronger. I have known many men recover at sea and in deserts who might have perished on land. The sea is clean.

So he smiled. 'Arimnestos. I knew you would get me here.'

I nodded. 'Lord, these men are my enemies, and I don't intend to give them the chance to betray their oaths to the gods.'

Cyrus smiled at me. He put a hand on mine, right hand to right hand. 'You are a good man,' he said. 'Why must we fight?'

'Change is the only constant,' I said. 'Some day, perhaps, we will be allies.' I stood up. 'I will have you swayed gently over the side, my lord, but the very moment you come to rest on that wharf, my men will back oars, and I will fly.'

Artapherenes nodded. 'My heart advises that what you do, you must do,' he admitted. 'That man's face held much hate. What have you done?'

I smiled. 'They made me a slave. I paid them back.' I rose to my feet and walked back to the helmsman's station. I took the oars from Sekla and said, 'Give me a moment here,' and he smiled and walked away.

Briseis watched it all.

I put my ship on a long, slow curve towards the pier to which the Carthaginian harbour officer pointed from his pilot boat.

I made a hand sign to Leukas, and the oar-rate picked up. The Carthaginian ships had come to a full stop to watch our talk with their elder, and they were slower and heavier, and we shot away.

'I am about to put your husband ashore,' I said.

She nodded.

'You could always come with me,' I said. 'I know you won't, but I'll curse myself for the next ten years if I do not ask.'

Briseis stood. Very softly, she said, 'Some day, I will live as your wife. But you do not want to humiliate Artapherenes any more than I do.' She smiled into my eyes. 'I do not love him with fire, but I love him none the less, Achilles. He is a worthy man.'

'He lay with your mother!' I said. See, the adolescent is never far beneath the surface, and I was suddenly angry.

She recoiled, looked away, and flushed. Then she said, 'You once swore to protect our family.'

Now it was my turn to look away.

She nodded. 'If the world were a simple place, none of us would have to make the choices that define who we are. Even when our choices are folly and hubris.' She shrugged. 'And would you have me abandon our children?'

'Children?' I asked.

She laughed. 'You are a fool, my Achilles.' She rose on her toes and kissed me, to the scandal of all the Persians. 'It is war,' she said. 'And in war, there is change. Didn't Heraklitus say so? Not this summer or next – but soon.'

'I will come for you,' I said, as rash as an ephebe.

She smiled. 'Good.'

We were three ships' lengths from the wharf. And as usual, I had put Briseis ahead of all my other concerns. Thankfully . . .

In many ways, despite everything that follows, it was *Lydia*'s finest hour.

First, because we rowed to within a ship's length of the pier – and suddenly, without warning or orders, at a single whistle, the port-side rowers reversed their cushions and we turned in our own length, slowing in the process to a stop and then continuing sternward at a walking pace. It is a wonderful manoeuvre – try training men to it, and you will find that it can take a summer to get it right once. Only a crew that has been together for years can get it just right, without broaching the ship or capsizing or breaking oars or wallowing.

All the starboard-side oars for the first six benches from the stern came in, and our starboard side sternward bulwark came to rest against the stone of the pier as if we were a child accepting the gentle embrace of a loving mother.

Before we touched, every marine was ashore. And Briseis – bless her – her voice barked like a fishwife's, and the women climbed the side and made the short jump while the lines were held. I clasped Cyrus's hand while Arayanam and Darius lifted Artapherenes on a bed made of spears and cloaks, and they stepped from the rail to the shore like sailors.

The three Persians saluted with their hands in the Persian way.

Briseis smiled at me.

I broke free of her gaze and made a single hand gesture to Megakles at the helm, and then at Leukas amidships. Leukas roared, 'Pull!'

Now, I don't know that the men of Carthage meant to betray their oaths. But I saw no reason to linger and test them.

The two heavy triremes were two cables astern, just getting up to speed. Three more triremes were launching from the sheds, and there was a great deal of commotion along the shoreline, and my heavy crew – with all the best men in their seats – knew the drill.

In five strokes we were at cruising speed.

There was a shout from the ship-sheds.

A sixth ship got off the beach under the sheds. I watched him – Phoenicians' ships are often male – and his oar-stroke was disgustingly ragged, and that made me watch him another few heartbeats. Only a certain kind of trierarch would have such a ragged crew. Phoenicians are generally superb sailors, but they have a few right fools and at least one evil madman.

Fifteen strokes and my oarsmen were pulling like the heroes in the *Argo* and I could see their oars bend at the height of the stroke. We were almost at full speed – ramming speed, as fast as a galloping horse.

I've said this other nights, but a sea fight seems to get faster and faster as you get closer to the moment of combat. I don't know whether this is some effect of the hand of the gods, of the spirit men carry within them, or merely a flaw in the flow of time's stream. Once thing I know – sometimes it is merely that the rowers pull harder as the ships close.

The two closest Carthaginians were suddenly five ships' lengths away. And closing at the converging speeds of a cavalry charge.

I had a ship that had been built for me – a crew I'd led for two wildly successful years, and trained the way a swordsmith hones a sword. And the harbour of Carthage isn't like the open ocean – it is like a mill pond. Flat. Weatherless. With no surprises. The moment I saw that badly handled trireme launch, I hoped it was Dagon. How many mad trierarchs could Carthage have?

I had a notion.

As we shot at the two Carthaginians, both altered their helms very slightly, to widen the gap between them so that I couldn't oar-rake the two of them.

It was a wise precaution.

But I had no intention of touching a Carthaginian that day. I had come into this harbour as an ambassador, and I had already done a great deed – I had kept an oath, and followed the bonds of hospitality. Cimon, I was sure, would praise me as a noble man. I had no intention of sacrificing all that for a moment's satisfaction in fighting. Let the Phoenicians break the truce and be cursed by the gods.

'Oars in!' I roared.

Always the last order before an oar-rake.

My oars shot in – my opponents might have asked why they came in so early, but no one ever does, in a real fight. The enemy helmsmen saw my oars come in and they each cheated their helms slightly

31

inward and ordered their own oars in, ready for the clash.

Every one of my marines and deck crewmen – and my twenty spare oarsmen – went and leaned on the port side of our trihemiola's deck rail. And I motioned, and Megakles put the helm hard over.

And we turned. Not the sharp turn of a low-speed rowing turn, like the one we'd just executed, where you turn on a single point, like a pivot – but a high-speed turn on the arc of the ship's length, drawing a geometrical figure in the water.

I might not have tried in the open ocean with real waves, but on the still waters of their inner harbour, I trusted to Moira and my rowers.

We shot across the westernmost ship's bow, so close that I could have hit their ship with an apple core. We were coasting, coasting ...

Ka held up an arrow and I shook my head.

Both of the enemy ships fell astern, turning as fast as they could.

'Oars out,' I called.

Have you ever had the moment come to you when you can *feel* the favour of the gods? When you are almost with them?

I had the sun and the sparkle of the sea – the stink of their barbaric sacrifices and the warmth of Briseis' smile.

I looked off to the west, where the four triremes were struggling to get all their rowers seated and rowing.

Sekla sighed. 'You're grinning,' he said. 'Everyone's scared, except Brasidas, who says you are like a mad priest.'

'Brasidas didn't say that many words.' I looked at Sekla, and his dark brown eyes were laughing.

'Whatever you are planning, I think it's my duty to point out that if you'd just turn out to sea, we'd run clear in five minutes.' Sekla pointed to the harbour mouth.

I nodded. 'Give me five minutes,' I said.

Sekla shook his head. 'Why?' he asked.

'Revenge,' I said.

We went west, no faster than a fast cruise. The wind was against us, and since our mast was a standing mast, the rowers had to work hard just to maintain speed. Leukas began to use the reserves to replace men as they tired.

I motioned, and Megakles cheated our hull south, towards the beach, by slapping his oars with the palms of his hands – just a few dactyls that would move the ship's hull south a little and then back on course before we lost way.

I needed all of my opponents to remain fixated on me.

And the gods were with me.

When the time seemed right ... It was like working a problem in mathematics, with Heraklitus watching over my shoulder, or Pythagoras's daughter Dano making little disapproving noises – I thought of her surprise to hear that a little man like me used her great father's theory of triangles.

But this was sheer guesswork.

I assumed it would take a certain time to turn my ship, even at this slow speed.

'Prepare to turn north!' I called.

'Starboard rowers, reverse your seats!' Leukas roared.

The ship was alive beneath me, and as soon as Leukas's hand came up to tell me that the benches were reversed, I pumped my fist – the starboard side oars touched the water, and Megakles leaned in his harness, pushing both steering oars together, and we turned.

The enemies to the west were slower. Those to the east – those we'd outmanoeuvred – were faster. Now I turned between them.

They all went to ramming speed with a clash of cymbals that carried across the water.

They were all very slightly astern of me, running at almost right angles, aimed a little ahead of me. I wasn't going very fast – in a ship fight, nothing loses speed like a hard turn. Every one of my rowers had his oar poised at the top of its arc, but none of them was in the water.

Bah. This is like having to explain the punchline of a joke. I confess that had they not been blinded by the gods, they would have smoked the trick or at least realised that I wasn't rowing.

Sekla said, 'This is insane.' He laughed aloud.

I lifted my hand. 'Now!' I roared.

Leukas's spear hit the deck.

One hundred and eighty oars bit the water.

One.

The six enemy ships swept at us like avenging falcons. No doubt that they meant me harm. No doubt they were coming for the kill. Fixated on it like predators – four from the west, two from the east. And the middle ship of the four was Dagon's – now I could see him standing amidships with a heavy whip in his hand. He had painted his ship red above the mid-deck oarsmen and white below, and the white showed brown and black stains – an ugly ship.

Two strokes. We were moving a little faster than walking pace, and the lead western ship cheated his helm a little to keep his ram in line with us.

Without a word from me, Megakles read my mind and steered a little bit to the west. I was looking at the sloppily rowed ship. There he was.

You know how you can pick out a woman you have loved or a good friend three streets away in a crowded city street – yes? The sway of hips, the particular way a man holds his hand or cocks his head, the slant of the forehead, the droop of a shoulder . . .

There was Dagon.

I knew him.

I laughed.

There are fools who do not believe in the gods, but I have seen them. And that day, in the harbour of Carthage, I felt Athena at my shoulder as if I was Odysseus reborn.

Third stroke. We were now moving as fast as a man can run.

I raised my fist and waved it at Dagon.

Fourth stroke. We shot out from between the beaks of the Carthaginians, like a hare that gybes so fast that the claws of the eagle close on empty air.

Except that there were six eagles, and they were on converging courses.

I watched Dagon as he saw the two ships to the east which had been hidden by my hull. And his own greed.

All six ships tried to change course.

One ship evaded the collision, but the other five slammed into each other – our two pursuers from the east into Dagon and the ships immediately north and south of his. They all collided – oars snapped, and men died.

We rowed out of their harbour, smelling their barbaric sacrifices and listening to the screams of their broken oarsmen, as their ships fouled the oars of the others, splintering the shafts, and breaking men's chests and arms and necks.

Brasidas came aft, and gave me his little smile.

Sekla was still shaking his head. 'Did you plan all that?' he asked.

I shrugged. 'I made it possible for the gods to show their hands,' I said.

The Spartan nodded.

★

I wasn't going back to Sybaris or Croton or Syracusa. So I watered at Lampedusa and again at Melita, and rested my rowers there. I intended to run for Athens, but at Melita, Brasidas asked me – with grave courtesy – if I could take him home.

And there was a man on the beach, nearly beside himself with fury. He was an Italian Greek, and an athlete. I knew him – everyone did, in those days. Astylos of Croton. He had won the stade and the diaulos at Olympia. He had a statue in Croton, his home city, and I had seen him pointed out to me there by Dano, Pythagoras's daughter.

He came to me as soon as we landed, put his hand out in supplication, and begged me to take him aboard as a passenger. The same storm that had dismasted *Lydia* had wrecked his ship on Melita's rocky shores. And he was desperate because it was an Olympic year, and he was due to compete. Athletes are required by the games to come a full lunar month before the first sacrifice – to prove they are worthy to compete. He was already a week late.

And his trainer was Polymarchos. Do you remember him from last night? A freedman who had trained me in Syracusa. I won't say he was the best swordsman I ever saw – that honour belongs to Istes, brother of Hippeis of Militus. But he taught swordsmanship better than any man I ever met, and he taught pankration as well, and running, and here he was on the beach at Melita.

He looked at me from under his heavy brows, like Herakles come to life – I've seldom met a man with the same weight of bone over his brow and yet such startling intelligence.

'You ruined Lydia,' he said. 'Daughter of Nikedemos, who took you into his home and welcomed you – and you ruined her.' He shook his head. 'Come,' he said to his athlete. 'I would rather miss the games than travel in this ship.'

I could see that his athlete felt differently. I walked to him, planted myself in his path, thumbs hooked in my zone. 'I have done evil deeds,' I said. 'But I have attempted to come right with the gods. Will you hear me?'

He turned his head away. His hands flexed at his sides, and his stance changed slightly – preparing to fight.

I knew his strength and speed. So I took a half-step back and touched my sword-hilt.

'Speak,' he commanded.

'Lydia is married to Anaxsikles the smith, and they have gone

35

to Croton to live.' I frowned. 'I helped Anarchos to arrange it. You must just have missed them. I provided the ship and the money. Polymarchos, I never intended that such evil befall her. But I accept that it was through my actions that she came to grief.' I shrugged. 'I have nothing more to say,' I managed, sounding very young in my own ears. It is hard to talk to a man with his head turned away.

'Nikedemos was a fool to turn her out of his house,' Polymarchos said. 'She was a fool to be so hurt by you, and you were a fool to play with a girl so young.' His eyes met mine. 'There are many fools in the world and I have been one of them. Are you sorry?'

Anger – anger born of resentment, anger at my own foolishness – bubbled up. I suppose my eyes clouded, and I'm sure my hands clenched, because I can still remember unclenching them. 'I'm more than sorry. I . . . lost something of what I thought I was.'

He rubbed his beard. 'Well – I never had you figured for a scheming betrayer, for all you're a subtle swordsman.' He glanced at his athlete. The young man was all but begging him. 'This pup will be much in your debt if you'll run us across to the coast of Elis.' He glanced at me from under his heavy brows.

'I've promised to take one of my men to the port for Sparta.' I pointed to Brasidas. He came over from his fire. He was candidly admiring the young athlete.

'Brasidas, this is Polymarchos, a hoplomachos teacher, a pankrationist, a wrestler – a fine coach. Polymarchos, this is Brasidas – sometime captain of my marines. A Lacedaemonian.'

Brasidas nodded graciously. Polymarchos matched his nod almost exactly. Then he turned to me. 'No matter how fast your ship – I'd have to ask you to run to Elis first, or even into the delta of Alpheos. The games are only a week away.'

I looked at Brasidas, and he smiled. He met my eyes and nodded.

'We'll take you,' I said.

Brasidas caught my arm – an unaccustomed gesture from the Spartan. 'I would see the Olympics,' he said. Quite a speech, from him.

Ten minutes' discussion on the beaches of Melita and it turned out that there wasn't a man in my crew who didn't want to see the Olympics.

Oh, what a pleasure it is to be rich enough and powerful enough to take a warship to sea with no better purpose than to go to the greatest games given in all the lands of the Hellenes! Mind you, I wasn't completely a fool. I loaded seventy great Melitan amphora of the best Chian wine I could buy. I'd never been to the Olympics, but there were men in Plataea who had – old Epiktetus, for one – and they all complained about the shameful bad wine and the crowds.

I remember that trip – less than three thousand stades, with a fair wind – as one of the more pleasant of my life. We filled our bilges with wine amphorae and then tucked up the nooks and crannies with water and salt pork and some bread, and we did what only Phoenicians usually did – we sailed the blue ocean, a straight line from Sicily to Elis. It is hard to reckon distances on the pathless surface of the sea, but my estimate was (and is) that it is almost three thousand stades from Melita to Olympia. And never a rock or an islet to get fresh water or rest your crew after you depart Sicily. We built a small floor of bricks in the bow and laid sand over it for a brazier, but you cannot cook food for two hundred men on a trireme and you can't even *carry* enough food for a week.

Still, our trip into the Western Ocean had taught us a dozen tricks for surviving in open ocean. One was that we knew we could go two days without food.

At any rate, Sekla and Megakles and I chose a course after some argument, and we put some scratches in the helmsman's rail to indicate where the sun should be at dawn, at noon and at sunset. After that, all we had was the straightness of the wake and the position of the stars, because there was no beach to rest at night after the first. The first night we touched at Sicily – we landed on the so-called Carthaginian shore south of Syracusa. Polymarchos took his young man out for a run, and a dozen of us joined him – Brasidas, of course, and me, and Alexandros and young Giannis. We ran under Aetna's crown, and smoke trailed away from the deeps within her. I have no idea how far we ran, but the young athlete effortlessly outpaced us all, even Brasidas. He was beautiful as he ran, and yet somewhat hangdog about it.

'Why's he so surly?' I asked Polymarchos.

The old fighter shrugged. 'We're farther from the Temple of Olympian Zeus than we were fifty days ago when we started,' he said. 'He's late. He may well be banned.'

It was the longest voyage I'd attempted on the Inner Sea – the longest made intentionally, with no storm to carry me where Poseidon willed. I sacrificed six sheep on the beach at Sicily – not far from where I'd once sat in the marketplace with Demetrios and

Herakles, selling hides – and stuffed my oarsmen with mutton, good bread, olives and good red wine.

And with the dawn, we were off. Our course was almost due east, into the rising sun, and we had the perfect wind. By noon, Aetna was almost gone behind us, and by dark, we were out on the great deep sea without land anywhere. The newer oarsmen were plainly terrified, and we served out wine and stale bread and dates.

The old hands – the oarsmen who'd been out beyond the pillars – laughed at their timorousness.

'You ain't seen nothing, young squid,' one old salt pronounced. 'A calm night like this on the great green? It's like being home in your bed.'

Polymarchos, that master of every weapon, looked green himself. He sat on the helmsman's bench – where Briseis had sat just a few days before – and groaned. 'I heard you say you were going into the open ocean,' he admitted. 'But I didn't think it through. Do you ... know ... where we are?'

I laughed. 'Yes,' I said. I pointed overhead. 'See the stars? Do you know they move?'

He nodded, eager to have his thoughts taken off the dark and moving waters.

I pointed at the Pole Star. 'You know that the heavens have a linchpin, like the wheel of a chariot?' I asked.

After watching for a while, he agreed this might be true, and I thought how odd it was that city men had so little idea of how the world worked. Perhaps a man has to live outdoors in all weathers to properly accept the role of the gods. And the way the world is made.

At any rate, after an hour or so, he accepted that I had a star that didn't move.

So I showed him a little of the knowledge I'd learned in the hardest school, as a slave on Dagon's ship, listening to Phoenician navigators talk about how to watch the stars. I showed him how to use a spear shaft, and how to use a cross-staff.

Finally, he laughed nervously – he, who could put me down in three sword-cuts.

'I don't know any more than I did when I started,' he admitted. 'But now I believe that *you* know.'

'Isn't that what you start with, when you teach an athlete?' I asked.

He frowned. 'Usually, that takes a year,' he said. 'It is a year before most young men really admit, inside their fool heads, that I can beat them – that they need to know what I have to teach.'

We both laughed. Then he put a hand on my knee. 'Listen – you are a good man. Why did you do such a foolish thing? To Lydia? And then you name your ship after her? What does that mean?'

I busied myself with the helm for a moment. 'It means that I refuse to let myself forget it,' I said. 'And I told myself a lot of lies about Lydia. I wanted two things. I wanted to sail to Alba, and I wanted the girl. But I can see now that she was the embodiment of something else that I wanted – a life as a craftsman.'

Polymarchos grinned, teeth white and shining in the darkness. 'I never thought you was really a bronzesmith. Nah – that's wrong. I knew you was. I just thought it was a hobby. You have aristocrat written all over you – even the way your muscles are formed. You've had gymnasiums all your life.'

Now it was my turn to laugh. 'Polymarchos, I was a slave from age fifteen to age twenty, and again just before you met me.'

He nodded. 'Sure. Many men spend time as slaves. Some it stamps indelibly, like a leatherworker's tool, and some it merely teaches a little humility. Gelon could use a few months as someone's slave.'

I raised an eyebrow. 'You left Syracusa.'

He nodded. 'Gelon is a brilliant tyrant, and he will make Syracusa great. But he took my citizenship. Fuck him. I spent half my life earning my way out of the slavery a bunch of pirates put me in, so that one rich bastard could take it again.' He glared at the dark water and the stars. 'Now I'll take this young Italiote to Olympia, and we'll win. And then Gelon will know what he has earned for himself by losing me. I could have won this for Syracusa.'

The next day, we had another day of pure, sweet sailing – the wind almost dead astern, the mainsail set and drawing well, the bow skimming along the waves. I found it hard to measure our speed – always a problem in blue-water sailing. It is difficult to work the geometrical figures for speed and distance when you don't know how far you are travelling or how fast you are going.

Leukas came aft for his spot at the helm. As soon as he had the oars, I took charcoal and began to draw on the deck, measuring the cord from Augusta Bay to Olympia by guessing the distance from Melita to Sybaris, based on a dozen journeys, and then making the same guess for the distance from Sybaris to Olympia. If, as I suspected, the two legs formed a right angle, then according to Pythagoras ...

Well, the figure I solved for was two and a half thousand stades. I figured it for an hour, and while I figured, I taught Leukas, who was coming along in his Greek letters, and Megakles, who could not read at all and wasn't interested. Leukas had never multiplied anything, but Sekla had, and he joined in, and then we were using the cross-staff to measure the sun's angle. It passed the time, and led the oarsmen to believe that we knew what we were doing.

We tossed wood chips over the side and tried to imagine how fast we were going based on how fast they fell astern. Our young athlete tried racing the wood chips down the length of the hull.

Astylos ran all day – even in the full heat of the sun. A trihemiola – a trireme with a flat deck and standing mast – has far more deck space than a trireme, but it is still only about one hundred and ten feet long. A stadion is six hundred feet long, so he had to run the length of the deck, turning constantly – and avoiding sailors and off-duty oarsmen.

At any rate – Astylos's performance against the wood chips gave me the notion that we were making about thirty stades an hour, which put us at over seven hundred stades a day, sunrise to sunrise.

Well – Poseidon's realm is immense. I knew that before I started figuring.

But from that day on, I began to see sailing and rowing as part of something greater, and this had many effects. First, because I taught Sekla and Leukas whatever I knew. Leukas was a far better natural sailor than I was – his guesses of our speed over water were far better than mine, and his notions of currents and his *feel* for the weather were better, but he was not very good at explaining things. However, he tried. Sekla knew the southern coast of the Inner Sea, and we began to discuss the possibility of exploring it. Greeks tend to know Greek waters. We're limited to what the Phoenicians allow us. Or we were then.

Not any more. Heh.

The ability to cross the blue deep without touching – I began to think about that tactically. We had often used a small round ship – the sort of ship that could be handled by four to six men – as a supply ship, and I determined to get my hands on one.

And I began to think about what war with Persia would mean. The last time that Greeks had tried to face Persia at sea, the Persians had outspent the Greeks, created a fleet with almost six hundred hulls – and purchased the treason of the Samnians. They won the battle of Lade hands down.

And now all those Ionian Greek cities were in their hands. In effect, that gave them a thousand good ships. My friends – my Athenian friends, who were, I hoped, just over the horizon, or headed for Athens, because I hadn't seen them in two weeks – my Athenian friends had told me that in my absence, Themistocles had seized the products of the Athenian silver mines and built a one-hundred-ship fleet for Athens with public money. A hundred ships was an incredible number for a Greek city. Rumour was that Aegina had another eighty.

Corinth might have another eighty.

Sparta would have ... none.

Even if the three mightiest sea powers among the remaining Greek cities united – they would have two hundred and fifty ships.

I looked out at the endless waves, and shuddered. In the whole of my life, Athens, Corinth and Aegina had never allied for any reason whatsoever.

The second sunset, and I saw seabirds. I was pleased, and said so to Leukas, who nodded.

Nonetheless, I was on deck all night. The night is a time when a man can think too much, and I had eight hours of darkness to smell the wind and think about Briseis. I could smell her hair on the wind, and I could feel her kiss on my lips, and I could wonder why I hadn't gone to her at night on the beach. I could think a hundred conflicting thoughts.

I could remember that she had said that some day we would live as man and wife.

I could take my Phoenician cross-staff and measure the heights of stars and their movement, and I could watch my wake and the sea.

I remember – that night, or the one following – I recalled a moment of wry annoyance when I realised that I had sworn to Apollo to learn the kithara or the lyre, and I hadn't done much with it. I didn't even have a lyre on which to practise. The gut strings are no friends to the sea – or rather, the sea air is no friends to wood and gut.

I thought about Polymarchos, and I thought far too much about the young slave I'd killed with my first cut on the beach of Africa. He hadn't deserved to die. He had mostly been in the wrong place at the wrong time.

He was the same age as my son by Briseis. I had seen the boy, carried by a nurse, in Thrace, when I killed the man I had assumed to be his father.

I had a son.

The bow ploughed the waves, and I thought about what Heraklitus the philosopher said about dipping our toes in the river. And we rushed on.

The next day was very long. We were already low on water, and all the salted pork was gone, most of the dates, all the bread.

My veterans had done all this before.

The new men, the former slaves – they were plainly terrified. I began to worry that they would mutiny again – not because they had any real chance of success, but because such behaviours can become a habit.

But an hour before dawn, I could smell land. I had the most exact scent of a charcoal fire, and the very first grey light of pre-dawn showed me the coast. I ran along it for an hour as the sun rose, and I became increasingly sure that it was Zacynthus. I'd run down that coast only three weeks before. I was almost sure, and the oarsmen were openly begging us to land, when I saw the temple of Poseidon at Hyrmine gleaming on the opposite headland. Brasidas confirmed it, and the newer oarsmen looked as if they'd been granted a new lease on life.

Sekla slapped my back. 'A brilliant piece of navigation.' He grinned.

I shrugged. 'Vasileos would have put the bow into the mouth of the Alpheos,' I said.

Megakles just smiled, as Laconic in his fisherman's way as Brasidas. But his smile was good praise. I was pleased. And before the men were too hungry, we landed on an open beach, bought sheep, sacrificed Melitan wine to Poseidon and a good cup too, and sacrificed the animals. We had a feast on the beach, and the new oarsmen kissed the sand, and the older oarsmen teased them.

But the shepherds were men of Elis, and they confirmed that the games started in four days.

We were still full of mutton while we pulled around the point and into the very narrow estuary of the Alpheos. There were a dozen merchantmen and almost forty triremes pulled up on the narrow pebble beach. Olympia nestles amidst mighty mountains, and the mountains seem to reach right down to the sea, as does Kitharon at home, and the beaches are steep and narrow and difficult.

Despite which, my heart fairly leaped with joy to see Cimon's *Ajax* and Paramanos' *Black Raven* and Harpagos's *Storm Cutter* and all the other ships we'd lost in the storm.

I waited for the men of Elis to choose me a landing place, and I enjoyed seeing the alterations they'd made to the beach. The hand of man can alter almost anything. That year was the seventy-fifth Olympiad, and the people of Elis had had three hundred years to make the landing area as comfortable as possible. Hellenes made the pilgrimage from Ionia and from Italia and Magna Greca and Sicily and as far as Massalia in the west and Ephesus and Sardis in the east, from Thrace and from Chacedon and from everywhere in Boeotia and Attica and the Peloponnesus. And for a moment, as I looked over the shipping and the tents and booths, I thought of my son – my son, running his stades and throwing his javelins in far-off Sardis.

And then my grand thoughts were ruined by the pair of Elisian factors demanding that I pay their outrageous landing fees. There may be an Olympic truce on war and strife, but there is none on greed, as I can attest. And it is fifty stades up-country into the mountains to Olympia, and I had thought to rent a horse, but I had to count my drachma – the prices were exorbitant, and I was feeding two hundred men.

My mother was sometimes a harridan, a harpy, an old drunkard. But she had the soul of an aristocrat, and she did teach me one valuable aristocratic lesson – there is a time to pinch pennies, and a time to let the gold flow through your fingers. A man is lucky if he attends the Olympics once in his life. I don't mean Spartans, or men of Argos – with a little effort, they can make the trip every year. But for a Boeotian, it is a once-in-a-lifetime opportunity – at any rate, I was on the beach, and I wasn't going to be dissuaded.

On the other hand – I had two hundred men trained to a high pitch, and I saw no reason not to use that training, so we stripped the ship, made packs, and marched up-country carrying our own shelter and all of our amphorae of wine. I spent my Illyrian loot freely, but we camped rather than renting flea-ridden lodgings. When we arrived on the plain of Olympia below the temple complex, a pair of priests emerged from the town and led us to a site where we could camp. I asked after Cimon and the priest smiled – he was a pleasant fellow – and nodded.

'Lord Cimon is present. The Athenians are on the other side of the treasuries. And your fellow Boeotians are just there, by the stream.' He pointed at the nearly dry course of the river.

'Thebans?' I asked.

He nodded. 'Yes.'

I didn't quite spit. 'Respected sir, I am a man of Plataea, and I would walk a dozen stades to avoid a man of Thebes.'

He laughed. 'It is a wonder that the Greeks have any common ground at all,' he said. 'Come – any man who brings two hundred followers to the games gets my attention. Are you the man who was at Marathon?'

I nodded.

He smiled. 'I thought so. I'll send a slave to tell Lord Cimon you are here.'

We'd come to the edge of the valley.

I had seldom seen so many people gathered in one place in all my life. I saw Cyrenes and Italiotes and Athenians and Messenians and Corinthians – and Spartans. More Spartans than you could shake a spear at. And with them, their women – tall, mostly blond, and all with the muscled arms and legs that mark Spartan women everywhere you meet them.

Women were not allowed to compete at Olympia during the main festival. They had their own festival later in the season, but in the Olympic year, this was the men's event. Nowadays, there is talk of forbidding women from watching, but in those days, women came right into the sanctuaries and cheered – not just maidens and whores, either, but married women. I think this is because in Sparta, men and women were more used to each other's nudity in games, and girls thought it no great matter to see a naked man. Athens is altogether more prudish. The men of Elis are of old allies of the Spartans and members of the Peloponnesian League, and they have many of their ways. At any rate, in that year, there were almost as many women as men in the tents, under shelters, or in the town.

Every house in the town had a porch built for ten or twelve beds. And sometimes rooms inside as well, and they would charge three or four drachma a day – for two wooden boards and some old straw, they charged a day's pay for an Athenian hoplite or an elite rower. And the more enterprising men of Elis and the surrounding region would put up big tents and offer space in them at similar rates, or they would build temporary buildings, with each peg and each beam marked with a number so that they could be taken down and rebuilt, like the wooden theatre of Dionysus in Athens. There was one great inn where a room cost twenty drachmas a night and only great men like Aristides were welcome.

All of my recent ex-slaves were earning their keep by hauling the great amphora of Chian wine, and when we had our campsite, my two hundred ran up our mainsail and two boat sails and four more military tents, and the smallest tent was quickly fitted with stumps and larger stones for men to sit on, and we began serving wine before we had our own quarters up, with a pair of marines on guard – not in armour, as that would have been impious – and with Alexandros and Giannis, who had a flair for such things, managing the pouring.

I oversaw the tents myself – and had to pay two hard silver coins for wood to make pegs, as we'd left all of ours on the ship, like fools. It was hot work, despite the altitude, and I was pleased to see that Polymarchos and his young athlete pitched in, working themselves hard, pounding pegs, and holding poles until the work was done.

I took the trainer by the shoulder. 'Come and have a cup of good wine with me,' I said.

He smiled. 'Later, Arimnestos of Plataea. For now I must take this young man to the temple of Zeus, so that he is officially entered for his races and events, or he will burst.' He shrugged. 'If they ask us about the storm – would you testify to the judges?'

I nodded.

I took the young man's hand. 'You have done very well with us,' I said. 'We measure a man by work, and not by good looks.' In truth, he was a beautiful young man, and not all my oarsmen – or marines – were immune to his looks. I grinned at him. 'You've hauled ropes, raised tents – you have been a pleasure to have aboard. So please consider camping with us, and you'll have two hundred fans to cheer you when you run.'

Polymarchos nodded. 'That's no small offer – men from Italy never have anyone to cheer them.'

The young man bowed. 'I am honoured.'

And they were off to the temple. I held it in his favour that he helped us with the camp before he went to face the wrath of the judges.

I went with Brasidas to get a cup of wine, and we were shocked to find that our canvas taverna had a line threading out of the door and all the way to the edge of the camp, with men pushing and shoving.

45

For complex reasons – reasons that this story will touch on, if you stay – it was one of the most crowded Olympiads in anyone's memory, and wine was already in short supply, three days before the first event was due to be run, and a day before the priests would burn the preliminary offerings. We had sixty big-bellied amphorae, and another six of oil, and we were charging what I considered a fair price that would gain us a large profit, and here were a thousand men, give or take, waiting in line for a cup of wine, with men joining the line so fast that in the time I take to tell this, another fifteen had joined the line behind Brasidas.

Several places behind me was a handsome young boy with dark skin and slightly slanted eyes. Those eyes were not common on the Inner Sea, and I knew him immediately. I smiled. 'Ganymede come to life,' I called out. Other men turned and looked, and the boy flushed. He was Cimon's hypaspist – a freeman, now, but originally purchased as a slave somewhere in the Chersonnese.

He bowed. 'Lord Arimnestos,' he said.

I shrugged. 'You are not a pais any more, and you needn't call any man lord,' I said. 'How is your master? Is all well?'

'He will be the better for knowing that you rode the storm and lived,' he said. 'I should go and tell him, but he was most insistent on a cup of wine. There is none to be had except a very bad local wine.' He looked almost tragically concerned, as young men are when they have been sent on errands.

I laughed. 'Please tell Cimon that I will make sure he has wine, if only he'll come and drink with me. Go – I'll wait.'

The boy bowed and ran off.

I turned to Brasidas. 'You don't think power has gone to Alexandros' head and he'll refuse us more than one cup?'

Brasidas smiled. But his smile was the only answer I got.

We waited as long as it takes a man to deliver the whole of his accusation in a law court – the sun sank appreciably behind the shoulder of the mountain – before we made it to the front of the line.

One of Ka's archers – the wounded man, Ata – was sitting cross-legged at a low table. He nodded without looking at us. 'A drachma a cup – lordy. It's the trierarch!' He shot to his feet as he looked up and realised he was addressing me.

Brasidas smiled.

I leaned over the low table. 'We're charging *a drachma a cup?*'

Alexandros grinned. 'Yes, sir!' His smile faltered. 'We're making a fortune, sir.'

I shook my head. 'We're not so greedy, gentlemen. Cut the price in half. Save six amphorae for our own use.'

Men behind me in the line cheered.

'Or double the price, and help fund the war against the Medes,' said a voice by my right ear, and there was Cimon. 'I'm a rich man and a eupatrid, and despite that, I considered leaving the temple precincts to run down the coast and buy any wine I could. Even if such behaviour is undignified.' He smiled at my pais, Hector. 'Handsome boy. Slave? I remember seeing him on the beach with you.'

I shook my head. 'Free. The son of a friend. A citizen of Syracusa.'

Cimon inclined his head. 'Forgive my use of the term pais, young man.'

My hypaspist, Hector, had been silent since the death of his father, and life on board ship – where he was mostly seasick and miserable – had left him literally unable to speak, but Olympus was recalling the boy to life and he flushed and bowed. 'My lord,' he said.

I put a cup of wine in Cimon's hand – he'd jumped the line with the natural greed of a great lord – and handed another to Brasidas and another to Cimon's hypaspist and yet another to my own, serving them all myself, like a good host. My mother had forced a few good manners on me.

'If Alexandros was selling wine at a drachma a cup, he has discovered a way of life more remunerative than piracy,' I admitted as we walked back into the magnificent red-gold light of the setting sun.

Cimon laughed – very much his father's, Miltiades', laugh. 'As honest pirates, we know that there is no better life,' he said. 'My visit to the Olympic games is being paid for by your Illyrian kinglet.'

'Is Paramanos here? Moire?' I looked at the line. Paramanos was a Cyrene – now an Athenian citizen – and Moire was my own captain and probably needed to be made a citizen of Plataea.

Cimon nodded. 'They're camped with me. The prices are exorbitant! And your friend Harpagos has a young cousin competing in pankration. And Aeschylus's young sprig . . .'

I shook my head. We had had young Aristides with us in our brief foray into Illyria, and there wasn't a man among us who hadn't found him tiresome. But it was like belonging to a city or being part of a village – I felt at home, even on the plain beneath the shadow of mighty Olympus.

Giannis, my young friend from Massalia, was transported. In addition to helping Alexandros make a fortune, he was seeing all the great men of Greece, and he looked as if he was atop Mount Olympus, with the gods, not at the base, drinking wine.

Cimon drank his wine. I could tell he wanted to say something and all this small talk was merely his way – the Greek way – of working around to the main topic. Brasidas shot me a look, which I interpreted as his willingness to walk off and leave us to ourselves, but I just shrugged at him.

'What are your plans from here?' Cimon asked with that elaborate casualness that marks a man who has a favour to ask.

'I'm for Plataea,' I said. 'But whether I go via Corinth or by way of Athens is dependent on many things.'

He nodded and looked away. His eyes followed a pair of eagles soaring high above us, well up the shoulder of the mountain. There is no better omen.

'Those eagles say that you should ask your question,' I said, in as light a voice as I could manage.

He bit his lip. 'Themistocles is here,' he said.

I nodded, the way men nod when they have no idea what other men are on about. 'I remember him well,' I said.

'You have been gone a long time. Themistocles has summoned – has requested – that all the great men of Greece attend these games – to talk about the Great King.'

I laughed. 'And I'm not invited? You could have told me straight out – I've outgrown the need to be the great man, Cimon. Your father always did it better than I ever will.'

But his face didn't change. 'No – I'm sure Themistocles will want you.' His eyes were evasive. 'Arimnestos – you are not an Athenian. And yet you are one of us – you led the way at Marathon.'

'Spit it out!' I said.

'Themistocles is working on a sentence of exile for Aristides,' he said. 'Aristides was ever your friend.'

I made the gesture that Boeotian peasants – and bronzesmiths – use to avert witchcraft. 'Aristides was ever my friend – but not yours or your father's by any means.' I tried to make my tone light. 'Cimon – we're at the *Olympics*. Could we suspend Athenian politics a while?'

Cimon turned and met my eyes. 'I held my peace all the way up the Adriatic and on a dozen beaches,' he said. 'I hadn't expected to find myself in the same camp as Themistocles while he bayed for Aristides' blood.'

I remember that I shook my head in disgust. Athenians are fine men – brave, noble, inclined to high ethics and beautiful rhetoric. But most of them would sell their mothers into the degradation of slavery in order to achieve political power.

'Cimon – Aristides hounded your father in the courts. The only thing the two of them did together was to win Marathon. That, and to fight the Alcmaeonidae. Eh?' I spread my hands.

He didn't laugh. 'Aristides is one of us,' he said. 'A gentleman. Themistocles is dead set to overturn the democracy and give power to the lowest orders. We will end with nothing – mark my words.'

I bit my lip. Really – viewed from outside, from Plataea – they'd be comic, these Athenian politicians, with their self-centred political greed dressed up as righteous political ethics – they'd be comic, I say, except that little Plataea needs its alliance with Athens, and when Athens catches cold, Plataea coughs.

And they were all my friends – Themistocles a little less than Cimon or Aristides, but he and I shared Marathon. And the defeat of the Alcmaeonidae.

Thinking of those events – six long years ago – put a niggling suspicion in my head. 'Aristides is the head of your party?' I asked.

Cimon nodded silently.

'Is your party the aristocratic party?' I asked.

Cimon paused. 'Yes,' he said.

'Does your party include Cleitus? And the Alcmaeonidae?' I asked.

Cimon shrugged again. 'Yes,' he admitted. 'Listen! Everything has changed!'

I surprised him, because I stepped forward through his protests and gave him a hug. 'Cimon – I have always seen you as the brother of my youth. I will always be at your side in any adventure – and the same goes for Aristides. My sword and my purse are at your command.' I grinned, and he grinned back.

'Just don't involve me in any of the shit you call politics. And don't put me in the same sword-space as Cleitus.' I delivered the sentence like a sword-blow. I meant it.

'If you understood what's at stake, you'd stand with us!' he insisted.

'Maybe he'd stand with *us*, instead,' Themistocles said. He was standing about ten feet away, and he had one of my horn wine cups in his hand. 'Considering that he's a friend to the thetis and he's been a slave. And he's no friend to the Persians and the Medes.'

Cimon glared. 'You can't pretend in a year of your fancy rhetoric that anyone in my family is a friend to the Medes,' he said.

Themistocles didn't give a dactyl. 'You come from a line of heroes back to Ajax,' he said. 'Your party serves the Great King and takes his bribes.'

'You lie,' Cimon said. 'And no amount of lying will change the reality – Athens cannot stand alone against the might of the Great King.'

I made a sign to my hypaspist. He understood at once, and slipped away.

'We can if we have allies,' Themistocles said.

'Allies like Aegina and Corinth? Our mortal foes?' Cimon asked.

'They are Greeks, like us. Cimon, you have fought the Medes all your adult life. Now you propose to make an "arrangement" with them.' Themistocles had a superb speaking voice – he sounded like the soul of reason. Cimon, by contrast, sounded arrogant.

'The Great King lives in Persopolis, half the world away, and he need never trouble me in my bed. You intend to overthrow the entire world so that you can have a fleet big enough to rival the Great King, and in the end, you will make Athens the centre of a maritime empire, where the rowers are the equals of the hoplites, and the hoplites are nothing but marines. A tyranny of the lowest orders, simply to row your fleet.' He all but spat the words.

Men locked in argument often ignore the world around them. In this case, Cimon was speaking, not just to Themistocles, or me, but to an audience mostly composed of my oarsmen, who were serving as tavern workers.

They began to grumble.

Hector returned with a fine Lesbian amphora charged with wine.

I stepped forward. 'Gentlemen,' I said, 'I am the host here, and I declare that both of you need another cup of wine.'

It says something about – well, about men – that I could agree with almost every word Themistocles said, and still find him a greasy politician; I could, as a non-aristocrat, feel insulted by almost every word that Cimon uttered, and still find him the better man. But if life were simple, we wouldn't spend so much time arguing, would we?

My hypaspist filled their cups, and Themistocles bowed. 'Arimnestos, you are the prince of hosts. I hope you will agree to come and sit at our council fire while we discuss the Great King's demands.'

I raised an eyebrow. 'Who have you invited from Thebes?' I asked.

He shrugged. 'One of their chief priests, and a dozen of their best men.' He looked at Cimon. 'At the Olympic games, one is seldom able to find any members of the thetis class on whom we all depend; but there is always a reliable number of conservative aristocrats.'

'As it should be,' Cimon said. 'The best is for the best men.'

'Really?' Themistocles asked. 'Wouldn't you like excellence to be for every man? Isn't that what Cleisthenes wanted?'

'Cleisthenes sought to allow the best men of the middle sort to be counted with the sons of the gods,' Cimon said carefully, but he was thinking through his words, and I think that shot from Themistocles went home.

'Don't you think that excellence breeds excellence? And that watching the best men in the Greek world compete could only make better men of every man?' Themistocles said. He said something like that. I've lost the elegance of his words, but I agreed.

And I said so.

'Cimon – you can't condemn men based on their birth. I ask you – look at our helmsmen. Birth does not make you a good helmsman. Only time and training and years at sea make you capable of commanding between the oars – eh?' I smiled.

He shook his head. 'Arimnestos – allegories always go the same way. The leadership of a city is not like the piloting of a ship. But even if it was – are you as good at piloting as Harpagos? Or that Alban of yours with the milk-white skin? They were *born* to the sea.'

I scratched my beard. 'You have the better of me there,' I admitted. 'But even though I was not – I can make a competent effort at taking my ship across the sea, or so men say.'

'You are merely an aristocrat pretending to be a bronzesmith,' Cimon said.

Themistocles frowned with real anger, I think. 'You bastards say that of every man who defies your narrow ideas of excellence. You just promote him in your minds to being one of you.'

The sun was setting. Cimon's face was red, but I thought it might just be the setting sun. Still, I didn't think that the two of them were headed in a useful direction. I waved for their cups to be refilled. The line into my canvas taverna now ran all the way to the temple precinct wall.

51

'I had Artapherenes aboard my ship a week ago,' I said.

That got their attention.

Themistocles glared at me. 'The Satrap of Phrygia?' he asked.

I nodded. 'The same. The storm wrecked his ship, and panicked the oarsmen.'

Cimon grinned. 'You *took* the Satrap of Phrygia?' he asked.

I shook my head. 'No – we're guest friends.'

Cimon nodded. 'Of course – I knew that. My father has spoken of it – and he is married to your – ahem – friend. Briseis of Ephesus.' He coughed.

Themistocles sputtered. 'Poseidon's rage! Are you all friends of the Medes? You – the famous warrior, the hero of Marathon?'

I laughed – Themistocles was easy to dislike. Cimon, like a gentleman, immediately appreciated that guest friendship overran any thoughts of ransom. Themistocles couldn't see beyond the advantage it would have brought to have Artapherenes.

I shrugged. 'You know I was a slave in Ephesus. Yes? Artapherenes ...' I smiled '... was instrumental in my freedom,' I said carefully. No lie there – just a carefully nuanced truth. I shrugged. 'Later, he saved my life. And the life of many people close to me.'

Themistocles shook his head. 'You have fought the Medes on many fields,' he said.

I smiled. 'And I count many of them among my friends, Themistocles. Almost as many as I have friends in Athens. Of the two, I feel the Persians are the more honest.'

'So despite all your fine words, you will support the aristocrats,' he said.

I looked at both of them. Talking about politics to Athenians is exactly like managing the helm of a trireme in heavy seas. 'No,' I said, right at him. 'I don't think that I will. But neither am I interested in a war for the emerging empire of Athens, Themistocles. This much I'll tell you both. The Great King is determined on war. He is building his fleets and his armies and his targets are Athens and Sparta.'

Cimon shook his head vehemently. 'No! If we send him tokens of submission – if we offer a small tribute—'

I had to take a step back to get his attention. 'No, Cimon. Don't delude yourself. The Great King is coming. It will not be next year – but it will be soon. Two years at the earliest, is what my friends say. Do you know that he's building a canal through the isthmus of Athos? Do you know that he's raising a fleet from the Ionian cities?

Do you know that he has promised two great satrapies in Europe? And one of those to Mardonias, or that's what I heard.' I shook my head. 'Cimon – you know what it is to decide on a voyage. You know how long it takes to gather your oarsmen, to get enough amphorae to ballast your ship in clay and fresh water, to lay in the sand, to gather salt pork, to find the right braziers and replace the broken oars—'

He held up a hand to indicate that he did, and my rhetorical device could be brought to an end.

'Think about a fleet of a thousand galleys and a quarter of a million oarsmen and marines. Think of an army of half a million soldiers. How long would it take to gather the supplies and scout the roads? And once you have started – once you have *spent the money and told your friends you are going* ...' I paused and took a breath. 'Do you imagine that he'll just stop because you offer a tribute?'

Cimon took a breath. 'And you spoke to him in person?' he said.

I nodded.

'And Briseis, of course,' he said, admitting to himself that I knew what I was saying.

'She said so, too. She would know.' I shrugged.

Themistocles looked at me suspiciously. 'You can't have convinced the eupatridae in one sentence,' he said. 'You are mocking me.'

Cimon was frowning. 'Themistocles – do you think it is possible for honest men to disagree?'

Themistocles thought for a long time, looking for a trap. 'Yes,' he admitted.

'I'm not pleased by what the Plataean has to say – but I have to believe it. I do not love your ... your democracy, Themistocles. But if Athens must fight for her life ...' He shrugged. 'If there is no hope of reconciliation with Persia ...'

'Your father helped create this war,' Themistocles said.

Cimon nodded. 'That's true. And because I know it to be true, I know it can be mended.'

Themistocles looked at me. 'What side will you choose, Plataean?' he asked.

I confess that I laughed. 'I'll be on the Plataean side, of course,' I said.

Themistocles stalked off soon after. Even though I could see that Cimon's mind was changing, Themistocles was such a domineering bastard that he wanted Cimon's absolute agreement – his slavish obedience.

In my observation, demagogues are the harshest tyrants. And you'll see how this comes out, if you stick with me.

I never liked Themistocles. He was too keen on his own power, and he made it a little too obvious to the rest of us that he was smarter than we and felt that we should leave him in peace to decide our futures – for our own good. I really, truly believe that's what he thought, in his heart.

Now, let me confess something to you, my daughter. He was smarter than almost anyone. He alone saw all the ramifications of building a mighty fleet for Athens, and he remained true to them. Other men made compromises – Themistocles was above such stuff. But in the world of mortals, there are no absolute answers, and so, when Themistocles became the saviour of all Greece, he had already planted the seeds of treason.

Hah! Aeschylus might yet write a play. It has all the great themes, does it not?

It is one of the little tricks of the gods that, as soon as a man takes part in some great moment, discussing the affairs of all Greece or considering ethics or philosophy, in the next moment he either has to deal with an angry child, an intestinal ailment, or a bureaucracy. Or perhaps all three at the same time. Just when you feel your most godlike, someone will come along to remind you that you really live in a Cratinus play, not an Aeschylus.

The evening began well, with Paramanos and Harpagos and Moire and some of my other friends and former associates in piracy joining us for wine. It had only been a few weeks since we had raided Illyria, and we were all rich and full of ourselves – which, I can tell you, makes for a fine symposium. We had couches of straw laid out, and the slaves and my oarsmen built us a fine fire of wood they collected high on the slopes – I remember Leukas complaining about how far the men had to go to get wood. Truly, with twenty thousand people on the plain, wood was hard to find.

And the place stank – have I mentioned that? Humans are not the cleanest of animals. I had Megakles pace off our camp and we dug latrines. Most other people didn't. If you catch my drift.

At any rate, I was just reclining on my elbow, with Hector pouring me some wine mixed three to one with water, while Harpagos was telling of our heroism at Lades. There must have been fifty men at our fire, and a few women – drawn not so much by my famous name as by the promise of free wine.

Out of the sunset came Polymarchos, like the proverbial ghost at the wedding.

He crouched by my pallet like a slave waiting on his patron. I could tell it annoyed him to be so subservient, and thus I could tell he needed something.

Power has many difficult aspects.

'Relax,' I said. 'What's the trouble?'

He shook his head. 'They're threatening to disqualify my athlete. You know he's late?'

I nodded. Like any Greek, I knew that athletes had to be present thirty days before their event, to train – very hard. In effect, to prove that they had the right to compete. Young Astylos was only four days early. I shrugged. 'He was shipwrecked,' I mentioned.

Polymarchos hung his head. 'Would you consider ... speaking to the judges?' he asked.

I misunderstood. 'I can speak about the storm, surely.'

He met my eye. 'I suspect they've been bribed.' He looked around. 'There're other men here who came late, and there have been many men admitted late over the years.'

Cimon, at my elbow, leaned in. 'Bribed is such a strong word,' he said with a smile. 'You mean that someone has an interest – perhaps a political interest – in strict enforcement.' He raised an eyebrow. 'What events are we discussing?'

Polymarchos looked annoyed to be interrupted, but he shrugged it off. 'Stadion and diaulos,' he said.

Cimon nodded. 'Athenians in both events,' he said.

Let me tell you how the world works.

In that one line, Cimon was saying that he – he, one of the most powerful men in Athens – had an interest in the two running events. It was all in the twist of his mouth, the light of his eye. But it was there.

As was – by implication – the question. Is this important to my friend Arimnestos?

I had become one of them. I understood the nuance of power. I was being asked – politely, one aristocratic pirate to another – if I was prepared to expend my prestige and patronage on Polymarchos and his runner.

No, pause and think. You must understand this, or you will never understand what happened in the years of the Long War, as we fought the Medes. Hellenes compete about everything. Small men will race turtles, and great, rich men and women race chariots, and those of us in between will compete with whatever comes to hand. So here was Cimon – a friend of my youth, a man I trusted absolutely – stating that he was not going to help me to help Polymarchos – unless I made it worth his while. And nothing bald had been said.

Greeks are not natural allies. That's all I'm trying to say. Business and political competitors; always looking for advantage. In business, in politics, on the seas or in the stadium.

I met his eye. 'I'd like to see this young man entered,' I said.

Cimon smiled. He didn't say anything as wild as 'what would that be worth to you?' but I was suddenly reminded of Anarchos. There were similarities.

He rolled to his feet with the agility of a trained man. 'Let's go and see the judges, then,' he said. 'I came through the storm, too. Perhaps they'll want my testimony.' He flashed me a toothy smile, and I knew I owed him a favour. He was going to help me put 'my' runner in the race, despite the fact that Athens had a competitor in that race.

But I owed Polymarchos. It is hard to say exactly why, or how. Part of my general debt to the gods for my mistreatment of Lydia, I think.

I had a name, then, but not nearly the name I have now. The same was true of Cimon. Yet, despite the fact that we were not yet truly famous men, it took us almost an hour to cross the camp to the temple. Night was falling – fires were lit across the plain. The smell of burning wood and the smell of dung – human and animal – and the smell of cooking onions and meat and the sweat of twenty thousand mostly unwashed and unoiled humans rose to the gods. Small clay oil lamps lit the camp, and sparkled in the falling twilight like a thousand tiny stars. It was a glorious night, except for the smell.

Polymarchos was impatient – he clearly thought that the judges would pack it in for the night. And he might have been right, except that I sent Hector running across the camp as my herald. So we walked, and men accosted us and offered us wine and praise, and asked us pointless questions so that we would speak to them, or asked us to make judgements on things about which we knew almost nothing. Such is the life of fame.

56

Eventually we made it to the temple, with Polymarchos all but bouncing up and down as we approached the broad steps. But the judges were still seated at their five tables, all lit by handsome bronze and silver lamps, and as we approached, most of the judges rose and bowed.

We were interrupting something official, that much I could tell. There was a man – a very handsome older man with the long, oiled hair of a Spartan aristocrat, and a woman – I assumed his wife, not beautiful, yet somehow magnificent, with arm muscles like an oarsman's and hair, thick and black as the falling night, piled like a tower on her head. She had the oddest eyes – one very slightly higher than the other, and both very slightly slanted, as you see in some people from the Sakje and the Aethiops.

I am not doing either one of them justice. He was dressed in nothing but a simple scarlet cloak pinned with gold, and she wore a fortune in jewellery – but for both of them their principal adornment was their sheer fitness. They looked like gods.

They looked angry. Deeply angry.

So did the judges. Who also, let me add, looked afraid.

Cimon nodded pleasantly to the Spartan couple, and the man – he was over fifty, and he had the kind of dignity that I've only seen a dozen times in my life – returned a small, but very genuine nod. He said, 'Under any other circumstance I would be delighted to speak to you, Cimon.' Of course, he didn't do anything but nod, but that's what he meant.

There were two more Spartiates – Spartan aristocrats – standing behind them, a middle-aged man in top shape and a much older man who had the beard of a philosopher and the body of an athlete. When the Spartan woman turned away from the judges with a look that might have turned almost anyone to stone, the other two followed her mutely. They wore their resentment more openly.

Cimon put a hand on my arm and we stopped. Cimon, who bowed to no man, inclined his head – as he might have to the gods – and the man and woman both stopped on the steps above us and returned the compliment. I'd like to think I didn't stop and gape, but honestly, they were … it is hard to describe. They were like Briseis. Greater than mere mortals.

Then they swept by us. Cimon didn't try to speak to them – it was quite clear that they had failed to gain their objective with the judges, whatever it was, and that this probably imperilled us, as well.

I didn't know precisely who they were, but I had a good idea I was watching one of the two kings of Sparta – Leonidas, the younger of the two, and his scandalous wife Gorgo. He was the right age, and her mismatched eyes were a guarantee. Men whispered that if she hadn't been the daughter of a king, Gorgo would have been exposed – killed – as a baby, because her face was deformed. Men whispered that she was a witch. A sexual deviant. A lust-mad, power-mad harridan.

Well, men whisper all sorts of crap when they are bored, and most of it is about women. Men also whispered that Leonidas was a usurper who had taken his throne illegally. No one ever expected him to be king – it is a long and particularly Spartan story, but he was not in line for the throne, and so he was sent to the Agoge, the particularly brutal school for aristocratic boys that characterises the Spartans. Where, let me add, young Leonidas excelled. And later, he was an effective warrior with an immense reputation throughout Greece. The day my father's poor Plataeans held the Spartans for a few moments on the plain by Oinoe, Leonidas would have been in the front rank. For all I know, he and my father crossed spears.

I'll digress, because although no one not born in Lacedaemon can pretend to truly understand the bloody Spartans, it is worth having a sense of their politics and their lives before I go on with my story. In my father's time – when Aegina, the island off Attica, was a close ally of Sparta, Sparta and her ally Aegina, backed by the Peloponnesian League, had mostly dictated Athenian politics. The manner in which they did this was complicated. I've spoken of it elsewhere, but suffice it to be said that only twenty years before I was admiring Gorgo's cleavage, which was superb, Athens had been, to all intents and purposes, a tributary ally of Sparta's.

Now, Sparta always had two kings. All of Spartan politics is a matter of balance, and they claim that their great lawmaker, Lycurgus, ensured balance in every form of government. Two kings to watch each other; a council of old men called ephors to watch the kings; an assembly of free men to watch the ephors, and whole nations of slaves – the helots – to do all the work. Sparta rules an area that had once been three separate states, and had enslaved two whole Greek populations. To some Greeks, this was hubris on a major scale.

To others, it was an ideal form of government.

At any rate – please pay attention, this is essential – the two kings of my boyhood weren't just rivals, but deadly enemies – Cleomenes,

58

who was the father of Gorgo, and Demaratus, who will come into this story again and again. And the focus of their rivalry was about their relations with Athens and with Aegina. Well, that and everything else. I leave the everything else aside for the moment.

Just before the time of Marathon, Persia sent ambassadors throughout Greece, requesting that every state in Greece offer earth and water – tokens of submission to the Great King. In fact, this was just after the time of my wedding. Aegina voted to send such tokens. Athens and Sparta had intense internal political disagreements about what to do. In Sparta – so men say – King Cleomenes, whose forceful and militaristic policies had animated Sparta for twenty-five years – had the Persian ambassadors thrown in a well, and told them they could get earth and water from it if they could climb out. By doing so, of course, he committed a gross impiety – the murder of an ambassador is an offence to the gods – but he also guaranteed that Sparta could do nothing but fight.

Still with me?

In Athens, the Persian ambassadors behaved with astounding arrogance. It was the talk of my wedding. I'll add that it is very un-Persian, and I suspect that someone in Susa or Sardis sent the wrong men. At any rate, there was a rape – and Persians were killed. I have heard a dozen self-justifications from men who were present. The murder of ambassadors is always a crime against the gods, no matter how you tell the story.

I've heard Miltiades suggest, in his cups, that it was done for the same reason that the Spartans did it – to make it impossible for Athens to do anything but fight.

Be that as it may be – it was the winter before the first coming of Datis and the Medes, and the men of Aegina were threatening to allow the Persians to use their harbours to conquer Athens. Cleomenes of Sparta forbade them to do so, and took hostages from the leading men of Aegina. Demaratus, his fellow king, felt that he had acted with hubris, and above the law.

Just to be a barracks lawyer, he was right, and any Spartan worth his salt will admit it. Cleomenes had a clear vision – right or wrong – of how Greece should be, and he was determined to resist Persia, and once set on that course, he was like a runaway chariot.

When the dust settled, Demaratus – the rightful King of Sparta – had been framed in a case that claimed he was illegitimate and not the King of Sparta. It was all a put-up job – a scandal at the time – but he was exiled. He ran to Persia, where he sat at the right hand of the throne of the Great King. More than a few Spartans left with him. There was an enormous split.

His younger brother was Leonidas. Leonidas was installed overnight, and after immense political manoeuvring, married off to a woman about a third his age – Gorgo, the wry-faced daughter of overbearing, hubris-filled Cleomenes.

Follow that? It's like a particularly juicy play about the gods at their worst. That's everyday life in Sparta. Murder, scandal, backstabbing, all with lots of pious sentiment and high moral tone and some ruthless athletics.

I'm not a fan. Mostly, their kings don't die in bed – or on the battlefield. They die in exile.

Like Athenian aristocrats, come to think of it.

Greeks. Power-mad fools.

The Spartans brushed past us and went off into the firelit darkness, and I was left pondering ... well, everything I just said.

Hector appeared. He bowed, and Cimon paused, so I paused too.

Cimon smiled at the boy. He was good – like his father, he was never too great to charm someone rather than merely command them. 'Speak, boy. What was all that about?'

Hector looked at me for approval. It was the oddest thing – we were on the steps of the great temple of Zeus, with all the judges of the games standing just above us in the lamp-lit interior of the great stone building, looking like supernatural judges themselves. Cimon decided to keep them waiting.

Cimon was far more an aristocrat than I.

I nodded to Hector.

'The King of Sparta,' Hector said carefully. He paused. 'Actually, the king's friend. But the king—'

'One of the kings,' Cimon said. 'Sparta is blessed with two.'

Hector nodded and bobbed his head. 'Yes, sir. One of the kings, and his wife, wanted to enter their friend's chariot. Late. Apparently they did not want to train their horses here, but chose to exercise them in Lacedaemon. To be truthful, sirs, I had trouble following the argument.' He shrugged, as boys will, even when being polite. 'The king claimed he had permission, and the judges refused him, and his friend.'

'Because he is late?' Cimon asked.

60

Hector bowed his head. 'That's what I understood.'

Cimon frowned. 'Arimnestos, why do these things happen to you? Now this is a matter of state. Not just about a few men pushing their athletes. You understand?'

I understood. Turning Polymarchos and his athlete down – that might be a small matter. Cimon and I had been prepared to put pressure on the judges. That made it a larger matter, but still small enough.

The King of Sparta?

That was a very big matter.

And bureaucrats hate to back down.

We climbed the rest of the steps. Young Astylos stood, disconsolate, by the end table. There were twelve judges, and they stood at their tables – some had scrolls, two had tablets of wood, and the archon stood alone.

A herald recognised Cimon. He'd clearly already spoken to Hector, so he raised his rod and announced us formally.

The judge-archon nodded. 'What matter brings you to the tribunal of Elis?' he snapped.

Polymarchos bowed. 'Sir, these are my witnesses to the power of the storm that shipwrecked us on Sicily. This is Arimnestos of Plataea, who rescued us, and this is Cimon, son of Miltiades, victor of Marathon—'

'I know who they are,' spat the judge. He looked like a man who had had a long, difficult day. He glanced at me.

'Sir,' I said. 'It was one of the worst storms it has been my ill-luck to encounter. I was blown all the way to the coast of Africa. Sir, I have sailed outside the Pillars of Herakles, my ancestor.' That's me, laying it on thick. 'This was as bad a storm as I have seen.'

Cimon nodded. 'I concur with everything he said. On the one hand, a heavy storm, and on the other, the coast of Sicily would have been a worse place from which to be blown than our position in the Illyrian Sea.' He smiled at his little rhetorical flourish – his one hand, other hand construction.

The judge narrowed his eyes. 'It seems to me that if Poseidon sends such a powerful storm, it is because he doesn't want an athlete to be at the games.'

Cimon nodded. 'The gods may have such disagreements. But Zeus is the god of judges as Poseidon is the god of the sea, and it is in the hands of Zeus—'

'Are you telling me the will of Zeus? Or my duty as a judge?' the man spat.

I had a brief flash, by all the gods, of the edge of my sword carving the man's neck. Why is it that small men, given a little power, will behave like petty tyrants? For a few days, this elder of Elis, a tiny city, had power over men like Leonidas of Sparta and Cimon of Athens. Instead of being honest and humble ...

Pah. I could see what he'd look like as his head fell off my blade. He made me that angry.

I thought Polymarchos was going to burst into tears. All that training, wasted – because of a storm, some rapacious Sicilians, and a dozen fools in the Peloponnesus.

Astylos had given up. I know how it is – when the fates are against you, and you know that you cannot win. He managed a smile.

I decided to brazen it out. 'I can name a dozen athletes who have been allowed to enter late – even this late,' I said. To be honest, I couldn't name one, but I was willing to bet that Cimon could. 'Unless you have some personal interest, sir, I think you need to explain yourself in detail.' I snapped that at him in my storm-at-sea voice.

Cimon raised an eyebrow, but he let me play my dice.

'Personal interest?' The old man's saliva actually struck my shoulder, he was sputtering so hard. 'Are you accusing me of ... acting against the will of the gods?' He shook his head. 'I am the archon of the games. I do not need to explain myself to you.' He waved his hand.

'Yes, you do,' I said. 'Or I'll come back with Themistocles.' It was an odd threat – but I knew he'd invited many famous men – to discuss the Persians – and I suspected he'd have more power with these men than Cimon.

Cimon, in the meantime, leaned down and spoke in the ear of the Italian athlete.

Then he nodded to me, and turned on his heel.

The judge said, 'How dare you – stop that man!'

But he was too late. Everyone had watched Cimon's expression of contempt – turning his back on the judge – and they'd missed Astylos slipping through the columns into the temple proper. He was in the sanctuary – from which he could not be removed by force.

Cimon spoke in a voice of iron. 'He will stay in the sanctuary until we have been heard. In an hour, every Hellene on the plain of

Olympia will have heard that you are barring competitors to influence events.'

'I will return with Themistocles,' I promised.

We walked down the steps. They were shouting behind us – but not at us, or at Astylos. The judges were shouting at each other.

'It's about the chariot race,' Cimon said as soon as we were clear of the temple. 'It must be. No one cares about anything else these days. The Spartans have kept their entry a secret. It must be a powerful entry. But the pretext used to disqualify them is the late-entry thing – I'm sure of it. Your man is simply in the wrong place at the wrong time.'

'By about thirty days,' I admitted.

Polymarchos had the good grace to look abashed. 'Gentlemen – I'm sorry to have involved you in this.'

I shook my head. 'It's not really about you. I'm for Themistocles. You?' I asked Cimon.

Cimon made a very odd face. 'I will present myself to the King of Sparta,' he said.

It was a busy night.

Athletes had to be entered before the parade, which happened before the opening sacrifices. That gave us two more days, but Cimon said, in parting, that he thought we'd have to make our case as the sun rose.

I went to Themistocles immediately. Sometimes the gods smile at the affairs of men – I found his tent with some difficulty, only to be told that he was drinking with the Plataean, Arimnestos. So I walked back to my own camp with my feet aching – a sailor can lose his love of the land very quickly – and I found him singing – very well, let me add – and at the centre of the party I had left some hours before.

I waited until he was done and had been well applauded before I cornered him.

'I was surly earlier,' he began. 'I came back to apologise and found you gone, but your man Harpagos—'

'Not my man any more. Very much his own man.' I couldn't help myself.

But Themistocles the democrat applauded. 'Yes – these are foolish notions of patronage of which we should rid ourselves. Well put. He is his own man. Exactly. But at any rate, he insisted I was welcome

– that any Marathon man was welcome.' He smiled, somewhat the worse for drink. 'I tried to do my bit.'

I laughed. Drunk, Themistocles was still a pompous arse, but somehow a much better man. He had a ridiculous garland of ivy on his brow and a big bronze wine cup – a Boeotian kontharos cup – half full of wine. My wine.

'I need a favour,' I blurted, 'but I suspect I'll do you one, just in asking.'

He nodded. And smiled. Greeks love a bit of messy logic.

'Is Leonidas of Sparta your ally?' I asked.

He played with his beard. 'Yes,' he admitted.

'He has arrived with a late entry into the games – a chariot in the four-horse event,' I said. 'The tethrippon.'

Themistocles was suddenly very sober. He sat up, his garland of ivy a little askew, and narrowed his eyes. 'And the judges have declined to let his team race,' he said. 'Look, I may not have loved the man, but he was brilliant. He saw it in a moment. Syracusa or Aegina – or both. They both have teams in the four-horse race. And they both hate Sparta.' He met my eye. 'At least, right now.' And he leered. 'And other reasons,' he added enigmatically.

'A friend of mine is trying to enter the foot racers, but he's being prohibited on the same grounds,' I said.

Themistocles took his garland off and put it carefully on the ground. 'Well,' he said. 'You are correct, Plataean. You have done me a favour. With a little care, I have the power – the friends – to remedy this, and thus do a favour for Sparta and for Leonidas.' He met my eye. 'I won't forget this.'

I sighed with relief. 'Themistocles, all I ask is that my man, Astylos, be allowed to race. I don't know him. But I owe his trainer.'

Themistocles rose to his feet. He lacked much of the immense dignity of Leonidas, but he was fit, with muscles upon muscles, and he, too, looked much younger than his years. They shared something, those two.

He walked off into the darkness. I turned to Polymarchos.

'What can be done is done,' I said. 'Have a cup of wine.'

In the dawn, we were all arrayed together in our best – I wore my Tyrian red cloak embroidered with ravens, and Cimon wore a garment so deeply died it seemed to vibrate – somewhere between red and blue. Themistocles wore a deliberately humble garment, a plain boy's chlamys in soft white wool – to show his body. And Leonidas of Sparta eclipsed us all, just by the way he stood.

We were waiting for the dawn ritual to be completed in the sanctuary – where, even then, my young athlete had been awake all night, clinging to a cold pillar – hardly the best training regimen for a man in his prime. But Cimon put my hand in the king's.

'Leonidas,' he said. 'This is Arimnestos of Plataea, son of Chalk-oteknes, son of Simonides. He led the Plataeans at Marathon ...'

The King of Sparta seized my arm in a two-handed embrace. 'What a pleasure it is to meet you in person,' he said. 'I am told that you, too, are a son of Herakles?'

I was almost speechless. The King of great Sparta knew of me? I think I stood there for two breaths, my mouth working like that of a fish out of water.

But Leonidas was too well bred to let me flounder. 'You are perhaps the most famous fighter against the Medes of all Hellenes,' he said. He smiled at Cimon. 'With the possible exception of your father, of course.'

I can't do justice to the way in which he said these things – force-fully. No one could mistake his comments for flattery. He spoke like a judge at a murder trial – and yet, there was almost always a wicked gleam in his eye, as if he knew a secret jest. Or perhaps found himself funny. He claimed he never wanted to be king, and I think that may be true. Perhaps he found it ... odd, and comic, to be king.

I recovered. 'Oh, my lord, I am merely another spearman,' I said, or something like that. 'The hero of the Plataeans is not Ajax or Achilles, but only Leithes, who gathered other little men around him to stem the rush of mighty Hector.'

He nodded. 'I remember the Plataeans,' he said. He smiled pleas-antly enough and then extended his great right arm to show a scar on his bicep. 'A Plataean spearman gave me that,' he said with a rueful laugh. 'In the Agoge, they told us that boys learn better from pain.'

As it proved, that was quite a long speech for him.

We walked up the steps, but the deal was done. The judges – with a great show of humility – admitted the Spartan team to the four-horse contest. Everyone made sacrifices to the gods.

It was all done in an hour, and the sun was a red disc on the horizon. Except that nothing had been said of my athlete.

Themistocles didn't make me ask. He nodded easily to the chief judge. 'I think there is another athlete who has been awake all night awaiting your clemency,' he said.

The judge wavered for a fraction of a heartbeat – long enough for me to realise that this vain old man was considering poor Astylos out of pure spite.

Themistocles raised an eyebrow. 'I would hate to have to bring all these men together again,' he said. His eyes were hard as rock – as hard as those of a man killing his way through defeated enemies. There was no mercy in them at all.

The judge considered resistance.

'But I will,' Themistocles said, his voice mild. In that moment, I saw who he truly was – a man who loved the exercise of power. For itself. I have known men – aye, and women – who live for the release of sex, for the balm of music – for the moment when you elude an enemy's spear and plunge your own into another man's guts – aye. All those.

In that moment, I saw that Themistocles lived for this.

The judge flinched. 'Of course your Italian boy can run. If he can stay awake.'

Themistocles smiled at me, as if to say: Now you owe me.

See? Hellenes, at the games of the gods. All fair and above board.

To be honest, age dims the memory. They were beautiful days, once I got used to the smell, and if there is a better life than lying in the sun with a broad straw hat and all your friends watching young men run their hearts out, I don't know what it is. After we won our case with the judges of Elis, I was elated – it is hard to describe – and I went and spent money in the market. Then I went for a run of my own, because I knew I had too much spirit. I ran a good distance – thirty stades or so, up and around the mountain and back. And went back to the market, collected my ivory Athena and my pair of fancy gold brooches from a delighted craftsman, and went to my tent to strigil and oil. I felt like a god.

Of course, most men were just waking up.

At any rate, the good mood didn't leave me all day. I lay on the bank of the stadium where the town of Elis now maintains tall grass banks for the spectators – so much more comfortable than wooden stands, or stone benches. I watched some boys wrestle, and then Harpagos and Sekla nudged me because they saw horses, and we gave our spots in the stadium to a group of Corinthians who were grateful to us and we walked down to the hippodrome, where we watched horses trot around and around. The trainers eyed each other, and none of the horses ran full tilt. It was much the same with the men – they watched each other, and tried to have bursts of speed without the others seeing.

By two days before the sacrifices to open the games, almost all the competitors knew each other like wicked brothers, and they had clear ideas of who was fastest, strongest, most dangerous. In sports like pankration, it often happened that most of the competitors would drop out, leaving only three or four remaining. Why get badly injured when you know that you can't take that big bruiser from Megara?

A few of the boxers sparred a little, and, as I say, a few of the young wrestlers, but most of the men and boys simply lifted weights, drew bows, and ran. They didn't want to match themselves against each other until the great day.

That afternoon, as it began to cool, I saw the chariot teams.

You may recall – if you've been listening – that I know how to drive a chariot. I'm not good at it – I'm far too large and I don't really love horses. But when I was a new-caught slave in Ephesus, I was trained by top men to drive a team, two-horse or four-. I don't know enough to win a race, but I know enough to judge a team, and this was a superb team.

That year, there were six teams. The Aeginians came out first that day, and many men cheered. Their horses were all white, matched with manes that stood up like the crests on men's helmets. They looked like Apollo's horses, and every man in the crowd thought the same. I'm no fan of Aegina, but I cheered those horses.

Then came the team of my friend Gelon of Syracusa. His team, as if in deliberate competition, was all black, and they were the largest, longest-legged beasts I think I have ever seen. I understood later that they were Persian horses, purchased by an ambassador, and they stood a fist taller than any other horse in the race, black as Hades. I suspected, while looking at them, that they were the most expensive team.

The third team was Athenian. It was a fine team of mixed horses – a dark chestnut with black mane and tail and three unmatched bays. They were the least remarkable looking of all the teams. They looked dowdy by comparison with Gelon's team.

Of course, no wreath of laurel is awarded for the 'best-looking team'.

The Corinthian team was driven by a black man – that alone was worthy of comment – and their horses were matched bays with their manes carefully dyed red. Perhaps most noteworthy, their African charioteer let them run – and they ran like a summer storm. He took one pole—

Have you never seen a chariot race?

They run on the same kind of course where men run. One stade, with two posts. You have to drive down the course and then turn at the post and come back. Not a round course – that would, apparently, be too easy. Not an oval. A straight track, a terrible turn, and a straight back – twenty-seven times. It is not a short race. In fact, the chariot race for four horses is the longest race at the Olympics, and horses have been known to die.

At any rate, the African took the turn on one wheel, and his offside chariot rail brushed the pole and he didn't even look at it. He was ...

Damned good. The Corinthians looked confident, and had that nice mix of showy and competent that suggests a winner.

The fifth team out of the pens was the Rhodian team from the islands, and they were too small and, frankly, looked like they needed to be fed. Sea trips can be very hard on horses, and these horses had seen better days. They were all piebald black and white, and they were a fist smaller than all the other horses.

And finally, while I was stretching and considering a cup of watered wine, the Spartan team came out.

They were good horses – unmatched, but well muscled, with square heads and big chests. I remember saying to Harpagos, who was with me, that they looked like Spartans – heavily muscled and red.

They made quite a stir. At first, I thought it was just because of all the bureaucratic uproar about entering them, but the man driving the Spartan team was, in fact, their owner, Polypeithes, a Spartan citizen. This hardly ever happened. Drivers were mostly professionals – freedmen or even slaves. The driver wasn't considered to be the competitor, in chariot racing – it was the owner who was the competitor. But most owners – the super-rich – didn't bother to get dusty.

This Spartan gentleman seemed to feel differently.

He drove his own chariot, and he drove well.

I rolled over to Harpagos and pointed.

He shrugged and handed me the wine.

'Watch the African driver,' I said.

Harpagos nodded, and motioned to Moire, who was with us. He nodded.

The African driver only watched the Spartans, and mostly he watched the Spartan driver. And when the Spartans were halfway down the track on the far side, the African cracked his little hand whip, and his team leaped – I swear it – from a high trot to a gallop, and tore down the track going the other way.

The Spartan had just let his horses go, and they were at full gallop as the Corinthian team thundered down the course in the opposite direction.

The African was testing the speed of the Spartan team in an indirect manner.

The two teams shot past each other, a chariot wheel apart. The Spartan raised his whip in salute, and the African matched it.

We roared. I'd say there were three thousand men in the stadium and we'd seen a great thing. It went by in a second, but it was great.

The Spartan team thundered to the post and so did the Corinthian.

The African leaned a little, just as he had before, and put his chariot up on one wheel, and it made the turn with all four horses leaning so hard you'd have thought that they were running sideways. The spectators had to look back and forth to see both ends of the stadium – the Spartan was farther from the post and his horses didn't lean as close. The Corinthian team was around while the Spartans were still slowing to make the tight turn, and the African reined in, sparing his horses. He knew what he wanted to know.

The Spartan came through the turn and he allowed his team to slow, aware that he'd been the slower of the two. But he didn't show any temper. He merely reined in his horses and saluted the crowd and trotted around the track a few times. I saw Leonidas with half a hundred Spartans sitting together, like a phalanx – and I saw Gorgo sitting with her knees drawn up while a helot held an umbrella over her head against the sun. Polypeithes saluted Leonidas, and then, as he drove down the course, he rolled to a stop by Gorgo. She was sitting just off the course, in technical obedience to the prohibition about women that wasn't really enforced anyway, but Spartans are often sticklers for religious observance.

She rose, the helot scurrying to keep up with her, and walked over to the chariot, and had a quick chat with Polypeithes. He bowed, and drove off. She shrugged and tossed a comment to her slave, who laughed.

I liked her instantly. Any man or woman who has laughing slaves is probably favoured of the gods. Trust me, thugater, I've been a slave.

That night we had another fine feast. Our food was already running short, and I was told there was nothing to hunt for ten miles – so my ill-got Illyrian gold went to buy mutton and kid. The farmers of Elis must be the richest shepherds in the aspis of the world.

That's not really what this story is about. But old men like to complain.

At any rate, I was the host, and I had half the famous men in Greece at my fire that night, and it was a delight – Polypeithes the owner and charioteer chatting with Brasidas, and Narses, the Corinthian charioteer, chatting with Ka. We had a dozen pankrationists with an admiring audience of amateurs listening to their every word, and for an hour we had two of the finest poets and their musicians singing comic elegies to non-existent athletes. Simonides of Ceos, whose verses I had always admired, was in sometimes friendly competition with my friend Aeschylus of Athens, and the two of them mocked each other – and everyone else – as the wine flowed.

It was a good night.

I fell asleep sober, and woke just as the first rosy fingers of dawn touched the sky far to the east. I remember – and the whole history of the Long War probably pivots on this moment – I remember that I had a desperate urge to piss. So, cursing the chill of dawn, I threw off my cloaks and rose from my warm bed and, disdaining even sandals, pushed out of my little tent and went to the latrine.

Of course, to reach the latrine, I'd have to traverse about half of our camp, and I'm sure I'd have set a bad example, except that other men were just rising, and I didn't want to be *seen* to disobey my own strictures.

I used the carefully dug trench and straightened my clothes and went back across the camp, still determined to see whether there was any warmth to be discovered deep in my cloak, when I saw ... Well, I shan't go into much detail, but I saw Gaia and Sekla, doing what men and women will do in the first light of dawn.

That was the end of sleep. Or perhaps it was the will of the gods that I wander out of our camp. But a glimpse of a couple making love – the expression on her face – and I was suddenly desolate. It wasn't that I desired Gaia.

It was that I desired not to be alone.

I think I probably groaned aloud, like some tormented soul in Homer. And then, embarrassed lest they had heard me, I ran.

And having started to run, running a good distance in the dawn seemed as logical a pursuit as any. I think I decided to run off my woes and start the day with good exercise. I pulled my chiton over my head and tossed it into my tent and ran down towards the river and then east into the rising sun, running along the valley of the Alpheos. There wasn't much water in the river, which left a perfectly flat flood plain clear, and in the cool of the early morning, it was easy running.

I was not the only one to think so. By the time I was breathing hard and having to concentrate a little on my run – perhaps six stades or so – I heard hooves behind me, and in about as long as it takes for a man to recite a hundred lines of Homer, a pair of horsemen passed me – naked, but already wearing big patassos hats to protect them from the sun. They waved and rode on – both entries, as it turned out, in the young horse events.

After they returned – with further salutes – I had the valley to myself. I ran along, avoiding the occasional goat, for another ten stades, and I felt better. In fact, as I turned at the base of a breast-shaped hill, I felt so good that I determined to run back to camp and find myself a porne. A flute girl.

So I was running west along the edge of Alpheos – I won't call it a bank, because there's almost no channel in Hekatombaion, a full nine moons after the New Year. I probably had a broad smile on my face.

I heard hooves.

I had time to think that whoever it was, was a fool for pushing his animals at full gallop this close to the races, and then the low dust cloud at the edge of the river disgorged a racing four-horse chariot without a driver.

I think I ran six or seven more paces at it before I realised that the driver was still in the chariot. The gods had decreed he not die – he was fallen in a curled ball in the base of the car, his head lolling dangerously over the back lintel.

Chariots are very light. The base of a good racing chariot is nothing but sinew woven as tightly as possible to provide a springy floor for the charioteer, who, if trained the way I was trained, drives standing with his toes on the yoke bar and his heels on the sinew.

71

Something had gone wrong. And the horses were utterly panicked – eyes wide, flecks of spittle all over their chests, sweat pouring down.

And it was the Spartan chariot.

Runaway chariots were a steady part of my young life on Hipponax's farm. We actually practised boarding and recovering galloping chariots. It happened all too often. One moment's inattention – horses are the dumbest brutes in all creation – and you are flat on your back on the dirt, and your team is vanishing over the distant horizon.

So I turned and ran south, away from the river – and then made a tight turn in, so I was running east again, into the rising sun, parallel to the river but ten horse-lengths away. The team was galloping right along the bank – horses can be like that – and while the offside leader knew I was there, the rest of the team was too busy being afraid of their own shadows.

While the chariot was still behind me, I ran – diagonally – across its front. I timed it well – by Zeus, I'd done it often enough – and the horses were tired already and slowing. I put up a hand, got a fistful of mane, caught the leather of the collar and leapt. In a heartbeat, I was astride the surly bastard – I mean the horse.

I had them walking in twenty strides. I was worried for the charioteer – I'd never seen a man fall inside his own chariot – but I was worried for the team, too. I turned them on the flat plain – from astride the offside horse. They were as happy to halt as I was to halt them, and then followed a fairly ludicrous time as I sorted out the reins and tried to calm them. All before I could look after the poor charioteer, who was, of course, young Polypeithes, the Spartan.

He had a bruise the size of an egg on the front of his forehead and he was breathing badly, and I discovered he'd swallowed his tongue. I got it out – I'd seen it done – and laid him on the grass by the river and splashed him with water, which accomplished nothing but getting him wet.

After a wait, I lifted him carefully – I still thought he might have a broken bone, or, worst of all, a broken back – and put him on the floor of the chariot, and then I drove it – slowly – back towards camp.

I came to the place where the valley really widens, just east of the hippodrome, where I could see – and smell – the camp, and it looked as if someone had kicked an anthill. The entirety of the Lacedaemonian delegation was out – a dozen on horseback, and the rest running or walking into the hills or along the river.

The one who found me was Gorgo. She was astride a horse like a man – or a Scyth – and she cantered easily along the river bed as soon as she spotted me, and reined in half a horse-length away.

She wore a man's chlamys over one shoulder and was otherwise naked. It must be noted – Spartan women do not live like Athenian women, and they train in public, take exercise, and apparently think nothing of nudity.

The ephors were quite right for not exposing her to die as an infant. Her body was ... remarkable. I'm not sure I'd ever seen a woman so graceful and yet so fully muscled. And she could ride.

I struggled to meet her eyes. There was so much of her to enjoy.

'How is he?' she asked as soon as she saw that I had the young charioteer.

'Nasty bump on his head,' I said. 'Deeply unconscious.'

She dismounted, threw the reins over her horse's back, and knelt at the back of the chariot, looking at the fallen man. She peeled back his eyelids with a Laconian practicality, and nodded.

'Doctor,' she pronounced. She sprang on to her horse. 'Follow me.' Then she paused. 'Will I start a riot?' she asked.

'Yes,' I said. 'I know a doctor.'

'Good. Come and tell me.' She paused. 'Please.'

Well, if you can't see the comic aspect to this, I think you're dead.

At any rate, I drove the four-horse chariot right to the door of a tent where Dionysus of Ceos – one of the men who'd been drinking my wine the night before – was just towelling his hair. He tossed his towel to a slave and knelt by the chariot for a moment, pulled up the eyelids just as Gorgo had, and nodded to me.

'I don't think he has any broken bones,' I said.

Dionysus ran his thumbs very gently around the edges of the contusion and then around the rest of the head, and nodded. 'Get him out of the sun,' he said. He looked at me.

I shook my head. 'I found him, and the cart,' I said. I pointed at the still-swelling contusion. 'Sling?' I asked.

Dionysus nodded. 'Oh – you're the famous soldier. I guess you'd know. Yes. Sling stone, or something like it. It might have been thrown, but it was perfectly round. Or near enough.' He scratched his beard. 'Who is he? A competitor?'

'Competitor and owner,' I said. 'Spartan. I met him last night. Polypeithes.'

Dionysus had the good grace to look impressed. 'His father was

73

a famous wrestler. I've stitched him up a dozen times.' While he spoke, his slaves brought cold water and laid cloths on the young man's head. Four of us – two slaves, the doctor and I – laid him on the doctor's bed and made him as comfortable as we could.

The doctor was looking at my leg. 'Wound?' he asked.

I nodded.

He shook his head. 'Beyond me. If only there was a way of stitching up sinew the way we can stitch flesh.'

I grinned. 'I can still run. Not fast, but far.'

He nodded. He was back to his patient. 'You are right – trust a soldier – no other breaks. Nasty bruise on his hip – that's where he fell.' He looked at me. 'You his friend? Partner?'

I shook my head. 'I met him last night. But I'll tell the Spartans. I promised their queen I'd report.'

'Who – Gorgo? Damn, there's a woman.' He grinned. 'Like an anatomy lesson come to life.' He laughed.

'You know her?' I asked.

'Everyone at the Olympics knows her. She's one of the best patrons here. Lacedaemon funds many events here, and medicine is not the least of it. If it were not for Sparta's involvement, Elis wouldn't always be able to pay the bills.'

He looked at the young man at his feet. 'He's with the gods, but unless I miss my guess or he is awfully unlucky, he'll be awake in an hour and have nothing worse than a sore head and a patch of missing memory for a few days.'

I left with a hand clasp and drove – still naked – around the stadium to my own camp, where I was much mocked by my so-called friends for driving a chariot naked.

'Ares come to life!' Megakles laughed. 'Or are you hoping some young girl will come and play Persephone to your Hades?'

Men made the horns against ill-luck because Megakles mentioned Hades, which he did at least six times a day.

Ka admired the team. 'Those are *horses*,' he said. He grinned at me. 'I could teach you to drive better.'

I laughed. 'Almost anyone could. Hector – a chiton and a chlamys, so I don't look like a beggar for the King of Sparta!' I motioned to Brasidas, who was stripped for exercise. 'Come with me. You can translate their silence,' I mocked.

Brasidas shrugged. He snapped his fingers at his body slave and the man ran for his clothes.

Brasidas joined me. His face was serene – as almost all Spartan faces are, at almost all times – but his body communicated his tension. 'I am not the right man to accompany you to the kings,' he said.

It occurred to me – not for the first time – that Brasidas' Laconic comments on the subject of his exile might have left out a great deal of detail.

I drove cautiously. Ka had watered the horses, but they were done – so tired that they only kept their heads erect with difficulty. Panic affects horses as much as men, and nothing tires a man like terror. Sometimes, I think that fear and fatigue are the same animal.

So I moved no faster than a man walking, and Ka ran along with us, talking to the horses – I began to suspect that Ka preferred horses to people – and we must have made a strange little party. Except that it was three days until the opening ceremony of the Olympics, one the greatest bloodbaths in the Hellenic world, and there were forty thousand men, women, children and slaves on the plain of the Alpheos, and every eccentricity in the Greek world was in easy sight. We probably weren't the strangest thing by a long chalk.

But we were odd – and magnificent – enough: a Spartan warrior, a Plataean in a magnificent cloak, and Ka – the essence of grace.

We crossed the plain to the Lacedaemonian camp. Unlike all the other camps, it was neat and orderly – almost four hundred small tents and a number of simple awnings and a few larger tents. I made the natural assumption that the small tents were for the 'average' Spartans and the larger tents for – whom? The royals and the 'nobles'?

In truth, like most Greeks, I knew nothing of Spartans or how they lived.

But as the chariot rolled to a stop in the small square in the middle of the larger tents, I recognised where I had seen the layout of their camp before.

Crete.

I'd spent a year training Neoptolymos – may his shade burn bright and go to Elysia! He and his father, old Achilles, were typical Cretan lords – rich, but living hard, in squads or 'messes' of ten aristocrats, doing nothing but making war and hunting. This is the Cretan way.

Around the central square of every town in Crete are the barracks of the aristocrats. Most of the aristocrats never go home – their wives live with the slaves, mind the children and the money, and the men hunt, and make war.

I thought all this in the time it took for the wheels to stop and a

75

pair of helots to leap out from under a low awning and take my reins with a matched pair of surly bows.

One of the helots snarled something at Ka. Ka ignored the man and came over to stand by me.

'I'll go back to our own camp now,' he said. I nodded, and he ran.

By the time I turned my attention back to the helots, Gorgo and Leonidas were there, as was Polypeithes' father, Calliteles. He was tall and broad with a heavy forehead and an enormous nose; he was one of the few ugly Spartans I ever met. Of course, he'd won the Olympics – and the Nemean games – for wrestling, so no one minded his heavy, dog-like face very much.

Brasidas dismounted from the chariot. He didn't say anything, nor did he turn white or allow his hands to shake – despite which, he gave me the impression of a man who'd have preferred to run back to our camp with Ka.

Gorgo put her hand on my arm with the familiarity of long as-sociation. In fact – and this is one reason that Spartan women are so very confusing to Greek men – I'm not sure that any other well-born Greek woman has ever put a hand on my arm in such an intimate fashion. Jocasta – wife of Aristides – might be accounted my friend, and I've sat in her exedra or at the edge of her kitchen many times, telling a story and even holding wool for her as she weaves, and never – never – has she touched me.

I'd known Gorgo for less than a day, and she put a hand on my arm with a disturbing warmth. This is why non-Spartans believe all Spartan women to be licentious. They are not – they are merely without so-called 'womanly' reserve.

Perhaps I go on too much, but you must understand what an impact the Lacedaemonians had on me. I affected to despise them – no, in reality I did rather despise them. But to walk among them was rather like a man walking among the gods. In a gathering of fifty Spartans, there was no man with flesh on his belly – no woman with sagging breasts. Their arms showed the muscle of high training. All of them. Their skin glowed with health and expensive oil. Their hair was long, impractical and scented – all the time. I suppose that I had considered Brasidas an exceptional man. Here – among his own kind – I realised that he was 'merely' representative of a kind.

Well.

Gorgo put a hand on my arm, and Leonidas smiled. 'Welcome, Plataean!' he said. He offered me his hand, and we clasped hands and then the hulking mass of Calliteles all but obscured the sun. But in that moment, Gorgo saw Brasidas. And the king saw her head move and the flicker of emotion around the corners of her mouth, and he looked. His lip twitched.

Then all I could see was the mountain that was Calliteles.

'I gather my son owes you his life?' he said. His voice was flat, eyes giving nothing away.

The pressure of his hand on mine, however, told a different story. Since I wasn't a Lacedaemonian, I smiled and shrugged. 'I suspect his chariot would have stopped,' I said. 'By the favour of the gods, he had fallen well – on to the floor of the chariot.'

Gorgo looked at me and raised an eyebrow. Let me say that now she was as well dressed as any matron in Athens – a superb wool chiton worn in the old Dorian fashion, heavily embroidered, especially on the fall of the peplos. She wore a lion-head bracelet on her right arm and a simple white linen fillet in her hair.

I took her raised eyebrow for interrogation, and I nodded. 'The doctor – an admirer, may I add, of you both – reports that until the young man awakens from his sleep, he is with the gods and there is nothing to be done.'

Calliteles nodded, face under control. 'Thank you, stranger,' he said.

I glanced around. There were twenty Spartiates in the square, by now, but they stood at a distance – I had only Brasidas, the king and queen, Calliteles and a pair of helots within earshot. I looked at the helots.

'Unyoke the horses and see to them,' Gorgos said without so much as turning her head to the slaves.

With a rattle of harness and wheels, the chariot moved off, the tired horses swishing their tails to keep off the flies.

'He was hit with a sling stone,' I said. My words were well covered by the movement of the chariot, but Gorgo and Leonidas heard me. The king's eyebrow went up. Gorgo smiled.

That was an odd reaction.

The silence went on. Lacedaemonians can be uncomfortable 'friends' in a social situation. They speak very little, and I had learned with Brasidas that one had to exercise a great deal of patience to have a conversation.

So I consciously relaxed my muscles and stood easily, waiting.

'I understand that you speak Persian?' the king said.

That was unexpected. 'Yes,' I said.

'Thank you,' said the king, inclining his head very slightly.

I nodded. Emulating the Lacedaemonians is a chancy business at best. But if they weren't going to be more talkative than this – well, I didn't particularly need them, either. And you'll note that they had not spoken to Brasidas or recognised him in any way. This annoyed me.

I suppose that I allowed my annoyance to show. I am, after all, a Boeotian from Plataea, and I have not been schooled my whole life to give nothing away on my face.

Far from it.

As I turned away, the king extended his hand, palm down – a rhetorical gesture that came naturally to him, I think. I paused.

'Why do you bring this man into my camp?' he asked.

'He is my friend. And a Lacedaemonian. It seemed natural enough.' I knew I was at the edge of being insulting. But I was, as I say, annoyed.

The king's eyes never left my face. 'Perhaps he was born in Lacedaemon,' the king said. 'He has chosen not to be a Spartan.'

Bloody Spartans.

'I'm sorry I took you,' I said.

Brasidas smiled. 'It might be best if you didn't take me again,' he said.

'I gather this means I'll have the continued pleasure of your company commanding my marines?' I asked.

'You use so many words,' he said. And shrugged. 'Yes.'

Astylos slept for a long time, and then he ran. He ran short, fast distances and then some longer ones – then he stretched, with Polymarchos helping him, and then he did it all again. I watched him, and I learned a great deal about stretching.

When the heat of the sun was gone, Polymarchos had a brief conversation with Ka, and Ka stripped to a loincloth – the Africans lack our views on nudity – and ran with Astylos. The Greek man was faster, but the African could stay with him through almost anything, and Astylos had to work very hard to put more than a stride or two between them.

Polymarchos stood with me. 'Really, it is a pity we can't find some way to make Ka a believable Greek,' he said.

78

One of the few requirements of the Olympics was that a man had to be free-born and Greek. The definition of Greek was sometimes elastic and sometimes very rigid – these things come and go. But at minimum, it required that a man speak Greek perfectly. The colour of a man's skin was not nearly so important.

Ka's stumbling attempts at sentences longer than five words would not have made him welcome anywhere – well, except perhaps a Spartan mess.

That night, Themistocles gathered almost a hundred men at his own fire. Cimon was there, and Aristides. I embraced the man that most Athenians, even those who hated him, called 'the Just'. He sometimes looked at Themistocles with undisguised loathing – but he was there.

So was Leonidas of Sparta. There were a dozen Corinthians, there were Megarans, there were two aristocrats of Aegina and a few Thebans. While I was controlling my urge to spit, the eldest among them came forward from the stool on which he'd been sitting. He was a bent old man with no hair on top of his head, and it took me a moment to recognise him, and then I crushed him in an embrace, despite his Theban ways.

'Empedocles!' I shouted – so loud that the King of Sparta turned his head. I'm sure the Spartans thought me a buffoon.

Empedocles laughed noiselessly. 'You are here? You live?' He shook his head. 'There will be some very disappointed men in Plataea, my son.'

His words gave me a chill in the warm summer air. 'Disappointed?' I asked.

'Your cousin's younger son has your farm,' Empedocles said. 'But there are men here who can tell you more than I. It is enough for me to clasp your hand – I feel ten years younger – nay, twenty!'

And behind the old priest in the firelight were a dozen Boeotians that I knew well. Perhaps best of all, I knew my own brother-in-law, Antigonus. He was standing a little aloof, looking at me.

I walked straight up to him and threw my arms around him. There was little he could do but respond.

At my shoulder, Cimon said, 'I told you!'

Antigonus just shook his head and crushed me to him. 'We all thought you ... were dead,' he said. 'By all the gods, Arimnestos – where in Hades have you been! Your sister mourned you for a year.'

He was still balanced between anger and love – like a mother whose child has vanished on a summer day, and comes back hours later.

'The Carthaginians made me a slave,' I said.

'And then he sailed around the world on his way to hurry back to Plataea,' said Cimon, always one to throw oil on a fire.

Antigonus looked away, and then turned back, and he had tears in his eyes. 'You *bastard*,' he said, but then he crushed me to him again.

Then I had to repeat the whole performance with Lykon of Corinth. He'd been in my wedding party – indeed, I'd expected my wife to prefer him. He had been the handsomest youth of his generation, tall, blond and beautiful, as well as good at sports and war and gentle, too. Easy to hate, except that he was so decent.

Now he was six years older, solid and dependable in the way no beautiful young man ever will be. I'm pretty sure he used the word 'bastard' too.

And finally, there was Old Draco – who must have been the oldest man at the Olympics, or close to it, but the wagon builder was still strong, and he walked without a stoop.

'If you weren't such a famous killer of men,' he said, 'I'd give you a punch on the nose, young man. Gone all the time – farm in ruins – no one exercising our phalanx – not a *fucking* decent bronzesmith between Thespiae and Thebes!' He glared at me.

Now, at that campfire, I was the great Arimnestos – hero of Marathon, veteran pirate, probably as well known as most of the warriors of my generation. Draco was a wheelwright who built wagons in an obscure town of which half of Greece had never heard.

But I quailed like a nine-year-old boy caught stealing apples.

Draco stepped forward, pushing me back by sheer moral authority. 'When are you going to stop playing boys' games and come home and do some work?' he growled.

I'd like to say I laughed, but I didn't. I all but cowered.

For some men, you are always a child. 'As soon as the Olympics are over, I will come home,' I heard myself say.

'Hmmf,' Draco grunted. 'None too soon,' he said.

The only other Plataean was Styges, of all people, and his greeting was far warmer. He hugged me, and shook his head.

'We knew you were alive,' he said. 'But seeing is believing.'

So much to my own embarrassment, I had to spend time telling the story of my enslavement and my eventual escape and the trip to

Alba and back through Gaul. I love to tell a story, but not under the eye of the King of Sparta and half of the elite assembly of Athens.

Despite which, it's a good story, and when I was done, Draco shook his head – frank disbelief on his face. The old man thought I'd made it all up.

Empedocles put a hand on my shoulder. 'You are touched by the gods,' the old priest said.

I shrugged, embarrassed. 'I made some good things in Sicily,' I said. Empedocles had given me my first steps as a smith for the god, and I showed him the sign for a master – in Sicily. He all but glowed. 'So you have not spurned Hephaestus for Ares?' he asked.

'Never!' I said. 'I am no scion of the bloody-handed god.'

Empedocles nodded again. 'Will you really return to Plataea?' he asked. Men were crowding around in the firelit darkness, and the King of Sparta was at my elbow.

'Yes,' I said.

'May I come and sanctify your forge?' he asked. And then, teasingly – 'And see if your mastery is good enough for Boeotia?'

I bowed. Greeks don't bow often – mostly to gods. Sometimes to great athletes, or great beauty in men or women. Never to army commanders and seldom to kings.

But he was a great priest. An suddenly, out of nowhere, the craft-longing was on me – to make something.

'I would be honoured,' I said.

The King of Sparta was on my right and Antigonus of Thespiae on my left. I grinned. It is not every day that you can out-aristocrat your brother-in-law.

'Antigonus of Thespiae, may I introduce Leonidas of the Agiad Dynasty of Sparta? Leonidas, may I introduce my brother-in-law, Antigonus Melachites.' It is not every day you can introduce the King of Sparta to your friends.

They clasped arms. It was an informal night – the air was full of mosquitoes and the fire was too hot and the wine was terrible, despite which we were all very conscious of *why* we were at Themistocles' fire.

Antigonus had the King of Sparta engaged – about horses – in moments. Leonidas *could* be made to talk, but I didn't know enough about any of the subjects that interested him.

Well – except one, as it proved.

At any rate, I was just turning to Styges to get an account of my cousin's usurpation of my farm when Themistocles stepped into the firelight and we all fell silent.

'Gentlemen,' he said, 'I have called you all together tonight to save Greece.'

We talked for four hours, and decided nothing.

I suppose all the thinking men in Greece could, by then, have been divided into four factions. A few were openly in favour of the Persians. Those were mostly old aristocrats who – publicly – accepted the Great King as a sort of 'first among equals' of the whole human race.

The second faction would be those who didn't see a crisis. Who refused to see that the Medes and Persians were on their way – that the war had begun. Because men are men, this group was by far the largest – at the fire, on the plains of the Alpheos, and throughout Greece.

The third group disliked the Great King and all his works, and believed that he would invade. But felt that it was hubris to attempt to resist, and intended to offer submission as soon as it was politically expedient. And wished Athens and Sparta, which could not submit, well.

And finally, there was the fourth group, who believed that the Great King was on his way, and intended to resist. The men who represented that faction were at the fire. Leonidas of Sparta was the chief – he continued to represent his mad half-brother's policy of aggression against the Medes. As the leader of the conservatives in the most conservative state in all of Greece, Leonidas was an odd ally for Themistocles.

But Themistocles – the leader of the popular party in Athens, the most persuasive orator of our day and the bitter enemy of aristocrats everywhere – was the other pillar of the idea of resistance to Persia. And truly, I think it unlikely that either would have succeeded without the other.

The men at the fire were, for the most part, committed to resistance. We couldn't agree on when, or how, we should resist. As an example – I will not bore you with a full relation – Cimon and I held the rostrum for half an hour, outlining the advantages of a forward naval strategy that would burn the Great King's fleet in its bases on the Syrian coast.

Back then, we thought the Persians would only come by sea, as they did in Marathon year.

I think we spoke well, but our views were ridiculed.

'The Great King has a thousand ships – by your own admission!' said a Corinthian. 'And yet you think that with a hundred ships you can reduce his fleet.'

Cimon scowled. 'Yes,' he said.

'And get rich into the bargain,' I added, which may not have been the wisest course.

More men were for forming a great league, and marching into Thessaly to fight the Persians.

'If they ever come, they will come by land,' insisted a Corinthian aristocrat. 'An army the size of the Great King's cannot be transported by sea.'

'Or fed by land,' muttered Cimon.

Leonidas watched it all, looking back and forth like a man watching an athletic contest, offering nothing.

At length, the same Corinthian rose – Adeimantus, son of Ocytus. 'I agree that we should resist,' he said. 'But these are Athenian tactics – the tactics of lesser men. In Corinth, we will not enfranchise the little men who are no better than slaves, just to have more rowers for our ships. We will not let *ships* decide the destiny of Greece.'

Most men growled or openly cheered. So much for a forward naval strategy.

'But,' he went on, 'how do we know the Medes are coming?' He raised a hand. 'The Persian empire is vast – yes. But it has its own rebellions and its own problems. Are we so sure? And if we are sure – I think every man here would like to know how much time we have?'

Themistocles glanced at me. He was standing quite near me – I think in support of my forward naval strategy.

'Arimnestos of Plataea can tell you more than I,' he said. 'As he had Artapherenes on his ship as a guest not a month ago.'

That was like kicking a hornets' nest.

But it was true. And I happened to look at the King of Sparta before I began – and in a glance I realised why he had asked me whether I spoke Persian. It was because he had already heard this tale.

So I began. I told the story simply – that my ship had been caught in a storm, and emerged to find the wreck of Artapherenes' ship close at hand and in the throes of a mutiny. I spoke of taking the satrap into Carthage and sailing out again, and I left out the difficulties.

Men frowned.

'Surely Artapherenes would have made a mighty hostage,'

Adeimantus said. 'Or are you some sort of secret Persian lover?'

There are insults that must be avenged in blood – although as I get older there are fewer and fewer of those – and then there are insults so ludicrous they deserve no more than a laugh. I laughed.

'I love Persian gold,' I said. 'But I find it easier to take it from them than to ask for it on bended knee.'

Cimon snarled.

'So you say!' Adeimantus shot back.

'If you had been at Marathon ...' I said, and let it go.

The king smiled at me. 'I saw the bodies,' he offered. 'At Marathon.' As usual, a short speech, but one that conveyed all the meaning he needed. He raised an eyebrow – just as his wife had. 'But – why?'

I shrugged. 'He was an ambassador, and his life was sacred. And – I owed him my life.'

Leonidas nodded. 'Good,' he said.

'And he *told you* that the invasion was imminent?' the Corinthian asked. I could see Lykon looking at the older man with distaste.

'Yes,' I said. 'He told me, his wife told me, and the captain of his guard – an old friend of mine, a guest-friend – warned me.'

The men around the fire spoke for some time.

I raised my voice. 'The Great King intends to build a canal across the isthmus under Mount Athos,' I said. 'And bridge the Hellespont.' I shrugged. 'So says his Satrap of Phrygia.'

Adeimantus was openly derisive. 'Bridge the Hellespont!' He laughed. 'I think you are trying to shock us with marvels, Boeotian.'

Even Cimon paused. 'That's laying it on a bit thick,' he murmured. 'A bridge over the Hellespont!'

Leonidas, on the other hand, looked at me with real interest. 'That would be ... glorious,' he said. His gaze was distant. Then his eyes snapped to me. He seemed an inch taller. 'You believe this to be true?' he asked slowly. 'I mean no offence. Different men will use words to sway other men.'

I nodded. 'A man I trust told me, and I believe him,' I said.

The King of Sparta nodded sharply. 'Then he is bringing a land army, and he means to have a real contest.' His eyes went to Themistocles. He implied that a sea battle was *not* a real contest.

Of course, to the Spartans, it was not – because it depended on the rowers and the helmsmen, not the hoplites.

★

84

Later, when the drinking was done and most of the men had gone to their beds – or their piles of flea-infested straw – I sat in the pleasant fireside air, blessedly free from the flies and mosquitoes which had descended like some curse of the Olympians at sunset and eaten us alive for three hours. Aristides sat by me – and Styges, and Lykon of Corinth and Cimon, Empedocles of Thebes, Calliteles the Spartan and a dozen other men. Brasidas was with me, too – ignoring Calliteles, who was studiously ignoring him.

The king had made me angry. I didn't realise it until he left in a swirl of red as his cloak settled about him. The arrogance of his cloak – was that it? I admired him as a man – and yet, the way he entered and left, as if he were king not just of the Spartans but of all Greeks . . .

I was stung by the words *a real contest*.

I lay on my cloak, allowing resentment to penetrate my maturity.

Finally I turned, ignoring what Styges had just asked. 'Why does your king call a land battle "a real contest"?' I asked. The king, of course, used the same words that we use for a race at Olympia. 'You are a Spartan, and you have seen a sea fight.'

Brasidas looked off into the darkness for so long I thought that he wouldn't answer. And why should he? It was an angry, rhetorical question.

But he coughed, and sat up. 'When I was young, and had just finished the Agoge,' he said, 'we went to war with Argos. It wasn't much of a war, really. We knew we would win, and so did the Argives – good fighters, but not like us. And we had more hoplites.' He turned, to make sure he had my attention. He looked into the fire. 'Cleomenes was the king. He was attempting to breathe new life into the Peloponnesian League and to let the allies have more say. One of the allied leaders made a suggestion about tactics.' He shrugged. 'And Cleomenes allowed the allies to follow this man – even though his brother, Leonidas, derided the notion as un-Greek and unworthy. So the allies marched off slightly to our left, and at a set command, they moved at an incline – very rapidly – like this.' His right hand was the Spartan phalanx, moving forward, neither slow nor fast, but inexorable.

I had seen it. Faced it. Nothing, in the aspis of the world, is more to be feared than the Spartan advance.

His left hand swung out wide to the left and then accelerated in from the flank.

Total silence had fallen. Brasidas never told a story – even those who did not know him paused to hear him. And Calliteles nodded, almost imperceptibly supporting Brasidas – *yes, it was as he says.*

'As soon as they saw themselves outflanked, the Argives broke and ran,' Brasidas said.

Many men nodded. Cimon looked like a boy who knows the punchline to the joke.

I shrugged. 'Outnumbered, facing Spartans, and outflanked?' I said. I nodded. 'I'd run, too.'

Brasidas nodded. 'They ran a stade – out of the jaws. Then they stopped. They reformed their phalanx.'

His eyes flicked to Calliteles, who was older. He was an Olympian, and that meant, I knew, that he'd probably been in the Hippeis – the Spartan Royal Guard – with Cleomenes.

He raised one eyebrow. 'Then they mocked us.'

Calliteles nodded.

'They sent a herald. They said, "O Spartans, mighty in war – have your arms lost their strength, that you stoop to trickery? Meet us chest to chest and shield to shield *in a real contest*, or march home and be damned."'

Brasidas allowed himself a small smile. 'We told the allies to stand aside. We marched down the field, and the Argives came to us, and we fought.' He nodded. 'We defeated them, of course. They sent heralds to offer submission and to request permission to bury their dead. We granted it.' He nodded.

Calliteles nodded also.

Cimon nodded in his turn. 'I know that I have heard this story told a dozen times,' he said. 'I was at dinner with Leonidas and Gorgo one night and an ephor told the story. I thought the point was that the Peloponnesian allies had wrecked the pincer movement by being too slow. I said so, and Gorgo looked at me – well, the way a wife looks at you when you say something foolish at temple.' He raised his eyebrows and spread his hands like a mime.

Brasidas looked at the ground.

Calliteles looked at the stars.

Styges had grown to manhood with Idomeneaus. He understood immediately – as did I, thanks. I had been with the Cretans. He leaned forward – a young man, and thus not quick to offer his views – but after several breaths, he said, ' I understand.'

Brasidas looked at him. 'Yes?' he asked. He sounded tired, as if using so many words had exhausted him.

'There's more to victory than occupying ground,' Styges said. 'My
... mentor, Idomeneaus, says that victory and defeat are ... in men's
minds. Some men die, and yet are not defeated. Other men kill, but
at the end of the day, they allow themselves to feel defeated.' His
dark eyes searched around the fire – looked at me, looked at Cimon
and then Brasidas. 'I have seen it, too.'

We all nodded. 'The Argives were completely undefeated by the
clever trick. Angered, but not even shamed. They had come to test
themselves – man to man – against the Spartans, not to dick about
with manoeuvre.' I had it, by then. 'Leonidas wants the Greeks to
measure their spears against those of the Medes. Man to man. Like
the Argives.'

Brasidas nodded. 'Not the Greeks,' he said. He shrugged. 'Or
perhaps. But mostly, the men of Lacedaemon.'

Calliteles had worked hard to avoid appearing to speak to Brasidas,
but now he couldn't help himself. He nodded emphatically, and his
right fist smashed into his left hand. 'To see who is best,' he said
simply.

I went to sleep and dreamed of Herakles. I remember it well.
Herakles was striding the earth, with the club on his shoulder, and
he was coming to Olympia to compete. It was a beautiful dream and
it was followed by another that had Gorgo, naked, riding a horse.

I don't need a priest to interpret either.

I awoke and went to piss, again, and again I passed from anger to
joy at the very early morning and the camp. I was used to the smell.
There was a gentle sea breeze creeping up the valley, and I dropped
my chiton and ran. My old wound hurt – it was my third day of
running – but I was determined, and I ground along the river.

After six stades or so, my right ankle began to hurt. By my tenth
stade, it hurt a great deal.

It is one thing to endure pain, and another thing to fear real injury.
Most men can endure enormous pain if they know the consequence.
What makes you a coward is the fear – the fear of permanent injury,
laming, rupture, loss.

My ankle didn't look bad, but I moved farther from the stream,
into the meadow where the ground was softer.

It grew worse.

Gorgo rode round the bend in the valley, her horse at a dead gallop. I knew her immediately, because she was a woman on a horse

with no clothes on, and there simply couldn't be so many of them. Even at the Olympics.

I forgot my ankle. This is how simple the male animal is. I forgot my ankle and flew.

Well. I thought that I flew.

She reined in by me. 'Arimnestos, if I didn't know that you had taken that wound fighting the Persians at Lades, I'd say that you were the most shameful runner I'd seen in many years.'

I grinned, suddenly delighted to have an excuse to stop.

'I see that in one way, at least, the Spartans are like other Greeks,' I said.

Gorgo shrugged. She backed her horse a step. 'How is that?' she asked.

'Women are more talkative than men,' I said.

She laughed. 'Shall I leave you to hobble home, then, Plataean?' she asked. 'I had not taken you for the sort who prefer to pretend that women have no wits.'

I stopped and laughed. 'No. But no man likes to be told he hobbles, when once he was young and fleet. Achilles never hobbled.' I held up a hand like a pankrationist who submits. 'Spare me, Queen! I'll walk by your side and endure your jests. Truly, my ankle is killing me.'

If she offered me any sympathy I didn't see it. 'You speak Persian,' she said.

'It is true.' Unbidden, the phrase 'nice tits', often used by Persian soldiers in Ephesus, came to mind. I turned my head to hide my smile.

She nodded. 'You have many friends inside the border of the empire?' she asked.

'And a few enemies,' I admitted. It is very, very difficult *not* to posture in front of an attractive woman. Luckily, she was above me on a horse.

We went along in companionable silence for a stade.

'I gather from my husband that I can welcome you to our League,' she said.

'League?' I asked.

'The conspiracy to save Greece,' she said.

I stopped and bowed as I would to a priestess. She was – hard to explain – like a priestess of Greece, if Greece were a goddess.

'I wonder if you would consider . . .' she began, and then frowned.

It was deliberate. I saw through it, because I knew women – not all women, but a woman like Gorgo. I knew Briseis. This was a woman used to getting her way from strong men – not by flaunting her sex, but by using her mind. The body was there to be admired, but it was only the bait.

Nor did I imagine that the wife of the King of Sparta was ... licentious. I can be a boy of nineteen with Briseis, but I am not utterly a fool. Gorgo wanted something.

It pleased me to play the Spartan, and walk along the valley with her, and act as if I hadn't heard her.

The camp came into sight.

'How did you come to count Brasidas among your friends?' she asked.

I thought this was a digression, but I liked the way it led. At least she had named him. 'I found him at liberty on the dockside of Syracusa,' I said. 'I needed a good man to captain my marines.' In truth, I had a good man in Alexandros. Brasidas was more like a force of nature.

She smiled. 'My husband hates him,' she said. 'Although it might be said that Brasidas hates my husband, as well.'

She smiled at me, daring me – I thought – to ask.

I had a hard time reading her age. But if Leonidas was fifty, she was thirty – with the body of a twenty-year-old. And the mind of an ephor – always scheming. Later I learned that she had one of the better spy networks in the Greek world, and when she and Cimon became allies, they, together, had the best information networks anywhere – equal to that of the Great King or the temple at Delphi.

I wasn't going to ask. You learn early, as a commander, that you *do not want to know*. If they tell you, well and good. If they choose not to tell you – well and good. And time saved, sometimes.

She shook her head. 'I gather you are immune to my charms,' she said.

I smiled up at her. 'I don't think your charms are on offer, Queen of Sparta? Or am I to imagine myself the new Paris – and seize you and carry you to my ship?'

She laughed and made an attractive face – pretending fear. 'It sounds exciting,' she said.

I shook my head. 'Look how it came out for them,' I said.

She laughed again. Gorgo's laugh was like Leonidas's voice – sharp, incisive, no quarter asked or given. 'And yet I hear you are a great lover of women?' she said. 'I told the king I could wrap you around my finger.'

'Did you?' I asked – flattered, in a way.

'I tend to melt Greek men,' she said, without immodesty.

'I am melted,' I said. 'If my ankle didn't hurt, I'd ...'

I met her eyes. There was something deadly serious there. The witty flirtation wasn't right.

'I'm sorry,' I said. 'I've missed the tone. May I help you and the king in some way?'

We went along for half a stade.

'I wonder if you would consider,' she asked carefully, 'taking a pair of Spartan heralds to the Great King?'

'To Persia?' I asked. I was ... shocked.

She sighed. 'I *have* handled this badly.'

'Brother, you look as if you've seen a ghost,' Cimon said when I hobbled back to camp. By then, my ankle was swollen. 'You've talked to Gorgo?'

That snapped me out of my state. 'What do you know?' I asked.

Cimon shrugged. 'Quite a bit,' he admitted.

'Poseidon, Cimon, if the Spartans are sending heralds to Persia, Athens is doomed.' I couldn't stop myself from saying it.

Cimon raised an eyebrow. 'Arimnestos, sometimes you do sound like a provincial hick and not like a cosmopolitan man of the world. Leonidas is the heir of Cleomenes and his aggressive foreign policy. He's unlikely to submit to Persia.' He looked at me and smiled. 'Is he?'

I had to admit that he had a point – and I knew enough to know that the cunning son of wily Miltiades would know more than I about what was going on. 'Gorgo just asked me to take the Spartan heralds to Susa,' I said. 'And to use my good offices with the Satrap of Phrygia to see them well treated.'

Cimon scratched under his chin. 'Yes. Well, you do speak Persian.' He looked away. And then back. 'Do you trust me?' he asked.

I smiled. I remember thinking of all the things about Miltiades that I hated, and those I loved. 'I'd be very careful of you if we were talking about Athenian politics,' I said. 'Outside of that – yes.'

Cimon grinned. 'No offence taken, Plataean. So – will you accept for the moment that I'm a member of the war party?'

I suppose I shrugged. As he was the leader of the conservatives who wanted war with Persia, it was not a sensible question. 'Of course.'

He sat back on his elbow, his long, aristocratic legs stretched towards my fire. 'You know what it will mean if the Great King actually marches – yes?'

I probably frowned. I do now. 'Yes. Hundreds of thousands of men marching over Greece and a ten-year war to push them out.' I nodded. 'Yes. It will be horrible.'

Cimon said softly, 'It will be the end of Greece as we think of Greece.' He waved a hand in the direction of the stadium and the hippodrome. 'They will cast down our temples and burn our cities and cut down our olive trees – destroy a generation of farmers, and loot us until we are even poorer than we are now.' He paused. 'And that's what will happen if we win.'

'If it is a land war,' I said.

He nodded. 'Your bridge – over the Hellespont – that idea frightens me, because I think ... I think it's true. I didn't believe you at first. Now – I can see it. A roadbed laid over sixty or seventy triremes.'

'Two hundred,' I said. 'It'd take two hundred triremes to bridge the Hellespont.' I laughed. 'Think of it as two hundred ships we won't be facing.'

'None of them will take the pirate's way and fight the Persians down at their end of the sea,' Cimon said. 'And when we suggest it, all they see is two men who will make their fortunes—'

'I already have my fortune,' I said.

'As do I,' Cimon muttered. 'But ...' he paused.

I waited.

I remember that Hector came out of his cloak, and brought us wine, and I remember that Cimon stopped talking altogether while the boy waited on us. And that told me a great deal.

Finally he pursed his lips grimly. 'The ultimate in forward strategy is to go to the Great King directly – and see if something can be done short of war.'

I sat back, deflated. 'We surrender?'

Cimon looked at me as if I were a fool. I had had a long day and too much wine and I suppose I was. I know a great deal about war, thugater, and one thing I know is that war is always bad. Good for broken fools and pirates and beautiful for young men who fear to be thought cowards. Horrible for women and children and everyone else.

It is one of the harshest truths that, in youth, the things you value – revenge, bloody honour, retaliation on your foes, manly prowess – as you grow older, you learn how hollow they are. Revenge? For the weak. Strong men have other things to do with their time – like live, till the ground, make babies, worship the gods. What is Arete? Are you excellent when you have another man's life on your blade?

I think not. And I have taken more lives than most men.

Cimon drew a bloody picture that night, as the Great Bear sailed over our heads – a picture of our world in flames. And the excellence that made us what we are – as sailors, as bronzesmiths, as athletes – even as warriors – burned away in the hot fire. With nothing left but the ability to fight – not like Greeks, but like desperate slaves.

Finally he shook his long hair. 'If they come – I will fight with my fortune and my hands. But better if they don't come.'

I nodded.

'How do we stop them?' I said, convinced.

'We prepare for war,' he said. 'And we appear as powerful, and as united, as we may. Only a strong front and the threat of a real fight will give the Great King reason to hesitate. And a good offer.'

It was my turn to scratch my beard and think.

'The new Great King – Xerxes – is young. We hear he is very ... emotional.' Cimon looked at me.

I shrugged. Artaphernes and Cyrus hadn't so much as mentioned him. My impression is that they didn't think much of him and had probably backed another contender. No one came to Cyrus the Great's throne without blood on his hands, and Xerxes killed his brothers to get to the throne – as was usual in the East. And, of course, contemptible to us.

'Are Persians religious?' Cimon asked me.

I frowned. 'Of course. Why ask me? You know as many Persians as I do!'

Cimon shook his head. 'I wish I did. I didn't grow up with them, and the Persian renegades at my father's court were not the men you describe. Renegades are seldom the true representatives of their culture – eh?'

I sipped wine and watched the fire. 'In truth, Cimon, their best men are very like our best men. Despite the stupid trousers.'

Cimon nodded. 'It will be dawn all too soon. I'll make my point. And Gorgo's. Do you remember Marathon year?'

I laughed. 'Isn't that a foolish question?'

'I prefer to think of it as a rhetorical question. You recall the Persian envoys?' He looked at me and I winced. 'I don't – but I have heard they were killed – in Athens and in Sparta.'

Cimon nodded. 'Cleomenes ordered them thrown in a well. You must know the story.'

I did.

'Most Spartiates believe he committed an act of gross impiety and that the gods are very angry at Sparta. I could list you off a dozen things the gods have withheld from Sparta – four bad harvests, a dozen minor failings, a bad earthquake ...' I was about to speak, but he held up his hand. 'Spartans are *very* religious, Arimnestos. Never, ever doubt it. I've been in and out of their messes all my adult life. There is *nothing* about superstition and religious observance that a Spartan doesn't believe.'

I nodded. Brasidas was a case in point. As usual. It put another face on his exile – of course, he was *also* cut off from full religious observance. I thought about that a moment, and lost the thread of Cimon's discourse.

'At any rate,' he said, 'the Spartans believe they are under a curse because of the murder of the heralds.' He leaned forward. 'One of the greatest signs of the displeasure of the gods is that Sparta has not won a single athletic event – not at the Isthmian games, not at Nemea, and not here – since the murder of the heralds. So – in the great sacrifice tomorrow, Leonidas will swear an oath to send his own heralds to the Great King – to do with as he pleases. Cleomenes is dead, but Leonidas may – I do not know – offer to send the Great King the men who killed his heralds.'

'A symbolic act short of submission,' I said. 'No earth and water, but—'

'And an act of piety to Zeus, showing that Sparta will atone for the stain. What is worse than the murder of heralds, sacred to Hermes *and* Zeus?' Cimon nodded.

I shook my head. 'I should sleep,' I said. 'There are too many secrets – Aphrodite, Cimon – and someone is throwing sling stones at Polypeithes!' I got up.

Cimon understood at once. 'Polypeithes' injury was ... the act of a man?' he asked. 'Son of a whore.' He looked away. 'That chariot is the best chance the Spartans have to win the laurel here. And we need them to win, Arimnestos. We need the old, conservative Spartiates to back Leonidas. Because Sparta has a pro-Persian party ...'

I nodded. 'Of course. There's a King of Sparta living at the Persian court!' I got it all, now. It was, as a plot, essentially Greek. It was as if Aeschylus were writing us our doom. The Spartans were the greatest military power in Greece. We all required them. And their house was deeply divided – Hades, Cleomenes only murdered the heralds to make it impossible for his rival king Demaratus to make peace!

Round and round. Plot within plot. Consequence within consequence.

Just the way we had been before Lades, when the Persians destroyed us and a third of our fleet defected.

I spat. 'We're contemptible,' I said. 'Not just the fucking Spartans. We'll fight among ourselves and plot for our own ends and the Persians will march in here and eat us.'

Cimon got up, too. 'Perhaps, and perhaps not, brother. But tonight, at the sacrifice, Leonidas will promise to send his heralds. As Delphi advised him. And they have asked *you* to take them – all the way to Susa if I have my way.' Cimon shrugged. 'And then, if one of the Spartan athletes can manage a win, I'd say we were on the way.'

'And someone here is trying to stop us,' I said.

Cimon shrugged. 'Not someone,' he said. 'Almost everyone.'

Too little sleep and too much wine. And a throbbing ankle, so I couldn't run. I needed exercise, and I walked out through the camp just after dawn. Slaves and poor men were cooking, and the rich were standing about looking tousled, or lying at ease in their blankets.

It was the great day. The day of the opening of the games, when we would all participate in the greatest set of sacrifices in the Greek world – more than a hundred oxen, all simultaneously on the vast altars. I could hear the beasts lowing, and I could smell them.

Walking doesn't heal a man the way running may, and it doesn't affect his essential daemon in the same way – taking a man to a greater height of spirit, I mean. I wanted a run. Instead, I had a hobble.

Nor did I see Gorgo, although I confess that I went closer and closer to the well-ordered Lacedaemonian camp and I suppose I had my reasons.

At the edge of the camp were twenty Spartiates, naked in the dawn. All of them had their sword-belts on. Every one of them had a chlamys over his left arm. They stood like statues, and then one of them – there was no obvious leader – barked a single syllable. It sounded very strange to me – not a Greek word at all.

Twenty hands went to twenty scabbards. Their swords – their short stabbing swords – appeared in their hands as if by magic, and as they drew, they cut – overhand, the blade rising up the body and flickering past each man's left ear and out – like the tongue of an adder – as their right foot glided forward, flat to the ground.

I had seen Brasidas practise the same movement. In fact, I had played with it myself. But I had never seen it done by twenty Spartiates.

'He!' grunted the leader.

The end of the down cut became a wrist rotation – a stomp of the right foot – and twenty swords thrust, point first.

'He!'

Every man pivoted on his hips and pushed with his aspis – in this case, each man used his chlamys draped over his left arm as if it were an aspis. I could see the attack – as a strong man steps with his left foot, he can slam the rim of his shield into you like a second sword. As a weapon, the rim of an aspis can break an arm or a leg or crush a skull.

The shield-thrust covered the flicker of the short sword up into an arc over each man's head ...

'He!'

The swords whispered down, this time on a steep angle that would have cut from eyebrow to hip, right to left – the opposite cut from the first cut. Every blade made a hissing sound passing through the air. Go and try it. Take a Laconian blade and try to make it whistle through the air. See how much strength and fine control it takes.

'He!'

Every man cut *up*, into the adversary's thigh and his manhood, the blade reaching under the locked shields.

'He!' he grunted, and twenty hands returned twenty blades to the scabbard. No one looked or fumbled or used his left hand – of course, you can't, with an aspis on your arm.

I can do that. A lifetime of practice. I'm a professional warrior and I can, on a dark night or with my eyes closed, put my sword back into the scabbard under my arm without pinking my own breast or fumbling.

But every Spartan could do it – even the young man of twenty who was running against Astylos.

When they were done they were all still for a moment, and then they relaxed and became human – one man stretched an arm and

95

laughed, and another murmured something and the three men near-est smiled.

A middle-aged man glanced at me, frowned – and looked back. He snapped his fingers and his helot ran to his side, and he pointed at me.

The helot ran all the way to my elbow. 'Sir – move along. Please. No trouble, sir – these gentlemen do not want an audience.'

I smiled at the helot. 'Then they shouldn't practise in a field at the Olympics.'

The helot didn't even take a full breath. He stepped in and put a hand on my shoulder . . .

And I threw him.

He rolled. Rose easily to his feet, and nodded. Almost companion-ably. He wasn't angry. It was as if he was saying, 'Nothing personal.'

He came at me again, now bouncing slightly on his toes.

My hands came up in a pankration stance and he reached to grab them – like lightning, let me add.

Well.

I stepped under his grab – passed my arm across his neck and swept his legs. He was a trained man, but not a really well-trained man.

To be fair, he was the best-trained *slave* I'd faced outside of Italy.

Now I had his arms. I put a knee deep in his armpit and he couldn't move. He was face down, and his left arm was hyper-extended.

'Ready to walk away?' I asked.

'No!' he shouted, and tried to flip. Which must have hurt his arm. He screamed with rage – and pain – and still couldn't overcome his position.

'If you keep trying, you will dislocate your shoulder,' I said. I blessed Polymarchos for showing me this wonderful pin. I'd expected to use it on drunken friends, but the helot was the perfect target.

Once more he bellowed – and he got enough purchase with his hip that for a moment, I thought he was going to make it off the ground – and then his shoulder gave.

'He has to keep trying,' said a low voice. I knew that two Spartans had come out of the group – I was very aware of them, and their swords.

'He knows he'd be killed if he showed fear or gave up,' the other said, conversationally.

'Why don't you tell him to stop trying?' I asked.

96

'Why?' he replied.

I stood up suddenly, stepped cleanly away from the helot – even desperately injured, he made a grab at my leg – and turned to face the two naked Spartans.

'Why don't you go away when you are not wanted?' the nearer man asked.

'I don't take orders well – especially from slaves. And rude men who are their masters.' I dusted some sand off my chiton. 'I am interested in your Pyricche.'

'Leave him, Bulis,' the bigger man said to the handsomer. 'He's some troublemaker.'

Bulis – I assumed that was his name – stepped inside what I would call my comfort zone – the girdle around me where a man can kill me.

I raised my left hand slightly to catch his eye, and succeeded. My intention was to take his sword out of his scabbard with my right hand. His was to strike me with his right hand.

It would not have gone well for one of us.

'Arimnestos!' called a woman's voice. 'Hades, Bulis, are you a complete arse!'

The Spartan paused.

As soon as he began to step back, I stepped back.

My hands were shaking.

So were the Spartan's.

For a moment, I couldn't think. I had been ... there.

So had he.

'You know the queen?' he said.

'And the king,' I added.

Bulis took a deep breath.

Gorgo – fully dressed, may I add – appeared just out of our range. 'Bulis?' she asked.

He nodded. 'I thought he was an arrogant piss-ant of a xenos, but I gather he's another of your friends,' he said.

'He's Arimnestos of Plataea,' the bigger man said. He smiled. He was older – almost forty – and had wide-set eyes and was missing a third of his front teeth. His missing teeth made my name sound exotic.

Bulis smiled – not the reaction I'd expected – and raised his eyes to the gods – and his hands. 'Ares' balls, sir. My apology.'

The helot was trying not to whimper.

The man missing the teeth knelt by his side, felt his shoulder and then – without any hesitation, and as fast as the strike of a snake – cut his throat, the draw from the scabbard flawless, the blade pulled across the helot's throat as if he were a human sacrifice, and just like that, the man was dead.

'He was a brave one,' he said, as he carefully wiped the blood off with the dead man's chiton. Then he poured oil from a flask – an arybollos, an exercise flask – and cleaned the blade and oiled it.

Spartans.

Gorgo put her hand on my arm. I think that she – as a woman – understood non-Spartans better than the men, and had – because she so often accompanied Leonidas – got an idea of what the rest of Greece thought about Sparta.

'He was badly injured,' she said calmly. 'And might never have been able to work again.'

'And you declare war on them every spring,' I said. I knew a *few* things about Sparta. Every spring, the ephors reminded Spartans to shave their moustaches – and to remember the war against the helots. The Spartans have a secret military organisation – like our religious bodies – to track and kill any helot whom they deem ready to revolt. They act quite regularly. They killed helots. In the night, in secret.

'Every man is at war with his slave,' she said. 'In Sparta, we tell the truth about it.'

I nodded. 'That, I understand, Despoina.'

She smiled. 'This is Bulis, son of Nicalaos. This brute without teeth is Sparthius, the son of Aneristus. Both front-rank men.' She nodded, and both men stepped forward. 'Spartiates, this is Arimnestos of Plataea. He is the man we have asked to transport you to the Great King.'

Sparthius had the good grace to groan and turn his head. Bulis smiled again. His eyes were a little mad. He reminded me of Idomeneaus in many ways.

'Well, now that they've tried to threaten me, I suppose we can all be friends.' I smiled at Bulis.

He didn't move. 'I never threaten,' he said. 'Threats are for the weak. There is only fight and not-fight.'

And again, there we were.

Gorgo sighed. 'It is a wonder women agree to mate with you,' she said. 'Bulis ...'

He bowed, elaborately. And backed up three steps. 'I make the Plataean uncomfortable,' he said. 'I'll speak to him from a safe range.'

'I'm sorry,' I said. 'I can't hear you.'

Sparthius laughed, a great booming laugh. 'We're going to be together on a ship? Delightful. I will learn so much. Bulis – heel, boy!' He mimed jerking a leash.

Bulis shook his head at me. 'No.'

'No what?' Sparthius asked.

Bulis came for me.

He came from three paces away, which is a long way in a fight. He was naked, and wearing a sword. I was wearing a chiton, but no sword. I think he was so contemptuous of my skills that he gave me three steps.

I was ready. He hadn't ever given a sign that he was turning off the fight – hence, I hadn't stopped being aware of him.

I don't usually kick, but he had long arms like an African ape and I didn't want to try him in a grapple – at least, not right away. I snapped a kick at his shin and pivoted and he reached with both hands.

My kick caught some of his shin and changed his balance, and his reaching hands caught my chiton at the pins but his balance was already compromised and I punched and he blocked and then we were circling. He had mostly ripped my chiton away.

Sparthius was swearing.

Gorgo just stepped back. I didn't see her, but I suspect that she had the look on her face that women wear when men behave like children.

I was aware that all the Spartans were now watching.

He had long arms, and he was quite content to box. He threw a flurry and I backed away. He threw another flurry – four punches in each. I turned. He threw another flurry ...

I tried to catch his left fist as it came towards me – the last punch in the third flurry. I missed, but my weight was committed, and we were locked in a grapple. His right hand went for my eyes.

They do that, in Sparta.

I passed my hands inside his and pushed his right elbow up and went for the throw, and he pivoted – Hades, he was fast – and tried to pass an arm around my waist. I raised my knee as if to strike his balls and my right fist backhanded him across the nose and I was away.

His smile didn't falter, and he didn't back up a step. His nose gushed blood.

I feinted a punch and kicked again. Again, I caught a piece of his shin – this time it was a better kick, and he had to back away, and I rotated, stepped forward and punched hard, forcing him back another step and then ...

I went for him. It was my best flurry – punch, punch, kick. The kick was a point-blank kick I got from Polymarchos, and unless you are a titan, you back away from a flurry.

He took one more step ...

... and went down over the cooling body of the helot.

I had planned it, so the moment he went backwards I leaped like a predator and was atop him. I caught his attempt to get a knee between my legs but the blow to my parts still stunned me – but my arm was across his throat and I had his right wrist.

He punched me with his left. It was like being hit with an axe.

I have been hit by an axe.

I pushed my right thumb up under his jaw.

Like the helot, he did not submit. He slammed his left into me – again.

I saw stars.

I really didn't want to kill him. It seemed ... unwise.

But I didn't really have another choice, and I didn't need another blow to my temple, so I shoved my thumb ...

His whole body went limp.

I waited perhaps ten heartbeats and then staggered to my feet.

I swayed.

And sat heavily. The world was swimming all around me.

Bulis hit *hard* – and that was his *left* hand.

No one applauded, but then, no one gutted me while I sat and breathed. My chiton was ruined – ripped from me early and now a rag on the ground. I picked it up and began to wipe myself down.

Bulis stirred.

I had hoped he was merely unconscious, but unlike many other things I've learned from fighting masters over the years, I had never actually used the thumb to the throat to put a man out. There's learning and then doing.

He coughed, rolled over, and threw up.

All the Spartans laughed.

While they were laughing, I tried to get up again, and I did better. My head hurt, but not with that feverish feeling that goes with concussion.

'Well fought,' Gorgo said.

'He's hardly our best,' Sparthius said. 'But Bulis is not bad. I'd say you were his match.'

'An even match,' Calliteles said. He stepped forward from the ring of onlookers – Spartans and helots. 'An even match in skill, but not in cunning.' He looked at the gathered Spartiates. 'How often do I tell you that a fight is what it is? There is no "unfair". Arimnestos saw the body and used it. Bulis should have known it was there.'

He had been an Olympian – the best wrestler in the world. I assumed he taught them.

Gorgo narrowed her eyes. 'You knew he was coming for you,' she said.

'Yes,' I said.

'You might have tried to dissuade him,' she said.

I managed to raise an eyebrow. 'Dissuade a Spartan from violence?' I asked.

'We're not Ares mad,' she said. 'We are a race of warriors, not a race of murderers. You might have ... smiled.'

'Backed up a step or two?' I asked. 'Perhaps I might have sent him a couple of heralds.'

She sighed.

I bowed politely to her and to Calliteles. 'If you'll pardon me, Spartans – I thank you for my morning's exercise.'

A helot produced a strigil. And an oil bottle.

Well – a gesture is a gesture. And Spartans love them. So I strigiled the dust and dirt and sweat off, scraping carefully, taking my time, and I oiled myself, while Bulis lay, barely able to move his lips. Then I handed the tools back to the slave and smiled my thanks.

My head swam from time to time – I had waves of dizziness, and then, suddenly, I'd be better. I put my hand to the side of my head and found that the left temple was mushy with blood.

I used my now-ruined chiton to fix that.

'I feel like a new man,' I said, lying. 'Anyone else?'

Gorgo's hand went up in front of my face as if to strike me. 'He does not mean that!' she said, as they all stepped forward. 'He is not challenging you. He does not know our ways.'

They looked disappointed.

Zeus, the Agoge must be something.

★

A little after noon, everyone – all free men, that is – begin to gather in the sacred enclosure. I wore a good himation – it was a formal occasion, after all. I led all my rowers – all free men, and with Draco's permission, cheerfully given – suddenly all Plataean citizens and thus eligible to attend. My head hurt.

Most of my oarsmen didn't even have a himation, but some did, and I put them in front, and we formed a contingent with old Draco and Styges and the two other Plataeans, both competitors – Antimenides, son of Alcaeus of Miletus who fell at Marathon, and Teucer, son of Teucer of Miletus, who also fell at Marathon. We went together to the stadium with twenty thousand other men, and then we processed to the temple.

At the temple precinct, an old priest was standing with Empedocles. Empedocles pointed me out, and the priest of Zeus pushed his way over to me. He was a man of Elis – older, but very fit, and clearly very rich from the gold chain he wore as a zone.

'Arimnestos of Plataea?' he asked.

I nodded. 'Reverend sir?'

He nodded. 'Empedocles of Thebes tells me you are a servant of Hephaestus, an initiate of the highest degree.'

I bowed. 'I have that honour,' I acknowledged.

'Empedocles says that you are the right man to make the sacrifice for Hephaestus. Indeed, we have six bulls for the smith god, and only three men to make the cuts.'

Empedocles had made his way to us – he was old enough that men would actually be polite and move aside for him.

'I'm a little old to swing the sword myself,' he said. 'But I'll say the words. You make the cuts for me.' He met my eye with a mischievous glint. 'There are not so many initiates of Hephaestos who can swing a sword, eh?' he asked.

'No, sir. Mostly we make them,' I said.

Both priests laughed.

I turned to Hector. 'Run and fetch the Raven's Claw,' I said. It was one of my first weapons – a heavy kopis, not long, but curved down like the beak of a big raven or any raptor, and sharp as flint.

The boy must have sprinted all the way to the tents. He came back scarcely able to breathe, bursting with pride. That pleased me – hard to say just why.

I took the sword and put the cord over my shoulder, and followed the priests out of the procession – or rather, to the front. There, the hundred or so men who would commit the sacrifices walked in splendour. It was almost the only occasion throughout the world when a man might wear a sword in public with a himation.

I was glad I'd worn so dignified a garment as a himation. I was in the same rank as the King of Sparta, and he smiled and winked as I was placed between two other Boeotians. The men around me were mostly hereditary priests, with a sprinkling of professionals – great aristocrats and powerful men. There, for example, was Adamenteis of Corinth, next to Leonidas.

It is, of course, an enormous honour to be asked to give a sacrifice at Olympia.

Just for a moment, I thought of my dead wife, Euphonia, who had been an aristocrat's daughter in Attika, and who would have *loved* to know that her bronzesmith husband would sacrifice alongside Aristides of Athens – five men to my left – and the Agiad King of Sparta.

I hadn't thought of her – just as a person, not an object of grief – in years. The thought of her simple pleasure in my achievement made me ... stronger. It was itself a gift from Aphrodite. I was not afraid. I was the husband of noble Euphonia, and I had every right to sacrifice in public as a priest of Hephaestus.

And something inside me healed.

We marched to the sound of flutes and horns, and we climbed the great steps.

Friends – what is life?

It is not the edge of the sword.

It is not all forbidden love and piracy.

That night – climbing the steps of the great temple of Zeus at Olympia with Leonidas of Sparta on my right and Aristides of Athens on my left – with Themistocles and Lykon of Corinth and a hundred other men I didn't know as well – with a sea of torches going back across the plain to the stadium and the camp – going to sacrifice to the immortal gods ...

I was with Greece.

Friends, this is hard to say. Someday, I will die.

Every man who was there will die. Most are long since dead.

All our children, all our wives, all our slaves. All will die.

But this must never die.

Why did we fight the Persians?

So that, rather than one man walking alone into his temple to sacrifice for his people to his gods – like the Great King ...

So that all men might walk into their temples and sacrifice to their gods. Together. Quarrelling about precedence and complaining about the mosquitoes, all the way.

That is Greece.

I was elated, but my hands shook.

Bulls are enormous.

Leonidas of Sparta sacrificed the first animal. By right of kingship, he was the senior priest of Zeus present. He raised his hands, no sword visible, and made the great prayer to Zeus.

And then, in front of twenty thousand Hellenes, he swore to send two hereditary heralds to the Great King. He swore it at the great altar of Olympia. He swore it to make restitution for Sparta's impiety. He didn't say as much, but there was a collective gasp as he recited his prayers, asking for the forgiveness of great Zeus, god of kngs and kingship, and Hermes, god of heralds and messengers.

I happened to catch sight of Adamenteis of Corinth at that moment. I marked him down as a Medizer. He glared at the Spartan king with unconcealed hatred.

If Leonidas saw him, he gave nothing away. With all Greece watching, the Agiad King of Sparta walked up to his animal – all white, as tall as his shoulder – and he placed his left hand on the animal, and it stopped calling to its mates. It raised its head slightly ...

The sword came from under his arm with the fluidity of water flowing. He never let the bull see the weapon – the sword rose and fell, not two movements but a single beat, and the bull – headless – fell to its knees.

Twenty thousand men roared to Zeus.

Not every man killed as cleanly as the King of Sparta, but every man killed his animal. Aristides – my friend, the priggish man of justice – was the only man to kill his bull as elegantly as Leonidas. He was of an age with the Spartan king, and as an Athenian aristocrat, he'd trained just as hard, and his cut flowed like water from a broken dam – sudden and yet smooth like planished bronze.

And then it was my turn. Forty thousand eyes on me.

I did not attempt to draw and cut like the king. I had my kopis loose in my hand, and raised my arm and rolled my hips and my animal fell to its knees, its head cleanly severed, and there was a roar – a beautiful roar.

Empedocles slapped my back with surprising strength. 'Beautiful, lad! Now follow me.'

I was ... not quite of the earth. Listen to twenty thousand Greeks roar their prayers to the gods and try to be calm.

He led me past Aristides, who clasped my hand, and past Lykon, who was still waiting his turn and didn't even see me – well down the line.

To another bull.

I think I grunted. The blow had taken a great deal from me – not just from my sinews, but from my heart.

I said, 'Another?' I looked at him. 'Isn't there some other man who wishes this honour?'

Empedocles shrugged. 'For Apollo, we have fifty candidates for every bull. Even for Ares, five. But poor Hephaestus ...' He smiled. 'I think the aristocrats feel he's not clean enough. Too much like a workman.'

I shook my head.

The bull could smell the blood on my blade. He began to move – he was chained by his neck, but he had lots of room. It is always better to kill early in a sacrifice. The later your turn, the more afraid the animals are.

Empedocles leaned over. 'Eight more to go. No one has failed yet.'

In a mass sacrifice like this, eventually someone fails. A blow is inept, or weak, and the animal is not killed cleanly. It is a bad omen. Not a shocking one – it happens all the time.

But in a great year, no one fails. That is a wonderful omen for the four years to come.

I had killed twelfth. No one had failed by then. Now I was down in the seventies – I couldn't keep count, and besides, just six places away on the great mound of ash and stone, an animal fell to its knees, head dangling by a thread, and blood gushed hot.

The crowd roared a prayer.

Quite spontaneously, many men – perhaps thousands – had begun singing the paean that all the Greeks sing when they are together. That sound – which I had last heard at Marathon – it raises the hackles on your neck. It is the sound before you commit yourself to death.

And yet, it is the sound that makes us Greek.

Euphonia and her Aphrodite – Hephaestus' wife, for all she was faithless – they got me through the first bull.

But the paean rose and my chest swelled.

The maddened bull flinched ...

And fell, head cleanly severed, the neck dropping away and the long spurt of blood from the main artery leaping from the still-living heart.

I have no memory of the moments in between, but I swear – *I swear* – that Hephaestus entered into me for those moments.

The paean swept on, roared by ten thousand voices.

I looked to the left. There were just six bulls to go on my side – six men. Even as I watched, the closest man to me made his cut beautifully, and the bull went to its knees, already dead, and the man wore the same look of elation I think I must have worn.

At the end of the row – the last man on my side – was a thin man, a mere stick figure. He was clearly afraid. It showed in his shoulders and his neck and jaw.

There was nothing I could do.

Third from the end cut, and his beast went down as if hit by an axe.

The smell of blood was everywhere, the roar of twenty thousand Greek men like waves of the sea on a stormy day, and the fires on the altars suddenly leapt as if the gods themselves inhabited them as a great gust of wind struck the fires.

The next man cut. I thought he'd failed – he certainly didn't behead his beast, and the animal seemed to turn its head aggressively – but then, with the grace of the dying, it fell forward and crashed to the floor, and the song went up.

Only the last man, whose arms appeared too thin to kill anything, remained.

As his arm went up, I tried to drive it for him. My hips rolled with his to put power into his stroke. He had a heavy blade. He knew how to use it.

It fell like the stoop of an eagle, and the beast dropped.

Far off to the right, there was another cheer – the two cheers crossed the crowd and met in the centre.

I had thought the song loud before, but presented with the spectacle of a hundred dead bulls – no one had failed – the crowd roared and they were half again as loud as they had ever been.

Temple servants brought us water scented with perfumes, and we washed the sacred blood off our hands – and our blades. A slave handed me a piece of sheepskin dipped in olive oil, and I used it to carefully clean and oil the blade before dropping it back into the scabbard. I must have taken too long, because Themistocles came and slapped me on the back.

'Two sacrifices in a single event – you must be blessed of the gods,' he said. He leaned close. 'Men pay a thousand drachma to be allowed to make a single cut.'

'Only for the fashionable gods,' muttered Empedocles.

Themistocles smiled at him. 'I like your wit, sir. Your accent is from Boeotia?'

'Not just the accent,' Empedocles said, and offered his hand.

Aristides came and we embraced. 'Two cuts!' He smiled and shook his head. Then, to my surprise, he embraced Themistocles, who returned his hug with every evidence of friendship.

I must have gaped like a peasant, because Aristides laughed.

'I only hate his foolish politics,' Aristides said.

Themistocles grimaced. 'There – something on which we can agree!'

The athletes processed into the temple – mostly they came by event, but not all; a few famous men came first, to the maddened applause of the crowd, and then the boys – the young boxers and pankration-ists and runners. They would be the first to compete.

After the boys – who were cheered as much for their beauty, as such things are reckoned, as for their coming fame – after them came the charioteers. They wore the long chitons that chariot drivers have worn for two hundred years, and the Cyreneian gleamed like polished stone, and the Spartan, Polypeithes, seemed steady enough, which pleased me.

After the charioteers came all the men who would ride horses, and then the handful of athletes – at least that year – who would compete in the pentathlon. Now, different men hold different events to be the most important – most aristocrats believe the chariot racing is the central event, because of old Pelops and the story of his chariot – most hoplite-class men prefer the running events, and many men prefer the pankration. The new race in armour – this was only the fifth time it would be run – was gaining tremendously in popular-ity with active soldiers – this is before men started using lightened shields and greaves as thin as parchment.

But the pentathlon is the best event. The men who win it are not just good at one thing, they are good at five things – running, throwing a discus, throwing a javelin, wrestling, and long jump – and all are each difficult events. A man who can do all five is a great athlete.

Once, before my leg wound, I could run. I've always been able to wrestle. My javelin-throwing is average at best, but average among men who are excellent. I have thrown a discus well enough to place with experts – but I cannot execute a good long jump. I have tried with and without weights, on sand, on dirt . . .

Never mind. I love to watch it, and I think the men who win are the greatest of all athletes.

After the pentathletes came the men who would run the foot races – the stadion, the diaulos, the long, brutal dolichos – and then the combat athletes, the boxers, wrestlers and pankrationists (wild applause), and finally the warriors from the last event that would occur on day four, the run in armour, the hoplitodromos.

And at the end, a trio of priests – the men who would officiate at the closing ceremonies and herald the next team of men of Elis who would prepare the temples and the city for the next Olympiad.

The high priest and the men of Elis led the athletes in swearing their oaths to the gods – they swore by Zeus to uphold the rules, to play with fairness in spirit as well as law, to act in such a way as to bring pleasure to the god.

Many of us made the oath with them.

And the flames rose into the gathering night, and the first sacrifices were thrown on the great fires, and the Olympics had begun.

The dawn of the second day saw the boys' events begin. It was a good day – full of heartbreak for some, such as the young boy from Crete who broke his arm from sheer exuberance and high spirits and missed his wrestling event – and full of wonderful drama, such as Epicradios of Mantinea's incredible win against much larger boys in boxing. He was as nimble as an Egyptian cat, and as quick, and in every fight he dodged and twisted and manoeuvred – and then suddenly his catlike one-two would lick out, and he'd be another step closer to victory. And when they put the laurel on his brow, he burst into tears.

Simonides wrote a poem about him, which we all heard that night at the fires. We ate beef – there was a lot of beef around, after the killing of a hundred bulls, and we had another hundred to go – and Aeschylus composed an epigram in his honour, and the boy wandered from fire to fire with his father and his trainer – he was the day's hero, and everyone wanted to applaud him.

I sat with Megakles and Leukas and Sekla and Aristides and Cimon – an odd mixture of races and classes, but that's the Olympics for you – and we toasted the boy and a dozen more, and finally I turned to Aristides when the newly famous athletes had passed my free wine and my fire, and said –

'I hear a rumour you are threatened with exile,' and smiled to take out the sting.

He shrugged. 'I have been on the verge of exile since first I raised my voice in the assembly,' he said.

'Men call you Aristides the Just!' I said. 'Why does Themistocles seek your exile? Why is anyone else foolish enough to vote for it?'

He drank. And smiled. 'Perhaps Jocasta seeks a rest from wearisome guests who prate endlessly about politics!' he said.

Cimon leaned forward. 'Last year, Themistocles put it to the vote – ostracism for Aristides. And he had the nerve to do it while Aristides was serving on the boule – standing right there, counting the votes. This thes – this lower-class arsehole – comes up and asks Aristides to help him write a name on the ostricon – the shards of pottery we use as voting slips ... Do you know what I'm talking about, Plataean?'

'We vote, even in boorish Plataea,' I said. No one likes being patronised, even by great men.

'You are spending too much time with the Spartans. So this fellow is illiterate, a potter or a vase painter of something, and he says, "Help me write *Aristides*."'

We all laughed.

Aristides looked at the fire, as men do when annoyed.

'And,' Cimon went on, laughing so hard he was spitting, 'and old Aristides here scratches his own name, just as deep and easy as if it had been Themistocles, eh?' He laughed. 'And when he's done, he says, "What do you have against Aristides, sir?" to the fellow, who clearly has no clue who he is.'

You must imagine that by this time we're all roaring with laughter.

'And the man shakes his head and says, "I don't know who in Hades he is, but everyone calls him 'the just' and that makes me feel unjust, and I hate him!"'

I spat my wine. It wasn't that Cimon's story was so funny – I mean, it was, but it's a pretty well-known story now – but the way he told it and the agonised expression on Aristides' face ... Aristides hated being talked about, while his enemy Themistocles loved it.

Hector moved around, pouring more wine, and Aristides raised an eyebrow as if to say *if you people are quite finished* and drank. 'As I was saying ...' he began.

It was something about his priggish air and his aristocratic manner, but that set us all off again, whooping and laughing.

I loved the man – but he could be an arse.

At any rate, when we were all done, he turned to me. 'Like Cimon, I believe that a naval solution to our problems is possible. Unlike Cimon and Themistocles, I think that such a solution would be a disaster for Greece, almost equal to failing to resist the Medes. We must best the Medes in a fair fight, man to man. Only that way do we prove ourselves worthy of the challenge – and only that way do we hold on to our political rights. If the oarsmen win the day, the oarsmen will be the new hoplites – won't they?'

Megakles looked away and smiled. Leukas didn't really understand Aristides' quick Greek amd Sekla pretended interest in the hem of his chlamys.

But I didn't. I sat back. Hector gave me a roll of bread with some olive paste and anchovies – a sort of opson-laden snack – and I ate it, and then I shook my head. 'Cleisthenes gave every Athenian heroic ancestors, didn't he? If the ships beat the Persians, surely all those thetes-class men will merely prove themselves worthy of the gift they have been given?'

I thought Aristides would snarl, he looked so angry. Cimon grinned.

'Well put, Plataean. Damn it, I should make you a citizen just to hear you argue with Aristides.'

Aristides frowned. 'I already have fifty men to do that, thanks.'

Cimon leaned in. 'Besides, Aristides is rich and from the oldest aristocracy, and Themistocles is rich and from new money, so they are bound to tangle. They represent different interests in every way.'

I looked at Aristides. 'At the time of Marathon, you were the enemy of any kind of faction.'

Cimon had the good grace to look away.

Aristides nodded. 'I feel the state is threatened.' He shrugged. 'To be fair, so does Themistocles. We agree on many things – but not at all on how to solve them.' He looked at me. 'One of us must go. I'm sure it will be me. I promise hard times and hard labours, and he promises free silver and an overseas empire.' Aristides managed a thin smile. 'Who would you exile?'

'You,' I said. I laughed.

Cimon nodded. 'But then ...' He looked around. 'I know Sekla. Can I trust these others?'

'I only trust them with my money and my life and my honour,' I said. 'Other things you have to be wary about.'

Cimon nodded again. 'If Aristides is exiled ...' he began, and Aristides actually reached out and put a restraining hand on him.

'Not even here,' he said. 'Not even to Arimnestos.'

I tried for half an hour to pry the secret out of them, and failed.

We all went to bed.

The third day dawned clear, bright and desperately hot. I went for a good run, my leg hurt me less than usual, and I didn't see Gorgo. And yes, I was disappointed.

I did run past the Lacedaemonian camp. And Sparthius waved at me, dropped his chiton and joined me for my run. Despite his lack of front teeth, he was a good talker and in top shape, and we ran along the river and he made more conversation than I'd probably heard from Brasidas in a thousand stades of ocean sailing. Mostly about chariot racing.

I left him at his camp before the sun was really hot, bathed in the shallow, clean waters of the river upstream of the temples and the camp, and then walked back and put on a clean linen chiton for the events. And then I went to see the games.

The third day is, in some ways, the first full day. The whole of the pentathlon is performed on the third day, and I watched it – indeed, I devoured it. I'm not sure I can tell you exactly why, but I walked back and forth around the stadium, watching the events – javelin, always my own weakest event, held me riveted to the spot like a hilt to a blade. The races were splendid, and the jumping was felt by many to be the best in twenty years.

No Spartan placed higher than fifth.

All the Spartans tend to sit or stand together in a single block, and they move together – like a taxeis of infantry, really. It can be imposing, until you understand that they feel themselves to be different and, like many different people, they are shy with outsiders. Sparthius, for example, having run with me, showed no reserve at all – he grinned when our eyes met and took my hand. He introduced me to four other men from his mess, and they seemed a pleasant, if silent, crew.

None of them spoke to Brasidas, but then none of them attacked him, either.

I went back to my campfire that night to find that we'd sold all of our wine, that I had a nasty sunburn despite my huge straw hat, and that I still hadn't had my surfeit of the Olympics. I was in love with the whole thing. I don't think that I had ever seen so many men demonstrate arete in so many ways. I don't think I had ever been so proud to be a Greek.

Themistocles, as is often the case, said it best that night. Aristides gave a dinner – note that I could afford to give men free wine, but Aristides could afford to have two hundred men to dinner – and when Themistocles spoke, it was about what it was to be a Greek. He was funny – there are, I promise you, many comic aspects to the Greek race – and sometimes trite or bigoted, but in the end, he said:

'Look around you, brothers! Where else will you find this – the contest of men against men, for nothing greater than honour – judged not by kings, but only by men like we ourselves. Here we are, at the shrine of the gods, and what we do here – this is *who we are*.'

He was a little drunk, but I thought it was well said.

And yet – I suspect the Persians said the same, when they raced their horses and shot their bows.

We all lay on rented kline in the oil-lamp-lit darkness and swatted the voracious insects and complained about the wine. I remember I was lying with Cimon, and we were debating whether to press our forward naval plan on Themistocles one more time, when a breeze made the lamps flicker and a group of Spartans approached. I was delighted to find that the young man who wished to speak to me was Polypeithes himself, and that he had made a full recovery.

'I owe you my life. We take this seriously, in Lacedaemon,' he said.

It is the special gift of the Spartans to give every utterance a spin that makes other men angry. I was tempted to tell him that we took such things seriously even in Plataea, but he was young and earnest and I merely pressed his hand.

'Will you race tomorrow, or use a charioteer?' I asked.

He smiled. 'Sir, I would rather come in sixth in control of my own team than win the laurel with another's hands on the reins.'

Cimon applauded. 'That's a proper spirit,' he said. 'If you go on in this vein, I'll have to cheer for you and not for Athens.'

While he was perched on my couch, I leaned forward. 'Any idea who hit you with a sling stone?'

Spartans are dreadful liars. He looked away and said, 'No!' and hung his head.

'Have you spoken to the queen?' I asked him.

He nodded. 'That is a Spartan matter,' he said stiffly, and rose from my couch.

I waved goodbye and let him go. His friends bowed respectfully – oh, it is such a pleasure to be a famous man! – and withdrew.

Later, at my own fire, I asked Ka to make some enquiries, and I raised the whole matter with Moire and Harpagos and Paramanos, all of whom agreed. I suggested to them that it was in our interest to figure out who had done it.

Paramanos's beard had a lot of white in it, suddenly. He looked old and wise. He sat back, accepted more wine from his own boy, and met my eye. 'Twenty thousand suspects,' he said.

I shook my head. 'More like fifty thousand,' I said. 'Slaves can use a sling, too. Even girls.'

They all shook their heads like the chorus in a tragedy.

'On a positive note, whoever did it is probably within half a mile of us right now,' I said. 'We know a few things. The guilty person was up very early, and went out along the river – that has to limit our potential group. I assume the attack was paid for by people who want Persia to triumph – or who want Sparta to submit.'

Harpagos grinned like the Chian fisherman he really was. 'Or someone who wants Athens to be defeated,' he said.

Moire laughed. 'Well – that's about everyone here.'

I already knew who I suspected. But I had no desire to poison their efforts – I knew that none of my captains could resist such a challenge, and I knew that all of them had rich resources in friends and business partners and foreign contacts.

Before I went and rolled into my cloak – alone, again, damn it – I had a whispered conversation with Sekla, Brasidas and Alexandros. We made our plans – to protect Polypeithes. It was – and is – funny to consider the four of us plotting to protect a Spartan, but something told me that not all Spartans were united in this.

★

In the morning, I took a staff and went for a long walk. I went up into the hills and talked to some sheep and came home by a roundabout course intended to put me on the plain in time to meet the Queen of Sparta out for her morning ride. I am as male as most men, and sometimes more so, and I won't deny that I looked forward to seeing her, but I had some business to transact, as well.

I saw her in the distance, already done and turning back, and I came down into the valley to meet her, as if by chance. I waved and she rode to my side.

'Good morning. You look like ... one of the more equestrian goddesses.' I smiled too broadly, and she frowned.

'Wouldn't it be a better compliment if you named one?' she asked.

I shook my head. 'No – that would only offer you more opportunity to disclaim the compliment and the giver. Aphrodite? No. Hera? Too presumptuous. Athena? Un-Spartan. Artemis?' I shrugged. 'In truth, you do not remind me of Artemis.'

Gorgo laughed. 'You are not like most Greek men,' she said.

I shrugged. 'I travel. Listen, o Queen. Do you have an idea who tried to kill Polypeithes?'

She nodded. 'Yes,' she said.

'Will he try again?' I asked.

She shrugged.

'You don't care?' I asked.

She looked away. 'I cannot be seen to care,' she said. 'For some very complicated reasons that have little to do with the matter at hand.'

I nodded, although in truth I didn't understand. 'Adamenteis of Corinth?' I guessed.

She blushed. Almost all of her.

'Why?' I asked.

'How do you know?' she asked.

I shrugged. 'I don't, but I saw the look he gave your chariot the other day, I saw his charioteer talking to Ka and asked Ka to ascertain a few things – and I saw the glare he levelled at your husband.'

'He hates Themistocles ten times as much as he hates my husband,' she spat. 'He wants his team to win any way he can arrange it, and he has accepted a fat bribe from the Medes.'

I nodded. 'Well,' I said. 'My second question is purely personal. Why do you want me to take your heralds to Susa?'

She looked at me as if I were a fool. 'So that they won't be killed, of course,' she said. She smiled – it changed her expression from serene self-possession to a nymph-like wonder. 'Do you really think that a pair of Spartan gentlemen who can make themselves disliked merely by walking are going to be a triumph at the court of the Great King? They are my friends, and my cousins. They are my husband's friends. They are making a brave sacrifice for our city – I'd like to keep them from paying too high a price.'

I looked into those laughing, nymph-like eyes, and somehow failed to say 'no'.

By the time we were entering the main valley, Gorgo and I, it was plain that something had happened at the edge of the encampment. Gorgo raced away – for the Spartan tents. I ran as best I could.

The cluster of men in the early light proved to be gathered around a corpse – a dead man with three feet of black arrow protruding from his head. He was quite dead. A pair of Olympian priests were already mourning him, and complaining that the blood shattered the truce and defiled the games. Even while I stood there, more priests came, and some of the judges. They were angry – even fearful.

A killing in the Olympics was no small matter. The impiety – the sacrilege – was so intense that men in the crowd spoke of the games being cancelled.

No one knew who the dead man was until one of the Argosian trainers identified him as one of the Corinthian grooms.

I said as little as possible and kept moving after that, because the dead man had a heavy south Egyptian arrow in him, and it virtually had to be one of Ka's. I jogged back to my camp, cursing my wounds, and found Sekla directing operations.

'I'm releasing the last two amphorae of wine,' he said. 'I've sent Ka to the coast to buy more.'

I understood immediately – Ka was out of camp and thus difficult to catch or question.

'I arranged for him to have a horse,' Sekla continued.

While Sekla spoke, I noted that Leukas had a sword under his chlamys – a long Keltoi sword – and several other men were unobtrusively armed. Sittonax was lounging on a spear, his wrist and left leg both curled lovingly around the shaft. Some men still used spears as walking staffs back then – Sittonax was taking advantage of that.

'What happened?' I asked quietly. I took Sekla by the arm and towed him into the back of the wine tent.

Quite loudly he said, 'It's foolishness to keep two amphorae for our own use. We can get a drachma a cup today.'

Then he lowered his voice. 'The man had a sling, and he went to use it on the Spartan charioteer. That's all I know. Ka made the call and killed him.'

It was an act of gross impiety – an attack on the Olympic grounds, during the truce. On the other hand, as far as I know, Ka had never believed in our gods, so perhaps he is immune. But if the attack were traced to me . . .

It is a difficult thing, having men who serve you. I gave them orders to protect Polypeithes. They did. Ka acted as he thought was correct, and now we had a corpse and some very angry Elisians.

'What is done is done,' I said. 'On my head be it. How is the Spartan?'

'I doubt he even knows there was an incident,' Sekla responded. 'Leukas followed him all the way to his encampment, dressed as a slave. He says the Spartans have thrown a cordon around their camp since the chariot returned.'

I poured myself a precious cup of our wine and sat on a leather stool. I beckoned to Sittonax, Harpagos and Leukas, all waiting visibly close. They came into the small back area of the tent.

I popped out and walked all the way around the tent to make sure we were alone. I caught Hector's arm – he was carrying a basket of bread for Gaia – and sent him to watch the tent from a little distance, to make sure we were not overheard. I took Alexandros off his duties running our watch against theft and placed him at the door of the tent. I summoned Brasidas to our meeting. Behind me, Sekla and Leukas continued a fairly unconvincing haggle about what to charge for wine.

Committing an act of impiety at the Olympics raised the stakes enormously. Suddenly, it was all life and death.

'Gentlemen,' I said when I went back. 'This is family only. Oikia, yes? Not for Cimon. Not even Paramanos.' I looked around, and everyone nodded. 'If Ka were to be taken, he would be tortured and then executed.'

That got to them. The south Egyptian was a very popular man.

'Sekla – well done getting Ka away. Now – what's our next step? It is five hours before the chariots run.' I waved at the Spartan camp in the distance.

Brasidas did not hesitate. 'Put a watch on the Corinthians. We have the manpower to do it.'

I had thought in terms of protecting Polypeithes. I had to smile at the Spartan-ness of his solution. I was prepared to defend, and Brasidas was, in effect, ready to attack.

'We watch them, but what more can we do? If two slaves leave their camp ...' I shrugged.

Sekla smiled. 'Every one of theirs who leaves camp is followed by a couple of ours. Do we have to be secret? Why not make it obvious? There are fewer than a hundred Corinthians here.'

I scratched my beard. 'We could end with a war between Corinth and Plataea,' I said.

Brasidas shook his head. 'Look – send a few men – led by me – to watch the Corinthian camp. And some boys as runners. Do the same for the Lacedaemonian camp. If the chariot leaves their camp – then we can act.' He shot me a hard smile. 'I doubt the Corinthians will try again, but if they do – we need to catch them at it.'

Hector's high-pitched voice shouted outside, 'Lord Aristides, master!' and I was outside in a heartbeat, smiling falsely.

Aristides looked as angry as an outraged husband. 'I would hate to think ...' he began, and I came out to find that I had half the noblemen of Athens in my camp. I sent Hector for stools and wine. Cimon gave me a sign that I needed to talk fast.

'They are saying in the camp that the Spartans killed the Corinthian groom. Other men say it was a Plataean. Others that it was an African,' Aristides said. 'This impiety must be punished.'

The problem with Aristides is that he was completely honest, and thus, he saw most issues in simple terms.

'I saw the corpse,' I said. 'Heavy arrow. Not anyone local.' I shrugged. 'Perhaps a Cretan or a Cypriote.'

Cimon's eyes applauded my lies. 'Cretans do use heavy shafts like that one,' Cimon drawled. 'I had forgotten that.'

Other men responded with the sort of spontaneous expertise that every man is capable of when he knows nothing – suddenly a dozen of them were experts on Cretan arrows.

Aristides didn't sit. He put a hand on my shoulder. 'I feel in my bones that you have something to do with this,' he said. 'I saw you look at the corpse. Tell me immediately, please.'

I shook my head. 'I can tell you only that the Corinthians have been trying to harm the Spartans,' I said quietly.

Understanding flooded Aristides. His body stiffened. He narrowed his eyes.

I shook my head. 'I'm looking into it,' I said. In truth, he was very difficult to lie to, and I was struggling, but with the stakes so high, I managed.

I turned to Cimon. 'Someone should watch the Corinthians, and someone else should watch the Spartans. To keep them apart, if nothing else.'

'You think the Spartans killed the groom?' Aristides asked.

I shrugged. 'You know that someone struck Polypeithes the charioteer with a sling stone – right?'

Aristides shook his head. 'I see,' he said, face closing.

Cimon took his arm. 'A slave is dead, not a Greek,' he said. 'Let's not make too much of this.'

He drank down his wine and dragged Aristides away, leaving me with Themistocles. The orator glanced at the Spartan encampment. 'You've taken ... measures?' he asked.

'No idea what you are talking about,' I said. 'But I have agreed to escort the Spartan ambassadors.'

'Heralds,' Themistocles said. 'Not ambassadors.'

We spent the morning and the afternoon watching the Corinthians. We had help from a dozen Athenians and we didn't hide ourselves particularly – that is to say, Cimon and I were quite open, and so was Themistocles – so open that Adamanteis came out in a cloak.

'We can see to our own affairs,' he said. 'We don't need Athenians interfering in our preparations.'

Themistocles shrugged. 'It is a fine place to stand and watch the games,' he said. 'And free to all men, I think.'

Adamanteis looked as if he might explode.

'Sir,' I asked, 'do you by any chance own in the chariot racing today? The four-horse team with the African charioteer?'

He nodded curtly.

I smiled. 'Ah, I see,' I said. I meant it. I did see. Gorgo had it all correct. 'May the best chariot and team win, then,' I said.

'I repeat – you needn't be here. We can protect ourselves,' Adamanteis said.

Themistocles shrugged. 'Perhaps it is not you that we protect.'

The Corinthian spun on his heel and walked back among his tents. Several men pointed at us.

I wondered whether he was enough of a fool to provoke a fight. At the Olympics, no less.

Meanwhile, we missed Astylos's day of triumph altogether, which galled me. We heard the roar from the stadium as he won the stadia, and Hector found us to tell us of the victory. Most of my oarsmen were in the south end of the stadium, roaring their lungs out for the Italian.

Two hours later, we caught the excitement even three stades away. Hector came to tell us that Astylos had won his first heat at the diaulos. Cimon and I cursed that we were missing a great moment. Themistocles made an excuse and left us to watch. He loved the running, and he wasn't doing anything but provoking the Corinthians. He and Adamanteis clearly loathed each other.

It broke my heart to miss the final race. More so as *two* Plataeans made the last heat.

But we accomplished our objective, because when two grooms departed the Corinthian camp, they did so just as the cheering reached a fever pitch, late in the day. They avoided our position by slipping under the edge of their back tents and creeping slowly along the ground until clear of the camp. Then they ran into the trees to the south of the river and began to make their way along the high ground towards the Spartans. We never saw them.

But Brasidas and Leukas did. The two were dressed as slaves, Leukas hawking wine and Brasidas serving it. Leukas's tattoos and barbaric Greek accent covered them both. They sent their pais – an Egyptian boy – running to us. I sent Alexandros and a dozen marines, all unarmed, to join Brasidas.

Then I put Leukas back on duty, this time with Sittonax and Harpagos pouring for him. It seemed possible that the first pair was a diversion.

With every possible arrangement made, I sauntered down to the stadium to embrace Astylos, who was so elated that he was with the gods. He had won two Olympic events in a single day. It had happened before, but no one could remember when, and he was, that night, the most famous man in the Greek world. And for many years thereafter.

Somewhere in the woods north of the sanctuary, Brasidas caught the two slaves. They didn't fight. He tied them to trees, questioned them, and then Alexandros took them to the Spartan camp. I would love to have been present when they were handed over, but it was all done very quietly and I didn't want my hand to be seen too broadly in it.

We ate and drank. The last of the wine was gone. The sun set. We changed the watch on the Corinthians. Brasidas assured me that the Athenians were watching the Spartans.

I went to my cloak, too tired to sit up with Astylos and Polymarchos and enjoy their moment of triumph. But the young man glowed, and Polymarchos look ten years younger.

I went to sleep. And rose in the dawn, to the last day. The day of the pankration, and of the chariot races.

I wasn't intending to miss the pankration, so I made my arrangements early and put Cimon in charge. And he dumped his command responsibilities on Themistocles, who, you will remember, had walked off to see the races. It would have been the perfect moment for Adamanteis to sneak an assassin out, but the world seldom works that way.

After all, Adamantheis had no idea whether his grooms had succeeded or not. Their orders – according to Brasidas, who questioned them fairly extensively (I'm sparing your finer feelings) – their orders were to injure the horses. They had slings, a bow and knives.

Enough. My point is that the enemy is not always all-knowing. In this case, I think Adamanteis was outmatched. He was one arrogant rich man facing a dozen arrogant rich men. Hah!

At any rate, the pankration was superb. Agias of Pharalas won in just four bouts – only six men were willing to match him, and two of them were out – badly injured – in two rounds. He was tall, heavily built, beautifully muscled, and very fast. He always attacked, and his movements were fluid and graceful – almost impossible for a man so big.

I was lying on the green grass of the stadium bank with a number of my friends, including Polymarchos and Astylos – crowned with laurel and bathing in the admiration of every man in the crowd, I can tell you. But Polymarchos pointed out the Pharsalians early.

'Rhadamanthius of Pharsala trains them,' he said. 'Men say he's the greatest warrior alive. He's a freedman – a former slave. You can always tell the men he trains – the way they move. Look at the lumbering bastard – he won't last a moment ...'

Indeed, as we watched, Agias took his opponent's left wrist in his right and rotated it up – just a little – and made his opponent rotate

120

on his hips – again, just a little – and at exactly the right moment, he seemed to step *through* the other man. Agias knelt suddenly, and pulled his opponent down – the man was forced against his will to rotate, to lose his balance, and to collapse back across Agias's out-thrust knee. He fell, and Agias rolled across him, a forearm across the downed man's throat. The big man was brave and strong – he struggled until he was unconscious. But the pin was complete.

Sadly that was the best of his matches. There really wasn't any-one who was worthy of him. One man he put down with a single, well-placed punch, and another he caught in a foolish extension and flipped over his head. All with an air of almost casual elegance.

Another Pharsalian won the wrestling. The two men enjoyed our plaudits, and walked the stadium receiving cheers and flowers and wreaths and small statues. Euthymos of Lokroi won the boxing. He was a fighter, and he fought three other men as good as he – well, not quite as good – but his fights offered more drama than the Pharsalians had. He seemed to just barely manage his wins, and yet, in the end, he had the same wreath of laurel on his brow and the same immortality. There's a lesson there.

And then it was time to walk down to the hippodrome and watch the chariots.

The order of events is not immutable, and I know that in other years, the chariots have run on different days. As men emphasise – or forget – the role of old Pelops in founding the games, the chariot races gain in importance or lose it again. Some new event – such as the hoplitodromos – will catch everyone's interest, or a particular athlete will capture the imaginations of the judges – and that can change the way the games are scheduled. In that year, with the fate of Greece blowing on the winds of fate, the chariot race for four horses was last.

Of course, we'd already had all the horse races, the donkey race, the race for colts, and the two-horse chariots. Oh, yes. Greeks will watch almost any kind of race.

But as I've already said, the four-horse chariot race is considered a sacred event. It takes a fantastically rich man to enter a team – to get four matched horses, you need to raise fifty, or so I'm told. Matched teams sold for enough money to buy a fleet or a small city.

Good charioteers were often Italian or Africans, because both of those somewhat backward places still used chariots in battle and for lavish display, and they had more and better charioteers. Even Asia had better charioteers then Greece – after all, I was one of them, however briefly.

At any rate, there were only the six chariots. So there was only one race, and the teams drew lots for their positions. There was no stagger, so the outside berths were seriously disadvantaged at the start – they had a great deal farther to travel, and they could not possibly get to the inside on the turns, so all other things being equal, the outside berths would be behind for a dozen laps.

And again, recall that on each lap, the chariot had to go straight down the hippodrome, turn at a pole, go straight back to the start, and turn again – not an oval. I think it is possible that the reason men loved to watch is that one or two chariots were always wrecked, and the value of a small city in horseflesh killed. Somewhere, a rich man was brought low. Lesser men could cheer for that.

That's a cynical reason. A better reason is that just one four-horse chariot makes the earth shake. Just one looks like the direct tool of the gods – the horses paw the earth and snort, their magnificent heads toss, and you can see Apollo or Zeus himself at the reins. Put six of them side by side, and the sound is like Zeus's own thunderbolts, and the waves of the sea.

The draws were announced while Cimon and I – and our friends – took up the ground that had been held for us all morning by a dozen of my oarsmen. On the inside, in the best berth, was the team from Ceos. As I mentioned, they were piebald horses and a hand smaller than the others, but the position at the inside changed all the wagering instantly. The charioteer wore a long white racing chiton with Tyrian red borders.

The next team out were the Corinthians, and they were magnificent, with the horses and the driver looking equally dark, glossy – and heroic. The charioteers' salute was sufficient to draw a wall of thunderous applause – the cheers roared on and on. His horses were calm, while the little horses of Ceos fidgeted and tossed their heads. The Corinthian wore a red tunic – all red.

The third team was that of Gelon of Syracusa – black as his heart, I might add. They were the most beautiful team, and men roared for them again. Their charioteer wore a pure white chiton and looked like the god Apollo.

The fourth team from the pole was the white team of Aegina. The horses were beautifully matched, and their coats had been brushed and brushed so that their bodies appeared to be some sort of flowing metal. Their charioteer wore a dark blue chiton.

The fifth team was the Athenians. Their horses were all beautiful, but unmatched. It was rather like a drama about Athenian democracy – the unmatched team. The Athenian charioteer wore a white chiton with blue borders and full-length sleeves, an older style the Athenians always favoured. I can tell you from experience that in a fall, those full sleeves can protect you from a great many abrasions.

And last – the worst position – came the Spartans. Every head in the hippodrome went to the Spartans, all sitting together.

They didn't react at all, and they all cheered the Spartan chariot. As did many others – all my men, and many of the Athenians, too. That brought some stares.

The six teams lined up carefully, and the judges examined every team. This went on long enough to make every man in the hippodrome anxious for his particular team and for the animals. I was hungry and thirsty myself before the judges cleared away from the teams, and the censor mounted the rostrum with a wand in his hand and raised it, and the tension in the hippodrome rose until it was like the tension between two phalanxes getting ready to close in mortal combat.

And then the wand dropped, and they were off.

The opening of the race held a layer of surprises like an Athenian wedding cake. The team from Ceos was off the line in perfect form – and they went from the stand to a dead gallop in six or seven strides, a superb performance.

The Corinthian driver had clearly expected to beat the Ceosian team off the line – to seize the inside lane and hold the pole for the turn for the beginning. And his team came off the line in beautiful style. But they could not beat the piebald horses down the stretch. It was amazing to see the four small horses run – they seemed to flow along the ground with something of the dancing grace of the Pharsalian athletes. They couldn't *beat* the bigger Corinthian team, but the Corinthians couldn't gain even a head and a neck on the Ionian team, and as the two began to come up on the first turn, if became clear that the Corinthian was not going to gain the inside lane.

He allowed himself to drop back half a chariot length, to cut inside and take the turn second. After all – I could read his thoughts – he had fifty-three more opportunities to pass.

The teams of Aegina and Syracusa duplicated the entire perform-ance. The Aeginians probably had the inferior team, but they were on their mettle, and the Syracusans could not cut in to gain the inside lane – you must imagine every chariot cutting hard to the left from the moment the wand was dropped.

The Spartans and Athenians were very slow off the line. Indeed, they seemed to merely trot while all four other teams galloped.

As a charioteer, I knew what that meant. It meant that they ex-pected trouble – collisions – and they wanted to be able to make big turns on the first lap, even if it lost time. In outside lanes, you need the help of the gods. I heard men hiss at them, but I felt the tactic was sound.

Especially when the Syracusan chariot refused to give way for the Corinthian. The whole pack of four was thundering into the first turn with two chariots trapped outside the pole. It is hard enough to turn with the pole – it can be harder to turn outside.

By the time all four had made the turn, both outside chariots had lost speed. The Syracusan's horses almost tangled with the Corinthian car, and there was a gasp, but the Corinthian flicked his whip back and struck the Syracusan off-lead, and the horse faltered, lost a pace, and the Syracusan fell back.

The Athenians were already in the inside lane.

The Spartans were comfortably behind them.

So the Syracusans had to fall all the way back to sixth. They were all around the first turn, and they thundered down the back stretch in line – Ceos, Corinth, Aegina, Athens, Sparta and Syracusa well behind, trying to get his horses back into their pace. They held this formation through the second turn, and they were one lap down.

To me, it appeared that the Ceosians and the Corinthians were running too fast. They set a terrible pace, and the Aeginians matched it. But the Athenian charioteer wasn't interested, and kept his horses in hand – fast, but not at the pace. He wasn't going to give a full lap, but he was saving speed.

The Spartan, Polypeithes, looked magnificent, his knees well flexed, his shoulders level, his hands steady, and he stuck to the Athenian. I thought he was wise.

Ahead of them, the Corinthian took aim at the Ionian as they entered the fourth lap. As he came out of the turn, he cracked his whip and let his horses go to their full stride, and they stretched out for him. We could hear him urging them, and they responded.

The Ceosian charioteer raised his hands slightly, and his smaller horses gave another spurt – and held their position. Just before the turn, the Corinthian had to fall back – again.

He thundered around the turn on the outside, his turn beautifully judged. But he lost ground with every stride, and now the Aeginians were in second place.

The Corinthians didn't go for the third place on the inside. They stayed outside, and ran. Down the back stretch, the Corinthians passed two teams, and on the turn into the fifth lap, they tried to close to the pole. The Corinthian was fully committed – he was leaning as far as a man can lean in a car, and his horse could not have had any more speed to offer. Nor will most horses give a magnificent effort more than once in a race – even horses have morale.

The African Corinthian went for all the knuckle bones.

He cut right across the Ceosians, and later it was said he flicked his whip at them. Perhaps. But the smaller Ceosian team baulked, and the Corinthians swept by. The Ceosians lost their pace and their tempo, and swerved – struck the turning post a glancing blow and slowed still further, and the Athenians pulled well out to pass. The team from Aegina was jammed in behind the Ionian team, unable to manoeuvre and forced to slow almost to a stop as the Athenians and then the Spartans and finally the Syracusans thundered by on the outside. By a miracle, no one was injured – no horse fell, no cart broke up. But by the time the Ceosian was moving again, the Ionian and the Aeginian were a full length – half the hippodrome – behind.

This sudden reversal of fortune – not uncommon in the hippodrome – left the Corinthians in the front by a whole chariot length, with the Athenians second and the Spartans third. The Syracusans were a distant fourth, and the Aeginians and Ceosians were well back. But with only five laps run, the race was barely a fifth done.

They ran four laps in that formation, and the Corinthian, now in front where he'd wanted to be, forced a terrible pace. He didn't plan to slow from a gallop, and he ran off the laps so fast that his opponents began to lose heart. The Athenians wanted to run a slower race with a fast finish, but the expert Corinthian charioteer wasn't having it.

Through the tenth lap, the Athenians, Spartans and Syracusans held the pace. But in the back stretch of ten, the Athenians – in second place and on the rail – began to slow from a hard gallop to a slower pace.

The Corinthian shot ahead.

The Spartans stayed with the Athenians, and the Syracusan made two attempts in the next two laps to pass them but could not, and the Ionoians and Aeginians were now too far behind to regain the distance unless a miracle occurred – the Ceosian team, in particular, looked very tired.

On the thirteenth lap, the Corinthian came up behind the other chariots and began passing them. He took the Ceosians after a brief struggle and many glares and some shouted words, and then passed the Aeginian chariot after a whole lap of racing side by side. On the fifteenth lap, he slipped by the Syracusans, suggesting to the crowd – as I already suspected – that the Syracusan charioteer wasn't as good as he needed to be at this level.

Sixteen laps out of twenty-seven, and the Corinthian team was a lap ahead of everyone but the Athenians and the Spartans.

Coming into the turn for lap seventeen, the Athenians moved into the pole, and just as the Corinthian team pulled out to pass on the turn, the Spartans – up until then almost spectators – pulled out as if to pass as well, blocking the Corinthian chariot. The Corinthian pulled out farther and again set his horses to run full out – he angled out to pass the Spartans.

The Spartan driver was thundering up on the turn, but he did not turn. In fact, he edged his horse a little farther outside. His very slight acceleration was either ferociously lucky or perfectly timed – the Corinthian was caught outside him and without room to cut back, and the whole car was briefly up on one wheel.

Then the Spartan abruptly decelerated and turned sharply – an incredible turn, shockingly dangerous. The Spartan car did not quite flip over, and seemed to turn at right angles – and left the Corinthian a whole chariot length outside the rail and at a virtual stop.

The Syracusans and then the Aeginians and then the Ceosians thundered by inside, and the Corinthian spent two laps getting back up to his speed. And now his horses were not running as well. The Athenians had lost no speed, and the Spartan team was less than half a length behind them, and as the censor marked the twentieth lap, the Athenian charioteer saluted the crowd, bent forward – and gave his horses some secret signal of hand or voice, and they were off.

They ran, not like the wind, but like a gale. They ate the ground between them and the Corinthian, and took him on the mid-lap turn in the twenty-first lap. It was a magnificent performance by the

Athenian charioteer, who showed his mastery – in his acceleration, in his timing, in his voice. He took the Corinthian at the very end of the turn. Then, as his car swerved in to fill the inside lane . . .

He slowed abruptly.

Again the Corinthian had to swerve, but again, there was nowhere to go. The Spartan team was already coming up outside. The Corinthian's mouth showed his anger – and he wilfully tried to slam his car into the Spartan horses, but the Athenian was decelerating too hard, and unless the Corinthian was willing to risk a messy death he had to rein in, and he did, cursing so loudly he could be heard in the stands.

Every Athenian was on his feet – many had their hands on their mouths, silent as their charioteer handed the race to the Spartans.

But by my side, Cimon had tears in his eyes, and he thumped my back.

Polypeithes got his team up to the fullest of gallops and blew past the slowing Athenian team just before the turn. He leaned, and for a moment I was afraid he wasn't up to it – but he shaved the post and completed his turn, his cart bouncing slightly as it skidded out behind the horses like an empty stone-hauling sled dragged on smooth marble by eager boys.

The Corinthian wasn't through.

He got around the Athenian on anger and will, and flicked his whip at his horses, and they responded one more time, heads up, willing, it appeared, to burst their hearts. They came down the front stretch of the twenty-second lap, and it seemed possible that they had kept a little in reserve. On the back stretch, the Corinthian made his move, whipping his horses repeatedly – and then striking at the Spartan horses.

Sometimes, men make plans. It was clear to every man in the crowd that the Athenians had agreed to support the Spartans.

But sometimes, the gods take a hand.

At the final post of twenty-second lap, the Ceosian team was stumbling. The horses were exhausted, and the charioteer was having trouble keeping them on the course and at speed. He didn't take the turn – for him, the last turn of lap nineteen – as close as he ought. In fact, he was ten feet off the post, and his chariot was moving at a trot.

And Polypeithes chose to put his team *inside* the Ionian team. He chose to cut from the outside position almost at right angles to the pole – a little like a man threading a needle in the dark.

Once again, he did the complicated manoeuvre he'd executed so well early on – he slowed, and pivoted his chariot on the inside wheel, the horses running through an elaborate double curve.

In the three heartbeats in which he executed the manoeuvre, he had every man in the crowd on his feet.

The Corinthian had to manoeuvre to avoid a wreck – the Ceosians got their heads turned back inward and went up the inside lane no faster than a brisk trot – and the Athenians were past the Corinthians on the inside and then past the Ionians on the outside – a magnificent double overtake – and then the Spartans and the Athenians were running free.

And perhaps the Athenians did not 'give' the race to Sparta, because those Spartan horses were *fast*. They ran, and the unmatched Athenians ran – they ran, and they ran, and the Athenians gained back a whole chariot length, so that when they crossed the final line and the heralds raised their wands, the lead Athenian horse was even with Polypeithes.

But no more.

And the Spartans swept to victory.

Cimon roared by my side, and even Aristides thumped my back. My Athenian friends, who had no doubt negotiated the 'chariot alliance' for King Leonidas.

Perhaps I've told my story badly. But as the Spartan team swept to victory, and the young Spartiate was granted the right to wear the crown of laurel – and to serve in the king's bodyguard all his life – in that moment, the Spartan peace party was defeated, and the alliance between Athens and Sparta – never, as you know, the best of friends – was sealed. It was sealed because Athens sacrificed an Olympic chariot race and because, as usual, a lot of Plataeans were doing the dirty work.

Susa – 483 BCE

Fierce as the dragon scaled in gold
Through the deep files he darts his glowing eye;
And pleased their order to behold,
His gorgeous standard blazing to the sky,
Rolls onward his Assyrian car,
Directs the thunder of the war,
Bids the wing'd arrows' iron storm advance
Against the slow and cumbrous lance.
What shall withstand the torrent of his sway
When dreadful o'er the yielding shores
The impetuous tide of battle roars,
And sweeps the weak opposing mounds away?
So Persia, with resistless might,
Rolls her unnumber'd hosts of heroes to the fight.

Aeschylus, The Persians 472 BCE

I didn't go straight to Susa. Nor did I mention that when Astylos won the diaulos, our Styges was less than a man's height behind him, placing third, nor that another Plataean was in the final heat. This was the best performance by Plataeans in the games for many years, and only the endless work of keeping Polypeithes alive and his horses uninjured kept us from the wildest party since the fire was brought to men. And, of course, we were out of wine.

The aftermath of any great event is a terrible crash, and the Olympics are no different. Every day, and every night, had been so fine – so much good talk, so many friends, so much camaraderie – heroism, and even beauty – that to break camp and pack and march with the crowds down to the sea seemed like the descent into Hades, and the want of spirit was dark for most men. But I had announced that I would sail for Athens with Cimon, and together we took many friends home. Aristides had business of his own, but we had Themistocles and all the Plataeans. I'm sure Draco came with me as much to make sure I came home as anything else. My beloved brother-in-law crushed me to him and demanded that I come and guest with him and then strode away after giving me the oddest look. He had business in Argos and would ride home. With his party went Empedocles, who gave me a great embrace and promised to visit me in Plataea.

We sailed south, into the same seas that had been so storm-tossed a month before, but now it was early summer, and the seas were packed with ships – Italiote traders, Illyrian tin ships, Corinthian merchantmen and warships, and Athenians – Athenian ships on every hand. We camped on beaches all the way down the coast of the Peloponnese, rowing all the way under the new summer sun and into constantly adverse winds, and my rowers, fat and hung over from a week at the Olympics playing at being gentlemen, discovered a new talent for grumbling.

But we weathered the Hand, the local name for the promontory, and turned east into the Laconian gulf and the wind changed, and our voyage took on a little bit of a holiday air. We camped on Kythera, enjoyed a feast of greasy mutton, drank the execrable local wine, and probably left a population increase. From Kythera we sailed across the blue water, our oars dry, all the way into Hermione, and spent the night under the pine trees by the temple, listening to a pair of musicians who were training there – beautiful stuff. A pair of oarsmen – Nicolas and Giorgios, who'd been with me since Iberia – left the ship to make a pilgrimage to Epidavros, and I wished them well and directed them to rejoin at Athens if they so desired, and we went due east for Athens, give or take a point, and had sweet weather, making the long blue water crossing in a day and a night so that we raised Piraeus with the rising of the sun.

So I had a week sailing home and another four days crossing the mountains to listen to Draco and Styges and all the other Plataeans tell me about how I should handle my family.

The long and short of it is that my cousin Simonalkes – you may recall him, as he murdered my father and sold me into slavery – took our family farm. When I returned in the year after the sack of Sardis, he hanged himself rather than face justice – or my spear. In Marathon year, his eldest son teamed with my Athenian enemies – actually, not my enemies but those of Miltiades – and came and sacked our farm and killed my mother. Simon, son of Simonalkes, died with Teucer's arrow in his eye, and we reaped his mercenaries like ripe barley, and I thought that was the end of them, but Simonalkes had other sons – three more, in fact, and Simonides, his second son, had come with Achilles, his third, and Ajax, his fourth, and occupied our farm. They came with force and money, and the archon, Myron, denied them citizenship at first, but they paid fines and went to the shrines and were, for the most part, forgiven.

I was, after all, dead, as far as anyone knew.

Styges, born a Cretan, wanted me to go back, collect some of my men and his master Idomeneaus, and go and wipe them out like a nest of hornets in a vineyard.

Draco wasn't so sure. I think we were in Attica, near my father-in-law's estate east of Oinoe, and camping in a sheepfold – the ship was left under Megakles and Leukas and Sekla in Piraeus, with orders to take a cargo no farther than Corinth and run it, and return to Piraeus. I'd wasted a day filling out paperwork for a number of men – such as Sekla, and Megakles – to hold Metic status in Athens, and I had Alexandros and a dozen oarsmen with me crossing the mountains – and Brasidas and Sittonax, who was as delighted to chase Greek girls as he was to chase Gaulish maidens. Giannis went off with Cimon – with the best will in the world I couldn't employ every young man. He was eager for adventure, and Cimon was pointing his bow for Thrace.

Draco sat on a folding stool and shook his head. 'You have become a lord,' he said. He smiled, but his tone was sad. 'Armed men at your tail, and ships, and cargoes. Like a little Miltiades. And all the great men know you – Cimon and Aristides and Themistocles and even the King of Sparta.' He drank some good Attic wine and frowned. 'I'm not sure I should have told you to come home. What can little Plataea offer you?'

In truth, I was thinking of Apollonasia, if that was her true name, whom I'd bedded against the very stone on which I was perched and who had, as far as I can remember, turned into a raven and flown away. My thoughts were not on Plataean politics, but I tore myself from her imaginary arms to listen to the old man speak, and when he asked what Plataea could offer me, I said, 'A home?' or something similar.

I wasn't so surprised, either. Listening to some of the younger men who had competed – Antimenides, son of Alcaeus of Miletus, for example, who had placed in the final heat in the diaulos and whose javelin throw had soared like a falcon – or Teucer's son Teucer, whose boxing was very good indeed – listening to them told me that my cousins were neither universally hated nor really very bad men. And listening to all the Plataeans reminded me – prompting a smile – that I had lived out in the wide world for a very long time. Plataeans can be ignorant hicks with the best of them, and Teucer's views on men loving other men would have made him a laughing stock among his father's friends – young Teucer flinched every time he saw men embrace. Sekla rolled his eyes.

But the next day, after we passed around the flank of Kitharon and rode down through the narrow streets of Eleutheras, none of that mattered, because I was home. Home is where all the fields look right and the grass has *that* smell and girls ...

For an old man of thirty-five, my mind ran to women a great deal. And to farms.

Boeotia is beautiful. It is a different beauty to that of Attica or Italy or Sicily.

We rode over the last arm of Kitharon. I did not stop to make sacrifice at the peak. Perhaps I should have, but I did not want to see black offerings there from my cousins. I had begun to flirt with the idea of reconciliation.

Does that give you pause? But consider. I have been a warrior all my life, and I have killed many men, but then, returning from Sicily – and Alba – I was tired of blood. I had killed Simonalkes and I had killed Simon – killed them, or caused them to die. One for Pater and one for Mater. Little Plataea – a town of five thousand citizens when it is at its very strongest – is not big enough for a blood feud. To my mind, I had two choices.

I could collect Idomeneaus at the shrine, walk down the road, and kill them to a man – men and children and possibly their women, too. That would end it. Leave none alive to grow to manhood and come back to wreak revenge. Nor did I doubt that I could do it – in my head, or with my arm.

That is who I am, child.

But if you have been listening, you know that for years I had been trying – really, since I went to speak to the god at Delos – trying to reduce the blood on my hands.

We came over the little ridge, then, and past the little mud-hole in the road where I had trapped the bandits. And we could see the low beehive tomb where old Leitos lay enshrined, and Styges ran ahead to warn his former master – and sometime lover – Idomeneaus, who had once been a kohl-eyed catamite and was now one of the deadliest men in Greece. Or the world. And who young Teucer thought a great man ...

I roll my eyes, too.

Draco waved goodbye and headed down the road, but all the young men stayed at the shrine with me for the night, and before the afternoon was many hours older, we had other men I knew coming up the ridge from the town – Ajax, who had fought *against* us in Asia, but was now a friend, and Bellerophon, who had been with us at Marathon, and Lysius, a veteran who had stayed and watched the town walls while we went to glory at Marathon. Idomeneaus hugged me until my ribs were threatened, and then demanded my whole story.

Before I got done saying that I had thrown myself into the sea, he raised his hand.

'We never thought you were dead,' he said. 'A man came – oh, two years ago – and asked a great many questions about you. I didn't kill him. He said his master knew you.'

I shrugged. 'Did this master have a name?' I asked.

Idomeneaus's mad eyes glittered. 'Who could forget a name like Anarchos?' he said, and I knew. I had shot my mouth off, and Anarchos sent a slave to check up on me – and all that information went straight to the tyrant of Syracusa.

Before I could begin again, a horse – an actual horse – trotted up, its hooves crisp against the stones of the road by the tomb. I felt as if I'd seen a ghost – it was Gelon.

'You – here?' I asked.

He laughed. 'Well – you made me a citizen,' he said. Gelon had been a mercenary – one of my cousin's men. I'd enslaved him, but freed him for Marathon. He was Sicilian. He laughed to find that I'd been a slave and a mercenary for years – in Sicily.

'I'm a farmer,' Gelon said. 'I married Hilarion's daughter.' He shrugged.

So I told my story – again. It was getting more polished with each telling, but I still couldn't hide that I'd mistreated Lydia, and men shifted or looked away. Heroes are supposed to be better than that. I left a few things out, but I told the whole of my recent meetings with Briseis and the Medes. Many of the men around the fire had lived through all my early days, and they deserved to know.

It grew quite late – we digressed a great deal. In the end, it was not Idomeneaus, but Gelon, who put the question.

'What will you do about your cousins?' he asked.

I shrugged. 'What do you think I should do?' I asked.

Idomeneaus spat. 'Kill them all. Right now, before dawn. Every man here will carry a sword.' He grinned his mad grin, and his teeth shone in the firelight. 'Listen, lord, we never stopped having the training just because you were … gone. We still have hunts on the mountainside. We've poured wine on the tomb for you – and every man here is one of ours. The Epilektoi.'

'You have not changed,' I said to him, and I smiled in case the mad bastard took it as an insult.

He wagged his head. 'Is there any other answer?'

I looked at Gelon. He looked away. 'You could try talking to them,' he said.

Idomeneaus spat in contempt.

'Would they talk?' I asked.

'They are not bad men, and they have brought money and work,' Gelon said, and Lysius nodded.

'They are not like Simon,' he said simply. 'They work hard.'

'By now they know you are alive, and here,' Idomeneaus said. 'Strike now, before it is too late. Plataea has politics, now. Myron is not what he was. Strike, and remind all these peasants what you are – who you are. Above the law. A lord.'

Bellerophon winced. 'Lord, I'll stand by you,' he said. 'But ...' He met Idomeneaus's eye. And held it. 'Glare all you like, priest.'

They all looked at me – even Hector.

I remember how clearly I saw what I would do. 'Tomorrow, I will go and visit my brother-in-law over by Thespiae. All of you go home.' I smiled at Idomeneaus. 'It's good to see you, you mad bastard, but I won't stage a bloodbath just to assuage your boredom. Go to sea with me if you need blood – we have buckets of it. I intend to try conversation. If that fails ...' I nodded. 'Then I'll kill them all. Not before.'

Almost everyone nodded. Idomeneaus simply got up, collected his spear, and walked off into the darkness. But I saw on his face that I had disappointed him. He paused. 'The sea is making you soft,' he said. 'These men have insulted you, and you must exterminate them, or be held weak.'

I remember that I shrugged. 'Only a fool thinks me weak,' I said. It was not a brag. It was true.

No one rose with the dawn. We'd sat up too late and there were hard heads. I looked around the clearing – now with a fine house and a small tilled field behind the tomb – and thought of Calchas and his cabin and his black broth. The exercises he made me do. I went to the smaller clearing among the great oaks where he used to drill me on my spear fighting, and I stood in the early morning sun and lifted weights and then practised the sword-draw I'd seen the Spartans do. I knew it, but the idea of practising it until the draw, the cut and the return to the scabbard were second nature – that was a very Spartan idea, and yet I liked it.

When everyone was up, we rode west, across the Asopus, skirting the town. I saw our farm. It was odd to see it without the tower I'd built, and with a new stone house stuccoed white in the sun. It was quite a pretty house, and already had a grape arbour.

My cousins had done well, and they'd been there a few years.

We took the road north and west, over the low hills, seventy easy stades to Thespiae, and we arrived at my brother-in-law's house in the late afternoon to find my sister Penelope waiting in the yard.

She had her hands on her hips, and she started telling me what she thought of my five-year absence as soon as we were inside her gate. And then she burst into tears and threw her arms around me, and I confess I joined her in tears.

'Don't you ever!' she cried, and other things that, when related, sound foolish, but at the time are very painful to hear.

My oarsmen and Brasidas had the good grace to vanish. Antigonus, who had met the Spartan at the Olympics, had beaten us home by a day by the land route, and he led my gentlemen into his elegant courtyard while admiring our horses and shouting for wine – really a superior display of aristocratic social skills, especially as he ruthlessly failed to save me from my sister's righteous anger.

Pen went on for a bit, describing what she thought of a man who tried to kill himself – she suggested that slavery at a Phoenician oar was *better* than what I deserved. I hung my head in shame.

Then she embraced me again, calling my name and praising the gods.

'And you don't even *ask* about your daughter,' she spat.

'Daughter?' I asked – rather automatically. I thought of Apollonasia again – a slave girl.

'My niece,' Penelope shot at me. Then she put a hand to her mouth.

It must have been on my face.

And then – well, then it all came out.

Euphonia died in childbirth. That I knew. But what I didn't know – in my post-battle blackness, in the soul-crushing horror that afflicted me when my wife died before I could reach her – what I didn't know was that she'd borne me a healthy daughter – as it turned out, perfectly healthy, even though she'd had the cord wrapped around her throat and almost died with my poor wife.

And they called the little thing Euphonia. We often do, in Boeotia, when a child takes its mother's place – that's a nice way of putting it, anyway.

Suddenly, my hands were shaking.

I had a child?

I do not remember walking into Penelope's house and into the women's quarters – only standing by a handsome pine table with a beautiful young girl bowing to me, and Penelope saying, 'This is your father, child.'

My little blond daughter smiled like an imp, hugged my outstretched hands and let herself be embraced without reserve.

'Oh!' she said. 'I've always wanted a father!'

Well.

Call me a fool if you like, but to my mind Euphonia – and her unreserved love, instantly given – was the gift of the gods to me for sparing my cousins. That's how I saw it then, and time has not changed my mind. Had I exterminated them in a night of blood, I promise you I would have found her cold and indifferent.

Believe what you will!

I'm not sure I had been so happy in all my life as I was that day, and I carried my daughter up and down stairs and hugged her and talked to her. She laughed and talked – and talked and talked – and I learned that she had two dolls, that she could read and write, that she was going to memorise all of the Iliad and the Odyssey and that she hoped to make a pot herself on the potter's wheel in Thespiae and ...

And suddenly she looked at me. 'May I go to Brauron, Pater?' she asked me.

No one had ever called me 'Pater'.

I swallowed.

My sister stepped in. 'Your father has a dozen friends to manage,' she said. 'Back to the exedra with you, my dear.'

'No – Pen – let her stay.' I grinned at her. Brauron is the great temple of Artemis near Athens. Young girls – maidens from age six to age twelve – go there to learn the sacred dances – and they shoot bows and ride horses and probably giggle like fools. My sister had not been rich enough nor had she the connections. Andronicus's sister Leda had, and she had been a 'little bear', as the girls were called – not once but three times. It was all very aristocratic and required an enormous donation of fabric and silver.

And friends in Athens. Phrynicus, the playwright – his relatives were priests at Brauron. I leaned back in my seat – women have much more comfortable quarters than men. 'Yes,' I said.

My daughter grinned her impish grin. 'Really?' she shrieked.

Pen glared at me. 'If you plan to spoil her, do it when I'm not here to see it!' she said, but Leda put an arm around her waist and nodded to me.

'It's a fine choice. She's a beautiful girl and well born. Her grandfather – Euphonia's father – can host her in Attica, and she'll have Athenian friends.'

So the next day, I hoisted her on my lap on one of Andronicus's better horses, and took Brasidas and Alexandros and Lysias and Ajax on other borrowed horses – and my brother-in-law himself. We wore fine cloaks and fine chitons and gold jewellery – well, Brasidas didn't, but the rest of us did, even Bellerophon – and we rode slowly so as not to raise dust. We crossed the Asopus and ate a pleasant meal in the shade of the sanctuary trees at the temple of Hera. We drew a great deal of comment from my fellow Plataeans, and I met briefly with a very anxious Myron, who was delighted with what I told him. I had a scroll and he signed it.

Then we rode over the hill – to my father's farm. I sent Hector – unarmed – to announce us.

He cantered back before we came to the fork. 'Your cousin Simon is waiting for you,' he said.

My daughter was delightful, chattering all the way and apparently unconcerned that my cousin might greet us with a shower of arrows. I was far more nervous. Twice, she leapt from my horse's back to investigate things – once, a kitten in the road which needed a scratch, and again, to pick flowers.

The old gate had been completely rebuilt. I rang the small bronze bell – my own work.

A slave opened the gate.

I didn't know Simon's sons at all – I'd seen them a few times in public, but never long enough to leave a mark in my head – despite which, I had to guess that the three big men in the stone-flagged yard were my cousins. I dismounted – there's nothing more aggressive than a man on horseback. My friends all emulated me, dismounting by the water trough where Draco and Diokles and Hilarion and old Epictetus used to sit and drink wine.

My cousins stood in a brooding silence, offering nothing.

I'd rehearsed a few lines, but none of them came to me. But when I reached to hoist my daughter down, I acted. I held her briefly in the air. 'This is my daughter Euphonia,' I said. 'I brought her to show I mean peace.'

Simonides – the man in the middle, and clearly the oldest – raised his chin. 'Then you are welcome, cousin.'

I stepped forward with my daughter in my left arm. 'You have done well with the farm,' I said.

'We found nothing but a ruin,' he said.

Achilles, the second brother, glowered. 'All our work,' he said.

Ajax, the youngest, shrugged. He was a very handsome young man. 'They all said you were dead.' He smiled – alone of his brothers. 'Well, all except the mad fuck on the mountain.' He wore a sword, and his right hand was very near the hilt.

I put my daughter down.

'You brought a great many men,' Simonides said. 'I gather we are dispossessed?'

Achilles looked around, as if counting the numbers. His older brother hissed something at him, and he fell back a step.

They were ready to fight.

'I'm here in peace, and I'm not here to seize the farm,' I said, and suddenly I was weary of the whole thing. 'My mother is buried here, and I will always love this place.' I raised an eyebrow. 'May I be honest, cousins? I could order you off, and I think the town would agree. I could buy it from you – this, and ten farms like it.'

'Not for sale,' bellowed Ajax.

'Will you shut up?' Simonides said. 'That's not what he's about at all.'

I looked them over. Achilles looked dangerous – dangerously stupid. Ajax looked handsome and a little shifty, but then, I was not predisposed to love any of them. Simonides was the spitting image of my pater as a young man.

And we are all Corvaxae – the black-haired men. Sometimes, blood is a little thicker than hate.

'I can buy another farm,' I said. 'But I do not really want a farm. I'm a soldier. And a shipowner.'

'What are you saying?' Achilles snapped. 'Say it and get out.'

Andronicus – remember, he was quite an important local man – stepped forward. 'Simonides, you have made a good impression in Plataea since you arrived,' he said. 'But your cousin here led us to Marathon, and his word will carry any council. Courtesy here would be your best path.'

Simonides took his brother by the arm and hissed, 'Shut up.'

'I agree that – as you are alive – it is your farm.' Simonides crossed his arms over his chest. 'But I want to hear you agree that we've done all the work.'

'I'll do better,' I said. I took out a small scroll. 'There. It is yours in law.'

I wondered whether my pater would send the Furies to pursue me. But really – I had enough enemies, and I didn't need a farm.

Then – and only then – did Simonides remember his manners and send a slave for wine.

The rest of that day was spent in Plataea. I met and embraced a hundred men – starting, of course, with my first true friend – Hermogenes. With Tiraeus, he had purchased the land across from Heron the Ironsmith and started a small bronze smithery. They had done well enough, but they made only small items – strap ends, small bells, buckles, eating knives – because they were poor and the land purchase took all their money.

The smithery was too small and too ill built. Because of that, they didn't get work that they should have – men like Draco took their work to Thebes or Thespiae. And Styges worked too far away – he admitted it himself – making war gear in a low shed by the Asopus, almost to Eleuthra. I told him I wanted him in the shop.

So after I exchanged signs and told them that I had been raised to master in Sicily, I went next door and offered four hundred drachma in gold darics to the widow of a wine merchant to sell me her house. And then I did the same on the other side.

It is great fun to be able to play the great lord. I spent money like water for a few days, and while my daughter played in the smithy, I hired workmen and was very bossy indeed. I ordered the badly built smith-shed torn down, and I ordered a stone building put up in its place, filling both lots. I had the wine merchant's house built into one end, and the other house torn down – it was abandoned – and rebuilt. I ordered equipment – anvils, bellows – sent for a carpenter for benches and toolboxes – and when I was done each day, I rode back to stay with Antigonus. I endured Brasidas's cold looks – he felt it was all helot work – and Andronicus took me aside to say that I should buy farms. Like an aristocrat.

But I was having a fine time.

Myron asked me – one of those days – if I was home to stay.

I shook my head. 'No,' I said. 'But I want a home here. My pater had a foot in the smithy and a foot on the farm. I'm not interested in farming. But I'll have a foot in the smithy and another on a ship.' I shrugged. 'I'd appreciate your help in finding a house.'

Myron nodded. 'You are still the polemarch,' he said. 'It would be good to have you here. There are new ... men in this city. And every time Athens sneezes, we catch cold. We live in ... difficult times.'

'What new men?' I asked, and Myron looked away.

'We lost men at Marathon and before,' he said. 'Some of the slaves Athens sent us are good men, and some are not. And many Thebans have purchased land. Some of them are good men, and some are ... Thebans.'

I brought Styges to the building site. He and Hermogenes were not always the best of friends – not all of one's favourite people can be made to love one another – but I reconciled them to the notion that it was my money going into the smithy. The tool shed was the size of a barn, and copied those I'd seen in Sicily and in Corinth – chimneys, hearths and bellows on the ground floor, lots of light, and space for ten men to work. In the second week, the new bellows came over the mountain from Athens – when you pay silver, you can get things in a miraculous hurry – and the new benches went in along the wall with a row of shuttered windows so that the whole shop smelled of fresh-sawn pine and oak. I had all the shutters painted bright red, and the doors, and I put the raven of the Corvaxae over the door in jet-black ironwork.

Heron was delighted. 'A place that big will draw business from Thespiae and Thebes,' he crowed. And he began to expand his own shop. Ironsmiths and bronzesmiths are not in competition for anything but eating knives, so it was fine that we were co-located.

Old Tiraeus laughed and watched the sheds being built. 'This is the second time you've saved me,' he said. 'I can work the bronze, but I can't make money.'

The truth was, Hermogenes was the same. A fine worker, and a gifted hand with the hammer – but not a man who could imagine what would sell, nor who could keep the bins stocked with ingots of bronze, or direct a dozen apprentices in pouring the sheet or pounding it out long before it was needed.

Styges was, though. On the battlefield and in the shop, he was a thinker. And so, while the new shutters went into the windows and the stucco dried on the outside and the two Athenian carpenters put their great pedal-powered bellows into the forge-fire hearths, I took my 'associates' out to dinner without Brasidas and his aristocratic notions. We sat and drank Plataean wine and ate oil on our bread and generally acted like the Boeotian bumpkins we really were.

I put Styges in charge of the shop, despite him being the youngest. Both older men frowned. But in the end, it was my money, and they agreed with no good grace despite the wine and the anchovies.

Men are men. You cannot tell a master smith that he should work for a younger man – even when Tiraeus himself admitted he lacked the skills to make and keep the silver.

At the end of the second week, the houses were done – rebuilt. One for Hermogenes and his wife, and one for Tiraeus and Styges, until one or both found a mate. I purchased them four slaves, and we all spent a day in the shop, playing with the bellows.

At the end of the second week, I sent for Empedocles, and that evening, riding home to Thespiae, I met a silversmith on the road. He was just come from a pilgrimage to Delphi. I didn't know him, but he proved to be a cousin of Diokles and quite a young man.

The next morning, he showed up at the stone smithery, and by the end of the day, he had his tools laid out on a bench and was quickly using up his store of silver making trinkets for the pilgrims who came to the temple of Hera – mostly women, and prone to buy jewellery. But his presence made Styges excited, because now he had someone to work silver, he could make fancier armour.

Myron's friend Timaeas offered me any of five lots for my own house, and I bought the house across from Myron's. I spent the money from my tin on that house – new everything, from slaves to statues to household gods. It had two things few houses in Plataea had ever seen – an in-town stable for four horses, and a water trough with flowing water. The house was big and spacious – too big for one man and his small daughter, no matter how rich. But I had the walls painted by professionals, and I spent money – more money – on horses, on silver plates, on good pottery and grain storage and then on grain.

It was like playing house, with real money.

I tell all this, as if all I did was concern myself with buildings, but in the main, what I did was play with my daughter and get to know her, and write letters to Jocasta and to Cimon and to Phrynicus asking for help putting her into the summer dances at Brauron, and before the late flowers were past budding and the first barley crop was in, I had a letter from Jocasta, wife of Aristides, informing me that my daughter had a place in the New Moon as a Little Bear, and that her husband was to be put on trial.

He is too proud to ask your help – but I well remember what you did for

Miltiades. *Themistocles will stop at nothing to see my husband in exile, and I cannot bear it. Arimnestos, bring your daughter to the temple and come and see what can be done for Aristides, and I will be forever in your debt.*

Jocasta

Unlike Gorgo, and the other Spartan women, who lived very much in public, it was almost unheard of for an Athenian woman to write a letter to a man – but Jocasta had a good head on her shoulders, and she had seized the excuse of my writing about my daughter (women's business) to make her plea.

I knew that things must be desperate indeed.

Cimon's answer came the very next day, and the tone of desperation was the same.

Of course we can arrange for your daughter to be placed at Brauron. But if you were to see fit to accompany her, you might find yourself requested to perform a miracle, as Aristides is threatened with ostracism.

I felt very wise, what with having made peace with Simon's sons and having brought some of my prosperity home to Plataea. Three weeks after my arrival, I had every mason in the town at work; the roofer was working from dawn to dusk, there were whole convoys of donkeys bringing goods from Athens, Corinth and even hated Thebes, and the new smithy rang with the music of the hammer on the anvil. My oarsmen – as well as Brasidas and Alexandros – had been formally invested as citizens at my behest. I helped Brasidas purchase a farm and the slaves to run it – never was there a less interested farmer.

I thought that it was foolish of Themistocles to continue the quarrel with Aristides – just when we needed both men for the war with Persia. I was in a fine mood, and I prepared my daughter to travel over the mountain to Attica while preparing in my mind the speeches of reconciliation I planned for Athens.

On the summer feast of Herakles, old Empedocles came and blessed the new building and the whole forge, even including the silversmith in his prayers, and he kindled all our forge fires. He had a Theban journeyman with him, and the young man beamed at everything he saw and helped the old man with the rites.

Then I made a cup. It had been two years since I had worked, and yet the power of the god flowed through me and I made a fine cup – with a flat bottom and sloped sides, and silver rivets on the handle, and the image of a priest blessing an anvil. And Empedocles laughed and then cried and complained that he was an old man, and we all drank a great deal. But I made a second cup and gave it to my daughter, and she shook her head.

'My uncle Andronicus can't make anything like this,' she said.

'He's an aristocrat,' I said.

And the next day, while my new slaves we repacking my new donkeys in my new yard of my new house, yet another messenger came, from the Agiad King of Sparta.

The truth? I rather looked forward to taking the heralds to Susa.

You must know I'd never been. But I had been to Sardis and I knew enough Persian to get good service and good food. I knew enough Persian aristocrats to expect to have friends at the Great King's court.

So I delayed my trip to Athens by a day so that I could say a proper goodbye – to Hermogenes and Styges and Tiraeus, to Myron and Draco – but most of all, to my sister and her husband. I arranged for my daughter to be retrieved after her time at the temple of Artemis. I promised to return.

'How long?' Pen asked. 'You only just came home!'

I nodded and looked out of the window. 'Look for me in the spring,' I said.

'A year!' my sister wailed.

My daughter clung to me.

I shrugged and my brother-in-law, who clearly felt I'd endured enough, said, 'My dears, he's been commanded by the King of Sparta!'

'I don't particularly care if he's been commanded by Hera or Zeus!' my sister said, but she relented, asked forgiveness for her blasphemy, and sent me on the road with her blessings.

I suppose I should have worried that Idomeneaus did not come out to wish me well. I prayed at the shrine and Bellerophon told me that the mad Cretan was hunting.

My six-year-old daughter was going to the temple of Artemis, and I was going a hundred times farther, to the court of the Great King. But she had six mules behind her, all heavily laden, and I had one.

And we stopped at the high altar on Kitharon, and I saw that someone had been making black offerings. I could guess which of my cousins was not yet done with our feud. But in my new-found wisdom, I was immune to such petty concerns. I brushed the bits of black wool aside and left my daughter to start a fire on the ash altar with her new hero, Brasidas – who would not worship a Spartan, at age six? Alexandros and I ran the mountaintop trails until we killed a deer. We didn't see Idomeneaus. We brought the deer's corpse back and opened it and burned the fat and the thigh bones on my daughter's fire. She had never sacrificed there, and it was a great adventure for her, and afterwards we all ate fresh venison.

She threw up.

Parenthood.

But in the morning, we went down the mountain into Attica, and the world was waiting for us.

I took Euphonia to see her grandfather. She was very excited to get to Brauron and she rued every day lost, sure that everyone else would be friends and she'd miss everything fun. But her grandfather – her mother's father – was a fine gentleman, still delighted with me. I was never asked where I had been for the last six years, and I won his heart by telling him that I'd stood next to the King of Sparta during the sacrifices at the Olympic games. And he loved his granddaughter. She was showered with presents – quite wide eyed, and yet perfectly willing to have more.

We stayed two days, and he agreed to fetch her from Brauron and keep her until Leda or Penelope came for her. My second night there I drank too much and cried for my daughter's mother, whom I truly loved. Her father was solicitous, and a little afraid of my grief.

But grief is only that. And it is better than emptiness or anger.

Ah, my daughter! You yourself learned the sacred dances in the groves and hills of Brauron, but some of your guests may not know the place.

Brauron is just a few stades south of Marathon on the same coast. And how that coast brought back memories for me. We met with Phrynicus and his wife – mounted on mules – just west of the city and we kept going, as a 'stop' in Athens could have embroiled us in politics very quickly. I had enemies in the city, among the Alcmaeonidae. The richest family in the world. But it was a great pleasure to revisit the days of our heroism together – how men love to talk about a shared adventure, my daughter! We lied and we lied – much as I'm doing with you now.

Hah, the looks on your faces.

At any rate, we crossed the mountains and rode across the great plain of Attica, and stayed the night in a fine house – that of a friend of both my father-in-law and of Cimon, and no friend of Phrynicus. A countryside aristocrat who swore that he had never in his life been to Athens. He was of the cavalry class, and he felt that the city was rotten with corruption. He all but fawned on Brasidas, asking his opinion on everything from spear fighting to the education of his son. And the man – Peisander – had a girl just seven years old going off to Brauron, as arranged by Cimon, and so we all rode off together the next day – Phrynicus swallowing his political views at every turn in the road, I can promise you.

It is hardly central to my tale, but I'll bore you with it a little, to help you understand how Greeks actually dealt with the coming of the Persians. Peisander had stood in his tribe's front rank at Marathon. He was a proven man – brave, and patriotic.

He fairly worshipped Aristides.

And yet, as we rode down the last ridge and saw the sea, he turned to me and shook his head. 'You are far richer than I – and a friend of the King of Sparta. And yet I understand from your silence that you support this foolishness – this war with the Great King. How can we hope to triumph?'

I smiled – winningly, I hope. 'Much the same way we carried the day at Marathon,' I said. 'Courage, and the love of the gods.'

He nodded. 'That's well said – piety like yours is rarer in these godless days, my friend. But – that was a raid. A punitive expedition. Men say that if the Great King comes, he'll have a million men. On our best day, Athens can raise fifteen thousand hoplites.'

I nodded. 'Sparta can bring twice that, with her allies. Thebes the same again, and Corinth and Argos the same again. With Athens as allies, we'll match anything Persia can get here.' I waved my hands. 'Greece is not Asia. They will have real trouble feeding and watering a giant army.'

He looked back at our daughters, riding side by side. 'Perhaps. Perhaps age makes cowards of us. But listen, my lord. Why not send the earth and water? We submit. Persia sends a satrap. So?' He shrugged. 'No virgins are raped.' He looked me right in the eye. 'No boys die on spear points.' Then he flushed, and looked back at Brasidas, who was close enough to hear him. 'I'm sure I sound like a fearful coward to you, sir.'

Brasidas shrugged. 'No man of Marathon is a coward to me, sir. But – I agree.' Brasidas looked at me and had the good grace to flash a wry smile. 'I do not understand, myself, why we must fight. Mere lip-service may suffice.'

'This from a Spartan!' my new friend said, and slapped his thigh.

Brasidas raised an eyebrow. 'I am a Plataean, now.'

I nodded. 'I can tell – you talk more.'

The priestesses of Brauron were not like other Greek women I knew. They were neither pretty nor ugly – in fact, the dozen I met ran a full gamut of feminine types – but they all had the air of command. Because of my time with the Keltoi, I recognised that they were free. They did not see me as husband, father or lord. But as a peer. Or even less. Interesting.

Sittonax said he found the priestesses to be the most interesting women he'd met in Greece, and one of the senior priestesses invited him to dinner. But not me – which was fine. I saw my daughter's quarters, which were very like a boy's military camp on Crete – in fact, my Spartan's eyebrows shot up and later he said it was like a politer Agoge for girls. And it was.

Euphonia had two advantages – her open disposition, which made friends easily, and Peisander's daughter Hermione, who was well known, from just across the mountain. I felt that I left my little daughter in good hands. But that night, riding back to a small inn kept for parents, I felt as if I'd just left Briseis. I felt as if a little hole had been ripped in my heart. I had only had a daughter for one single month.

If you are expecting me to talk about how I rescued Aristides from ostracism, I'm sorry to say I did not. Phrynicus and Peisander shared only one political issue – they both detested the ostracism. I kept them to that subject all the way back across the plains of Attica, but it was increasingly clear to me that my friend was doomed.

Despite being in favour of the war with Persia, Aristides fought the creation of a large and powerful Athenian fleet tooth and nail, rising every day in the assembly to rally the old families and the aristocrats against Themistocles. Men said he planned to take the tyranny to stop the democrats.

Men like Peisander thought that would be a fine thing.

We stayed another night with the aristocrat, and then Phrynicus and I and his charming wife rode slowly down towards the sea, crossed the ridges until we could see the magnificent acropolis rising in the distance, and then down again into the city.

'Themistocles wants to build walls,' he said.

His wife rolled her eyes.

'He has been a good friend to us!' Phrynicus insisted.

'As long as you write his panegyrics,' she commented. She smiled at me. 'He is caught in the middle. He was friends as a boy with both.'

'You know that when Themistocles was a boy, he was not allowed into the main gymnasium because his mother was foreign,' Phrynicus said. 'So he took to exercising at a small palaestra just outside the old walls by the statue of Herakles. More and more of us went there with him, until it turned out we'd basically taken all the students out of the main gymnasium.' Phrynicus shot me his wry smile. 'I think we gave him a taste of power and he's never looked back.'

'And Aristides was one of the boys who saw him shut out of the aristocratic gymnasium?' I asked.

Phrynicus wrinkled his nose. 'Can you imagine Aristides the Just doing any such thing? But they've always been rivals. Rivals for girls and sometimes boys, rivals for commands. Aristides is a far better soldier. Themistocles is a better orator and, frankly, sees farther ahead. Aristides is more honourable. Themistocles is more capable of making the hard decisions. Aristides is a better negotiator.' He rolled his right hand back and forth as he read off this litany.

'Together, they make one perfect man?' I asked.

Phrynicus's wife snorted.

I went and lived with Paramanos, who was very prosperous and had a fine house in Piraeus, with a dozen slaves and sixteen rooms in two storeys – three wings around a tiled courtyard, very elegant. I didn't recognise it at the time, but my greatest disappointment in Plataea had been that Hermogenes and I were no longer close friends. There was some wall between us – and I blamed silver and fame.

I had no such reserve with Paramanos, and that was all the odder, as we had not started friends and, in fact, we had been closer to allies than philoi. He'd been my slave and then my freedman – helmsman in my ship, and then sub-captain. Now, as a rich Athenian merchant – Miltiades had arranged citizenship for him and his Cyrenian-born daughter – we were peers.

Paramanos had purchased the contract of a beautiful young hetaera – five years. He confessed to me in private that he would

149

probably offer her marriage. She was younger and, like Gorgo and the priestesses at Brauron, very open. She sat in a chair while we dined, made jokes both coarse and clever, and played. She also told Paramanos when he had had too much to drink and laid out for him what he needed to do to help his daughter along towards her wedding.

I liked her. We flirted and debated some philosophy and she fairly doted on me when I said that I had known Heraklitus. She was, for a woman, very well read – she was better educated than some Athenian men.

But I digress.

I had to sail to Sparta to pick up my charges, and time was of the essence because I needed good sailing weather. But – obedient to my orders – none of my ships were available. *Storm Cutter* and *Lydia* were both running small cargoes. Paramanos's *Black Raven* had once been my ship – but it was Paramanos's ship now, and he regularly carried silver to the Ionians and brought back dyed wool – an excellent trade for a fast, well-armed ship.

So I had days to wait, and I politicked for Aristides. I went up to the city from Piraeus and visited the assembly. Oh – I was a citizen of Athens. I can't remember whether I've said, but after Marathon, Athens had made me – and a dozen other Plataeans including my brother-in-law – Athenian citizens. Perhaps the finest thing was that they had the priestess of Athena Nike pray every morning for the 'City of Green Plataea'. I know, because I so swelled with pride when I learned this that I rose the next morning in the dark and walked up to the town. I was the only worshipper in the temple – nothing so fine as what is now planned. Afterwards, an acolyte came and took my donation.

'Are you by any chance a Plataean?' he asked, and I grinned and admitted I was. He was delighted.

As I left the little temple, I noted that I was being followed. I did nothing about it – I went down the other side of the acropolis, past the festival site, and walked into the area where the rich had their homes – like a little parkland in the city. My two followers moved from wall corner to wall corner. If they had simply strolled, they'd have been much harder to spot.

I was alone – rare for me, but I hadn't wanted Brasidas or Alexandros or any of the others at my shoulder in temple. So I moved as if unaware of my tail, and went to Aristides' house.

We embraced, but we'd just been together for two weeks, and Jocasta gave my hand a squeeze – like a massive embrace from that very proper aristocratic lady. I heard it all over again, but Aristides was resigned and clearly was working to bring Jocasta to this point of view. I had never seen open discord between them, but Jocasta was sufficiently moved to disagree – flatly – with her husband in front of a third party. Aristides looked hurt.

I pretended not to be there.

Eventually, Jocasta walked away to see to a servant's injury. Aristides waited until we could hear her bare feet on the marble of the foyer, and then he leaned close.

'I have to say this, my friend. Themistocles and I are not friends – but I have accepted this exile. I will go with you to the Great King. Athens cannot be seen to send an ambassador. But a man in exile – a conservative?' He nodded.

And I understood.

It had always seemed odd to me that, whatever their differences, these two leaders of the resistance party were at loggerheads. I had smelled the rat, but I hadn't come to the correct conclusion.

'You should tell Jocasta,' I said. 'She keeps all your other secrets.'

I said it deadpan, and he, being Aristides the prig, didn't find it funny. But I did.

Eventually, I left, being unwilling to invite myself to dinner. I'd had three cups of wine and I wore no weapon, and so I picked up one of Aristides' sticks by the door and flourished it at him. 'I need to borrow one,' I said.

'He never leaves home with them,' Jocasta said. 'But every time he visits our farms outside the walls, he walks home with a new one.'

'I like them!' Aristides said ruefully.

You might think that, as one of the richest men in the world, Aristides could be allowed to own as many walking staffs as he liked – but if you think that, you've never been married.

They were waiting in the near-dark, just north of Aristides' house, and they had knives.

I slipped through Aristides' house as silently as a thief and left by the back gate, which Jocasta held for me while looking as if she doubted my sanity.

I poured a little oil on the fire by saying, 'Your husband has something to tell you,' and once out through the back gate I walked through the alley – used only by slaves and tradesmen – with twelve-foot stone walls towering over me on either side. It was almost dark.

I lay down at the corner and looked around it at ground level. That's how I know there were four of them, all well armed. I assumed they were sent by bloody Cleitus, of the Alcmaeonidae. I didn't feel like fighting three younger men, and besides, I didn't need to fight them.

I slipped across the alley and vanished into the sacred precinct of the unfinished temple of Olympian Zeus. The Pisistradae had started it and left the drums for the columns lying around like children's toys. Young couples came to ... well, to use the columns. I was treated to more than my share of erotic breathing as I crossed the space, and emerged on the east slope of the acropolis, which I skirted. Twice I doubled back in the dense street grid, and I sat in one of the fountain houses, watching my back trail. Things you learn as a slave stay with you for life.

That night I ate with Paramanos and my people – and with Giorgios and Nicolas, returned from their pilgrimage. Next day I attended the Athenian assembly and voted against ostracism for Aristides.

We lost. Aristides was exiled for ten years.

His exile did not include forfeiture of any property – his wife could continue to live on the east slope of the acropolis and his managers could continue to run his farms. By Athenian standards, it was lenient, if you left out the crushing unfairness of it. The problem was that men like Aristides had had the habit of making themselves tyrants for more than a hundred years. Aristides had it all – money, good looks, a war record, and oratory skills. I suspect that, even if he had not been chosen as the secret ambassador, he would have had to go. Perhaps the secret mission to the Great King was a sop.

Frankly, Athenian politics always appals me. They punish the best men and raise fools.

Mind you, in the same assembly, I voted *in favour* of spending the year's excess from the silver mines on building new triremes – the second or third year they'd done that. I must have been one of the few men in that assembly to vote that way – against ostracism, in favour of the fleet. Most Athenians saw these as conflicting interests, because they were too close to the problems.

Well.

Late that afternoon, *Lydia* swept into Piraeus with a hull full of hides and Ionian wine, and the next morning I had her laded with white Athenian leather, fine bronze wares and pottery. I arranged a farewell dinner with Phrynicus, and sailed away west, for Sparta.

I don't remember anything about the sea voyage. I suspect it was fraught with the usual perils and probably had as many irritated rowers and magnificent dolphins as every other trip across the Aegean, but what I remember is Sparta itself.

I suspect that most people do not imagine Sparta as beautiful; Athens is beautiful – she has the acropolis and two hundred years of magnificent architecture. Plataea is beautiful because of Kitharon and because of the green fields that stretch away, the visible signs of Demeter's blessing to man and Hera's blessing to Green Plataea.

Sparta is also beautiful. Did she not give birth to Helen? And are not the women of Lacedaemon all Helen's daughters? High up the vale, with mountains rising on either hand, the carpet of olive trees rolling across the valley – Sparta has a unique wonder.

But I cannot abide the helots. Or rather, the Spartans themselves. On every hand in Sparta, one sees them – and they are somehow more wretched than slaves in Athens or Plataea. Perhaps that is merely my own prejudice, but few helots are ever freed, and the enslavement is racial, not by chance or war-capture. Many have been slaves for so many generations that they think their state is natural – as do their masters. I admire Sparta for many things – but the enslavement of the helots casts a shadow, and that shadow, to me, is at the core of who they are.

I left Brasidas on the ship with Sekla. Spartans are less forgiving than other Greeks in matters of skin colour. I took only Alexandros and Hector, and we purchased horses by the beach at Gytheio where *Lydia* was selling her wares. When we came in stern first, there were a pair of Carthaginian triremes on the beach to trade, and two more over by the Migonion. But they wanted nothing more from us than to buy our goods, and there was not a sign of Dagon. I rode north to Sparta with no greater concern than to pick up my passengers and make haste before the autumn storms hit.

We entered the city on the main road, as well paved as the Panathenaic way, and rode past the temple of the Dioscuri, which was every bit as elegant as anything in Athens – the local stone lent itself to the remarkable quality of the Peloponnesian sunshine. It was high summer, and just before midday, when most Spartan citizens rested in the shade, and even slaves seemed to dart from shadow to shadow. The three of us wore straw hats with brims so wide we seemed to be in tents.

The agora was as busy as any in Greece – the goods unloaded on the beach at Gytheio were already on sale in the capital. In the agora, the midday sun was ignored – there were hundreds of men and women moving about, and long awnings. It was here that I saw the main difference between Sparta and Athens. Sparta has magnificent temples but too little shade, and Spartans are too proud to pretend to need a stoa. In fact, I saw mostly helots sitting under the old oak trees that ringed the agora. Citizens stood proudly in the sun, as if daring Helios to do his worst.

I wore a big hat.

We dismounted at the edge of the agora, and it was there that I got my first taste of helot life. An adolescent Spartiate – probably in the last years of the Agoge – demanded water from a helot woman, and when he didn't get it fast enough, he said, 'Obey, bitch,' and struck her.

Instead of screaming for help, she cringed away and fetched him water.

Perhaps it was not a representative incident. Perhaps I misjudge them.

At any rate, we asked directions.

If I expected a palace for the two kings, I was wrong. The kings live well – they have the kind of staff one associates with the richest Athenians. But their homes are private houses, and Leonidas lived in a beautiful house with three wings around a courtyard with its own olive tree and a small fountain. The courtyard had three arcades of columns, one on each side, for shade. A wall and a set of barracks for slaves, and a small warehouse, took up the fourth side of the complex.

We were ushered in by a helot butler, and brought into the court-yard. There we were served a marvellous water, full of bubbles from some god-touched spring. The helots served Hector as freely as they served Alexandros and me.

Alexandros smiled at Hector. 'I think you are in for an easy few days.'

I laughed. 'Am I such a hard master? But perhaps we could send him to the Agoge.'

Another helot came in. 'Masters, the Lady Gorgo wishes you to know that she will join you directly.'

Indeed, the lady herself followed hard on the slave's message. She was dressed simply, in a long yellow chiton pinned in the Dorian manner. She wore a girdle of gold tied with a Herakles knot and wore a diadem in her hair.

'Ah, Helen,' I said. I said it lightly.

Her eyes crossed mine the way a man's do when he is ready to draw a weapon.

'In Sparta, no woman is ever compared to Helen,' she said. She nodded agreeably. 'Pardon me. Your words took me aback, and I should have nothing for you but praise. The king is at exercise and will join us soon, as will some of your other friends here.' She nodded pleasantly enough to Alexandros and to young Hector.

I intervened to make introductions. 'My lady, this is my captain of marines, Alexandros, a gentleman of Plataea, and this is my hypaspist, Hector, son of Anarchos, now also a citizen of Plataea.'

'Ah, Green Plataea. I intend to make a pilgrimage to the temple of Hera in the spring.' Gorgo smiled. 'I love to travel. But I thought that you had another captain of marines?'

I was a little shocked that she should mention him. 'I have several ships,' I said.

By this time, slaves were appearing with nuts, honeyed almonds and wine. Gorgo led us, as if in a procession, through the courtyard to another wing and in under the portico to a tiled alcove not unlike the edge of the Athenian paleastra – stone benches like those athletes use. The benches lined two walls, so that quite a number of people could sit and converse – a very civilised notion.

We sat and munched nuts.

'We must speak of payment,' Gorgo said quickly, as if discussing a distasteful ailment with a physician. 'I realise that a man does not run a ship the length of the Inner Sea for nothing.'

I had already discussed this in Athens with Cimon and Aristides – and Jocasta, who was more interested in the life of the Spartan queen than any story I'd ever told her. We'd agreed that I would charge the Spartans nothing.

This is politics. Generosity matters. In fact, I could ill afford to sail for several months without making a profit, but with some 'help' from rich Athenians, we – the Athenians, in this case – could appear generous and supportive.

'I will carry a cargo each way,' I said airily. I met her eye – so odd to look a woman in the eye every time you spoke. I think that's why

Gorgo reminded me so much of Briseis. 'I do not intend to charge you anything for taking your heralds to Susa.' I nodded. 'Think of it as little Plataea's contribution to the defence of Greece.'

This obviously pleased Gorgo a great deal, and she took my hand and pressed it.

Leonidas returned from exercise, wearing only a chlamys, like an Athenian ephebe. His body was as near perfect as a man's can be – although his lower legs and shins were a mass of ugly bruises.

I took his hand. 'Pankration?' I asked.

The King of Sparta laughed. 'How did you guess? And worse tomorrow.' He raised his eyebrows briefly in an expression of self-knowledge. 'It is harder at my age to pretend to be a hero of twenty-five.' In fact, the Agiad King of Sparta was nearer sixty than fifty.

I nodded ruefully.

'You should come!' Leonidas said. 'Many men here would seek to measure themselves against you.'

I laughed. 'I'm sure they'd beat me black and blue,' I answered.

'Better you than me,' said the king.

Leonidas was introduced to Alexandros and to Hector, who was open mouthed with wonder at being in the presence of the Great King of Sparta. I confess that I was more than a trifle awed myself.

He turned to me and sat on the bench where Gorgo had been sitting. 'You know I sent a delegation to Delphi last year?' he asked. 'I wanted to hear from the oracle what was to come for us if we resisted. And do you know what she answered?'

'No,' I said.

'Good, because if you did, I'd have quite a breach in my security arrangements.' The king smiled ruefully. He was very easy to like – he had a kind of magnetic charm coupled with humour that was very appealing. He nodded and lowered his voice. 'She said that if Greece was freed, she would owe her freedom to Green Plataea. And she said, *"The strength of bulls or lions cannot stop the foe. No, he will not leave off, I say, until he tears the city or the king limb from limb."'*

I winced. 'That's ... not the prophecy I'd have wanted to hear,' I agreed.

Leonidas shrugged. 'The gods do as they will. But when I heard that you spoke Persian and had ships, I wondered if you were the tool by which Green Plataea would serve Greece.'

I suspect I grinned. 'I'll do my best, o King,' I said, and bowed.

*

156

I had expected to pick up my two heralds and go, but in fact we dawdled a week in Sparta, and I'd have stayed longer. There is much to love there, as I, as a man who enjoyed watching women, must tell you that there are more beautiful women in Sparta than most places, and when you stare at them they stare back. One old hag of thirty, fresh from hard exercise and wearing nothing over her loveliness but a chiton of linen, caught my eye and shocked me by crossing the agora and asking me my name.

That wouldn't happen in Athens.

'Arimnestos of Plataea,' I said.

'I guess you like what you see,' she said. She laughed. 'At my age, it is always a pleasure to catch a worthy man's eye.'

Indeed, my eye was caught. She turned away, but her eyes didn't leave mine until her head was fully turned.

I almost followed her up the hill.

Men – Spartiates – mostly live in barracks like Cretan noblemen, and their wives keep house (with helot slaves) and mind the children (mostly done by slaves) and run the estates by which the men pay their mess bills. Odd as this arrangement might seem, it works as well as any other. To a Plataean, every Spartan woman seemed like the very epitome of athletic beauty, and Hector spoke for us all when he said (watching the old crone of thirty sway delightfully away from us), 'If I were a Spartiate, I'd never spend a minute in those barracks.'

I suspect we all three of us sighed.

It was also impossible to guess whether any of these remarkable women were available. By the standards of Athens or Plataea, they were all so forward that they might have been porne. And I could remember Plataeans who had been to Sparta on pilgrimage making claims about their lusty infidelities – but none of the women I met seemed – somehow – the types. They were direct – it is true. And sensual and athletic. But not, more's the pity, licentious.

Like upper-class Athenians, the men were more prone to run mad over a pretty boy than over their wives, but – just as in Athens – it was hard to tell how much of that was emulation and prowess, and how much was really … love. Or whatever passed for love in the hothouse world of barracks and Agoge.

At any rate, on my second day in Sparta, the king took me to meet his mess and dine with them, which was accounted one of the highest honours in the Greek world. It's good that it is such an honour, because the food was terrible. I think they make a special effort whenever a foreigner comes. The black broth tasted as if pig excrement had been involved in making it. I *never* had such foul bread in all the years of my slavery. The Phoenicians give better food to their oarsmen.

But I digress.

I was also invited to the exercise field, a little less civilised than one of the better Athenian gymnasiums, but you have to realise that the Athenian upper class often emulates the Spartan aristocracy. So the gymnasiums are not so different. The sun is hotter, and you cannot smell the sea air.

I boxed a little with the king. That was a great honour, too – despite his bruises, he didn't spar with everyone. And by boxing with me, he made me anyone's equal, and so men virtually queued up to fight me. An older man – one of the king's guard – slipped past me with a beautiful feint and broke my nose – this in the first minute – and then was most solicitous in fixing it. He said something, reached out and pulled hard, and reset it.

And then he expected to go back to our contest.

Spartans.

I took a dip in their cold water to clear the pain – I don't think I impressed my opponent at all – and to get the pain-fatigue out of my muscles, and then I went back, towelled dry by helots, and chose a younger man for a bout of pankration. I knew I had to – there's no avoiding pankration in Sparta, and if I ever planned to walk among these men with my head high, I had to endure it.

Spartans, of course, bite and gouge and do other things in a pankration match that are forbidden elsewhere. My young opponent was quite heavily built and fresh from the Agoge, and I'm pretty sure, given my swollen nose and the ease with which my first opponent had downed me, that he saw me as easy prey. He was very polite.

I let him catch my arms, gave a twist I'd learned from Polymarchos, and threw him.

He bounced to his feet. I got a nice cheer – a buzz – from the other men watching.

I backed up a couple of steps, and my opponent came at me.

Now that I'd taught him not to grab at my hands, I raised them, and when he refused the bait, I threw a flurry of punches. I caught him twice and stunned him, which allowed me to catch his right arm in my left and then pass my left hand under his elbow.

And down he went. He tried to resist, and got some muscles

pulled for his pains. I could have dislocated his shoulder or dropped him on his head, but I was a guest.

And he tried to grab my testicles.

I had been warned – many times – and I had fought the helot at Olympia. I really should have known. He hit my testicles a glancing blow as I rolled my hips away, and kneed him – all the while wrenching his right shoulder, which must have been in agony.

So I rolled the arm down, hit him in the ear with my left hand – pretty viciously, I confess – and then put him in the sand face first, with a knee in the small of his back.

He tried to kick me – backwards.

I looked at the king. I had my opponent in the full hold – and his kicks were only ruining his own shoulder.

'How do I make him stop?' I asked.

Men laughed.

One of the older men stepped forward with a polite nod to me and tapped the young man with his staff. Instantly, the young man went limp.

I got up.

He tried to bounce to his feet, but his right arm wasn't fully responding to his commands. Nonetheless, he stretched forth his hands as if ready for another bout.

I looked at the older man with the staff. I saw a slave with a water ewer, and held up my hand – walked to the edge of the sand and took a drink of water.

The king waved at the sky as if stating a pleasantry about the weather. 'You have to go a third fall. It will humiliate him otherwise.'

I suppose brave and foolish young men are much the same everywhere. Just more so, in Lacedaemon.

I stepped back on to the sand, nodded to him, and we circled a few times. In fact, I was not going to rush him – both for his ego and because I had a suspicion that Spartans practised fighting hurt.

Sure enough, when I offered him an opening he raised his right hand, all but offering it to me, with all the prospect of pain that would go with it – and then stepped in deep with his left side, intending a fast throw and using his own injury as bait.

I snap-kicked his left knee. I hit his right bicep with my left fist, and turned, making him follow me. It had been an excellent move, for a wounded man, and he responded well, but he had almost no strength in his right side and now he was a little white around the nostrils.

I caught him on the turn – and pinned his right hand low with my left, a wrist grab. I meant to avoid further injury to his right. I can be a good man.

My right hand went for a lock on his left, but he was too quick, so I thrust it deep, so that my right hand clipped his jaw and went past, all but touching his left shoulder as my right foot went behind his feet, and then I threw him – backwards – with my out-thrust right hand. I followed him down, pinned his left under my knee, and put my right hand to his throat.

He tried to hit me with his right fist.

I think I shook my head. He had no strength in that fist at all. But he was still fighting.

I had just spent fifty days training with Polymarchos. I'd probably never been as good as I was just then.

At any rate, the ephor with the stick came and tapped him, and again he went limp, but he sprang up again, and took my hand. And I noted the way men looked at him when he strode – strode – away.

He'd made the grade. Spartans aren't all about winning. It is more, for them, about the manner of the contest. When it became clear that he couldn't beat me, then it was a different kind of contest, and in the eyes of all the Spartiates – all of us, really – he had triumphed. Over his own pain.

That was Sparta.

I wrestled a fall with old Calliteles. He stepped through the crowd and said, 'So far you haven't faced our best. I'm an old man, but I'd be pleased to fight a throw.'

He was big – he had two inches of reach on me, and few men can say that, and he outweighed me by several stone. I was careful while we circled, and I was in my fifth or sixth fight of the day and blessing Polymarchos and all the exercise I'd got building things in Plataea.

We circled for a long time.

Twice he grabbed for me, and twice I evaded him. This was wrestling, so I couldn't keep him at a distance with kicks and punches, and at the third attack, I saw an opening and pounced.

Hah, hah! I was face down in the sand a moment later with his whole weight atop me. Some opening. But he forbore to break my arm, and he slapped me as I rose. I took up a guard and he shook his head.

'One fall a day. That's all my old knees can take,' he said.

'Mine too,' I said, somewhat ruefully.

And then Bulis appeared. He came through the crowd quickly, and pushed into the space in front of the king.

'I'd like a go,' he said. 'Unless you are too tired.'

His delivery was Laconian – flat. In fact, I was tired – the broken nose had taken a great deal out of me, and the young pankrationist had been very strong. And I thought Bulis meant me harm.

'Of course,' I said. It occurred to me, in a somewhat reptilian moment of which I'm not proud, that if Bulis broke my arm or injured me, I could save six months of my life and not take him to Sardis or Susa.

It was hard to read Bulis. He was not giving off the signals I'd have taken for violent aggression. His face registered very little emotion, and he merely inclined his head. He might have been cold, angry – or shy.

'What would you like to do?' he asked.

'Pankration,' I answered. I'm not a great boxer, witness the nose.

Bulis stepped straight in with a punch aimed at my nose.

I tried to trap his punch.

Neither one of us was successful. He rotated on the balls of his feet and threw his left, and I kicked at his left knee, and both of us half turned and returned to our guards – and backed away.

He grabbed for my throat.

I grabbed for his, and we had several very intense heartbeats while our arms intertwined, looking for a hold.

He rolled – a feint, and I caught that it was a feint in time to raise my leg and block the kick to my crotch. I'd been shown a beautiful move by Polymarchos – a kick-lock – and since I had my left leg up, I flicked my own kick at his testicles and then tried to catch his left leg and encircle it with my right. But I hadn't practised it enough, and I missed the hold. We passed each other, and he got a weak left into my gut, and my structure held.

In truth, we were well matched.

I knew a few tricks that I didn't think were taught in Sparta, and it was time to dust them off. But I needed another clench or a flurry of boxing blows, and so, of course, I got neither. We circled, and then we exchanged kicks, and then circled.

I stepped in. It was the first time I'd initiated the action, and he was ready – but a little over-eager, and I deceived his right hand, and got my left in a smashing blow to his shoulder, and I tried my gambit, passing deeply with my left foot. I went for a left armlock which he easily evaded, and he caught me a fine left jab to the temple.

It was my turn to fight through pain. I got my instep around his right heel, passed my left arm behind his head, missed my jab as he ducked his head – and then I pivoted on the balls of my feet, so that my left knee came in behind his right knee, and I bore him down to the ground. Gaining control of his left arm as he struggled for his balance.

He tried to reverse the hold and to throw me left to right, but the grip is inexorable, and I had him face down in the sand.

He tapped. Like a normal person.

Later I learned that Spartiates – full Spartiates, who have seen battle – are allowed, even encouraged, to tap, while the young are forced to fight to full submission or unconsciousness. I suppose I see the point, although they must lose some good youngsters that way.

He got up and smiled at me.

I've seldom been so surprised. It wasn't a 'now I kill you' smile, but merely a smile of appreciation.

Then he came at me hard.

We had a ten-heartbeat flurry – fists, kicks, and then a fast series of grabs – he got me over his hip, and I rolled rather than fight it, and he wasn't – quite – fast enough to pin me as I rolled through his fall.

That drew applause, which was my downfall. I like applause, and I slowed –

bang.

Down I went. Of *course* he was right behind me as I rose from my roll, and he got my shoulders from behind as I hesitated in my turn and threw me – literally pulled me on my back and fell across me.

I laughed.

He laughed.

I dived at him, got a knee in my thigh, and then tried the same infighting technique I'd just used – but from the front – using my shin to force his shin back. He stumbled away – but he broke my attempt. I threw a strong right at his retreating face and caught him, and he threw a right – I grabbed his arm, we both missed holds and stumbled together and then – I can't remember how – we were on the sand, grappling on the ground like boys.

The Spartans know all about ground fighting, but they disdain it, because on the battlefield it can get you killed, and combat sports, for Spartans, are about battle, not about games. I might have had an edge, but my opponent – sheer luck – caught my broken nose with his elbow, and I was fighting in a red haze and anger and pain.

I have no idea how long it went on.

But the ephors separated us. I was tapped on the shoulder, but I didn't know the signal, so the next thing I felt was a blow to my calf.

I stopped struggling, realising that my opponent was not moving.

Luckily, the gods have graced me with good wits and some humour – so I got to my feet as best I could and embraced Bulis before he could say anything.

He smiled again. 'Good fight,' he said.

I didn't fight in the king's gymnasium again. It took me two days to recover from the first time, and my nose took weeks to recover fully. But after that day, men greeted me in the agora and in the streets, usually calling out, 'Khairete, Xenos!'

And I received an offer to dine with Bulis and his mess.

Sparta is not devoid of small talk, gossip, song or good fellowship. I lay on a couch in this, a more 'average' mess, and was served food that was merely bad and entertained by Sparthius, who was Bulis's partner and a very funny man. Sparthius was irreverent and sometimes nasty, mocking Gorgo's mismatched eyes and my limp, suggesting in some fairly obvious ways that as I was Hephaestus, all my women would cheat on me. He told a story about a drunk buying a fine wine to pour as a libation on the grave of a friend, and then offering to pass it through his body once first – he mocked Sparta and he mocked Athens.

At the same time, he mocked the gods. And he knew songs – ribald songs, dirty songs, marching songs ...

Bulis just lay beside him and smiled from time to time and sipped his wine.

We all drank a great deal, and I came to know the other men in his mess. They weren't average, all being members of the elite Hippeis. All of them were handsome, and all of them were over thirty, and married. They struck me as being ... young. Most were my age, and yet – the Spartan lifestyle allowed them a boyishness that I had probably lost while I was a slave, or perhaps at Sardis. They laughed at farting. They mocked a helot with a misformed penis, but it was not particularly cruel, especially when they offered to send him to Corinth to get it 'treated' at the temple of Aphrodite. They drank like boys, too – on and on, mixed only one to one with water. As the wine flowed, Sparthius became louder, and, I confess it, funnier, kneeling on the tiled floor and begging (in the character of a Macedonian) for Helios to stay away, stay away. 'Oh, it burns!' he shrieked, and everyone laughed.

Macedonians, of course, come from a land of rain and clouds and their fair skin burns in the sun.

Bulis turned to me. 'My wife finds you very attractive,' he said. 'She enjoyed your flattery.'

Gulp.

I hope I smiled. 'The lady I met in the agora is your wife?'

He nodded. 'We were married young. Our fathers arranged it – almost as soon as we were born. They were ... you know. Erastes and Eromenos.' He sipped more wine, his eyes elsewhere.

That was all. At the door, when I was handed my cloak by a helot, he embraced me. 'We should fight again,' he said. 'My wife was right about you.'

Leonidas had a number of meetings with my passengers, and I assume he briefed them extensively on his views on a number of subjects. I was not invited, and in truth, I can't imagine why I would have been included. I went riding with Gorgo – the closest I've ever come to loving horses – and I drilled with Bulis's mess on three different days. Their Pyricche was different from ours – different music, and much more chorography. In fact, I learned that where Plataea has a single, fairly complicated dance, Sparta has seven. I learned one well enough to practise it with Bulis and Sparthius on board ship.

I also began to practise their quick draw with the sword. On one of their practice fields, they use a row of polished shields so men can watch themselves as they train, and I did so, cutting a post, and several times men would stop and correct my posture or my footwork. It was one of the curious things about Sparta that training is seldom done by one man. In Athens, as you probably know, each taxeis hires a professional trainer to improve their spear fighting or their drill. But in Sparta, any man who has seen battle can correct any other man, especially if that man is younger. Virtually all of the older hoplites were very capable men, and they tended to wander around the drill field, like a hundred hoplomachia teachers instead of just one or two. As long as I was on their field, they trained me as willingly.

And in the agora, I heard more – and better – philosophy than I heard in Athens. Well, in Athens before Anaxagoras came, but that's another story. But with the helots to do all the work, men had little to do but exercise, and in Sparta they exercised their minds as well as their bodies.

In truth, Briseis should have been born a Spartan.

Late in the week, I was introduced to Leotychidas, the other king – the Eurypontid king. He was sober and very grave – almost sixty years old, and still as solid as an oak tree. He lacked Leonidas' charm, but he had a great dignity, and I could tell that Polypeithes, who was kind enough to introduce me, fairly worshipped him.

'Ah,' he said. 'You are the foreigner that Gorgo fancies.' He frowned. 'That woman always gets her way.'

There really wasn't an answer to that, so I bowed.

'You speak Persian?' he asked.

I admitted that I did.

He nodded, lips pursed. 'I suppose someone must. Do you think Xerxes will march an army into Greece?'

'Yes,' I said.

He nodded. 'As do I. Nor do I think that sending a pair of my best men to die will help in any way.' He shrugged. 'Can you keep them alive? Are you a friend of the Great King's?'

I had to shake my head. 'No, my lord,' I said. 'I knew his father's brother. And a few of his soldiers.'

He rocked his head from side to side, as if considering me from different angles.

'Hmm,' he said. 'Well, if you knew a few of my Spartiates and my father's brother, I'd give you a hearing. That's the best news I've heard all day. What will you say on our behalf?'

I almost choked on my tongue. 'I'm sorry, lord?'

He was watching me as if I were a not-very-bright boy. 'If you gain the ear of the Great King before my two Spartiates wander in, what will you say? I tell you, I'd rather they weren't killed.'

I thought it through for a number of heartbeats. I could hear Polypeithes breathe by my side. Finally I shook my head. 'I'm sorry, lord. I can't say anything on the part of Sparta. I am not a Spartan.'

The Eurypontid king's eyes were fixed on mine. 'Would you be shocked if I gave you my permission to say *anything*? Be my guest, Xenos. Say what you like, and claim it comes from me. If you think that it will buy us peace, or keep these two young men alive. Anything but my submission.'

He said more, but that was the gist, and when I had a last dinner with Polypeithes, Leonidas and my two passengers, the Agiad king said much the same, and after dinner, when the mess was drinking toasts, I was summoned to the king's house and found Gorgo sitting in the courtyard under the stars.

Nearly invisible helots brought wine and nuts.

I have no doubt belaboured this point, but if an Athenian matron had invited me to her house and met me in the garden with a chiton open down the sides, drinking wine neat and eating honeyed almonds, I would assume I was welcome to more than the nuts.

Gorgo did not seem that way. So I sat on a bench and repeated some of Sparthius's jokes, and eventually she came to the point.

'What have the kings told you? About the Great King?' she asked.

I shrugged. 'I'm not a Spartan, lady. I am not your ambassador.'

Gorgo wouldn't be swayed. 'You *speak Persian*.' She raised an eyebrow – an impossibly attractive look, given the very slight unevenness of her eyes. Impossible to explain why, if you haven't seen her. 'Do you know that there is a Spartan king living in the Great King's court?' she asked.

'Yes,' I said. 'Demaratus.'

She looked away – not as if evading me, but as if seeing events unfold. 'He was deprived of his kingship – illegally,' she said. 'Bah. It had to be done. But he is not such an evil man. I wonder if you would carry a message to him from me.'

How in the name of all the gods had I got mixed up in this?

'Of course!' I said.

She gave me a wax tablet. It was blank. She smiled.

I didn't want to know. I handed the tablet to Hector after summoning him.

We sat up for some time, and eventually she sat on her bench with her knees drawn up to her chest and listened as I spoke of Sicily. Somehow we got on to Athens.

'How they hate us,' she said.

I shrugged. 'Athens and Sparta are similar enough that, like angry brothers, when they look at each other, they see only their own flaws.'

She grinned. 'Did you make that up yourself?'

If Spartan men were boyish, Gorgo was very 'girlish'. She was spontaneous and mercurial, and often hard to follow. But I smiled back. 'In fact, just this once, I did.'

She nodded. 'I like it. I should like to go to all the places you have been. Sicily. Athens. Perhaps Athens most of all.'

I laughed. 'My friend Aristides – do you recall him?'

'A fine man,' she said. 'My husband admires him.'

'As do I,' I answered. *When he's not an insufferable prig.* 'His wife longs to meet you.'

'Really!' she said. She giggled. But I think she was flattered. 'You should ask her to meet me at Plataea. I go in the spring, to the temple of Hera. If Plataea is to be the saviour of Greece, I wish to know why.' And she shrugged. 'I have a son, but I should like another child.' Her eyes met mine.

I didn't get it. I still do not. Was that a proposition? I could not tell. But I began to think ...

'You do not speak of Brasidas,' she said.

It was the second time she'd brought him up.

I shrugged. 'He's my friend, but it does not seem to be in good taste to mention him.'

Gorgo nodded. She sat back. It was very dark, and the air itself was perfumed with summer.

My hands shook a little. I was preparing myself to kiss the Queen of Sparta.

'I'm arranging to lift the ban of his exile,' she said.

I sighed. 'He will no doubt be delighted,' I said. Somewhat annoyed.

'He will no doubt throw my husband's offer in his face like the stiff-necked bastard of a dog that he is,' she said pleasantly. 'But we owe you a great deal already.'

We were almost nose to nose. I could feel her breath on my face.

A hand came to rest on my shoulder.

'Sir?' Hector said. 'Alexandros is very drunk.'

I got up and clasped her hand. In a flash, I had decided that ... that Hector's arrival was from the gods.

She laughed. 'You are a good man, Arimnestos.'

In the morning, we rode south. We were on the beach before darkness fell, and we ate lobster and fresh fish with the oarsmen, who had eaten and drunk their fill for a week and were, all taken together, penniless and hung over.

And we took another five days returning to Athens, because we had to land for food and water every night, and the wind was resolutely against us. I had a good load of Phoenician goods purchased by Sekla in the markets, and there were not many Athenian ships that called at Sparta. I hoped to be first into the Athenian agora with my goods.

Nor was I disappointed. Indeed, I never made it to the Athenian agora – a pair of middlemen, friends of Paramanos, bought my whole cargo, but my profit was enough to suggest that piracy was *not* the best way to make money at sea.

My Spartans were good passengers. They took turns at the oars when they saw that the rest of us did, and they were better than polite to Brasidas. He was the one who seemed rude – he was aloof with them in a way he never was with young Apollodorus or the others. And Sparthius continued to be a comic, while Busis was mostly silent. When he did open his mouth, it was to ask questions. He'd never been to sea before, and he wanted to know *everything*.

After we sold our cargo, I arranged that the Spartan heralds should be housed by Cimon, and I purchased a small, tubby merchantman. In our expeditions in the western Mediterranean and the Outer Sea, we'd learned how handy it was to have a store ship to carry water and food – even running to Sparta and back across the Gulf of Corinth had brought that lesson home, with wasted days crawling around the periphery. I gave the command to Megakles, and gave him Giorgios and Nicolas from the oarsmen and a couple of my Syracusan deck crewmen. We fitted the merchantman out with a cargo of Athenian luxury goods – mostly pottery – and a deep tier of water amphorae. I bought dried meat and dried fish and grain, and stored them in layers, mostly in pottery with waxed tops.

Moire and Harpagos came in with their ships, and I got them cargoes, although by now I was dealing in credit – Cimon's credit. I was out of money.

I rode over the mountains to Brauron, and paid my daughter a final visit. She was tanned and hard muscled as only a young girl can be, and while she was happy to see me, she was anxious to go back to her friends.

I didn't know enough about children then not to be hurt, but I let her go. I stayed the night with Peisander and on the way back I stayed with Jocasta and Aristides, who was ten days from starting his exile. He seemed quite light hearted. She did not.

Whenever I visited Aristides, there always came a moment when, by common consent, I would go off to the women's area and sit in the late afternoon sun with Jocasta and help with her wool. It was when we talked – when she gave me her marching orders for her husband, usually.

'The Queen of Sparta would like to meet you,' I said.

Whatever she was going to say, it went right out of her head. She laughed. 'That's lovely!' she said.

'Queen Gorgo asked me to say that your husband is a fine man, whom her husband admires, and she'd be delighted to meet you at the temple of Hera at Plataea in the spring, after the feast of Demeter.'

She clapped her hands together. 'I'm sure ... oh!' she said. 'I could see Aristides then, as well!'

I nodded. 'I thought of that at sea. Come and stay with us – my daughter and me. Or with my sister Penelope and her husband Antigonus.'

'Aristides has spoken of them. Is it really possible?' she asked.

I grinned. 'I'll come and get you myself,' I said.

She nodded. 'I like having some hope of seeing him again. He's very "stiff upper lip". I'm not so cold.' And then she leaned closer. 'You know he's coming to Susa with you,' she said.

Piraeus, at dawn.

My ships had taken on stores at Zea and then been rowed around the night before to wait on the beach. My oarsmen were rowing heavily laden ships – they didn't need the additional weight of a hull soaked all night in water.

Bulis and Sparthius were as curious as cats, prowling among the last hemp nets of cargo, unfolding a linen boat sail, and inspecting the equipment of my marines. I had eight men in each ship and a pair of professional archers, and then I had Ka and his six men – all good archers, and also willing deck crewmen.

Aristides owned his own ships – not just one, but two, big, long, narrow sharks. The very height of Athenian shipbuilding, which, back then, six years after Marathon, was just developing into the very best in the world. He had his own oarsmen and his own followers who turned out as marines. The splendour of their equipment utterly eclipsed that of my men, who looked merely practical – although through the influence of Brasidas, my men had matching rust-red cloaks and matching red, black and white horsehair crests. The Spartans are great ones for uniformity of equipment.

But if Aristides wanted to tell the voters of the assembly what they were doing when they exiled him, the display of his two warships

– only the very richest men could own warships – fully manned with citizen oarsmen whose wages he paid, and protected by marines who were his 'gentlemen' …

Let me pause in my story for a moment. I, in fact, owned three warships and a round ship. Those of you who have been listening know that I didn't *pay* for any of them except the merchanter. I took them from other men. When I took slaves, I often used them as oarsmen for six months or a year in lieu of the price of their freedom. I have been a pirate for most of my life – a pirate whose actions were often sanctioned by Athens or one of the other states. But Aristides was a true aristocrat, who spent his fortune on the good of his city, sponsoring athletic contests, contributing to temples, paying for the chorus in the Dionysian plays, and buying warships.

Themistocles didn't come to gloat. But Phrynicus did, and he was one of the orator's closest friends. He came down to the beach and hugged me, and he gave Aristides a letter. They talked for some time, and in the end embraced.

I tried not to stare, but what I saw confirmed my notion that Aristides' exile was, at some level, contrived.

I had Harpagos and Moire under me as trierarchs, and Megakles as the captain of the *Swan*. Aristides had Heraclides, one of my oldest mentors, as his second trierarch.

With five triremes and a stores ship, we were probably the most powerful squadron in the Aegean that summer, and the pity of it was that we were bound on nothing more profitable than an embassy to the Great King – and even I suspected that pillaging some Egyptian ships and a few Carthaginian or Tyrian freighters would *not* enhance our reception at Susa.

But as we ran along the coast of Euboea and east to Skyros, on the balmy summer zephyrs, the sea was full of potential prizes, and my oarsmen looked at me as I stood amidships – watching a pair of Carthaginian biremes bound for the Hellespont, watching a Tyrian merchantman wallow in the soft breeze, downwind and easy prey.

When they grumbled, I'd catch someone's eye and point to the wreath of olive at the bow.

I had in mind a little scouting on my way to Tarsus. In fact, all the men who could navigate were scratching their heads. Tarsus is south of Rhodos and around the corner from Cyprus and beyond.

On the beach below the temple on the rock – I never caught its name – Aristides and I laid out our plans for our officers.

'Our first intention is to see if Xerxes is really building a canal behind Mount Athos,' Aristides said bluntly. 'Second, to see if he is bridging the Hellespont.'

Bulis's face gave nothing away, but Sparthius laughed. 'So – we're suddenly hoplites in an Athenian naval expedition?' he asked.

Aristides got along well with both of my Spartans – of course he did. He admired their way of life. So he shook his head. 'Nothing of the sort. On the one hand, we all learn about how advanced the Great King's plans are; on the other hand, we look at his defences. The sailing season is young. We have more than a month to reach Tarsus and start inland.'

I have to mention that, before I knew that Aristides was coming, I had made the plan to go to Susa or Persepolis via Tarsus. There were a number of reasons for this, but the most important was simple distance. It is much easier to travel by sea than by road. Most Greeks going to the Great King went to Tarsus, which placed a man almost two-thirds of the way to Persia, or at least to Babylon.

I had also dispatched letters – to Artapherenes, to Briseis, and to my friend Cyrus, asking for letters of safe conduct and permission to use the messenger stations on the Royal Road.

When Aristides announced his intention of joining us, I told him of my plans, and he agreed.

'I had no notion of safe conducts,' he said.

And that was that.

The sailing weather was perfect. But keeping my men together – that was harder. The voyage offered no chance of heavy profit, but once news of our intention to scout the Great King's preparations made its way down to the oar benches, every man knew that we were running risks.

So that night on Skyros, when we were done briefing the officers, I assembled the oarsmen – all of them – and gave a speech. I can't quote it – but I told them the truth. I told them that we were the first ships of a free Greek navy. That we had to do what we were doing for every free man and woman in all of Greece. And that it was just as important for them to behave themselves well in Asian ports as it was for them to row well as we slipped along the Thracian coast.

When I was done, no one cheered, but they walked off into the darkness in a sombre mood.

Aristides shook his head. 'You could be a fine orator,' he said. 'Your voice is high pitched, but you make men listen.'

Bulis lay on the sand by my fire, his head on his hands. 'You believe that?' he asked me.

'Yes,' I said.

He nodded. 'Do you think we can defeat the Great King?' he asked.

'Yes,' I said.

'Good. So do I. So do all the Spartans. It is the other Greeks for whom I have concerns.'

We spent the next night at sea. We had the store ship, and she had a bricked hearth for cooking. It is not easy to feed six hundred men out of one hearth, but with cold meat and bread, we got them fed.

We laid to for as long as it took to get a good rest and get food. I spent the entire time worrying about that fire on *Swan*. Fire, at sea, is not man's friend.

Then we ran almost due north. I had the stars as a guide, but these waters were relatively unfamiliar to me. Not so for Harpagos or Moire, who had sailed to Thrace for slaves and hides and everything else all the years I'd been gone. I followed the Pole Star as the Carthaginians taught, and in the dawn, Sekla slapped my back and called me the king of navigators as Mount Athos rose out of the sea, due north.

Our warships stood off, well over the horizon from any but a watcher on Athos's highest peak, or the gods themselves, and the tubby *Swan* bore in as if sailing for the Chersonese. We sailed parallel and a little farther out to sea – a standard trick of piracy when scouting a potentially profitable coast.

We didn't have to close the Athos peninsula to see the Persian preparations. Megakles did, because he's an excellent sailor and a daring man, but before the mainland was more than a smudge, we could see the shipping all along the coast – small boats, round ships and galleys.

Perhaps fifty sails in view. For the wilderness of Thrace, that was ... incredible.

We swept north on a favourable wind for Thassos, and I began to have real apprehensions about the Persian invasion.

As in – was it imminent?

Nor did I any longer think our five ships were the strongest squadron in the Aegean.

We had our sails down as soon as we began to see warships, and we rowed – oarsmen cursing – under bare poles. Aristides had a different rig from mine and unstepped his masts.

Nothing irks an oarsman like rowing when the wind is favourable for sailing.

I lived in fear, moment to moment, that the Persian fleet would send ships to look at us. We were too far for me to see what ships they were, but I had to guess most of them were Phoenician.

All afternoon, I cheated my steering oars to the north and east, trying to be invisible, while one tiny sailing ship did the work, going right in among them. In late afternoon we landed on Thassos and bought sheep from shepherds so barbaric we couldn't understand their Greek. We had all our marines in armour, and Aristides – an old campaigner – taught me a new trick by building a small tower on the headland, which would give us precious warning of an attack.

But we were not disturbed in our sleep, and in the morning we watched the sun rise in the east and we dried our hulls, all our cargo stacked in the bright sun on the beach – waiting for Megakles.

And waiting.

Noon passed, and the oarsmen slept, and the Spartans ran up and down the beach. My marines didn't exercise – they were still on duty, sleeping in watches. As Bulis – well ahead of his friend – turned at the rocky promontory to run back, I saw him pause.

He was saying something to Brasidas.

Brasidas shrugged and continued towards the tower – really, just a set of poles tied together with a floor of boughs, but it placed a man at treetop height.

Bulis came running back down the beach, but during the time that he and Brasidas spoke, Sparthius had passed him, and now they were both sprinting, flat out, for the campfires and the line of boats. Men got up from their midday naps to cheer the Spartans, who looked like gods.

And that started a whole set of contests. Men wrestled and boxed and even fenced with oars – a very popular and very dangerous oarsmen's game.

I stood on the beach and worried.

I was still in shock at what I had seen the day before.

After midday, Aristides came with several of his young men. He sat on a rock, and his hypaspist poured wine from a skin.

'You worry too much,' he said, but he had the same lines under his eyes as I had.

I shrugged. I remember looking around at his friends – I didn't know most of them, although I knew his nephew, and I knew Aeschylus's younger brother and of course I knew Heraklides. 'I saw a great many Persian ships yesterday,' I said.

Aristides rubbed the top of his nose – a much-imitated facial tic in the Athenian assembly.

'One thing to hear of it and another to see it,' he said.

We shared the wine, and I heard that Aeschylus's younger brother was planning to go into politics, that the youngest man was actually my enemy Cleitus's youngest sibling Alcibiades. He was a handsome devil, and he had that look – arrogance, yes, but also a total disregard for the opinions of others – that sets young men apart and makes them so easy to hate. He and his older brother Cleinias were both followers of Aristides. They were also rich and powerful enough to own ships, and they were with us to 'learn the ropes'. Athenian aristocrats worked pretty hard, back then.

The two Alcmaeonidae watched me like hawks, but their fascination wasn't devoid of respect. If Aristides even deigned to notice, he paid them no heed.

And while I thought all these thoughts, distracted for the first time in hours, Megakles crept over the horizon in his little *Swan*.

'Elaeus is *full* of ships,' Megakles shouted, before he leapt over the side of *Swan* and swam ashore like the fisherman he was.

Naked and dripping, he emerged like Poseidon himself. 'There're *fifty* warships in Elaeus bay, and another six or seven rowing guard. All Phoenicians. Nicolas saw two more hulls he thought that he knew – Samian Greeks.'

'Could be worse,' I said. Athens had as many ships. Aristides and I exchanged looks and then we were off, gathering our athletic oarsmen, pulling down the tower, and racing to sea – like pirates.

From Thassos we ran downwind, under sail, to Samothrace, and we kept the shoreline out of sight to the north all the way. We saw fishing boats twice, but no more warships, and we made camp on the south side of Samothrace, with a tower and guards, and doused fires as soon as the food was cooked.

And in the dawn – a cold, grey dawn with rain in it – we were off again, this time running under sail into the mouth of the Hellespont. If the Medes saw us – well, they saw us. You cannot hide in a body of water six miles wide.

It was late afternoon by the time we were near Troy. And now, despite our efforts at stealth, it was impossible to hide our presence. We had fishing boats all around us from the towns on the Bosporus, and we had a dozen military triremes – Ionian Greeks – patrolling the waters in the difficult, choppy sea just south of Troy.

I watched the ships as we ran in, looking for a sign that one of them was Archilogos, once my master, then my friend, and now my sworn enemy. It was hard to define how we all knew that these were Greek ships and not Phoenicians or Carthaginians or Aegyptians, but Sekla knew, I knew, and Aristides knew, and we ran down on them with all our rowers at their stations and all of our marines in harness.

They paid us no heed at all, so with a flash of oars, we turned on the opposite tack and sailed north into the main channel. I can only assume that they thought we were part of the Persian fleet. Why would they not?

Who expected Athenian ships in these waters? Cimon and Miltiades had been driven from here six years before.

We ran north, but again, we already knew what we would find.

The reality, however, was far more chilling even than what we had seen off Mount Athos.

First, the narrow Hellespont was choked with shipping. I stopped counting at a hundred boats – warships, merchant ships, fishermen. Access to the Euxine makes this one of the busiest pieces of water under the sun – I had lived and sailed here for years – but this was extreme.

And fifty stades north of Troy, we came in sight of the greatest concentration of shipping I had seen since we fled from the Persian fleet in the disaster at Lades.

I turned to Leukas, at the helm, and made a turning motion with my hand.

'Ready about!' Leukas screamed. Marines on the top deck threw themselves flat so as not to go over the side – neither triremes nor trimiolas have railings on most of the deck – and the deck crew ran about like ants in a disturbed nest trying to get the mainsail down.

The port-side rowers reversed their cushions, and Hector signalled frantically to Harpagos, the next ship aft of us.

There were at least two hundred warships at Abydos on the Asian side. I didn't wait to learn more.

Xerxes was coming.

★

Two days later, we were sitting in the palace in Mythymna, on Lesvos. My hands had stopped shaking, but the terror was real. We had seen three hundred warships. Off Mount Athos, it had been possible to see an Athenian fleet stopping the Great King's fleet, but with three hundred ships already at sea, and they only the harbingers …

'It doesn't matter whether he's going to build bridges or simply ferry his army a taxeis at a time,' I insisted to Aristides. The Athenians were a talkative lot, and they were debating what the great fleet meant, and whether Xerxes was really bold enough to try and bridge the Hellespont.

Bulis fingered his beard. 'I would like the kings to know of this,' he said.

So we agreed to send Moire home in *Storm Cutter* with a cargo of Lesbian wine and oil and some Chian wine and mastic. He was ordered to touch at Athens and speak only to Cimon, and then go on to Sparta. Bulis wrote him a letter on papyrus.

Aristides was shaken. 'Is there any point in going to Susa, if the Great King has set his mind on war?' he asked. 'I do not want to be cooling my heels at the Great King's court while his troops lay siege to my city.'

The Spartans felt the same way, but the lords of Mythymna had some useful knowledge. Lesvos was Persian – it had been conquered and treated harshly. Mythymna had no Persian garrison because Mytilini had resisted so long and the Persians were spread thin in Ionia, and we were welcomed there. I had friends all over Lesvos, and the son of Epaphroditos, Axiochus, came from Mytilini in a fishing boat when he heard I was there.

They gave us all the news they had. And what they knew was a little reassuring. Their ships had been summoned for the *next* season. They were to attack Athens in the *next* spring.

We rested our rowers for another day and Sekla sold most of our cargo on the beach – not the luxury goods, but all the heavy stuff. We made a good profit, which was mostly consumed by the oarsmen.

We ran down to Chios, and Harpagos saw his cousin, as did I. The Persians had been even harsher on Chios than on Lesvos, and we had to be very careful. Most of the Chians I knew were dead, but when we asked men, they admitted they'd been summoned for service in the next spring. Harpagos got us a copy of the letter from the satrap.

Let me add that none of this was meant to be secret. But some news travelled quickly, and other news hardly travelled at all. It is one thing to hear a rumour of war, and another thing to see the satrap's letter. Signed by Artapherenes.

I will say a little of Harpagos's cousin. I had offered to take her to Plataea, once. She and I had been lovers – not for long, and mostly because of the death of her older brother, which hit her hard. She had been a wonderful, cheerful, lawless girl – a fisherman's daughter, and a fine young kore. Now she was a silent, bitter woman, aged before her time, with nothing to say but curses.

Friends, I have said before that the Persians are men like us, and in many ways more honourable. But I have to also say – in her eyes, I saw pain and humiliation, and the future of Greece, if Persia ruled.

We were very wary, south of Chios. Once, we Greeks had owned these waters. Now, all of them belonged to Persia.

Tarsus is one of the oldest cities in the world. They worship the horned and winged lion, Sandon, there, and it is a very rich province of the Persian empire.

I had never had reason to touch at Tarsus before, and our squadron was careful on approach, all of the other ships hanging well off the port while I took *Lydia* in with all my benches manned. But as soon as the somewhat withered olive wreaths were visible, a pilot boat came out of the harbour and on board was a senior officer of Hydarnes' household – Hydarnes was the Satrap of Tarsus and the surrounding region, and one of Xerxes' favourites according to rumour. From my Persian friends, I knew he came from one of the oldest families and that his father had helped put Darius on the throne.

His steward bowed low on my command deck. 'My lord, I am commanded by him whose servant I am to present you with these safe conducts, issued by the Great King under his imperial seal. And with this writ commanding that you and your servants be allowed to pass down the Royal Road and to be served at the post houses. And I also offer you this letter from the satrap Artapherenes, who has further sent you an escort of his noble cavalry to take you all the way to Susa.'

Hector stepped forward and took all the scrolls and tablets.

The steward bowed deeply once again.

I returned his bow, in the Persian way. When you bow to a man's servant, you are bowing to him – the Persians only throw themselves on their faces for the Great King in person, but they salute a senior servant almost as if he were the man or woman themselves.

'I thank you for your prompt service. May I add that I have a cargo?'

The steward, a Babylonian by his olive-skinned good looks, smiled. I gathered he'd dealt with Greeks before. From his own belt he pulled a very small scroll. 'My master has decreed that your cargoes will be passed uninspected and untaxed, as part of an embassy.' He handed me the scroll. 'There is a berth for your ship.'

'I have five ships,' I said, as much to see whether I could puncture his smooth delivery as because I was afraid we'd swamp Hydarnes' hospitality.

'So many?' the steward asked. He looked out to sea.

'The Ionian sea is full of pirates,' I said. I tried not to smile.

He was a young, fit man, despite his odd trousers and perfumed beard, and he wore a sword. And he met my gaze without hesitation, and smiled.

'That's what I hear,' he said, looking pointedly at my rowers.

I liked him.

Ashore, on the open ground, paved in marble, that ran down to the military piers of the harbour, stood an escort of twenty armoured men. They wore tall, conical helmets that tapered to points, and armour of bronze scales. The officer had blue enamelled scales of Aegyptian work in alternating rows, and a magnificent beard, and he slid from his horse and embraced me. In truth, it had been less than a year since I had seen Cyrus – but we met like long-lost brothers, or at least cousins.

'Let me look at you,' he said. 'You look like a king, or a prince.'

I had hoped that Artaphernes would send me an escort. Persians measure power in many ways but most of them have to do with favour – with the power of your relationships. Artaphernes, by loaning me his own household cavalry, was putting me 'under his shield', as we say in Greece. I hadn't expected Cyrus in person, but I had hoped for him. He would help me avoid foolish pitfalls on my way to Susa, and deeper and subtler ones once I made it into the Great King's presence. I raised my hands and prayed to Zeus and Hermes right there in the seaside agora, and then I began to introduce my own friends.

Bulis was as closed as a locked trunk. I had learned enough of the man to know that he was merely being careful, dignified, giving nothing away that an enemy might make use of. Sparthius was open, effusive and talkative, and he exchanged hand clasps with Cyrus.

'My first real Persian!' he said. 'He is your friend?' Sparthius asked me.

'Friend and guest-friend,' I said in Greek, and then translated into Persian.

Aristides was almost as cautious as Bulis, but he had better manners, and he was not unwilling to bow as the Persians do, although neither of the Spartans would bend even by an inch. Sallis, the steward, was introduced, and provided each of us with an interpreter. Every one of them was an Ionian Greek slave.

Take what message you like from that.

We climbed up the streets of the lower town and Sallis showed us a few of the sights. The temple of Sardon was magnificent, if a little gaudy even by Boeotian standards.

'The central sacred precinct is more than a thousand years old,' Sallis told us. I suspect we craned our necks like hicks, because he laughed aloud. 'If you pass Babylon, you can climb the temple of Marduk. It is more than three thousand years old.' He shrugged.

Something crossed Bulis's face. He glanced at me.

I walked next to him for a while.

'It is not what I expected,' he muttered. 'I have been to Mycenae and it might have an old wall that is a thousand years old.'

I remember nodding. 'These people are very, very old. But not the Persians. They are as young as we Greeks, or even younger. Indeed, some say we are related.'

Sparthius laughed behind me. 'Nothing worse than near relations, in a blood feud.'

Hydarnes did everything in his power to welcome us. We were housed in the satrapal palace. Hector laid out a fresh linen chiton – it was hotter than any place I'd ever been, and damp, and everything seemed to droop in the heat. A slave took me to the bath, and a musician came in and began to play.

In the bath.

Musicians will sometimes play in public baths in Greece. But I'd never had one all to myself, and he played almost anything I knew. He, too, was Greek.

A pair of women came in. They were fine-looking women, with

good breasts and small waists, muscled legs – really, I was very interested. They came naked, and there could be no doubt of their roles.

But they were both Aeolian Greeks. As soon as they saw I was Greek, they threw themselves at my knees and begged me to rescue them. It was, just possibly, the most humiliating moment of my life, because I fancy myself the sort of man who rescues the weak, not oppresses them further.

Hector heard their story later. They were a Chian nobleman's daughters, and they had been 'employed' in the satrap's palace for four years.

In fact, as we moved around the corridors and unpacked, it became obvious that every low-level slave in the palace was Greek.

We met Hydarnes in person just before dinner. He had a great feast prepared – iced wine, whole deer, antelope, and the head of a lion. Whole sheep in saffron and raisins, and a dozen more dishes. It was a dinner for six hundred men – and women.

We could smell the feast, and Hydarnes sat on a low throne flanked by golden statues of the local god. I went first, and I bowed – as an equal to another equal.

He waved a hand, as if dismissing my insolence as puerile. 'I gather you are guest-friend to Artapherenes,' he said. He leaned forward. 'I gather you were once a slave.' He meant it to put me in my place.

I bowed again. 'Two years ago, I was a slave of a Carthaginian tin trader,' I said. 'The gods decide men's fates.' A year of dealing with the bigotries of Sicilians had made me immune to this sort of thing.

He looked at my friends. 'It is interesting to meet so many *free* Greeks. I only know them as slaves. Greeks make excellent slaves.'

I nodded. 'As do Persians,' I said. So much for diplomacy.

But he threw back his head and roared. 'Hah! Good for you. Yes – I suppose that if I was taken, I would make a fine slave. I know how to give orders *and* to take them. This is the power of our empire.'

After me, he was introduced to Aristides. He smiled and rose from his throne and came down to take Aristides' hand. 'I understand you have been exiled,' he said. 'My king offers you his hand in friendship.'

Aristides took the proffered hand. 'For myself, I would like nothing better than to be the king's friend,' he said. 'But I remain an Athenian.'

Hydarnes nodded. 'So few Greeks seems to feel as you do. They come to us and betray their homes for a few pieces of silver. But you are a nobleman.'

Aristides frowned, but Hydarnes went on to the Spartans. 'And you – men of Lacedaemon! Will you be friends of the Great King? Are you exiles?'

Bulis looked at me. We'd discussed some responses to questions like this. He said, 'We are heralds of the Kings of Sparta, with a message to the Great King,' he said.

'A message of friendship?' Hydarnes pressed on. 'From the Kings of Sparta?'

Bulis looked as cold as ice. 'The message,' he said slowly, 'is for the king your master, and not for you.'

Hydarnes frowned.

Soon after, we went into the great hall to dinner. We lay on couches in the Greek manner, but women sat in chairs. There were at least a dozen Persian, Median and Babylonian women. Not many among six hundred men, but enough to draw comment from the Greeks.

Aristides was sharing my couch, and Hector was waiting on us with Aristides' hypaspist, Nikeas.

I remember that the wine was odd. First, too sour, and then too sweet.

'You know who would love this?' Aristides asked me, while using a fold of bread to shove more mutton in saffron into his mouth. He laughed like a boy and chewed politely.

'Cimon?' I asked. 'Miltiades?'

'Jocasta,' Aristides said. 'She craves travel and adventure. For her, this would be like ... meeting Odysseus.' He leaned closer, as Hector poured wine and thus covered us from observation. 'Do you think all the Greek slaves are a message?' he asked.

'Yes,' I said.

'I pray to Zeus you are wrong. And to Hermes, god of heralds and ambassadors.' He sat back. 'You no longer think it can be stopped.'

I shook my head. 'I never did, once Artaphernes said the Great King was determined to make war. He's already spent the money. Can you imagine how much it costs to have three hundred triremes at sea a *year* before you plan to attack?'

Greek slaves averted their eyes while serving us, so that we would not look into their faces. But some cried.

One young boy broke down while serving Bulis. Bulis put a hand on his head and whispered something in his ear.

Hydarnes looked at the Spartan from his dais. 'Come, my friend,' he said. 'You must talk to us, and not to our slaves. Tell us all why you men of Lacedaemon decline to say you will be the friends of the Great King. You have but to look at me and my fortune to see that the king knows well how to honour merit. In like manner you yourselves, if you would only make your submission to the Great King, would receive great gifts and land from his hands, seeing that he deems you men of merit.'

Bulis rose to his feet. 'Hydarnes,' he said, 'you understand less than half of the story. You tell me that if I am a good slave, I will be rewarded for surrendering my freedom, and that may have been your own experience.'

I had never heard Bulis speak so well. But Spartans are full of surprises. Bulis's interpreter stumbled when he reached the insult – the sting in the tail, as we Greeks say. He fell silent.

I stood up and finished Bulis's statement in Persian.

Bulis raised his voice to continue. 'I am merely a citizen of Sparta, and perhaps I misunderstand. But it seems to me that you have all your life been a slave to this king, and since you have never been free, you have no idea how sweet liberty might be. Because if you had tasted it,' Bulis said, and he smiled at the boy who had cried, 'then, as I see you are a man, you would have fought not just with your spear for freedom, but with axes and knives and even with the nails on your fingers.'

So he answered Hydarnes. As I translated, I was quite sure that I had the same smile on my face that I wear when I fight.

Hydarnes was obviously annoyed, and equally obviously unwilling to show it. But at the end of dinner, he stood and waved at me in a way that had to have been insulting.

'Tomorrow I hunt lion,' he said. 'A great man-killer is preying on my slaves. Come ride with me, and let us see who is a man, and who is a slave.'

He hadn't included the Spartans. That made sense – as heralds, they were exempt from all challenges and all contests. And sacred.

I was not, so I rose and bowed. 'I would be delighted,' I said.

Later that night, I lay in bed and listened as Greek slaves were beaten with rods in the courtyard. I'm sure they beat the boy – he had laughed aloud when Bulis spoke, and Hector liked him.

But there are ways and ways of scoring one's victories. The next day, I hunted in the mountains with Cyrus and Hydarnes. I could tell that neither liked the other – indeed, I had seen Cyrus grin like a daemon when Bulis's insult went home, so I understood that we had some latitude here. But I was determined that I would rescue something from here.

My goods – Athenian goods – had fetched shockingly high prices on the wharves. Sekla reported to me in the dawn as we mounted our horses for the hunt, and I knew that I had silver. So, when our dogs had run the lion and it was cornered in a stand of trees – alien trees, of a kind I'd never seen before, with yellow flowers – while the party sorted out their weapons, I turned to Sallis, who was with me most of the time.

'If I wanted to buy a few of the Greek slaves who have pleased me, what then?' I asked.

Sallis made a face – the face Asians make when they are prepared to haggle. 'If they are the Great King's slaves, we may not sell them,' he said. 'If they are my master's slaves, all is well.'

I described the boy and I named the two Aeolian women – Sappho and Lysistrata.

Sallis shrugged. 'But you didn't lie with either of them,' he said.

I found Sallis to be – it is hard to say what I found him to be. Comprehensible? Easier to understand than Hydarnes? A fellow sufferer under the yoke of Persia? A man with a sense of humour? Perhaps all of these things.

'They are the daughters of a man who was my friend,' I said. That stretched the matter a little, but not much.

He nodded in complete understanding. 'Ah! If you appealed so to Hydarnes, he might give them to you.'

'I would prefer to buy them,' I said.

'You do not want to owe my master anything?' he asked. He looked past me to where one of Hydarnes' guardsmen was handing out spears. 'You are wise, for a Greek.' He looked away. 'Babylon revolted just last year, and one of my cousins was taken for the Great King's house.' He shrugged. 'Among us, it is no dishonour.'

A guardsman, face wrapped against the dust and wearing the most ridiculous trousers I'd ever seen – and I had seen Gallic noblemen – handed me a spear so magnificent that I lost the thread of our conversation for a moment. It was steel, blued with care, inlaid with gold, and the sarauter was of solid silver. It was a lonche, just seven feet long, and the head was sharp enough to cut like a good sword.

'My master bids you take this spear and join him for the kill,' the guardsman said.

I slid from my horse. Sallis was suddenly fighting his.

It was the terror of Sallis's mare that gave me space in which to live.

I have to tell this tale backwards and say that the lion, cornered by dogs in a stand of trees, was an old and wily campaigner, and he had, in fact, killed two dogs and then slipped away from the pack, gone down the ravine behind the woods – a ravine we hadn't seen – and now, like the man-killer he was, he was stalking us.

He'd come up the ravine, and his scent panicked all the horses at once. Men were thrown. Better riders, like Sallis, had their hands full.

In Persia, one is supposed to kill the lion with a spear, from horse-back or on foot – usually after the dogs have softened it up a bit.

I saw the beast. He was coming at us through the grass, with the swagger of a killer and the eyes of a madman. His head was low, but he was scarcely troubling himself with concealment. He'd picked his quarry, and he was intent only on his kill.

Hector.

Hector saw him. But he froze – his feet seemed to have grown roots.

I'd never faced a lion before, so I did everything wrong. I didn't expect it to be so fast, and I rather expected it to ... I don't know, to hesitate, or to pause, or to *ready itself* before attacking.

Instead, two horse-lengths from Hector, it went from its swaggering lope to a leap. It was in the air.

Calchas and Polymarchos saved Hector. A lifetime of training and nothing else. I don't remember anything but its stinking breath and the cat dead, my spear cleanly impaled so deep in its neck that it emerged at the back, and I had to do a little bit of undignified scrambling to avoid the dying energy of its claws, which still got my thigh – see these scars, thugater? Four lines all parallel.

It was a three-day wonder, and the infection that Apollo shot into my thigh was a two-week wonder and more, giving me strange dreams and making riding an agony. But that was in the future. At that moment, I stood in the grass with the dead lion at my feet, and turned to find Hydarnes behind me, empty handed because in the commotion caused by the panicking horses he hadn't got a spear.

I'd been living with the Spartans for some time, at that point. I'm very proud of what came next. I turned to my host and bowed, with the dead lion at my feet and my own blood running down my leg.

'Good spear,' I said.

That night I was feasted like a god. The wound had not yet begun to trouble me. And when the feast was over, and Hector had cleared away my gifts – a fortune in cups and the spear I had used – I went back to my chambers only to find Sallis standing at the entrance.

He handed me three clay tablets. 'I have arranged that all three shall be sold to you. My master accepted your offer of three mina of silver without quibble, and your slave Sekla has already paid me.'

Sekla was no man's slave, but he was a good actor.

I offered my hand. 'May I offer you my guest-friendship? Among Greeks, this is a sacred thing.'

He looked surprised. But he took my hand. 'With thanks, my lord. I am but a servant—'

'You are a good man,' I said. 'Come and feast with me in Greece, when all this is over.'

Sallis bowed. 'My lord – I will.' He nodded. 'And I ... if you pass Babylon, let me send a letter to my sister.'

So I made Sallis a friend. And went into my chambers, to find two beautiful women and an eleven-year-old boy, all weeping together. They had Hector weeping too.

All of them – except Hector – came to me on their knees, thanking me and praising me. Now, every man craves the good opinion of others, whether he admits it or not, but these three – it was too much.

I was gruff, and sent them away.

Hector came to me a little later. The wound was just starting to bother me. Hector waited silently until I gave him leave to speak, which I did with a wave.

'I could take the boy,' he said. 'I could use the help. You are a demanding master.' He spoke solemnly.

It is true that Hector was my manservant and my armour carrier and my signals officer and sometimes my secretary. And like most men with slaves and servants, I'd provided him with freedom and some real benefits, but I hadn't really noticed how much he did.

'He's free. I suspect he's nobly born. He may not want to be the hypaspist to a hypaspist.' I raised my eyebrows.

'He wants to be a warrior,' Hector said.

185

I nodded. 'He was born in the right time,' I said.

Hector frowned and looked at the floor. 'So do I,' he said. 'But the lion ... I was ... I was ...' He turned his head away and the word came out as a sob. 'Afraid.'

I laughed. I agree, it was probably the wrong thing to do, but really – adolescent boys and their fancies. As bad as girls. *The same as girls*. Who puts these ideas in their heads?

Homer, that's who.

He flinched from my anger and I grabbed his shoulders. It was really the first time I'd hugged him. I know that sounds odd, but he was a very grave boy, and he'd lost his father. His reserve was very ... adult.

But I grabbed him and wrestled him into an embrace as he burst into angry, humiliated tears. I said all the things older men say to boys about courage, and he didn't listen – like all boys.

Lysistrata and her sister appeared with their bedding. They drew the wrong conclusions and withdrew, but as Hector began to recover, Lysistrata came back with a bowl and a towel. She paused in the doorway and met my eyes. She was a fine woman – intelligent and sensitive and tough enough to survive in a harem.

Hector fled.

Lysistrata came in and made the sort of bow that women make to fathers or husbands at religious ceremonies – at least in Plataea. I agree that in Ionia they can be both more and less formal.

'I have some small skill at healing, my lord,' she said. 'And the wound on your thigh is more dangerous than you think.'

I took the bowl and started to wash my thigh, and considered how to get her into my bed without taking advantage of my power over her. Of course, we all know the answer to that. But I am as human as the next man, and just then, I didn't want her healing powers. Or rather, I wanted her to heal me of the stare of the lion's eyes, because they held my death.

She mistook my hesitation. 'I will not fawn on you, my lord. But ... what care has this wound received?'

I shook my head, embarrassed by my own desire. 'I wiped it with grass,' I said.

She shook her head, all business. 'Lion's claws carry every kind of disease,' she said. She had me lie down, and then, with Hector and her sister helping, scrubbed the wounds until it was all I could do not to scream. She put honey into each wound after dribbling wine on them.

I suspect she saved my life.

When the other two were gone, sex was the farthest thing from my mind. I *hurt*. She rubbed my upper back for a little while. 'My sister and I would like to sleep in your apartment, lord,' she said, somewhat dreamily.

I agreed. Of course they wanted to escape.

The next day, I was almost speechless with fever. The fever lasted three days, and when it passed, I was as weak as a child. Despite which, our party was ready to ride for Susa via Babylon, three thousand stades away.

I sent the two Greek women to my ships. I had a farewell conference with Sekla, and directed him to meet me at Ephesus in late winter. I gave him a letter for Artaphernes and another for Briseis, and wished him – and Meglakles and Harpagos – well. I took Brasidas and left the rest of the marines.

If it came to a fight, we weren't going to cut our way out of Persia.

I sat my three Spartans down on the tiled porch of my magnificent apartment in the palace. My thigh was alternating cold and hot, and I had had two dreams of Herakles and one of the lion's eyes. But I wasn't dead, and I needed these men. Because of my wound, I was blunt.

'I need all three of you to get along well enough to serve together. This is not about Sparta only, but about all of Greece. Bulis, I ask you to treat Brasidas with honour.'

Bulis's face was as absent of emotion as the lion's had been. 'I will do Brasidas all honour,' he said in his eerily flat voice.

I looked at Sparthius and he laughed his comedian's laugh. 'Don't look at me. I have always honoured Brasidas.'

Brasidas looked at me with the slight smile of a man who has received an unexpected injury from a friend.

I thought, *Damn it! Why did I get this wrong?*

But the three exchanged a kiss of peace and a hand clasp, and I thought Bulis and Brasidas lingered for a moment.

When they were gone, Hector approached me cautiously. He looked at Brasidas, just walking down the front steps and being greeted by Cyrus. The two were obviously discussing the pack animals.

'You tell me never to listen to the gossip of slaves,' Hector said.

I raised an eyebrow. 'I agree that it's hard advice to follow,' I said.

'Sparthius's helot has been teaching me some wrestling,' he said, which neatly implied that I hadn't. The young are very good at placing the knife. 'He says ... he says Brasidas exiled *himself*. He says that Brasidas refused to pay his mess bill and left. But he doesn't know why, except ...' Hector had the good manners to blush, since he was now repeating pure hearsay. '... Except that he's heard of Brasidas referred to as the only man in the world who hates Leonidas.'

I nodded. I could barely think – I was still fevered.

'And I want to thank you for saving my life,' he went on, as if that was the less important item. 'I want to apologise for breaking down last night. Sappho says ...'

I raised both eyebrows.

He turned bright red.

'Oh,' I said. 'It's like that, is it?' I shook my head. 'I'm sending her home to Chios, my lad. I'll send you to the ship to say your goodbyes.'

He stammered something, but he went to the ship eagerly enough.

Youth. Wasted on the young. Or perhaps not.

Riding was agony – first because of my thigh, and second because I was dizzy all the time, but I couldn't send them on without me, as Cyrus was *my* escort, not theirs. And the first three days were all climbing – up and up and up into the highlands. We passed a number of ancient monuments in those three days – a statue of an Assyrian king, lording over a slave; a small pyramid that marked some feat of arms by an Aegyptian king – it was like a road of wonders. Truly, northern Syria is where all worlds meet – Persia and Babylon, Urarit and Phrygia and Palestine and Aegypt – and Greece.

Lysistrata had left Hector with thorough directions on my wound, and we put infusions on it, and I drank tea – tea made of something like sage, although it had a bitter taste that was only saved by honey. But the first two weeks of that journey are lost to me, and even the Spartans commiserated, which suggested to me that I was doing well in the endless contest of manhood.

In fact, my recovery dated from the first day we reached a post house on the Royal Road. The Royal Road runs from Susa to Sardis, and does not go south to Tarsus. So we spent two weeks riding north to catch it in central Lydia.

My fever broke – for good – in a small stone post house at what appeared to be the top of the world. I ate, and Hector pressed my hand, and Cyrus admitted that he had feared for my life. It was all very gratifying.

I also discovered that I had slowed them all down. Because after two days on the Royal Road, when I'd eaten a huge meal of mutton and then demanded a few gallops to cheer my restless horse, Cyrus announced we were going to move faster – and suddenly, despite our forty men and ten pack animals, we began to make real time, travelling as far as two hundred stades a day.

The second or third night on the Royal Road, I found that Aristides had put his bedroll next to mine. And Bulis moved Nikeas's bedroll over two places, and he and Sparthius moved into my corner. Only important royal guests received the right to live in the post houses – which were like small inns. Most people slept outside them, and indeed there were rows of small shelters of varying degrees of craft built outside, and while some post houses were empty of visitors, others were packed with people and herds.

Indeed, the roads and the post houses were among the greatest wonders of the empire.

At any rate, when the satrap's guardsmen settled down, Aristides rolled as close to me as a lover. 'It is good to have you back,' he said. 'Have you looked in the store houses?'

I hadn't even seen a store house.

'They're stuffed with grain,' he said. 'I looked in the grain barn here – it is also packed. There is enough grain in that barn to feed ten thousand men.' He squeezed my shoulder. 'I know what I'm saying – I'm a farmer.'

Bulis spoke out of the dark behind me. 'He's getting the road ready for his army,' he said.

I chuckled. 'Perhaps we could arrange for an army of rats,' I suggested.

Bulis all but hissed. 'That would not lead to the contest we desire,' he said.

As we descended from the mountains into the valleys of the Tigris and the Euphrates, the preparations of the Persians and Medes became more obvious. At every town, men were conducting inspections. Every forge was busy making spears and armour. Horse herds were being moved into the autumn grazing, and the harvest was coming in, and there were government men everywhere, collecting, enforcing – the power of the Persian bureaucracy was staggering compared to anything I'd seen in Greece, and their taxation was the heaviest I could imagine on the Babylonians.

It was hot and sticky, and my hip still hurt. I had aches in my back that seemed to connect with my pelvis, and even regular massage – in this, at least, the Persians are our brothers – didn't seem to fix the injury. Muscles had been damaged. My body was far more deeply hurt than I had thought.

The area between the rivers was the most intensely cultivated I had ever seen. It made Boieotia and Green Plataea appear a howling wilderness. Laced with canals and irrigation ditches, the fields rolled away in an endless embroidery of man's handiwork on the face of the earth, and the canals and irrigation ditches were *old*. We passed the ruins of cities that our guides told us were more than two thousand years old – one they claimed was four thousand years old.

Cyrus rode by my side. It was the longest time we'd spent together since my youth, and he was eager to see his home and his father. And we were delighted to find that the friendship of youth had been built on stone, not sand. We fenced with sticks and wrestled and raced our horses and even shot bows, and we were well matched at all but the last, where he was utterly my master.

And I began to be serious about Hector's training. With no less than three Spartans, we were quite the travelling school of martial prowess, and as the three Spartans seemed disposed to share their knowledge, Hector had two months of the finest instruction that a man could have on wrestling, boxing, grappling, the use of the sword and knife, the spear and the bow. Cyrus joined us every day, although public martial exercise was not a Persian notion, and men – and women – would emerge from their travel shelters, or in town would come out of their houses to watch us exercise.

In one town in Mesopotamia, Brasidas spent the evening hours in the most mosquito-infested place I'd ever been, teaching spear fighting to Babylonian youths. There was some wrestling, and when he finally joined us, he looked grave.

'These men are very well trained,' he said. 'They are not Spartans, but they are not soft.' He glanced at Bulis. 'Who is it who says the Medes are soft?'

Bulis shook his head. 'Only a fool,' he agreed.

It was an hour before I realised that I had seen Brasidas and Bulis speak to each other.

But Cyrus, who shared my chamber, laughed. 'These are not Persians or Medes,' he said. 'These are Babylonians. By our standards, they *are* soft.'

Because of my letters for Sallis, we detoured a little off the Royal Road to visit Babylon. Greeks have been coming to Babylon since the time of the poetess Sappho or before – her brother served there, as you all know. We've all heard of the hanging gardens and the temple of Marduk and we know that Greeks lie.

The men who had seen Babylon only lied by diminution.

First, it was the most populous city I have ever seen – even more so than Thebes in Aegypt. I cannot imagine how many men and women live in Babylon – slaves and free, they are uncountable. But the temple of Marduk towers over all, and the gardens are like a mountain covered in plants, as the designer intended, for the story is that they were built by a great king of Babylon for his wife, who missed her home in the mountains.

And the temple of Marduk? Or, to be specific, the *ziggurat*? It is a mountain made by men for the gods. Perhaps it is as tall as the acropolis of Athens. Perhaps it is not.

Neither one was the greatest marvel of this city.

And on the plains outside the gates was an army – a magnificent army of horsemen and chariots and armoured infantry. Cyrus told me that Babylon was on the edge of revolt – that despite being one of the core kingdoms of the Persian Empire, Babylon craved its independence.

We were breakfasting on the walls, drinking the very sweet date wine and eating little rolls of wheat flower with butter and honey. If Babylonians are a little soft, they should be forgiven. Truly, it is a land of plenty.

Cyrus was watching the army drill.

'It was a mistake for the Great King to permit them to assemble,' he grumbled.

Now, to be honest, I had almost never heard Cyrus criticise Xerxes. That's merely good policy – I might rant against bad government in Plataea, to another Plataean, but I would not air my dirty laundry to a Spartan or a Persian.

Nonetheless, I had seen signs that Cyrus and his men did not love the current regime. For one thing, it was as plain as the nose on his face – and Cyrus had quite the nose – that he detested Hydarnes. Cyrus, far from resenting the Spartan heralds, seemed to enjoy Hydarnes' discomfiture.

And there had been a day or so at Hydarnes' court when it

appeared that the satrap would be with us on the road, and Cyrus had writhed in annoyance.

But this was overt criticism.

I leaned out over the railing. We were guests in one of the Great King's many palaces. Slaves bustled about, seeing to our needs with a level of obsequious fear that I found unpleasant.

'Why?' I asked. 'They seem like a mighty host.'

Cyrus shook his head. 'Xerxes seeks always to please all men,' he said. 'He is not as sure of himself as a Great King must be. The Babylonians remain loyal to us only when they fear us. Babylon and Persia are *not friends*. If these men drill together, they will only convince each other that they must resist us.' He met my eye.

I smiled. 'Which would be the best thing for Greece, would it not?' I asked. That famous Persian honesty could be used.

Cyrus was no fool. 'Oh, revolt in Babylon would stop the invasion, at least for a time.'

In fact, what I saw out there on the plains of Mesopotamia was an army of almost fifty *thousand* men, most of whom were armoured. Almost a quarter of them were mounted. The charioteers outnumbered the entire phalanx of Plataea.

I watched them exercise, and Bulis joined me. We watched them all day.

Towards evening, they passed back into the city through the main gate to the cheers of a crowd so huge I couldn't count them.

'Do you want to fight them?' I asked Bulis.

He smiled – the man who never changed expression.

'Yes,' he said.

The army of Babylon was incredible. Vast, well armoured, and beloved of their people. But that was not the most magnificent spectacle Babylon had to offer.

I was lying about in Babylon because the heat and the insects had put me back into my fevers, and I was sick for several days, and spent them watching the army drill. But on my fourth day in the largest city in the world, I rose, took Hector and a pair of local slaves, and went to the house of Sallis's sister with his letters to her.

I have no notion of what Sallis said to his sister in those letters. But like saving Polypeithes' chariot on the plains of Alpheos, it was one of the pivotal moments of the war. The world turns on the whims of the gods, and on the actions of men of whom no one will ever hear.

Sallis had impressed me as a gentleman, but he'd never mentioned wealth or power, and he seemed to me to be a senior servant, so I suppose that I had imagined his sister as a portly matron of forty, living with her husband the dye merchant in some narrow but attractive street. Indeed, when I gathered my little group to attend her, I worried that Hector and two slaves might appear too long a tail for her and might make me seem arrogant.

In fact, Sallis's sister was the wife and widow of a man who might have been King of Babylon, and she lived in a palace larger than the one in which I was housed, hard by the great temple. It occupied the whole of a low hill, and had its own garden – this *inside* the walls of the most densely populated place in the world. Nor was the complex a single building or even three or four around a central yard. It was a dozen buildings – a hall, a small temple, a stables, a barracks for slaves, another for soldiers.

I stood and gaped like a hick. In fact, Babylon made me feel a bumpkin every minute.

I was rescued by my borrowed slaves, who ran – in the most intense heat I'd ever known – into the slave barracks and came back with directions to the 'main' palace. And a further escort. And then we were briefly interrogated by military retainers in fine armour – coats of bronze plates, some tinned to look like silver. They wore pointy helmets that made them look like exotic animals, and officers wore turbans of linen wound around the peaks.

No one spoke Persian but my borrowed slaves. So all conversations were three sided.

In the end, I met a supercilious major-domo who took my letters and dismissed me like a slave. I shrugged – I still, at that point, was not sure that Sallis's sister wasn't the wife of a senior servant. I really wasn't any too sure what my slaves were telling me, and Hector was as confused as I, and we had a good laugh about it when we returned to the Great King's palace.

Ah, what a fine question, thugater! Of course, the Great King almost never came to Babylon, and at that moment, Xerxes, King over Kings, was hunting lions in the valley below Susa, another thousand stades away. But his palace in Babylon was kept open for visitors and messengers and ambassadors.

At any rate, Hector and I lay on a couple of kline and mocked ourselves to Brasidas and Cyrus and Aristides, who were entertained.

Aristides actually broke through his reserve and had to swing his feet to the floor as Hector described the Hero of Marathon, stammering to a bored Babylonian slave driver.

But that was not the end of the letters. Before the evening came and the oil lamps could be lit, the very same major-domo appeared, ushered in by the Master of the Palace, a Persian gentleman who'd greeted us on arrival and had scarcely been seen since.

Aristides was still there, helping Hector with his rhetoric.

The major-domo threw himself on the floor at my feet.

I laughed. Greeks always do, when foreigners do this thing. It's comic. A man's arse sticks up in the air – anyway, it is most certainly not Greek.

But the Persian fetched Cyrus, and we had a four-sided conversation, from which I eventually understood that the major-domo had mistaken me for an unimportant slave, and his mistress, upon reading the letters, had sent him with a sword that I could use to kill him if I so desired.

The Master of the Palace – yet another Darius, of course – told me that this was merely good manners, and assured me that I was welcome to kill the man.

'Are you a slave?' I asked the man.

He raised his head. 'No, lord.'

'He sounds like a slave to me,' Aristides said.

I raised the man and took the sword. 'Translate for me,' I said to one of the Babylonian slaves. 'In Greece, from where I come, one of the greatest sins a man can commit is to treat a free man like a slave. We call it hubris.'

The man closed his eyes and tensed his neck muscles.

'But no one is allowed to execute a free man for hubris.' I shrugged. 'I forgive you. I am a foreigner and you had no idea who I was.'

It was a superb sword. It was made with that pattern welding that the chalcedonies do so well. The hilt was odd – not my style at all, with no cross-guard to protect the hand. I gave it to him.

'Please keep the sword, master, as a gift from my lady. And I thank you for the gift of my life, and it would be my extreme pleasure to escort you to her. In fact,' he said, suddenly quite cheerful, 'in fact, unless you have another engagement, she insists.'

His change of demeanour was very much in keeping with everything and everyone I knew in Babylon. They were ... mercurial.

I took a little trouble over clothes and cloak, although without trousers I looked like a freak to every man and woman on the streets – no one wants to wear an embroidered wool cloak on a hot summer night in Babylon. I wore the sword I'd been given.

The Master of the Palace, who seemed to be quite slow to Cyrus, provided me with a train of slaves – a dozen – and I took both Hector and his young apprentice, who had filled out on the road and shot up a foot with the plentiful meat that came from the bows of my Persian escort.

To make a better show – at the Master of the Palace's suggestion – we rode horses.

This time, our greeting at the gate was utterly different, and we were ushered directly to the main hall after a very embarrassed captain of the guard had given me his personal apologies in the most astoundingly bad Persian. I left Brasidas to attempt conversation, and one of my multilingual borrowed slaves.

After all, it seemed like a golden opportunity to gather some information. I no longer believed we had a chance of convincing the Great King to keep his armies out of Greece, and that, in turn, meant that our next duty was the collection of information.

And then I went to meet Sallis's sister.

The main hall was ablaze with torches and lined in heavy columns of green marble shot with white. Two of the columns had gold – actual gold – inlaid in them, and they framed the lady as she sat in splendour on a dais, surrounded by women in magnificent layered robes.

Not a fat merchant's wife, then.

There were a dozen armoured men in the spaces between the heavy pillars. The warm air was spiced with incense, and the women around her were beautiful. She herself was no older than twenty-five, and she wore enough gold to pay a taxeis of mercenaries for a year. Her eyes were slightly slanted in the Eastern way, almond-shaped and black. Her brows were also jet black and they shone against her skin, which seemed as if it was golden in the torchlight.

I gave her the bow I had not given to Hydarnes, touching my right knee briefly to the marble floor.

She rose from her throne – it looked like a throne to me – and came forward and took my hand and kissed me – on the mouth.

'A guest-friend of my brother! Staying with the Persians! I assume you found my house unacceptable, and I am mortified.'

A clever person can say one thing and mean another. She spoke excellent Persian – better than mine – and to me, her meaning was clear – *We've had a misunderstanding and it is time to move on.*

Her kiss burned on my lips.

I met her eye, and like Gorgo, she looked back without flinching or dropping her eyes.

'I am very sorry for any misunderstanding, my lady. Your brother asked me to carry his letters, but said nothing further.'

She smiled at me. 'Of course he did not. And I understand that you are guests of the Great King, and thus it may be more politic to stay in the Great King's palace and not share my poor food and flea-ridden beds.' She curtsied. 'I am flattered that you have come at all, and hope my poor house is worthy to receive you.'

I sighed. 'I am but a foolish barbarian and your sarcasm is wasted on me,' I said.

She leaned in close. 'I have never found sarcasm to be wasted on a Greek,' she said. She made a motion with her hand, and the soldiers marched away. 'We will be served a private dinner. Will you dismiss your slaves?'

'Yes,' I said. 'But several of them are not slaves. The young man and the boy are free men – my shield bearer and helmet bearer. Noble youths.'

Women came forward. 'They will be suitably entertained,' she said.

As private dinners go, it was tolerably public. I think I counted forty servants waiting on us. We dined in a tent made of gauze, which admitted the light of sunset and the breeze, but kept the insects at bay, although every tray of food coming into the tent probably brought a new battalion. We had six courses and wines, and as the evening wore on, the need for privacy seemed tolerably remote.

Despite which, Sallis's sister Arwia was beautiful. It was more than beauty, however. I was captivated as soon as I heard her speak, and nothing about her was less than desirable, so that as the meal wore on, I had to count horses and stare at servants and at one point excused myself and walked around her garden.

Nor did the lady in question do anything to encourage me, beyond meeting my eye from time to time and laughing a great deal. Few things encourage a man like a woman who will laugh at his jokes.

She was a fine listener, and not just a slavish one. I have known women who ask questions automatically, because they have learned that it is their role to entertain men, and men like few things better than to talk about themselves. No – you needn't deny it. But Arwia asked questions and then asked further questions, searching, probing – sometimes mocking, sometimes dismissive or even acerbic.

She would stare into my eyes and ask another question, and another, and it was as if she were getting closer to me. She was not. She sat cross-legged on the other side of a low table and each of us also had a sort of elbow table where slaves placed our wine. We were separated by the table and by cushions, as both of us half sat and half reclined, and for part of the meal, owing to a religious custom, she sat partially screened by a fine net.

It did not screen her eyes, or her voracious questions.

'You are Jawan?' she asked, quite early.

We had to feel our way through Jawan, which turned out to have a meaning not too dissimilar to 'Ionian'. In fact, it turns out to be the Babylonian/Assyrian word for Greeks – if you allow that Asian Ionians are Greeks.

When I thought about it, it was rather the way we kept expecting Persians to behave like their cousins, the Scythians.

We then passed half an hour as I described the Greek world, and the Mediterranean. She listened with perfect attention and at one point summoned a slave to write some things down.

'Where is Sparta?' she asked. Sparta was, it turned out, the only western Greek city of which she'd heard, and when I told her that it was scarcely a city, but more like an assembly of four rural towns, and that the greatest cities in the Greek world were Athens and Corinth, she shrugged. She'd heard of Corinth, and sent a slave to get a jar, which proved to be the old Corinthian ware of my grandfather's time.

'There used to be just such a pitcher on my mother's table,' I said.

'What happened to it?' she asked.

'My brother knocked it off the table with his elbow,' I admitted.

'Ah! You have a brother. How old is he?' she asked.

In truth, I scarcely ever thought of him, but I said, 'He has been dead since I was thirteen. Twenty years or so.'

'How did he die?' she asked, tearing at a round of unleavened bread with which to take her next course of food.

'A Spartan killed him,' I said.

'And then your people were conquered by the Spartans?' she asked. 'And yet you are the lord of the embassy, and the Spartans are your servants.'

I think I nearly spat my wine, and I'm glad that none of my Spartan friends were there to hear her. 'We are allies,' I said. 'The Spartans never conquered us. We came to an equitable peace.'

She snorted. 'Equitable peace?' she asked. 'What's that?'

Occasionally I used the wrong Persian word. It was not my first language, or hers, so we had some very funny confusions.

And through it all, she ate. This woman, who was not very much above five feet in height, managed to eat every bit as much as I ate. She drank wine, and the wine was particularly odd – heavily spiced, with odd ingredients. The more of it I drank the more awake I became, the more fluent I felt, and the more intoxicated I became with my hostess.

Her eyes had begun to shine in a way that women's eyes are spoken of by the poets, but seldom appear. I had just paid her some compliment – flattered her beauty, I suspect, and she put a hand to her mouth and giggled like a girl.

'Among the Jawan, do you use the poppy in wine?' she asked.

I shook my head. 'No. We water our wine, and sometimes we add spice or honey if the wine is a trifle off. Poppy juice is for medicine.'

'Hemp seeds?' she asked. 'Lotus flowers?'

I shook my head. 'I have heard of all these things being given to wounded men,' I said, 'Or women in childbirth.'

She giggled again.

We drank more wine.

We had some amazing confection of ground pistachio and almond in honey – at least, that's what I think it was. It filled me with energy, and I began to talk very quickly. By then we were on to war, and I was explaining – probably with wide-mouthed pomposity – the manner in which Greeks made war.

She nodded. And asked about our siege equipment.

'How would a Greek army go about taking Babylon?' she asked.

I remember being amused. 'No Greek army could get here,' I said.

'We have had Jawan mercenaries. Good men – as good as Carians. Head to toe in bronze.' She was lying back, now, and her eyes were almost slits.

'And you have an army many times as great as any Greek army I've ever seen,' I said.

She waved dismissively. 'The Persians beat us like a drum,' she said. 'They killed my oldest brother and my husband. And unlike you, my dear, I do not forgive or forget.'

A slave came and removed the screen that separated us, and the table.

Another slave put an iced dish next to me. I ate it. It was superb. It was iced berries in some sort of frozen water, like snow. It may even have been snow. On a hot summer night amidst incense burners, an iced drink makes you feel you are one with the gods.

'If the army were beaten, my Greeks would still not be great enough to surround this city,' I said.

She was half asleep. 'The Persians can surround us utterly. They can bring a hundred thousand men – two hundred thousand.'

'No king on earth can feed two hundred thousand men and all their slaves and pack animals,' I said.

She sat up. 'Yes, he can,' she said. 'He can fill the plains from here to Ninivet with men. The Great King can raise a million men – and feed them.' She lay back. 'I know. You must believe me.'

I shrugged. Always humour a lady. 'I'm not sure there are a million Greek hoplites,' I said. 'Or even a hundred thousand.'

She shook her head lazily. 'But you have a great fleet,' she said.

I thought of Athens and Aegina – mortal foes. 'Only if we can agree among ourselves,' I said.

About this time it began to dawn on me that I was very drunk. And further, that all the lights were gone except the oil lamps on our elbow tables. And finally – that we were alone.

She rose on one elbow and looked at me. 'You have fewer than a hundred thousand soldiers?' she asked.

I nodded.

'And ships? Five hundred triremes?' she asked.

'In the whole world of the Hellenes, there are not four hundred triremes,' I said. 'Perhaps if we were allied to Gelon of Syracusa.'

'He is Jawan?' she asked.

It was my turn to wave dismissively. 'Not really,' I answered.

'How many soldiers does *your* city command?' she asked, and for the first time she leaned towards me. Her unbound breasts pressed down against the fabric of her gown – a very fine linen.

'Fifteen hundred on her best day,' I said proudly.

She laughed – surprised and not well pleased. 'And the Spartans?' she asked.

I shrugged. 'Five thousand Spartans. Perhaps thirty thousand Peloponnesian allies.' I leaned forward too.

I knew she was working me for information. But I could not see her as an ally of the Great King. And I wanted her. I just kept leaning a little closer.

She laughed, and her breath was warm and wine-scented on my face. 'You will fight the Great King with four hundred ships and fifty thousand men!' she said. 'You are insanely stupid or very brave.'

I leaned one more inch and put my lips on hers.

For a long time – perhaps three or four beats of our hearts – our lips just touched.

And then she gave a little moan of pleasure and rolled off her pillows and into my arms.

We kissed for a long time. I had just moved my hand to roll my thumb around her nipple when she looked up into my face.

'How soon could your fleet attack?' she asked.

Perhaps the most erotic question I've ever been asked.

No one interrupted us. Allow me to say that as a nobly born widow in Babylon, the lady had no strictures to her behaviour – she entertained me quite publicly, and bragged that she'd set a fashion for having a foreign soldier as a lover.

Let me also say that she was beautiful. Her shoulders and neck were muscular – she was, in fact, a passionate huntress and archer – and her great dark eyes and shining black hair were magnificent.

She never stopped. In the middle of the most indecent intimacy, she would turn her head almost all the way around and say, 'Where do the Jawans get their golden hair?' or equally, 'Can you sail from the Jawan seas to our sea?'

Her passion – besides the obvious – was revenge on Persia for the death of her husband, whom she had obviously loved very much. He had been a senior military commander, and had been executed. She could tell me about him while I fondled her. She could chat about the possibility of a Babylonian revolt . . . Never mind. I'll make you all blush. And it was the possibility of the Babylonians revolting again that got me to tell all this in the first place.

She wanted me to bring my fleet to the aid of her city.

I related all this – less the salacious details – the next day to my Athenian and Spartan friends while we played Polis in the sunshine. I had had no sleep at all, and somewhere deep in the morning, Arwia had admitted to me that I'd been drinking drugged wine since the evening began.

Brasidas snorted his wine.

Bulis looked away.

Sparthius laughed his easy laugh. 'Trust you to get a princess while the rest of us are bitten by insects.'

Aristides raised an eyebrow. 'I will leave to the side the abrogation of your responsibility to your guest-friend for the preservation of his sister's honour,' he said coldly.

For perhaps the first and last time, Bulis rolled his eyes.

I looked down. 'I promise you that the lady's reputation will suffer no harm from me,' I said. 'Customs here are different.'

Aristides sniffed.

Bulis leaned towards me. 'If the Babylonians are really ready to revolt,' he said. He looked around.

Sparthius nodded. 'Everything I see says that the Great King is ready to march on us in the spring. Everything is ready. Armies, food, roads, ships – the canal and the bridges.'

I nodded. 'Everything but the adversary,' I said. 'We Greeks are not ready.'

Aristides rubbed the top of his head. 'Just so,' he said. 'And we wouldn't be ready in the spring if we flew home now under Hermes' outstretched arms.'

Later that afternoon, Cyrus kept me from a nap that might have saved me and sat me down in the courtyard.

'You spent the night with the Lady Arwia,' he said.

I smiled a smug and probably unwise smile.

He nodded. 'She is wicked, that one,' he said. 'She is a rebel, and the Great King should have shortened her by a head when he killed her husband. What did she tell you?'

I shrugged.

'Come, brother. What did she ask you to do?'

I chuckled. 'Modesty forbids,' I said.

Cyrus smiled, then. 'You pleasured each other? That is all?'

'She asked me a thousand thousand questions about the Jawan and their lands, even when I was riding her,' I said.

He nodded. 'But no ... politics?'

I shrugged. 'I heard her speak fifty kinds of treason. Who minds what a woman says, when she is willing?'

He nodded. Bluff, empty-headed, woman-using Arimnestos – eh?

'I hope to see her again tonight,' I said.

'Indeed, your invitation – with all your Spartans and Athenians

– is in the palace even now.' He rose and we exchanged bows. 'Tomorrow we will ride for Susa. I need to get my head out of this crotch of pests. Into the mountains where the air is clean and cool.'

There are women – I'm sorry even to repeat this, but I've had some wine – there are women who you desire with all your being – until you've had them, and then the charm wears away. In the cold light of day, you see a thousand flaws – sometimes in them, and sometimes in yourself.

There's a brilliant Persian poem about it, which I can't remember.

But Arwia was not one of those women. The thought of her inflamed me, and when I was in her presence, I was like a boy – unable to take my eyes off her, nor to behave myself.

She seemed to revel in it, and we flirted outrageously.

But she was so skilled as a hostess that she could flirt to the point of open licentiousness with me, and still make Aristides love her. He was not besotted, but he never spoke slightingly of her again. The Spartans were utterly charmed.

Something happened which, among other men, might have led to blood. I tell this that you may better understand the Spartans.

Sparthius decided he wanted her. He knew full well I'd bedded her the night before, but he set himself to win her – with humour, with flattery, with anecdotes. He showed his muscles, he won her laughter.

He was very good.

Nor did he hide his intentions from me. As Arwia was in no way 'mine', I didn't make some feeble remark to that extent, but at one point, I did poke him sharply in the arm.

He grinned at me. 'Let the best man have her,' he said. 'I've seldom seen her like.'

She entered fully into the spirit of the thing, too. Once she realised she had both of us captivated . . .

There are some powers one should not grant to mortals.

With Aristides doting and Sparthius and I besotted, she began to target Bulis. He drank steadily, but his face remained carved in stone. I had seen him turn his head to hide his amusement at his friend, and perhaps at me, but with the lady he was careful, cautious and correct.

She had dancers. They danced. To say that they danced lasciviously would be like suggesting that the sun gives light.

First girls . . .

Then boys ...

Then boys with girls.

At some point Aristides excused himself. It was all tasteful – none of your flute-girl tricks with vegetables – but he went for a turn in the garden.

The Spartans sat and watched.

I realised that Arwia was using her erotic dancers to measure them. I watched her watch them, and I thought – *This is a very dangerous woman indeed*. Dangerous, and yet ...

And yet, we were on the same side.

After the iced drink was served, Arwia went and sat by Sparthius. He reached for her and she laughed and slipped away and put a hand on his arm. She said something.

He laughed very hard.

Then she sat by Bulis. He met her gaze with level gravity. She whispered in his ear, and he nodded – and smiled.

And finally she went and sat by Aristides. From her neck, she took a magnificent necklace of lapis and gold. She put it in his hands. 'This is for your wife,' she said.

He tried to laugh. 'How do you know I'm married?' he asked.

'Oh, for all I know, all these gentlemen have wives,' she said lightly. 'But you love yours.'

Aristides beamed. I had no wife, but I knew what she had just said, and I felt its justice.

A dangerous woman indeed.

An hour later I lay in her arms – under the stars. Under a billowing tent of gauze. With a bowl of iced fruit by my elbow.

Pah! I brag like a pimply boy. It was ... wonderful.

She lay back, snapped her fingers, and a slave disconcerted me enormously by appearing, wiping her all over with a moist towel, and vanishing into the perfumed darkness. A second slave began to wash me.

I almost leaped out of the tent.

She laughed. She laughed a great deal.

She grabbed my ankle and pulled me back into her arms. 'I know you have no fleet,' she said. 'And I know that you cannot sail from Sparta to Babylon.' She pressed her lips to my ear. 'But let me pretend you can.'

I would like to take credit for what came after. But the truth is,

Arwia saved Greece, and I had very little to do with it. We did spend the rest of the night pretending that I was going to lead a great army of Greeks through the Persian empire. She made suggestions about where they were weak, and I promised to rescue Babylon from bondage.

Oh, Babylon.

I never did learn what she said to Bulis. I know she told Sparthius that she was not woman enough to lie with both of us together. He laughed about that until his dying day.

The next morning, we rode away from the insects and the perfume and the sticky heat of love, and started up the roads into the mountains of Persia, on the last lap to Susa. Cyrus had a message from court. We were wanted.

Until then, Susa had seemed impossibly remote. Now we were less than two weeks away. And my Spartan friends, who were each as brave as men could be, suddenly seemed a little more detached. Bulis spent more time training Hector. It became a passion, pothos. Sparthius began to purchase strumpets in the way stations. He had never done any such thing.

One night Brasidas accused him of comforting the enemy. Sparthius reacted angrily. They were outside, and I began to pull my cloak around me.

Brasidas laughed. 'Every child you make with these women will be half a Spartan,' he said.

Sparthius laughed – and laughed.

At some point, Brasidas and Sparthius and Bulis had come to terms. I'd seen it happen, but it had been so gradual that I'd missed the nuances, and I didn't know what had divided them in the first place.

The trip from Babylon to Susa is not so far – a little less than two thousand stades, and all on excellent roads. Susa is the Persian winter capital – in summer, they move high in the mountains to Persepolis, which, I regret to say, I never saw. A day out from Susa, and we were on cooler plains with the mountains visible in the distance and the river at our feet, and the air, as promised, was crisper and clear and cool, even though we could all but *see* Babylon behind us. I exaggerate, but we could see far across the plains before the daytime heat shimmer struck.

We had ridden for eight days through a flood of soldiers – slingers, archers, spearmen – horse and foot.

I missed Arwia. I mention this because, for a two-night affair that a man might dismiss, I was still beyond smitten or besotted. At every stopping point, I considered making an excuse to ride back. Only Gorgo's words – that we were a conspiracy to save Greece – held me to my task.

Brasidas rode next to me as we ploughed a furrow through the soldiers of the Persian Empire.

'Do you still think that Greece can match the power of the Great King?' he asked.

'No,' I said.

He laughed. 'We're wearing off on you, Plataean. That was a Laconian answer.'

I shrugged.

'Will you try to buy peace from the Great King?' he asked.

'No,' I said. I smiled. I was getting better at playing Laconian.

'What, then?' he asked.

'We'll fight,' I said.

'And then?' he asked.

'I suppose we'll die,' I said. I was riding in a river of potential enemy spearmen. The road to Susa and Persepolis was choked with soldiers. They were everywhere – Assyrians, Elamites, Mesopotamians and Medes, horse and foot.

That night, I dreamed of Arwia, her magnificent shoulders glistening with sweat, riding atop my hips. She was, by far, the greatest wonder of Babylon. Not just as a lover – but as the force that saved Greece.

You'll see.

Susa was beautiful. It lacked the majesty and the squalor of Babylon. And the size. In truth, Susa was a fine city with a noble waterfall and two beautiful bridges, but it wasn't a great deal bigger than Plataea and it was certainly smaller than Corinth, for all that it had a more cosmopolitan population than any city in Greece save possibly Athens. The agora teemed with men – and women – from every part of the empire and many parts adjacent, and there were Greeks – and everyone else.

It is not important to this story – but I need to mention that in Susa I met both Aethiopians and Indians. I met an Indian merchant who told me that his country was one hundred and forty-four thousand stades distant, and that, on the Outer Ocean, there was a current and a set of constant winds that would move a ship from Aethiopia to India in the summer and back in the winter. His name was Abha, and we talked for days – I told him how to sail west from Ephesus, and he told me how to sail east from Bahrain. He sold me some fabric and a fine quantity of pepper, and I traded to him my last Athenian arybolos, some British pearls and a Rhodian perfume. We agreed that it did not really matter what we exchanged – our goods would be priceless rarities at their destinations at opposite ends of the earth.

Abha's role – well, if I continue to tell this, you'll meet him again.

Pardon my digression. We were met at the gates by soldiers. They were 'Immortals', as the Greeks call them. In Persian, they are called Anûšiya. Which has the same meaning as our Hetaeroi. They march with the Great King, everywhere – on campaign, on the hunt, and even in the bedchamber. There are ten thousand of them – that's true – but they come in two ranks. The Outer Companions are armed with a short spear that carries, as its sarauter, a silver apple that makes a deadly mace. The Inner Companions, the true Anûšiya, number only one thousand men, and they carry the spear with the golden apple.

There is no 'Horse Anûšiya' or hippeis, as we would call them. Every Persian noble has his own retainers, and the Great King has his own, as well, but as the Great King – at least among Persians – is far more a 'first among equals' (rather like the Kings of Sparta, in fact!) his cavalrymen are also his friends. And the Immortals are soldiers – some are nobly born, but most are commoners and some are foreign despite their Persian dress – Medes, Babylonians, even a few Greeks. They are chosen purely by military merit.

We were met at the gates by six of the Inner Guard, with golden apples on their spears, magnificent scale corselets – but without our shoulder yokes, which makes them appear far slimmer – and beautiful over-robes. Their over-robes were wool, embroidered with silk.

Silk is a kind of textile – or just possibly a form of metal – woven by spiders far to the East. I bought some in the market. It is sometimes available in Aegypt, but all of it comes from India and even farther east, in legendary Kwin.

Well! It was a day of wonders. You must let me tell it my own way.

All traffic through the gate stopped for us. Six imperial guardsmen were sufficient to guarantee us instant passage through every checkpoint. The leader of the Anûšiya chatted with Cyrus.

Suddenly he turned to me and bowed. 'I am sorry,' he said. 'My lord tells me you speak Persian, and I was treating you as an ignorant person. We never see Greeks who speak our tongue.'

I nodded. 'May the light of the sun always shine on your face,' I said.

He grinned. 'You have the accent of my home!' he cried, and slapped his thigh in delight. 'Did you learn from a man of Fars?'

I nodded. 'I have the honour to be a friend of Artapharenes, brother of Darius the Great,' I said.

Cyrus nodded. 'It is true. He was a young scamp, but we took to him. Only the gods know why. He saved my lord's life, too.'

The Anûšiya bowed low. 'Truly,' the leader admitted, 'we seldom meet a Greek of worth. Most are slaves – and better so.'

One of the soldiers looked up at me – we were mounted. 'Are you a Spartan?' he asked. 'We hear they are very good. Good fighters – men of honour.'

I pointed at Brasidas, who was just behind me. 'He is a Spartan.'

The leader nodded. 'The Spartans will be with us, when we fight. Their king-in-exile is close to our king. They hunt together.' He nodded as if stating a profound truth. 'The Spartan king is an honourable man – and a fine hunter. Very brave.'

Well, we all delude ourselves in war. Why should not the Persians delude themselves?

'What are they saying?' asked Brasidas, and the two heralds pushed their horses forward. I translated.

The Spartans all smiled, and Sparthius slipped down from his horse. 'Immortals? These are Persian Immortals?' He looked over the officer's equipment like a man buying an ox at a fair. 'Ask him if I can hold his spear.'

The Persian courteously handed the Spartan his spear.

Sparthius – ignoring the crowd of onlookers we'd drawn at the edge of the Susan agora – began to whirl the spear.

'Superb balance,' he said. 'Short – but a good head.' He tested it with his thumb and smiled. He handed it to Bulis, and who looked at the head – and smiled.

'Good steel,' he said.

Before the gods, the Immortals made the Spartans happier than Arwia's beauty and all her wit. Bulis called to me – in Greek – his voice full of life, lilting like a boy's.

'These are worthy men.'

By which, if you haven't figured out the Spartan mindset, he meant – these are men worth matching spears with.

In truth, the Great King's palace at Susa was splendid, and had I seen it before Babylon, I would have gaped. But I'd been to Babylon, and Arwia's great hall with its winged lions and green marble columns was – truthfully – grander than Darius's palace at Susa. And when you left the temple-like hall for the guest quarters – it was more like a stone-built barracks, which, in fact, it was. The Great King had almost a thousand guests, and we were packed in like travellers in the caravanserai along the Royal Road, with Indians and Bactrians and Jews . . .

At the same time, the guest barracks was wonderful, because we all mixed together at mealtimes as if we were some kind of exotic army, and the conversation was a delight. I didn't meet a fool there, and I met many men far better travelled than I. Aristides all but held court – his wisdom was apparent to all, and he quickly gathered a group of high-minded men who discussed issues like the value of excellence and the purpose of human life.

I don't want to suggest that I wasn't interested. But I was in the capital of the greatest empire on the aspis of the world, and I was there to learn all I could about the enemy, not about the mind of man. Each day, when the sun was halfway to the middle of the sky and the shadow of the horse statue in the Foreigners' Courtyard reached a certain point, the palace major-domo would come and announce the list of guests who would be received by the Great King. And as soon as this ceremony was performed, Brasidas and I would pack ourselves cloaks and hat and go out into the agora. We visited Cyrus at his father's house and had a tremendous meal with a man who had ridden with Cyrus the Great and had, himself, been to the borders of India. He was a courteous, dignified old gentleman who was nonetheless not too fine to flourish his akinakes and show us just how he slew a prince of the Scythians.

We went with Cyrus to the barracks of the noble cavalry and watched them at exercise.

Cyrus said, 'It might seem foolish of us to show you everything – our armament, our tactics. But the Great King believes that if other nations see our power, we can avoid bloodshed by your submission.'

In truth, just on the plains around Susa, the Great King had more – and better – cavalry than all of Thessaly and all of Greece could ever raise, better mounted, better equipped, with bows which none of our horsemen had. One day, Cyrus took us to see Persian archers.

I grew up watching Persian archers, but the Spartans had not.

Brasidas stood silently while twenty men lofted shafts so fast that the third one was in the air before the first struck. And when they struck, they struck deep. Persian bows were bigger and more powerful even than Scythian bows, as those of us who had faced noble Persian archers at sea had every reason to know.

And Cyrus embarrassed me by telling the men on the archery range that I had charged Artaphernes' guard at Sardis – and lived.

'Tell us!' men insisted, so I told the story, hiding, as much as possible, the fact that there had been only ten of us in the charge.

'And Marathon?' asked another. 'The battle on the plains of Athens? Were you there, as well?'

I admitted I had been, and then we were swapping lies – or at least half-truths – because he had ridden with the cavalry at our end of the line.

In the end, we agreed that no two men see a battle the same way, But I agreed with him that, had the ends of the Greek line not pressed forward so fast, the Persians would have triumphed. This seemed to satisfy him that I was a reliable witness.

They served us wine, and we were like comrades.

The next day, in the market, a street sweeper – a low-caste half-Mede – told me that soon I would have his job.

'Now you are an ambassador,' he said. 'Soon, you will be a slave, lower than me. I see it every day. Put your neck under his foot and get it over with!' The man laughed a gap-toothed smile. 'I need the help.'

And that day or the next we were invited by Shahvir and Mayu – I think I have those names correctly, they were officers of the Anûšiya – to a mess dinner at the barracks. I was enjoined to bring all the Spartans, and I did.

Shahvir was a fine companion, but as soon as we'd had a cup of wine, he showed us several sets of Greek panoply. 'You have seen us ride and shoot,' he said. 'Let us see the Greek way of war.'

I protested that he must have seen hoplites – in Babylonian service, if nowhere else.

'I myself have fought the Ionians several times,' he said. He shrugged. 'Too much armour, too little training.'

I turned to Bulis. 'He'd like us to demonstrate the phalanx.'

Bulis nodded. 'With three men and a foreigner?' he asked. Note that well, friends – we were in Susa, in Persia, and he called me a foreigner. It is hard to love the men of Lacedaemon. At any rate, he shook his head at me.

'You do not know our dances,' he said.

'I know the seventh dance,' I said. 'I learned it from Sparthius.'

Sparthius nodded. 'He's better than most boys,' he said. 'I say let's do it. With four of us we can look like something.'

Brasidas looked as displeased as I. 'I am a Plataean,' he said.

In that moment, I loved him.

Bulis didn't change expression. 'Of course. Your view is noted. Will you dance with us, Plataeans?'

I looked at Brasidas, and he nodded. 'Yes,' he said.

It is one thing to dance the Pyricche in the agora of your city, or some clear space under the walls. At Plataea, we dance it at the corner of the enclosure of Hera, and the goddess herself, I think, watches us when we are at our best.

But even when we stumble or miss the time, we dance for three thousand men and women, and we know them all by name. When a young man is particularly skilled or good, women – and some men – cry, '*Kalos! Kalos!*'

It is different, when you dance the war dance for enemies. And you must believe me, friends. By that night in Susa, we knew that we were a few Greeks in a sea of enemies. They were good men and women – decent, honourable – but they were – from the Great King we had not met to the meanest slattern – cocksure that they would conquer us and make us slaves.

Nor was the armour good stuff, nor did it fit well. In the end, I asked Mayu for his scale shirt – we were of a size.

'But it is not like your gear,' he said.

'I have one just like it hanging from the rafters of my house,' I said.

'Where from?' he asked.

'Marathon,' I said wickedly. No one should ever have sent me as a diplomat.

Bulis commanded us. He made us stand perfectly still and simply tap the floor with our sarauters for what seemd like an eternity. He wanted us to have the rhythm correct.

I have said that the Spartan Pyricche is not like ours. I'll say more now. In Sparta, they have ten – or, for all I know, fifty – Pyricche, not just one. Each dance has a particular storyline, and each dance teaches a set of lessons to a boy – or a man.

So the seventh dance of the Lacedaemonians is the dance of the shield press. In it, the two lines exchange thrusts, but only to offer the opportunity to use the aspis as a weapon. It is the one I chose to learn because it teaches the lessons so well – how to turn your aspis like a table, how to cut with the outer rim, how to break an opponent's body-structure with a push offline.

For a moment, as we stood ready, I couldn't think of the opening sequence, and so I was late – terribly late – entering the first step.

Hah! But after that, I was into the rhythm of the thing, and we were like gods.

There is a moment – just as in the Plataeans' Pyricche – where we all step together, stomping our right foot heavily as we push. Our four feet were like one foot – or like hundreds, all together.

And on the last step, we stopped. All together, and no shuffling.

The Persians applauded us. Mayu hefted an aspis and made an odd motion with his head. 'You couldn't do any of that in combat, of course,' he said. 'You'd be too closely pressed together.'

I translated for Bulis, who shrugged. It was a shrug of contempt. 'Only militia and slaves huddle together,' he said. 'Our men keep their places in the line.'

Quite a long speech for him.

I'd like to say that the Persians were so impressed with us that they stayed home and didn't invade Greece. But we all know that's not what happened. Instead, Mayu made it clear that he thought our dance was pretty, but nothing to do with war, and over food and wine, Shahvir explained to me that Marathon had been a fluke caused by the unreliability of some of their Greek subjects.

Well.

Bulis sat in silence, and Brasidas asked for translations, and sometimes smiled. Sparthius looked angry, and drank too much. I suspect we were sullen – I was surprised at how hostile the Anûšiya were, and as we walked home, Cyrus apologised.

'They are not gentlemen. Merely warriors. I see what your dance teaches.' He shrugged. 'I suspect in time, Mayu will see, too.'

We cooled our heels for two weeks. It was a glorious time, and if I hadn't been pining for Babylon, I suspect it might be one of the favourite times in my life. Everything at Susa was an adventure, and I tasted saffron, drank rare wine, eyed noble beauties, and saw the most beautiful horses I'd ever seen.

Really, Persia is a fine place.

A little less than two weeks after we'd arrived, Brasidas disappeared. He left a note to say that he was going to visit a friend. Bulis and Sparthius looked ... knowing.

And told me nothing.

A few hours after he left us, Hector brought me a message he'd received from a slave.

'A Greek slave,' he said.

It invited me to a meeting at a time and place. There was no signature.

I have been a slave, and that gives me a natural tendency to caution in these matters. Besides, after our somewhat hostile reception by the Anûšiya, I had become aware that I was sometimes followed.

I shrugged. 'No,' I said.

The next day, a helot – I'd know those Messenian features anywhere – plucked at my elbow in the Foreigners' Courtyard of the palace.

I ignored him.

'Just come with me?' he asked.

'No!' I said. It had to be a provocation. They'd pretend there was a slave revolt, or ask for money – we all knew our turn with the Great King was coming, and we all knew about Xerxes' little ways. He tested his guests. And then killed a few.

'My master asks to see you,' he said.

'Who is your master?' I asked.

'Are you dense?' he spat, in a very unslave-like way. 'Demaratus!'

I presented myself to the former King of Sparta in an olive grove six stades south of the city. His helot had taken me out of the palace grounds to a brothel. I chose a girl – none of your business – and was escorted to a room, from which I was then escorted out through another door to a waiting donkey, and we rode out through one of the military gates past the great bridge. That's all I remember of the route.

Demaratus, contrary to the propaganda of the last few years, was a handsome, older man, did not have a hunchback or a limp, and looked like what he was – one of the greatest aristocrats in the world. He was richly dressed, even in an olive grove. Brasidas sat under a tree, with a scroll, looking for all the world like an Athenian gentleman reading philosophy.

I didn't bow. He wasn't my king. But I did present my wax tablet. 'From Gorgo,' I said. 'Wife of—'

Demaratus laughed. 'I know whose wife Gorgo is,' he said. 'Are you ready to see the Great King?'

I believe I shrugged.

'I have spent a week flattering him into letting the two fool Spartiates live,' he said. 'The murder of his father's envoys was an incredible insult at the time. Even today, it is widely remembered.'

'And Aristides?' I asked.

'Athens is doomed,' the former King of Sparta said. 'Everyone in this city lost someone on that beach. Athens will be destroyed. All the omens foretell it. But I would see Sparta saved.'

I frowned. 'Aristides will be killed?' I asked.

Demaratus looked at Brasidas reading. 'If I have my way with the Great King, all of you will be loaded with presents and sent home,' he said. 'He is ... mercurial. Curiously not in control of himself, for a man with such power. Oddly in need of the good opinions of others.' Demaratus shook his head. 'He is not Darius, but then, almost no one is.'

I must have looked surprised. He raised his eyebrows.

'Not what you expected, Plataean?' He shrugged. 'I can never go back to Sparta. I was treated worse than a helot. But I will not be an agent of my city's destruction.' He waved the tablet at me. 'With your permission, sir?'

I stood back and watched him turn away. He went to Brasidas, and they talked for a moment – there was a loud snap – and then both of them were looking at something. The former king nodded.

'I broke your tablet – foolish of me. I'll send a new one with you. For Gorgo, you understand.' He nodded.

I nodded in turn. It's not always good to tell people everything you have guessed.

'May I ask one more question?' I asked.

He laughed. 'Plataean, I am retired – an old man. I have nothing but time.'

'Is there anything we can do to induce the Great King to make peace?' I asked.

He didn't hesitate. 'No,' he said. 'The coin is tossed. The soldiers are ordered and the fleets are gathered. Your arrival at this time is viewed as a piece of foolish effrontery. A year or two ago – perhaps. Now – if it were not for me, you'd have been refused, seized as enemies, and crucified.' He shrugged. 'Perhaps not you. Artaphernes got you a safe conduct by name. That means something here.'

As always, Artaphernes saved my life.

I nodded. 'I never thought we could make peace,' I said. 'But it seemed worth a try.'

Demaratus scratched his beard. 'I truly doubt that Xerxes can move an army from here to Corinth and then seize Corinth – much less reach Lacedaemon,' he said. 'But Athens will fall. Sparta ... can hold.'

'I hope you are an ill prophet,' I said.

'Everything has come about as I told that fool Cleomenes when he *first* started to challenge Persia.' He shrugged. 'I was a King of Sparta. War is my business. Without the direct intervention of the gods, Greece cannot stand against Persia.' He shook his head. 'Aristides has made himself very popular with the magi. His knowledge of Greek and Aegyptian philosophy will probably save his head. The magi are very powerful here.'

Brasidas got up. 'I'll go back with him,' he said.

The former King of Sparta smiled. 'It has been good to see you.'

They did not embrace. I had decided that Brasidas was his son, or perhaps his lover – I revised that.

We went back to another gate, led by the helot, who took me into the kitchen of the brothel, where I emerged into the common room to be heckled by a pair of Babylonian Jews for riding the best girl for three hours. I bought them wine and we were friends.

Brasidas watched it all with interest. On the way back to the palace compound, he shook his head. 'So now I've been in a brothel,' he said.

This from a man of thirty-five.

The Great King summoned us.

We dressed carefully.

The summons was to me, as the 'Ambassador of the Greeks'.

Aristides as my mage.

The Spartans, as 'heralds of the Spartans'.

These titles were settled by the court chamberlain, and I read into them that Aristides was not to be killed – because his being Athenian would never make the court calendar. In fact, despite being in every way the senior member of our party, he was being dismissed as a functionary.

But there is my name, in good Avestan – Airyaman Navazhar, of Palatay in Jawan. Noble-minded light-bringer – that's me.

It was Mayu who appeared to lead us to the Great King. He shook his head at our naked legs and offered me his own trousers.

The king's hall was roughly on the same layout as the palace in Babylon. We entered through a magnificent cloister of pillars – arcade after arcade, like the great trunks of an old forest of marble. We processed through the entry hall with censors and the major-domo, and we were with twenty other foreign guests to make the auspicious number of twenty-four. We were the least important and came last, after a delegation of noble Saka, who looked about them with thinly veiled contempt.

Or perhaps they were merely the nomadic version of Spartans, and gave nothing away. We passed up a short set of very broad, very deep steps. I'm guessing that the architect did that on purpose to make me feel small, but everything was on such a scale as to make me feel small.

We passed from court to court – through the first court, where the law was pronounced, to the second court, where sometimes the king's mother held her own divan, and into the third court, where military matters were settled. Each one of them was as big as the temple of Artemis at Brauron. Everything was hung in Tyrian purple and decorated with pure gold, and after a while the eye simply declined to take it all in, although the frescoes – which were, as far as I could see, fired clay with permanent tints, done as tiles and assembled like a meta-mosaic – were superb – as good as anything in Hellas.

And then we processed back through the second hall to the first, just in case we were not sufficiently impressed.

Altogether, the whole was the size of the Athenian Acropolis. All gold, and purple and tiles.

And then we entered the throne room.

It was not so much a room as a corridor, with cross-corridors, like a huge iota or a tau. So from the entrance, you couldn't see the men standing in the wings – the functionaries and soldiers and judges and scribes waiting for orders. You could only see him.

The Great King.

He wore cloth of gold and purple, of course, and on his head was a tiara of pure gold. He was a handsome man – but I didn't know that at the time, because of the golden throne with the winged lions.

Much like Babylon. I think, had I not seen Babylon first, all this would have stolen my senses. Now it all seemed . . . extreme. Affected. And a little like the Persians aping the manners of the Babylonians, right down to the winged lions. I have no idea who had winged lions first. Having faced the more prosaic variety in tall grass, I had no wish to face one with wings.

Xerxes received each group of guests – accepted their gifts and promises of men and material for his war against Jawan. That was us. And we were waiting until last.

And it went on and on.

All told, we must have stood for four hours. I was delighted that I wore a linen chiton, and so, I can tell you, was Aristides. Our bare legs stood us in good stead. With the crowd of functionaries and the torches, it was as hot as any place I've ever been.

And as we drew closer to the throne, it seemed to me more and more likely that Demaratus was wrong. And we were going to die.

We were certainly being humiliated. All the other delegations were brought wine, beer and water. We were not. All the other delegations were offered dates and sweetmeats and honey – we were not.

No one would look at me, or meet my eye.

Slowly, inch by inch, we moved down that long, dark cavern of a hall towards the gold-lit man in the robes. He sat six feet off the floor, and his feet rested on a table.

Finally, the Saka threw themselves full length in front of him and mumbled something. They began their own ritual – gifts, which looked to me like braided halters but turned out to be horses. And promises of ten thousand horsemen to ride against Jawan.

The Great King spoke platitudes, and they echoed from the ceiling. He sounded like a god.

I thought his architect had been heavy handed.

I also thought that, had I been taken directly into the sacred presence of the Great King, all this might have struck me harder, but four hours of waiting wilted even fear. From time to time, when the line moved, my heart would race. I was ready to die. But then, I'd grow bored.

Even summary execution can seem dull.

I also occupied my time translating what I could hear and understand for Aristides and the Spartans. Early on, I was told to be quiet by a chamberlain, whom I ignored. Later, Cyrus emerged from the crowd to tell me not to speak.

'You translate, then,' I said.

Cyrus winced. 'It is the custom of the King's Presence not to speak,' he said.

'You are speaking,' I said.

He smiled. 'I am a full Persian.'

I went on translating aloud, and in fact I began to raise my voice slightly.

Aristides spoke under me, twice – once to agree with the Spartans that if they took us to kill us, we would die with dignity and not struggle. The other time, to agree that we would bow, but not perform the proskynesis.

And eventually, the Grand Chamberlain motioned me forward.

We had no gifts.

I happened to have gifts, in fact, and several functionaries had *offered* us gifts to give. Just to make the ceremony work.

But Bulis insisted that we were not offering any form of submission, and Aristides agreed, and now, in that moment, it was my time to explain this to the Great King.

First, I bowed.

There are many forms of bow, in Persia. You can incline your head – equal to equal. You can bow at the waist. You can bow so deeply that your right hand brushes the ground.

You can throw yourself on your face.

I had observed – in four hours – that the Persian nobles bowed with one hand touching the floor, and all the ambassadors, who were after all making or renewing formal submission, performed the full proskynesis and threw themselves on the floor. Some crawled forward and kissed the table on which the Great King's feet rested.

I decided on my course and I went forward with the Grand Chamberlain, and when he brought his arm down on my shoulder, I slipped it – he wasn't a fighter – and I bowed at the waist and placed my right hand fully on the floor.

Like a great nobleman.

Or a friend of mighty Artapherenes.

The silence wrapped me like a shroud.

What I didn't know was that behind me, neither Aristides nor the two Spartans so much as twitched. They didn't even incline their heads.

Oh well. I'd been a slave among Persians, and I couldn't make myself be that rude. I rather admire the Spartans in retrospect, but at the time I made my choice, and they made theirs.

One of the chamberlains grabbed at Bulis, and attempted to force his head to the floor, and Bulis threw him – softly, over his hip – and then laid him quite gently on the floor.

The Great King laughed.

'I see you are my jesters, today,' he said. 'That was a fine throw, although Nasha is hardly our finest wrestler.' He leaned forward. I was so close to the throne that I could hear the gold cloth rustle. 'Why do you not bow?' he asked. He pointed at the Anûšiya, who were ready, spears raised, to kill us.

Bulis spoke – although we'd all agreed I'd do the talking.

'We only bow to gods,' he said. 'You, Great King, are after all but a man.'

Bulis said the words – in Greek.

I got to translate them.

Xerxes looked away. He was, in fact, looking at someone I couldn't see, in an alcove by the throne. Demaratus, I'd lay any wager.

He smiled. 'What curious men you must be.' He shook his head. 'You are Spartans?' he asked.

'We are heralds of the kings,' Bulis said, through me.

'And although you have kings, you do not bow?' he asked.

We all nodded.

He shook his head and frowned like a man who mislikes a bitter taste.

'Very well,' he said. 'Speak your piece, men of Lacedaemon.' He said the last very well – he'd practised it.

Bulis nodded to me.

I said, 'O King of the Medes! the Lacedaemonians have sent these men to your court, in the place of those heralds of thine who were slain in Sparta, to make atonement to thee on their account.'

Xerxes nodded. And tugged his beard and looked again to his right – and then to the left. I could not see who stood on the left.

He straightened himself and leaned forward. 'I do not concern myself with the impieties of the foreigners,' he said. 'It is not for me – Great King, King over Kings – to act like the Lacedaemonians, who, by killing the heralds, have broken the only laws which all men hold in common. As I hold you in contempt for such barbarism, so I will never be guilty of it myself.' He leaned forward more. 'I will make war on you, and wipe you from the face of the world, and I will *not*, by killing you, allow the gods to let you escape from the consequences of your outrageous impiety.'

I confess I still think it was a noble answer – for all that it was composed by Demaratus, as a slap at the policies of Cleomenes. That is how it was – four thousand stades from Athens, we saw Spartan diplomacy play out in the throne room of Darius.

Xerxes motioned at the Spartans – dismissal. He wasn't angry. But he ignored them, and when a pair of guards motioned for them to leave – they turned, and left. Both were in shock. They were prepared to die with dignity, but ill prepared, I think, to be treated as contemptuous wrongdoers.

They were evicted.

The Great King turned his liquid brown eyes on me for the first time.

'And you,' he said. 'You were a slave?' he asked.

I smiled. 'I was,' I agreed.

'And you have saved my friend Artaphernes from death – and saved the entire delegation of noble Persians travelling to Tyre in Libya.' He waved. 'Why have *you* brought me no gift?' He meant – I seemed to have more sense.

I bowed again. 'My lord, I am not rich enough to give you any more of a gift than I gave when I saved your envoys.'

He looked away, and smiled, and looked back. 'You sound more like the other Greeks I know – a ready answer for everything. Will you serve me?'

I shook my head. 'As a man – in any way my lord commands. As a Greek? Never.'

Cyrus – just at the edge of my peripheral vision – gave a nod, and I knew I'd made a good answer.

Xerxes smiled – he was charming, for a tyrant – and nodded. 'Strong words – the better to *negotiate*. Isn't that the Greek way?'

He looked off to his left, and I saw a man – I'd seen him at a distance in the Foreigners' Courtyard, surrounded by soldiers. Mardonius – the king's most trusted counsellor and the most open advocate for war with Greece.

Now, at a signal from the king, he came forward to stand beneath the throne. He bowed low – but did not quite throw himself on the floor. He wore long robes of white and red, with red trousers. He was heavily muscled, like an athlete, and yet I found him faintly ridiculous in his trousers – some habits of thought are difficult to overcome.

'What level of power or wealth will buy you, Greek?' he asked. His Persian was different from the king's. He spoke a northern dialect of Persian. He was one of the few courtiers to wear a sword.

The guardsmen were still standing with their spears in both hands, points aimed at me, like men hunting wild boar on the flanks of Kitharon. But I truly doubted that Xerxes would kill an accredited ambassador, more especially one with a safe conduct.

I bowed again. 'Great King, I am neither a wealthy nor a powerful man – so there is no point in offering me such things.'

Behind me, Aristides snorted.

Xerxes had to know that Aristides was the true ambassador – the man of wealth and power. Yet he ignored him. I suspect that Xerxes' hatred of Athens blinded him as effectively as my notions of men in trousers blinded me.

Aristides leaned forward and very quietly, in Greek, whispered, 'Mardonius is going to seek to trick us into something – an impiety, or an outrage.'

I could feel that, as well.

By one of those ironies so dear to the gods, Mardonius was in the same position that Cleomenes had been with the Persian ambassadors. He wanted war – and if he could arrange to kill me, he'd have put the Great King in a position from which he could not withdraw. I saw this – a little too late, but better late than never – as Aristides spoke.

Mardonius bowed – again – to the king. 'May I question this Greek, Great King?' he asked.

Xerxes smiled at me. 'Be my guest.' He sat back and a slave put a cup in his hand.

Mardonius nodded affably at me. 'Is it true you were born a slave?' he asked.

I shook my head. 'No.'

Someone had given him the wrong information.

'You were a slave to Artapherenes,' he said.

I bowed – again. 'No, my lord. My lord is misinformed.'

I thought he'd explode. His tanned skin flushed with blood so fast I suspected it would burst from his eyes.

'You have been a pirate?' he began again.

I ignored him. 'Great King, King over Kings, I am here as a representative of the peoples of Plataea and other places in Greece, to speak of matters of peace and war. I am not here to discuss my personal life with your servants, however charming.'

All throughout the hall, there was a rush of muttering like the first gust of wind in leaves.

But the Persians are brave men, and they detest cowardice as everyone does. Cultures are different, and my feeling, since youth, has been that they mistake our Greek love of talk for a form of fear – they think that our negotiation and our business dealings and tendency towards both argument and compromise are signs of weakness.

And we, in turn, think they are a nation of slaves, heedlessly obedient to the whim of one tyrant.

I doubt we, either of us, see the other clearly, but one thing I knew from having served Artaphernes, and that was that the Persians prized straight talk, bluntness and boldness.

At any rate, the mumbling went on, and Xerxes raised three fingers, and the hush that fell was absolute.

'Yet,' Xerxes observed – genuinely curious, I think – 'yet you have been a slave. You admitted it to me.'

I nodded. 'Great King, out beyond the rule of laws that makes your empire great, there is a wide world with no law. If a man is to sail the seas and trade, he must needs run the risk of slavery and death. I have been a slave twice.'

'No man born a slave can speak in this assembly, and to do so invites a charge of impiety and sacrilege in the king's sacred presence.' Mardonius was a hothead, I could see.

I thought of Heraklitus and his views on slavery. I managed a smile, even though I was growing afraid that Aristides and I were to be the sacrifices at this feast. 'My lord, I was not born a slave, nor am I one now as I address your king. Yet to us, lord, you are but a slave. You do what your king orders you – every one of you. You have no assembly in which to vote and not one of you plays a part in the creation of your laws. To a Greek ...' I shrugged, knowing from the rumbles that I had offended nearly everyone present. But the voice of Heraklitus in my head pressed on, and I said his words. 'And – taken another way – what man here present is anything but a slave – to time, to the gods, to his own appetites and desires?'

Aristides put a hand on my shoulder.

I braced for the spear point. But I'd rather be slaughtered as a lion than a lamb, and I had a feeling that Xerxes was a man for a big gesture.

Xerxes sat back – and smiled. 'Artapherenes chooses his friends well,' he said. 'Go back to Greece and tell them to submit and I will be merciful. But my armies are formed, and my will is set. I will march.'

I bowed, but I stood my ground. 'Merciful, Great King? To Sparta – and Athens?'

He shook his head. 'No,' he said. 'For them, nothing but salt and ash. I vow – before the gods, and may my crown be taken from my head—'

An older man emerged from the right of the throne. 'Stop! Great King, I beg you not to swear.'

The Great King glared at his counsellor. I didn't know who the man was, but he was beautifully dressed.

Mardonius looked at the man as if a heap of dung had materialised at his feet. 'How dare you interrupt the king?' he hissed.

'An oath to the gods is not like a statement of policy, my lord,' the old man said. 'It has effects that ripple through all of the universe. I beg you not to push the king into such an oath.'

Mardonius put a hand to his chest like a bad actor. 'The king but reacts to the arrogance of the Greek ambassador! I have nothing to do with this sort of manipulation.'

For less than a single beat of a desperate man's heart, Xerxes' eye caught mine. A hint of amusement – and fear. It was not all pomegranate juice and slave girls, being the Great King.

I watched them – and managed to glance to my right and left, to see the courtiers around me, the palace officers, the soldiers. In a single sweep of my gaze, I saw the depth of the central division in this court. I had no idea what had caused it, what factions existed, but I could see approval and disapproval, anger and fear and outrage and hope, writ all about me. There was a war party and a peace party – that much was clear.

If I had five years and a million darics to spend, I suspect I could have exploited it. But I had neither.

The Great King sat back and raised his hand for silence. 'Very well, old friend. I will not swear to the gods. I will merely state the obvious – my armies are ready to march, my ships have been summoned to their duty, and there are stockpiles of food throughout my realm. Let Athens and Sparta shake with fear, for my hand is not light. My spear is long, and I will take my bow in my hand and my chariot wheels will roll over their armies as a farmer threshes wheat.'

It seemed to me a dismissal, and I stood straight – waiting for the blow, or the motion of his hand – whatever it might be.

But as the silence lengthened, I realised that they were all waiting for me to speak in reply.

I had in my hand the caduceus – the bronze staff of a herald.

I did not bow.

'Great King!' I said. 'I have come seeking peace, and been promised war. So be it. My land is poor and yours is rich, and your reach is long. You have a thousand thousand slaves and fertile land that stretches away with uncountable riches, and my land is girt by the sea and has little to offer but rock and stone.'

I held my staff over my head. 'But before the immortal gods, Great King, Greece is far, the world is wide, and we, too, have spears.'

I threw my staff on to the marble. It rang like the hammer of Hephaestos on the anvil of the gods.

Then I turned on my heel and strode from the hall. Aristides walked by my side. We expected to be cut down at every step, and no one would meet our eyes, but behind us, the king was silent.

We didn't make it out of the second hall. We were moving swiftly when a dozen guards – fully cloaked and with their faces covered by the tails of their headscarves – surrounded us with spears. They didn't even speak.

My knees grew weak. Why not? My friends, I was unarmed, and these men were in armour, and I knew I was going to be executed in some back hallway.

I was terrified, but I knew I had to do something or die, so even as they moved in around us and directed us toward a side corridor, I began to look at them with professional desperation. I was looking for an ill-hung sword, any available weapons – a spear I could seize.

I jostled Aristides with my hip and our eyes met.

We were taken into another, even smaller corridor, and I was lost – I think we were in a servants' area, but there were no frescoes.

I heard the sound of running footsteps, and the guard nearest me – not a royal guardsman, unless he was wearing a disguise – turned to look.

I hit him in the ear with the palm of my hand – very hard – grappled close, and grabbed his spear. Without stopping, I turned the shaft to kill the man behind him, but the man had also started to turn to see who was running up behind, and my spear's metal butt caught him in the head and laid him out.

Two down and ten to go.

Aristides got the second man's spear before his body hit the floor.

The guardsman closest to me was very good – he dropped his spear and drew a short akinakes from his belt – he was inside my spear – and cut at my head. Aristides saved my life by covering me with his spear shaft.

But that one attack wrecked any hope we had of escape, and we were two men surrounded by ten.

'Stop!' ordered a voice. 'Stop!'

It took me a whole ten heartbeats to realise that he was shouting in Greek, and it was Cyrus.

He appeared around the last bend in the corridor, and his eyes took in the scene.

'Hold!' he roared in Persian. 'Stop! Put your weapons down!' he then said in Greek. He knelt by the two men I'd felled and put a hand to their throats.

'No one is dead. No one *needs* to die.' He looked back and forth. 'These are the Queen Mother's men, and they have orders to protect you.' Cyrus turned to the man with the drawn sword. 'He speaks Persian – why did you not speak to him?'

The man looked at me with undisguised hatred. 'It never occurred to me that he and his companion were so uncivilised as to use violence in the Royal Palace.'

Cyrus looked at me.

'I thought we were about to be murdered,' he said.

Aristides laughed. 'As did I, Lord Cyrus. Come – if we are all friends, here is my spear.'

He handed it to the captain of the guard, who glared at him – and took the spear.

'The queen will not thank you for mistreating them,' Cyrus said, but we were prodded – almost beaten. Our guards were angry and afraid, and men were left to look after the two men we'd put down. I took a number of knees and fists in the dark corridors, and then we emerged into the light, and I was blind. Cyrus walked between us, a hand on his sword.

'This is not going well,' he admitted.

The guards took us across a courtyard I didn't know and into another palace. A dozen more soldiers surrounded us, and then we were put into a windowless room – quite forcibly. My shoulder was hurt – two men took my arms, and I tried to struggle and failed.

And then we were alone, in the dark. And Cyrus was locked in with us.

'This is not what was supposed to happen,' Cyrus said. 'The Queen Mother wants you to go home alive. Because she does not want Xerxes to be guilty of any more impieties, and because she is an old friend and ally of my master.' He sat against a wall and fingered his beard by the light that came in around the door. Once our eyes adjusted, it was not so very dark.

'And those were the Queen Mother's guards?' I asked.

'I don't know. This is not ... I have not been here in a long time. Things were not done this way in the time of Great Darius. He was master in his own house.'

We sat in the dark for a long time.

Eventually, Aristides put a hand on my shoulder. 'You spoke well,' he said. 'I particularly liked your piece on slavery.'

'I don't think Mardonius liked it,' I said.

And later, when it had begun to get darker outside, Cyrus told us a great deal about the inner workings of the court.

'When Lord Xerxes took power,' he said, 'he had to make many agreements to win over some of the Persian and Mede vassals. He offended some of Darius's best officers by promoting younger men. It is almost always the way – so my father tells me. But Xerxes – it is not that he is weak, rather that he is changeable. Today's alliance may be tomorrow's enmity. Men say that the only council that he trusts is the last council to reach him.' He shrugged. 'This prevarication is not the normal way of a Great King. Mardonius and Atosa the Queen Mother and his brother Haxāmaniš all seek to dominate, him or at least influence him.'

'And Artaphrenes?' I asked.

Cyrus shook his head. 'My master is too wise to play these games. He is a loyal man and he rules his provinces, levies taxes, raises troops – and stays away from all this. We thought ... perhaps you would help us to stop this war.' He frowned at me. 'Why make such inflammatory answers?'

But Aristides leapt to my defence. 'What else could he say? We hoped for some private talks with the king or his people. None were offered.'

'Mardonius had had you followed night and day – you, and me, and every one of my men. One of my men was killed in a brawl that has no obvious cause – when I was attempting to send him to the Queen Mother.' He shrugged. 'Mardonius will stop at nothing to provoke this war. He is to be Satrap of Europe. The war is his reward for service and his stepping stone to empire.' He frowned at me. 'Some of us think he covets the empire for himself.'

'By Hermes!' I said. 'Why am I only finding this out now?'

Aristides frowned. 'Yes,' he agreed. 'It is late to have the politics of this court revealed. A week ago we might have done something. Or prepared different speeches.'

Cyrus shook his head. 'Meeting the Queen Mother was to fix everything. Now – I'm sorry – I think we have been sold to Mardonius. I don't know why. I regret that my death will lead to open conflict within the empire, but my father will not leave me unavenged. I have sons.' He smiled. 'I cannot regret having been your friend, Arimnestos.'

The door opened.

I prepared myself to die.

But the world is never that simple, and instead of executioners, there were three slaves. They had clothes – fine clothes, all Persian. And food.

We ate.

After some discussion, we changed into Persian dress. We were dressed as guardsmen, in the hideous trousers and the long jackets. I felt like some sort of effeminate, and Aristides was worse – his long legs were too long for his trousers.

The lead slave wrapped our heads in coverings and pulled the ends over our faces, and we were out the door. There were spears leaning there and we took them and followed the slaves across the courtyard we'd crossed earlier.

At the last moment, there was a shout, and the slaves froze. Two soldiers – Immortals – ran up, swords drawn.

'Don't you know that all movement is forbidden?' one growled.

The slaves flinched. 'My mistress ...' the lead slave whimpered.

'Dog of a Mede!' I snapped. I used Mardonius's northern Persian accent. It sounded barbarous. But I knew the Immortal was not a Persian. 'Be about your business, or let us go to Lord Mardonius and see who has the right to give orders.'

The two Immortals looked at each other.

'Move!' I said to the slaves, and pointed my spear imperiously.

They let us go. They didn't love us, or even – quite – believe me, but we moved quickly and they didn't choose to arrest us.

And then we were in the women's palace. I knew what it must be as soon as we were in the doors – women smell different from men, and I don't mean perfume. It was a different reek – laundry and kohl instead of sweat and leather.

We were taken down a short corridor and up two narrow flights of stairs where our spears were very inconvenient, and then into a room where we were in the presence of a dozen masked guardsmen. The room was lit by a hundred oil lamps and the walls were frescoed with pictures of bulls.

The guard parted to reveal Atosa, the Queen Mother.

I bowed to the floor, complete with my hand touching the stone.

She smiled, and her face was beautiful. She must have been only slightly older than forty, with access to every refinement, and she was lithe and smooth skinned. She wore long robes of silk, in layers, and her face was bare. She wore a silk tiara edged in gold and silk trousers that disguised very little of the shape of her legs, and behind her, on pillows, were a dozen of her ladies, each prettier than the last, with arched eyebrows and straight noses and sparkling eyes – I doubt that in fifty years of sailing the bowl of the earth I've seen so many beautiful women in one place.

Despite which, my eyes were only for the Queen Mother.

She stood looking at me. She gave me a small smile and the most fractional inclination of her head, and then she turned to Aristides.

'You are the great lord of Athens, whom my son has chosen to ignore?' she asked.

Aristides bowed. 'My lady, I am an exile.'

She nodded. 'I lack the time to play this kind of game, Athenian lord. My son is on the edge of a great error, and he is badly counselled.'

Aristides was not at his best with women. He was on edge – but he rallied. 'My lady, I cannot pretend to negotiate for Athens,' he began.

She snapped her fingers. 'I do not care a fig for Athens,' she said. 'It may endure my son's wrath or it may go on to future greatness, and it is all one to me, if only my son does not fritter away our birthright and our empire on overextending his power.' She looked at me. 'Mardonius intends to take you and murder you – tonight. His people and mine are playing a deadly game of hide and seek even now.' She smiled. 'My two unfortunate men are both making good recoveries. May I say that – despite any consequences – had you killed them, I'd have fed you to the dogs.'

I nodded. 'I think your dogs would have found me stringy,' I said.

'I'm a little past my prime, myself,' Aristides said – you can tell the depth of his discomfort by the fact that he actually managed a witticism.

She waved our attempts at lightness away. 'I will not allow Mardonius any more power over my son.'

I had to try. 'O Queen of Persia, is there any way in which we can – by explanation or discussion – prevent this war?'

She pursed her lips. 'I do not want my son to commit an act that might damn him with our gods,' she said. 'And I would do much to help Artaphernes, who stood by my husband at all times. But please do not imagine that I wish to see anything but the destruction of Athens. Let every stone be torn from every other stone. Let her temples be destroyed as ours of Sardis were destroyed.'

So much for peace.

Only then – in the Queen Mother's apartments in Susa – did I fully understand that we'd never had a chance. The Ionian Revolt, the burning of Sardis, the destruction of Euboea and the Battle of Marathon were like stepping stones across a raging torrent – and each step took us closer to the moment when the Great King's armies marched.

'I will save your lives,' she said. 'But I will applaud when I hear that the Acropolis is afire.'

Aristides bowed. 'O Queen,' he said, 'Athens has done nothing but defend herself and her people from your husband and now your son. I am sorry for the wreck of Sardis. It was ill done. I was there, and I would have prevented it if I could have. Your own sometime subjects, the Ionians, were the guilty parties. And I stood on the plains of Marathon and did my best to stop Datis and his army from sacking Athens – after seeing how he destroyed the cities of Euboea and sold her citizens into slavery.'

She cut him off with a wave of her hand. 'Please. Save your breath. I care nothing for your arguments, nor am I here to negotiate. I had you brought here because Mardonius would never dare search my apartments. Now you can escort me to my summer palace, and I will, I hope, never have to see you again.'

Cyrus bowed. 'Great Lady, what of my men, and the other Greeks?'

She smiled. I suspected she would make a terrible enemy. 'I have them all safe,' she said. 'The Spartans were taken on the very steps of the throne room. Your men, their horses and all their kit await you in the mountains.'

Aristides nodded. 'Then, Great Queen, what can we do but offer our thanks – as enemies?'

Her eyebrows raised. 'Ah! Nicely said. Let us go. I have been pining for the mountains.'

We moved fast, and I have very little to relate beyond a tale of fatigue and near-complete disorientation. We filed down the main stairs and formed the escort around her litter, and she was carried in state across four courtyards to the royal stable block, where, to my astonishment, she mounted a horse.

She rode as well as Gorgo, or better. She rode astride, and she seemed one with her horse – and all of her decorative ladies mounted as well, a cavalcade of beautiful centaurs. Horses were brought for each of us, and Aristides proved an excellent horseman – no surprise.

'Put the Greeks in the middle,' the queen said. 'They do not ride like us.'

Well – I suppose it is true. There was something . . . organic about the way Persians rode. We were stiffer. But then, I've never loved horses. Aristides did, and even in the torchlight he looked more like a Persian than I did.

Some things cause me more fear than others. I've never been great at public speaking – although I can manage a good thing on occasion – and this sort of escape probably caused me more fear than all the battles I've ever seen. We were stopped four times by soldiers – but on each occasion, a single glimpse of Atosa was enough to render the guards impotent, and our little caravan wound down the hill, through the streets, and out the northern gate. We rode in the moonlight along the river, and when the sun rose, we were already in rockier terrain, and there were hills rising on our left.

We rode all day until we reached an extensive horse farm. We changed horses in a stable attached to a fine estate, where Cyrus found his entire cavalry detachment, and I found the Spartan envoys, as well as Brasidas, Nikeas and Hector.

There was a great deal of back-slapping. I'm not sure, until we found each other in a barn north of Susa, that any of us expected to make it out alive.

Cyrus joined us where we were gathered. He drew me aside.

'Atosa is leaving in half an hour. She intends to ride north into the hills. I would like to leave her here and go north and west across the Masabadan – the land of the Medes. By staying in the hills, we can avoid most of their searches and slip up the Euphrates to Dura.' He waved at his men. 'With twenty of the best, we'll be fine – especially as Atosa has offered me sixty horses. A rich gift indeed.'

He watched me for moment. 'You hesitate?' he asked.

'I had hoped to return via Babylon,' I said.

'Arwia's palace will be watched – indeed, it was watched before you ever arrived. She is a snake, that one. She, not her husband, should have been given over to the sword.' Cyrus shrugged. 'I would not advise you to pass Babylon. Or rather – I will not go there, and I'm willing to compel you to come with me. I promised Artapherenes.'

I shrugged.

'I promised Briseis, as well,' Cyrus said.

'Let me talk to my friends,' I said.

I walked back to Brasidas, Aristides, Bulis and Sparthius. The two Spartan heralds were not good riders, but they'd had almost two months to harden, and they were better than they had been.

I laid out the choices for all of them.

Sparthius pointed at my trousers and laughed. 'It really is hard to take you seriously that way,' he said.

I pointed at his.

Aristides frowned. 'Gentlemen, we are not schoolboys. Arimnestos, our duty is to return with what we have learned.'

I shrugged. 'I confess I might be self-interested, but my thought was that Greece might be saved in Babylon.'

Brasidas nodded. 'I think the same. Babylon is smoking like a pile of sticks just before they ignite.' He narrowed his eyes. 'I think I know how to provide the spark.'

I suspect I looked jealous. 'You?' I asked.

He laughed. 'I have a message for a certain lady of Babylon from a former King of Sparta. Not all plots concern you, Plataean.'

Neither of the other two Spartans looked surprised.

But Aristides took me by the shoulder. 'Brasidas knows his way around this plot,' he said.

I looked at him, and he smiled. 'I do, at that,' he said. 'I'll go to Babylon. You go home and make the Greeks move.'

I suppose I might have protested more – but to be honest, I had had enough of the East. Babylon was a lush memory, but it was not a place for me.

Aristides – the least underhanded of men – nonetheless was the one to point out the flaw in our plan. 'Cyrus will not want us to send aid to Babylon. He may be willing to help us, and happy to do Mardonius a disservice, but he's still a loyal Persian officer.'

Brasidas cursed.

We all stood there under the sun, tired, dispirited despite our escape, in alien territory, heads down.

Very, very quietly, Hector spoke up. 'You could ... just say ... you are going ... er ... back to Demaratus at Susa.' Hector flushed. 'I'm sorry, lords. But Cyrus knows that Brasidas ... knows the Spartan king.'

Brasidas brightened. He smiled again, and Bulis tousled the boy's hair.

'Odysseus born again.' He looked at Brasidas. 'How will you get to Babylon? You don't speak any language but Greek.'

'It won't work,' I said. 'You'll never get there from here.' I stared at them. 'We have to go somewhere near Babylon – remember how far across the plain you can see it? Then Brasidas slips away and we cover for him by dressing Niceas here as a gentleman. We only need to give Brasidas a day's head start.' It occurred to me in a single breath – that I could slip away in the same way – and that I'd be missed much sooner than the taciturn Brasidas.

At parting, the queen sent me a guest-gift. Her chamberlain delivered it.

'My mistress sends you this, a treasure of our house, that no Greek will be able to return to his people empty handed from the court of the Great King. She says – go, return to your homeland, and tell them of all you have seen, and the glory of the Great King, and tell them to give their earth and water and become loyal subjects.' He bowed deeply – as if I were a great noble – and handed me a cedar box inlaid in silver.

I handed it to Niceas without looking at it.

The chamberlain sneered. 'It will be the handsomest treasure in Greece. And you are too foreign to look at it? Or are you Greeks merely dead to beauty?'

Aristides vaulted into his saddle like a man twenty years younger. 'We have beautiful things in Greece,' he said. 'Hills, valleys, waterfalls, the sea, and women.' He shrugged. 'We're not much for treasures.'

Bulis laughed. 'We're too poor!' he called.

And we rode away, leaving the chamberlain to his contempt. Myself, I think it was one of Aristides' prettiest speeches.

So in the end, we all rode together, dressed as Medes – up into the high country west of Susa, up the valley of the Eualaeus, past the walls of Hulwan, and then down into the plains at Me-Turnat, a journey of almost fifteen days – some days so slow that at the end of the day we could see the previous day's campsite in the clear air, and always short on water. We slept on the ground and hunted every day, and I was astounded to watch the facility with which the Persians shot from horseback.

Me-Turnat to Babylon is five hundred stades, and the roads were well marked. Indeed, we saw a column of spearmen, and when I spoke to their officer, he described his travels and in the process told us exactly how to reach the great city in the middle of the plain.

We began to ride due west across the plain, and summer was ending. In the mountains it had been cool, but here, despite the sun, the heat was also less, and the turning of the seasons reminded me that I had another two months' journey to reach the coast, unless we took the Royal Road, which Cyrus feared to take. Even as it was, he wanted to skirt the plain instead of crossing it, staying at the fringes of the highlands.

When we reached Dura on the Tigris, the gods took a hand in our affairs, and sent us a pair of Phrygian merchants with a convoy of goods travelling by river to Babylon. They spoke Greek.

We pooled our money and Brasidas vanished on to the docks. There was no time or place for long farewells. I was afraid – afraid I was sending him to his death, and afraid that I was sending him to my fate when I could have done his job better. But Aristides was unrelenting in his insistence that my role was to get them all back to Greece. They were my ships, and, as he pointed out, my relationship with Artapherenes.

I watched him vanish into the untimely autumn rain with mixed feelings.

Late that night, Cyrus awakened us and dragged us out into the inn's courtyard, on to horseback, and we were away, still blinking away sleep. He himself was already wet to the skin, and we rode north, cold, wet, miserable, and wondering what had occasioned this untimely ride. As the sun began to rise in a pale grey imitation of daylight, he came back down the column to me.

'Apologies, old friend. The Great King has not forgotten you, and there are cavalrymen on the roads. Someone talked.' He shrugged. 'It is hard to hide half a dozen Greek men, no matter how I dress you.'

I passed this on to the other Greeks.

Aristides said quietly, 'It couldn't be better, despite the lost sleep. All we need to do is pretend that we don't know where Brasidas is, either.'

I had a hard time adjusting to Aristides the schemer – a man I'd have said was unable to tell a falsehood of any kind. As it proved, he was full of deceit for those he perceived as his enemies. The next morning, he had me tell Cyrus that we'd lost Brasidas, and there followed a certain amount of bad playacting as we worried about him.

In the end, we all decided that we could not go back. I think Cyrus felt we were a little callous about it, but we all have trouble reading foreigners, and Cyrus had trouble reading us.

Brasidas was either in Babylon or caught, by that time, and we had six thousand stades of riding ahead of us, and we tried to avoid the Royal Road.

But for most of the route over the Taurus Mountains and farther west, there *is* no other route. The Royal Road wanders a bit, but it goes over the *only* practical passes. And in places, it is only one or two horsemen wide. Ten men could hold some of those passes for days against an army.

We ended up creeping along valleys, crawling up heights, and then dashing along the road. Horses died, to Cyrus's intense annoyance. The queen had given him magnificent horses – his gift, which he was burning up protecting us. I doubted very much that Cyrus's head was on the line.

After ten days in the mountains, it felt as if it was the only life I'd ever known. Some days we bought a sheep or a couple of goats; some days we got warm bread from an oven, or wine. Most days, we ate grain by the handful – boiled until soft. The water boiled before it was hot when we were high in the air, and we had snow one day, all day, and sat and shivered in our summer clothes.

We arrived at Melitene on the upper Euphrates tired and saddle sore and much thinner than we'd left the plains, and the reports of merchants scared me. In effect, in ten days in the mountains, we hadn't got any closer to Greece. But I didn't know the terrain, and I certainly trusted Cyrus.

One of the few things I remember of that desperate trip was that I trusted Cyrus and had to convey my trust to the others, every day. Bulis, especially, was constantly on the brink of turning on our escort. And they grew increasingly tired of us – six foreigners who were the cause of all their discomfort. But they were honourable men, and true to their salt – a Persian expression, because salt for them is the sign of hospitality. However much they loathed us, they kept going.

At any rate, we made Melitene and rested for a day. We all bought heavy local cloaks and rolled wool hats, and even the Spartans made some concessions to the weather.

Cyrus sat with me and we shared a cup of wine.

'I'm going to try the road,' he said. 'We have to beat winter into the high passes. Winter is close.' He shrugged with obvious discomfort. 'If it comes to a fight – well, there're not many men who can beat my demons.'

Indeed, after ten days of hunting and riding with Cyrus and his men, I doubted whether there were better cavalrymen in the entire world. It was in the mountains that the quality of their horsemanship became fully evident. They could ride up – and down – slopes I would have said were too steep for a horse even without a rider. I spent a lot of time clinging to my horse's mane in something very like terror, and at one point Cyrus laughed, slapped my back, and informed me that this was fair repayment for our time at sea.

Our fourth day out of Melitene, we descended sharply down a series of switchback trails to the Royal Road, and then we moved like the wind. With three horses to a man, we rode fast – trot, canter, walk, trot all day, a brief break every hour and then a new horse. I would guess we made almost two hundred stades the first day on the road. We passed the way station without stopping even to use the well.

The next day, we made half again as much, passing no fewer than three way stations. At the third, we stopped, and drank from the well, filled our canteens and rested our poor jaded horses. Cyrus looked grave when he emerged.

'I didn't fool the post-master,' he said quietly. 'There are still patrols out looking for you.'

He sent a pair of his best men well ahead as scouts, and the next day, at midday, he dragged us all off the road into a narrow pass somewhere in Kataonia. We saw the patrol before we heard them, far off on the road, and we stood by our horses' heads until they were well past. Then we got back on the road and went as fast as we could.

But it wasn't fast enough, and of course we left tracks, and the enemy had a rearguard. They must have hidden from us as successfully as we hid from them, but they warned the main body. By late evening, it was clear that we were pursued.

Cyrus cursed. 'I don't want to lose a man here,' he said. 'Nor do I want to kill men whose only fault is serving their king too well.'

We made the post house, and Bulis suggested that we could poison the well – which caused Cyrus to look at the Spartan envoy as if he were some sort of hardened criminal. 'Nothing,' he said, 'would induce me to poison a well.' He stomped off, his flat leather boot soles making a flapping sound in his irritation.

We slipped away before first light with six men covering us from the heights. The enemy patrol was hot on our heels, probably having ridden all night to close the gap, but they had to stop to water their horses and we slipped away.

But later that day, as we wound our way through the Comana valley, they struck. They charged our rearguard – not quite by surprise, but their total commitment was fearsome, and they killed two of Cyrus's men at the first encounter – and then it was a fight. Bulis and Aritides had doubted whether, when put to it, Cyrus would fight. I never doubted it. But Persians are as given to blood feud as most men, and after the deaths of Altris and Eza, two of our younger Persian escorts, the rest turned to fight with a will.

Cyrus laughed grimly, loosening his sword in its sheath. 'Mardonius must have offered a mighty reward for you,' he said. 'Nothing else would cause these men to risk everything like this.'

They came on recklessly.

For their part, Cyrus's men waited patiently. No word was spoken for a long time, and even I wondered whether it was possible that we were betrayed – Bulis was growing restless, and Sparthius already had his sword in his hand.

And then, without a word spoken, both sides began to loose arrows, and for a moment we were in a hail of shafts. I had faced Persian archery before, but it was worse mounted – because my horse took two arrows before I had any notion that we were being hit, and she reacted by throwing me over her head.

By Apollo, by whom I seldom swear – that was a heavy fall, from a horse on to rock, and jagged rock, at that. I lay unmoving for too long, and suddenly there was a cavalry melee over my head, and I, the vaunted warrior of the Greeks, was lying on my back almost unable to rise from the pain in my hip where it had struck the rock.

I was stunned. I couldn't get up.

Hector saved me. He stood his horse right over me, and when the enemy charge came home, he used his spear like a hero, keeping a pair of Medes at the point of his spear – one of them missed a cut with his sword and clipped his own horse's neck, and his horse bolted – and Hector put the other down with a fine thrust. I was nothing but a spectator.

Nor, to my shame, could I tell the two sides apart at first. Dust rose all around us, and every one of them had their facecloths buttoned across their faces against the biting cold and the blown grit. Sparthius had an arrow in his thigh and was out of the fight, and Bulis and Aristides were swapping swaggering sword-thrusts with a pair of Medes – Bulis, the better swordsman, was getting the worst of it because he wasn't a good horseman, and Aristides, who had a magnificent horse, was steadily pushing his opponent back, turning him, until the man's horse stumbled and went over the lip of a gully, never to rise again. Some of the Persians used their bows at point-blank range, instead of spears or swords. Aristides' servant, Nikeas, took an arrow in the face and went down.

My mare, despite the two arrows in her, had tossed me and then stood stock still, within reach. How like a horse, eh? I must have twitched, because Hector – with a courage few could have emulated – *dismounted* to help me up. He got her reins and handed them to me and I got her head around and with a gut-wrenching wave of pain I got my left leg over her back and turned her to face the next wave of enemy, Babylonian sword in my hand, to drive Sparthius's opponent off him. He was badly hit and barely in the fight; his strength was ebbing, desperation on his features.

I couldn't reach his opponent, but I could reach the rump of his opponent's horse, and I cut down into the horse's hindquarters mercilessly and the horse gave a great shudder and fell, one leg clawing the air and the other apparently ruined by my cut. I hate to hurt a horse – but Sparthius was about to go down, and I got an arm around him and put my horse into the man fighting Bulis. By ill luck – for him – he'd just turned to deal with Aristides, and I cut him so hard in the neck I almost severed his head, but my Babylonian blade was too flexible for such a cut and it bent – but didn't break.

He fell dead, and the blade returned to shape.

Hector speared a Lydian who was about to throw his spear into Cyrus's unprotected back.

And the fight was over.

Horse fights with bows are deadly. Most of the enemy force were dead – or were dead a few moments later when dismounted men cut their throats. We had six dead and another three with mortal wounds – most of them from arrows.

Nikeas, blessed by the gods, had a nasty and disfiguring scar; the arrow had ploughed a furrow along his forehead and torn a length of scalp the width of my hand, so that it hung free – and knocked him unconscious. But the boy's skull was thick and well formed and turned the point, although we were all treated to a sight of bone itself.

Aristides – Athenian gentleman of many talents – came to the fore. As Cyrus's men killed their mortally wounded, there was a young man – too young, I thought – with an arrow lodged deep in his chest. He was incredibly brave – sitting with his back against a rock, making jokes.

I caught Cyrus looking at him, and he turned away. 'He knows the mercy stroke is coming,' Cyrus said, and he choked on the words.

But Aristides, who was crouched over Nikeas, looked up. 'What?' he asked. He left his hypaspist on the ground and went to the Persian boy. He made a measurement with his fist laid against the centre of the boy's chest – and looked back at me.

There was a man – Amu. He was the largest of Cyrus's men, with a big hennaed beard. I had spoken to him several times, mostly to hear the tales of his life in the East, because he came from the mountains above mystical India. He stood behind the boy with a wicked knife in his hand – and frowned.

Aristides looked right at Amu. 'No!' he said.

Amu spoke no Greek. Arisitides spoke no Persian.

But Cyrus was there, and he shouted 'Hold!' in Persian and leaped to put his hand on the big man's arm. Amu paused. Every one of the surviving Persians looked at Arisitides.

'I can save him,' he said.

He opened the boy's jacket. Without warning, he struck the arrow – hard – with the palm of his hand. The head burst out the boy's back, and there was blood – but not too much blood, I felt.

Every head followed Aristides as he moved around the boy, holding his shoulder. He leaned the boy forward. He was chatting away in Greek – I have told a poor story if you don't know that Aristides never chattered, but now he spoke of the weather, the trees, the boy's bravery ...

I knelt down and translated it all. The boy watched me as if I were a priest of his god of light, and suddenly Aristides said:

'Tell him, "Be brave. There will be a lot of pain."'

I repeated his words. With Amu's help, Aristides seized the arrow and cut it at the entrance wound with a tool they used for horses' hooves, and then pulled by the head – unbarbed, by the gods – and it came out with a wet sucking noise.

He pushed honeyed wine into both ends of the wound and put pads of combed flax – which we had in abundance – on both entrance and exit wounds.

The boy's eyes never left mine, and he never uttered a squeak. Amu sat down by him – knife carefully sheathed – and praised him.

'It's his son,' Cyrus said. 'Pactyans, from Argosia. Hard men.' He put a hand on my shoulder. 'Tell your Athenian I thank him. We all thank him.'

I watched Aristides, now sewing up his hypaspist's scalp. 'We got you into this,' I said.

Cyrus shrugged. 'We say *co istādehi daste oftādeh gir* in the north.'

It was an expression I'd often heard. '*As long as you are standing, give a hand to those who have fallen.*'

He shrugged. 'Yes. But also, it is hard to see which comes first. Mardonius is my master's enemy – and a man whose actions are, I believe, bad for the Great King and bad for the empire.' He met my eye. 'But I sense that we are soon to be foes.'

I could tell you some marvels of that trip – the monster we killed in the high passes of the Antitauros Mountains, and the spiders of the high plains of Cilicia – but that is not tonight's tale. We rode for fifty days from Melitene, nor did we escape winter unscathed, and those shivering nights along the Paroreios come back to me on cold nights here, lying under three blankets with the wounded boy between me and Amu; hiding for a day in a highland village because Sparthius's wound had become infected and Aristides, who'd become our doctor, wanted honey to put on it. The mountains seemed full of armed men – the reward offered for us must have been immense enough to engage the interest of every bandit in the hills.

I have never been so cold. But as the boy Araxa fevered, grew worse, and then – very slowly – began to recover, Amu grew closer to us, and then the natural bonds of a fight and shared food saved us, and by the time was saw the green fields of the upper Kogamos, we were comrades – Spartans and Athenians and Persians all together, and Sparthius's recovery – he was emaciated but growing stronger by the day – was as much a cause for cheer to Karesna, one of the Persians, as the boy Araxa's recovery had been.

By a quirk of fate, we were all hale – aside from some virulent head colds and a lot of coughing – as we rode down out of winter into the green valley that led to Sardis.

Two days later, I stood before Artaphernes.

He looked terrible.

He had circles under his eyes and his skin looked grey. His face was puffy, and he had a paunch, and he clearly found movement difficult. His son – also Artaphernes – waited on him – and glowered at me.

The Satrap of Lydia and Ionia returned my bow of thanks and waved his eldest son away. 'Go and embrace Cyrus!' he said. 'I must talk to Arimnestos alone.'

We were served cups of hot cider by a slave who spilled some, and then we were alone.

'I should ask you about your trip, but you are here, and that is all I need to know. Cyrus says you fought your way out. That Mardonius has put a price on your head. Unofficially, I already know this, and when the courier comes – any day – I will not be able to pretend I don't know where you are. So you must be gone.'

'Are my ships in Ephesus?' I asked.

He looked pained. 'I don't know. If I were you, I would not go to Ephesus – Archilogos would like nothing better than to be the means of your arrest.'

He paused, winced, and I thought he looked ... old.

'I can go to Phokaia,' I said. Athens bought alum from Phokaia for her tanning industry. Athenian ships called there all the time.

'In winter?' he asked. He raised a hand, clearly tired. 'My friend, I'm sorry. Sorry for all of it. But we are, to all intents, at war, and any hour now, I will be ordered to seize you. My son wishes you taken immediately.'

I didn't even know his son. 'Why?' I asked.

'There is a rumour – as yet unconfirmed ...' Artapherenes looked at me and scratched his beard. 'Do I treat you as a friend, or a dangerous enemy? Do I – by telling you this – aid your cause and work against my own king?'

I shook my head. 'I have no idea of what you speak,' I said. I took his hand and kissed it, as I would have that of my own father. 'Thank you for Cyrus and the others. Without them, I would be dead.'

He nodded. 'Well – without you, we would all be dead. Our tale of exchanged favours goes back many years, young man. You wish to go and pay your respects to Briseis. I recommend that you be brief – and circumspect.' His voice grew harder.

I got up from my knee. 'I am always at your service,' I said.

He laughed. 'You are a fine man. Try and stay alive in what is coming – and remember that if ever you wish to bend your stiff Greek neck, I have a place for you in my house.'

'I can certainly serve cider better than the boy you had here – I wouldn't spill any.' I laughed, and for the first time since I'd come in, Artapherenes smiled.

'Oh, Ari,' he said. 'When this war comes, it will be the end of everything for which I worked.'

He caught my hand. In a low voice he said, 'When I die – you must take Briseis. My son will kill her.' He looked into my eye – not pleading, but with the resolve of the warrior. 'Swear to me.'

'I swear by all the gods in Olympus,' I swore, having learned nothing, apparently, about swearing oaths.

'And until then, do an old man the grace of keeping your hands off her,' he said with a hard smile.

I swallowed.

He nodded. 'Go. I may not see you again – or if I do, it will be in Greece.'

Briseis was, I think, thirty-two that year.

Motherhood had mellowed her – had filled in her stomach a little, perhaps, and made her breasts lusher. It had not changed her eyes, or her neck, or her shoulders, or the quality of her smile – that complicated instrument she wielded as I wield a spear.

She rose with her accustomed grace as I entered, and she kissed me on the lips – a brush of her lips on mine that struck me like a Persian arrow.

Nothing ever changed.

She put the back of her hand on my chest when she kissed me, as if to ensure that I didn't crush her to me, and even that small warmth went to my heart like a Levin bolt.

'I must go,' I said foolishly. 'Artapherenes asked me to … come for you when I hear he is dead.'

'His son wants me for his own, and hates me for my contempt.' She shrugged. 'It is, I think, an old story.' She took my hand – oh, the softness of that hand, and the cool warmth of her touch – and drew me on to a kline. 'Cyrus will not let me die so easily, nor be used so ill. Neither will any of the old guard. I am not afraid.' She smiled. 'But I will be happy to have you as my last husband, my dear. The Greek ambassador to the Great King! Friend of the King of Sparta and Lord of Plataea!'

'I am not the Lord of Plataea. Plataea is the size of a large farm and has an assembly of a thousand bickering old men – older than me.' I laughed. 'But I served at the Olympics as a priest.'

'Oh,' she said, with complete seriousness. 'You are a great man, now – not just a great sword.'

'Will you still be my wife if I am a penniless exile in Italy?' I asked. 'Because if Xerxes has his way, there will be no Athens, no Sparta – and no Plataea.'

Her smile fell away. 'Yes,' she said. She met my eye and bit her lip, and for perhaps the first time in all our years together, I saw her hesitate. 'Yes, Ari. Our world is coming to an end. The world of Sappho and Thales and Heraklitus – of Melitus and Ephesus and Mytilini.' She held my eye. 'What will come after? Imperial Persia, and the Great's King's winged lions on every doorstep?'

'No,' I said.

She smiled. 'You truly believe – even after Lades – that Greeks can stop the Great King?'

I nodded. 'Athens and Sparta,' I said. 'We are not ready for what is coming. I have seen the Great King's preparations. I cannot count his soldiers. I'm sure his fleet will be greater than five hundred hulls.' I was suddenly bitter. 'I sailed to Alba – do you know that? For tin. For … a pothos. Better that I had been here, working to build a resistance to the Great King among the Greeks. Now – it is too late. In three months, he will march.'

She bit her lip. 'No,' she said. She looked around – again, showing fear for the first time I could remember. 'No, he will not march in the spring.'

I felt the blood rush to my ears as if I'd taken a blow. 'Why?' I asked.

She leaned closer – I thought to kiss me. 'Babylon is in revolt,' she said.

That was all she knew.

I tore myself from her sight, took my Spartans and my Athenians, and fled for the coast. I learned – much later in life – that the Great King's messenger came two days later. Artaphrenes was sick – and his son turned out all his father's household troops to pursue us.

But the gods had other ideas. The gods had their own plans for Greece, and for Persia. It was like ... like living in mythology, except it was real.

We rode across the plains of Sardis and over the mountains to the coast like a storm. By then, even the Spartans were excellent riders – we'd had five months on horseback with expert teachers.

And I have to tell you, my friends, that the sight of the sea – even in winter, blue and blue, rolling away into the west – made us all weep.

Aristides pulled his riding cloak over his head to hide his face. When he had mastered himself, he said, 'I will never come to Asia again – not willingly.'

We rode down into Phokaia about the time that Artaphrenes' household guards began searching for us in Ephesus.

And there on the beach of Phokaia was my *Lydia*, and when we cantered along the coast road, one of the first men I met was Leukas.

It can seem, in a tale like this, as if I was the hero – the great hero, or perhaps even, if I tell it awry, the only hero. Let me say that I was surrounded by heroes, and that many, many other men said, and did, the right things.

Megakles and Sekla and Leukas were three of them. What might have happened, if they had not used their heads? They took *Lydia* into Ephesus at the turn of the seasons with a cargo of white Athenian hides and Phoenician dyes, and they sailed away two days later, leaving a pair of trustworthy oarsmen and a light boat to find them if I returned. The open hostility of Archilogos – the richest shipowner in Ephesus – made the harbour there unhealthy for them. So they rowed up the coast to the port that had the friendliest relations with Athens, and rented a portion of the beach for the winter – bought a small house, sold their cargo, and settled in. They had men in every port from Samos to Lesvos, and they were collecting rumours like professional spies.

Sekla, as it proved, knew more of what was happening in Babylon than Artapherenes, the satrap. Because Phokaia had alum – most of the dyers' alum in the world – and thus it had merchants who came from Susa and Babylon and Athens and even Syracusa. Sekla's news of the revolt was first-hand, from an eyewitness.

I got it as our rowers pulled us out of the harbour into a cold, sunny winter day. There was rain on the northern horizon and storm heads out over the Aegean.

I chose a multitude of compromises. Megakles concurred. We put the bow due north – and sailed within sight of land, all the way around the great bow, as Greeks call it – the coast of Asia, and then the coast of Thrace, under the lee of magnificent Samothrace and then down the coast of Thessaly to Euboea and Athens. It is a very, very long way to sail and row compared to skipping from Lesvos to Skyros and then to the coast of Euboea, but it has the signal advantage that if a squall hits you, you might survive a swim to the shore. And every storm-tossed day, there's at least the possibility of an anchorage or a beach.

With adverse winds, winter storms and fog, we were almost thirty days sailing home – and our rowers were as thin entering Athens as we had been coming down out of the hills on horseback. No fishing boats in winter means no one from whom to buy fish – no shepherds on the hillsides, no mutton on the fire.

We left Aristides on the coast of Euboea. I sent him to my house with Hector and Alexandros and a pair of marines.

We landed in Piraeus, and while Sekla sold our cargo, I rushed to Themistocles.

I think that what I remember best is that when I said Babylon was in revolt, he slammed his right fist into his left.

'Now,' he said. 'Now we have a chance.'

Corinth – 481 BCE

In which of the local glories of the past, divinely blessed Thebe, did you most delight your spirit? Was it when you raised to eminence the one seated beside Demeter of the clashing bronze cymbals, flowing-haired Dionysus? Or when you received, as a snow-shower of gold in the middle of the night, the greatest of the gods, when he stood in the doorway of Amphitryon, and then went in to the wife to beget Heracles? Or did you delight most in the shrewd counsels of Teiresias? Or in the wise horseman Iolaus? Or in the Sown Men, untiring with the spear?

Pindar, Seventh Isthmian Ode, 454 BCE

After Athens, I returned to Plataea for the longest time I had spent there since my wife died.

In my heart, I was preparing my home for a bride again. And my bride was to be Briseis.

By now, some of you must wonder whether I am a complete fool, that I should seek this woman's favour so often, and so often be turned away. But however brief our encounter in Artapherenes' house in Sardis, I knew – I *knew* that the contract was signed.

And my house in Plataea was beautiful. The frescoes were done, and the house was stocked with grain and oil and full of light and life, because my daughter was there with her nurse Phoebe, a charming local girl, a priestess at the temple of Hera. Phoebe had made the mistake any girl can make, and had a baby without a father – but her milk had saved Euphonia, and as my daughter grew, Phoebe had, in some ways, matured with her.

I confess that, besides my daughter, her body slave and Phoebe, mine was a very masculine household. I had found a place to beach my ships in the Corinthian gulf – over by Thisbe – and with my brother-in-law I'd bought warehouses and barracks there. Because that put my oarsmen so close, and because they were – with Myron's help – all Plataeans, I tended to have a dozen of them around at any given time – on errands, or simply seeing the city of which they were (miraculously, to many) now citizens.

Sekla – who had collected quite a bit of money over the preceding few years – purchased a house in Plataea that spring.

I unpacked my few treasures from Persia – some silk, which went into stores, and my lapis, and the cedarwood box from the Queen Mother. I had never opened it, and when I did, I convinced my new slave butler that I really was a man of consequence.

It was a two-eared cup, as tall as a man's hand to the wrist, big enough to serve to ten guests at a drinking party, made of solid gold. On one side, a mounted man – a king, from his high crown – killed a lion with his bow. One the other side, a pair of winged lions were engraved surrounding an enormous emerald, the largest I'd ever seen, and beryls and other stones were set all the way around the rim – just below it, so that a man could comfortably drink from it. It was slightly bent, from where I'd fallen on it in the fight in the mountains, and I shocked my major-domo by taking it directly to the shop and truing the circle of the rim. My silversmith saved me from cracking the mounts that held the jewels – what does a bronzesmith know of such work? – and then we all marvelled over the quality of the workmanship. It was worth … well, about as much as the whole town of Plataea.

I exaggerate. Perhaps only half as much.

It impressed Aristides. He looked at it for a long time, and even put it tentatively to his lips. And then he looked at me over the rim.

'The hillside of Kitharon is more beautiful,' he said.

I had Aristides as a long-term guest – I had returned from Susa to find him in one of my rooms with a pile of scrolls under his elbow, reading Anaxamander as if he, not I, was the owner. But he was an excellent guest, and – having run a rich household for many years – he was an endless fund of information.

Aristides, Sekla, Megakles, Leukas, Sittonax – who had a dozen tales to tell of his adventures in Asia; Hector and Nikeas and Alexandros – and all my local friends, such as Ajax and Gelon and Lysieus and the three smiths, who had made more money in one year than they had imagined possible – Tiraeus and Styges and Hermogenes, much recovered in his old self thanks to prosperity—they were all present. Wealth may not buy happiness, but it certainly beats poverty.

And I had truly begun to enjoy wealth.

We went through a great deal of wine as that winter gave way to spring, and the bitter rains gave way to warm sun. The sun dried the stones, and my gardener – a freedman from Sicily, of all places – provided me with jasmine and roses and a hundred other flowers and shrubs, as well as making my olive tree shine like Athena's gift to my house. Aristides – as anxious for his wife to arrive as I was – helped me with every detail, and when the guest house was finished, we watched the fresco painter – and annoyed him mightily, so that he muttered at us every day.

My guest house was decorated with scenes from the Odyssey – the return of Odysseus, the loom of Penelope, and the moment at which Penelope takes her husband in her arms. My daughter loved them, and did her best to 'help' the artist, who might mock or curse me but was always bright and pleasant with her – even when her dirty handprints marred Penelope's face.

Storm Cutter returned very profitably from Aegypt with the onset of spring, and Paramanos told Moire where to find us and he took a cargo for Corcyra and came right round to Thisbe. My African navarch announced himself by riding into my courtyard on one of the handsomest horses I'd ever seen – he had Ka behind him on another – and Jocasta, wife of Aristides, mounted on a third.

When I'd known him well, Moire hadn't been much more fulsome than a man of Lacedeamon, but six more years among Greeks had broadened his vocabulary and his confidence. He sat easily on a kline with a cup of wine, and chatted with Aristides about Aegypt as if he were an Athenian gentleman of the bluest blood – but that was, in those days, how the explosion of sea trade was changing Athens. Navarchs and helmsmen were suddenly men of property and wealth, and merchants – Athenian, Metic or freedmen – were growing to be as wealthy as the old money – or wealthier.

In some ways, it didn't seem right. I had taken an embassy to Susa and brought back almost nothing – I'd preserved some fabrics from India and Kwin, and one packet of spices – but while I'd spent my fortune on a failed embassy, Harpagos, Moire and Megakles and Sekla had made me a fortune moving goods from Athens to Aegypt and Asia. Our piratical triremes made poor merchantmen, but the sudden demand for luxury goods could make even a trireme's voyage profitable. And the pause in the endless naval war between Athens and Aegina – according to Moire, the rumour in Athens was that Sparta had ordered Aegina to cease operations – made shipping safe, or at least safer than it had been in twenty years.

At any rate, I sat home that spring, and my captains made me more money. Moire purchased a pair of small round ships in Corinth, stowed them with Boeotian barley and shipped it up the coast of Illyria with *Storm Cutter* as a watchdog, while Harpagos and Sekla took *Lydia* and a larger round ship that could carry two *thousand* medimnoi of grain – a good size hull and the proceeds of two successful voyages – and laded her for Aegypt.

Moire brought us reports of the failed revolt in Aegypt and the ongoing revolt in Babylon. When Sekla sailed, he had orders to pick up any information he could gather. It is not part of my tale to explain the workings of shipping – mine or anyone else's; merchanting is a dull business, unless there're pirates or a storm – but I will mention that Sekla, who was from somewhere on the coast of Africa, had met Greeks and Phoenicians who traded up the Nile where he found merchants from the Erythra Thalassa and the Great Eastern Ocean, and he was afire to go. My reports from Susa and my discussions with Abha made for some fine spring conversations, a cup of wine on my knee, in my own garden.

Sekla, eyes afire, leaned forward. 'When all this war is done, I say we take two triremes and a store ship,' he said. 'Carry our goods up the Nile, and build ourselves ships on the Erythra Thalassa and try the Great East Sea.'

'That is a mighty dream,' I said.

Sittonax laughed. 'You sailed to Alba,' he said. 'Why not India?'

The Galle was becoming a geographer.

I laughed, but Sekla looked off into the darkness. 'Doola would sail to India,' he said.

And I thought it might be true. That's when that dream began. It is another story, but I'll tell it to you some day.

Jocasta's arrival changed the house in every way. First, a great Athenian lady does not travel alone, and she had six women with her – joined within hours by my sister Penelope and my sister-in-law Leda and *their* servants.

I remember standing under my portico, looking at my garden, and poor Euphonia caught my hand. 'I don't *want* to go and weave with the ladies,' she said. For almost two months, she had stayed up too late every night and listened to tales of sailing the world with a dozen men who catered to her every whim, and the arrival of a houseful of gentlewomen had catapulted her back to her life as one of them. 'I want to sail to Aegypt with Sekla. A pox on all this weaving.'

But I won't make a mockery of femininity. The air of the house changed for the better, and Jocasta and Penelope got more work out of my servants and my slaves than I ever had. Pen fired my cook and bought me a Thracian – imagine having a tattooed killer as your cook, but I did, and he was very good.

We laid in more wine.

I did enjoy the moment when Jocasta entered the andron to set up her loom, and there was the Persian cup. She started.

She looked at me as a nine-year-old girl looks when she wants one more piece of honeycomb and doesn't dare ask.

I took it down and handed it to her.

She held it for a moment, and handed it back. 'A remarkable piece of vulgarity,' she said.

'A gift,' I said.

'Oh, well.' She smiled. 'People do give the oddest things.'

The oarsmen were sent to find their own lodgings.

Hangings went on the walls for the first time – I hadn't missed them – and one day, Jocasta and Leda and Penelope went to the agora with a dozen servants and four slaves and spent – I can't remember how much, but it seemed a great deal – on a wine service in silver and a complete set of the sort of overly ornate Athenian ceramics that I carried in my ships and avoided owning – all scenes of the gods and everyday life in lurid red and black. I liked plain black ware and I liked my good Boeotian pottery – thick, heavy and solid as Old Draco or Empedocles himself.

By next morning, I couldn't find a scrap of it in my house.

You see – like all men, I've turned to mockery of women, when what I really want to convey is that my sister and Jocasta and their friends made my house beautiful and civilised enough to receive the Queen of Sparta. I had to admit that the Athenian ware was pretty enough, and the cups were light in the hand, well crafted. My rooms were full of light and air – but decorated in the latest taste – and the women set up looms and prepared for me a set of matching drapes for my couches with a sort of ruthless efficiency that reminded me of a well-run ship. Really – watching Jocasta direct a dozen women weaving on four looms was much like watching Paramenos direct a ship in a storm – no hesitation, no anger, just a single-minded concentration on the task. They wove wool, and then they wove all our spare flax into towels, and then ...

And then Gorgo came.

She came to Plataea with a dozen Spartan women and two men – Sparthius and Bulis. She arrived quite late in the evening, having celebrated the Epikledeia in Corinth. The queen was tired, but we stood with her people in my small courtyard and gave her Plataean kykeon, wine with barley meal and grated goat's cheese, and she laughed that laugh and was visibly delighted by everything – including a suddenly shy Jocasta and my daughter, who kept grabbing the great queen's hand and dragging her to see the most ordinary things – which she accepted with a good grace.

When she was gone into the guest quarters, led by Pen and Leda, I put the two Spartiates on kline and we sat and drank most of an amphora of wine. I told them what I knew of the revolt in Babylon.

Finally, I turned away another bowl – Hector nodded, as if to tell me in his fifteen-year-old wisdom that I had chosen well – and cocked an eyebrow at Sparthius. 'And Brasidas?' I asked.

He looked away. Bulis looked at his feet. These were men who could defy the Great King and fight anyone to the death.

I let it go.

Eugenios, my new slave domesticos, purchased over my bewildered objections by Penelope for roughly the price of all of my other slaves combined, came in and escorted the Spartans to their room. They had to share – even my house, which seemed as vast as a cavern when it was just me and my daughter and her nurse, was now as full of people as a hive is with bees. It was not too late at night.

It was probably better that way. We didn't sit up late, as the Spartans were tired – so we had a fresh day in which to renew acquaintance. But as soon as Eugenios escorted them out, Leda and Pen joined me and sipped my wine, sitting on a kline and swinging their feet.

'A symposiast at last,' Leda said, stretching. 'I declare I shall wear ivy on my brow and sing a lewd song.' She looked at me from under her brows and made me laugh.

Pen poked her. And turned to me. 'Fancy, having the Queen of Sparta in our house.'

Our house. Well, it made me smile.

Leda got up and stretched again. She and Pen were just thirty – matrons. Both were priestesses of Hera and busybodies, so they were fit from walking. Each had borne just one child – both sons. Pen's son Euaristos was new to me, just five years old. Leda's son was six, born to a man she never mentioned. I noticed that they were fit – and lovely – but neither was as fit as any woman among the Spartans.

All this was by the way. Leda was, I thought, stretching to catch my attention. And that was a kind of trouble I didn't need. But I liked her smile and her wit, and I probably grinned at her like an old satyr.

They went off to bed chattering.

Morning came early.

I met Gorgo playing with my daughter in the garden, less than an hour after dawn. Euphonia could barely sleep for the excitement of having the Queen of Sparta in the house, and her doting nurse helped her dress and loosed her on the world.

The queen rose early.

'I hope you are not planning on going riding,' I said.

Gorgo laughed, long and hard. 'I was hunting,' she said. 'I had a beast in view.' She shrugged. 'You took my boys to Susa and you brought them home. And helped with the chariot. All in all, I owe you.' She smiled down at Euphonia. 'She is charming. She was telling me about Brauron. You should send her to Sparta for a summer.' She nodded. 'She's athletic enough. Some girls can't take the pace of the races and the dance, but she could.'

'Can *you* tell me anything of Brasidas?' I asked.

Gorgo looked away. 'He is still in Babylon,' she said. 'I doubt Demaratus can save him now.'

'What did he *do*?' I asked.

Gorgo shook her head. 'It is not my place to speak of it. And I regret that. We are deeply in your debt, Arimnestos of Plataea.'

We talked for some time about the situation, and Euphonia, bored, slipped away into the garden and vanished to the stables.

At some point, I thought of Demaratus, and the tablets, and I sent Eugenios to fetch them. He brought them to me – somewhat hacked about. The string that held them together had been cut, so that they were simply three individual wax tablets, one double sided, and one with a carved cover. I held them out to the queen with a bow.

'I'm sorry, my queen. These are from the former King of Sparta, Demaratus, and I was to deliver them to you immediately – and I have failed. I forgot them. And indeed, I can't imagine that they have much of import – I confess I've read his note on the wax – it used to be clearer – and all it contains is directions for the factor of one of his farms.'

The queen took them. She sat suddenly, as if overcome by emotion – she, a Spartan – and she held them in the skirts of her chiton. Then she took the cover, and flexed it between her powerful hands, so that the frame splintered.

She took a sharp knife from her zone, and slipped it between the wax and the board beneath, and peeled the wax away in one neat rectangle – and the board beneath was covered in dense black writing.

She laughed aloud.

'I should not have let you see that,' she said. She raised her eyes. 'Swear you will not tell.'

Well, I'm telling you now, but I think everyone involved is dead, now.

She peeled all three boards clear of their wax, and Eugenios carried the wreckage away. I have no idea what the former King of Sparta said to Gorgo in a three-page letter, but I'll guess that he sent her a list of messengers and codes. Because from that day forward, she always seemed to know more than anyone about the Medes – and especially about their fleet.

Just as we tidied up the last splinters, Aristides joined us – shocked, I think, to find the Queen of Sparta alone in the garden with a man, much less with me. His wife joined us soon after.

She came across the garden, and I could see that age sat more heavily on her than on Gorgo, although they were much of an age – thirty or thirty-five, whereas their husbands were fifty-five and fifty-eight. She had more grey in her hair, and child-rearing had flattened her breasts, widened her hips and added to her weight. She was a handsome woman with a straight back and a dignity unmarred by time – but Gorgo appeared ten years younger – or even fifteen.

Gorgo smiled at her and took her hand, and they embraced. And Jocasta giggled – something I would not have thought possible – and whispered to Gorgo, who shrieked as if bit by an adder and then laughed so hard I thought she might fall down. She took Jocasta's hand and put it on her right breast, and the two dissolved in laughter.

Aristides was embarrassed. He looked at me, and then looked away, and then walked out of my garden, calling for Nikeas. I followed him, passing a yawning Leda under the archway. She paused to smile at me – a full-face smile – and then I caught sight of my Athenian exile.

He kept walking – out of my house, out of the gate, towards the town wall. I followed him, and eventually caught him up.

'It is unseemly,' he muttered.

'Have you given her the necklace?' I asked.

That gave him pause. 'No,' he admitted.

'Or anything else from the time we were away?' I asked.

Aristides glowered. 'She was behaving like . . . like . . . a man.'

I shrugged. 'Your wife is making friends with the *Queen of Sparta*. The rules for women in Sparta are very different.'

He put his hands on his hips – fidgeted – and put them down by his sides. Finally he turned and started walking back to my house. 'You are right, of course,' he muttered. 'But she is always ... so ... reserved.' He turned. 'I love her ... dignity.'

'As do I,' I said. 'But it is a cloak she should be allowed to put off, from time to time.'

Aristides chewed on that for perhaps forty paces, and then said, 'You get in a good thing, now and then. Dignity as a cloak – that's good.'

We had the Queen of Sparta in Plataea for five days.

As with Jocasta, one of my favourite moments was created by the cup. Spartan women often sit with men, as I have mentioned, and several times we all sat in the guest house, or the garden, but one night we assembled in the garden and the insects were too much, and we moved into the andron, and there, glowing in golden opulence, was the Queen Mother's gift.

Gorgo went and took it down from the low shelf on which it sat.

'I want to drink from this,' she said. 'From the Great King?' she asked.

'The Queen Mother,' I admitted.

Bulis laughed. 'The Persians are so rich they don't even know they are bribing us,' he said.

We all laughed. And there we sat – the Queen of Sparta, the just man of Athens, and the heroes of Marathon, and drank to the cause of the liberty of Hellas in the cup we'd been given by the Queen of Persia.

Three of the days she was with us, Gorgo went with Pen and Leda and Jocasta and paid worship to Hera at the temple.

Every day, she was feted – by Myron, by Antigonus, by the temple of Hera itself. She made a great donation, and she was, to all intents, pleased by everything she saw. She kissed Boeotian babies and watched my Epilektoi dance the Pyricche.

Bulis walked among the young men and talked to them. He was like a different man – charming, with compliments for every boy on their physique, their bearing, their skill. Later, he lay with me on a couch.

'This is a fine town, I think. More like Sparta than I would have believed. Small – and thus good.' He raised a kantharos cup. 'See? You make me drunk, and I talk.'

And Sparthius told Ajax and Lysius that the young men were good. This praise, from a Spartiate and a professional warrior, went straight to their heads, and they got very drunk and made fools of themselves very publicly, which was a nine-day wonder in Plataea and had no other effect on any of us – or them.

Early on the last full day, I put all the women up on horses – the splendid horses Moire and Ka had brought – and we rode up to the shrine of Leithos, and Gorgo made a sacrifice of wine. An odd thing happened that I cannot explain. Gorgo poured her libation on the precinct wall, and the tomb rang – as if with laughter. I had known that tomb since I was a boy, and never heard the like. Some of the men flinched.

Idomeneaus came down from his hillside to see the queen. She looked into his mad eyes and spoke quietly to him. He asked her something, and she nodded.

Later he came to me, and nodded. 'She says you served her well,' he said. 'The hero – he is very pleased that she is here.'

I thought he looked madder than ever, and I didn't linger near him. He smelled odd, and not of the hillside.

Then I took Gorgo up Kitharon, and we rode to my family's altar – twenty of us, the queen, and Jocasta and Pen and Leda and Artistides and the two Spartan men, Gelon and Alexandros and Idomeneaus and Styges, of all people. And we made a sacrifice of a deer we'd speared on the way – Styges got it – and then we rode slowly down into the gathering twilight of a late spring evening.

I rode side by side with the queen.

'I do this a great deal,' she said, as if I'd asked a question. 'Leonidas is a hero, but sometimes that stands between him and other men. I go to small places and great, and I visit women, and woo men – for the cause.' She turned to me in the gathering darkness and she did not look downcast. 'But I tell you, Plataean – this is a fine place. Your people are good people. The Pyricche and the women's dances, the wine and the barley and the festivals and the temple ...'

As always, I was tempted to say that I did not need a Spartan's good opinion to know my home was good. But instead I smiled.

'I'm glad you see all these things,' I said. 'To me, it is merely home.'

She nodded. 'Next spring, we'll have an assembly of all the free Greeks. At Corinth, I think. Please come, with Myron.' She smiled. 'My husband wants you there as much as I do. Listen – we've made a good beginning. Most men accept that we must resist. Your reports and ours have spread far and wide.'

On the last night, she led a torchlight procession around the women's shrines, and then she returned to my house. I had kline in the garden – all of them I owned and four borrowed from Myron, who joined us. I had a scandalous dinner – a mixed dinner, with men and women together. In Lacedaemon, it was sometimes done, and in Italy it was the norm. In Etrusca, a man and his wife might make love on their couch at the end of a meal and no one would think it odd.

Antiochus pretended to be scandalised, but Myron joined in with a will, dragging his shy wife from her chair and making her lie beside him. After a cup of wine she giggled as much as Gorgo and Jocasta.

We ate and drank. We spoke of nothing deep, or meaningful, except about children, and their upbringing. Gorgo smiled at Jocasta's description of the perils of choosing tutors. Of course, Jocasta was far more directly involved in her son's education than Gorgo, who had probably handed hers off to slaves minutes after childbirth. That was the Spartan way.

Yet despite a thousand differences, Jocasta and Gorgo were instant friends. It was odd – and somewhat miraculous – that Gorgo had somehow discerned this from a few descriptions, but their alliance helped all of the events that follow. Leonidas forged an alliance with the democrat, Themistocles. Gorgo made hers with Aristides' wife.

When Gorgo and her train had ridden away – headed to Thebes for another social visit – Pen fell on to my lap in unpretended exhaustion. Myron sent a slave to ask all of us to dinner – because, the slave explained, he assumed we'd be too shattered to cook. He might have been right, although I suspect it was my cook and Eugenios who needed the night off.

That was the queen's visit to Plataea. Ever after, Plataea was much more favourable to the Laconians in all their dealings. Thebes was merely polite, and Sparthius stopped with us one more night while Gorgo visited Thisbe – to tell me that the Thebans had been rude.

Nothing pleases a Plataean more than news of foolishness in Thebes.

'They're going to accept the Great King,' Sparthius said.

I shook my head. For a Plataean, that was a major threat.

I took my daughter to spend her summer at Brauron by sea, in *Lydia*, and promised to pick her up again myself and not to spend all summer at sea.

You would think – after all we reported, and after Moire took *Storm Cutter* home early and reported on the Persian fleet in Thrace and the number of ships in the Bosporus – you'd think, I repeat, that all Greece would have rung with the sound of mallets driving pegs into new planks, of men straining to learn how to wield an oar, of legions of Jocastas weaving sails.

You'd think.

You'd think that the knowledge that only the bravery of the men of Babylon had kept the Persians from our doors that very spring might have served to alert Greece.

But Greeks like to talk. And everything had to be talked through, and every one – everyone who mattered – had to be allowed to speak, and when I entered Piraeus that summer, there were, in fact, forty triremes under construction – but only because of Themistocles and his silver mines.

'I only got these by swearing that if the Persians didn't come, we'd storm Aegina,' he said. 'Before the gods, all men are fools.'

I drank to that, and we discussed what he knew from all the captains who carried goods from Asia or Ionia. He said that the revolt in Babylon had been crushed, and that the Great King had ordered most of the nobles involved, and their wives and children and children's children, put to death. Every Greek mercenary taken was executed as a rebel.

'Now he'll come,' Themistocles said. 'And we still won't be ready.'

'Gorgo says there is to be an assembly at Corinth,' I said.

'Only because Adamenteis is the most ruthless politician of our age,' Themistocles said – this for a man who exiled all his opponents. 'He told the Spartans that attendance at the Isthmian games by an entire Spartan delegation was his price for hosting the affair.'

I shrugged. 'It must be somewhere,' I noted.

A day later, I was in Piraeus when the sky to the east and south began to turn black – not grey, not even a dark grey, but black, like coal or charcoal. I have seldom seen a sky that colour.

As the winds rose, I gathered what oarsmen I could and got the *Lydia* into one of the new stone ship-sheds, where she was snug, high off the water, and dry. Her hull was waterlogged and had worm, and the ship-sheds were the very best place for my *Lydia*.

What followed was one of the worst storms I've ever seen. The wind was from the east, as strong as a northern gale, but longer and shriller. Noon on the second day we had shrill winds and an orange sky, as if the gods meant to burn the earth away.

Seasoned captains got their ships off the seas. Far to the south, off Crete, Harpagos took our pentekonter freighter into a little port for refuge. Moire ran *Storm Cutter* back into Corcyra despite having just left the sea wall. Megakles took *Swan* into Mytilini, and *Lydia* was safely in a ship-shed.

Far to the east, the storm smashed into the bridges on the Hellespont, and wrecked them.

At the time, I stood at the eastern edge of the Piraeus harbour and let the storm soak me to the skin as I watched it come in. I could feel its deadliness and the force of its winds and I prayed to Poseidon to preserve my friends and my ships. And eventually, I was wise enough to pray for any man at sea in such a storm, with a little more humility.

For four days the waves pounded Piraeus. For four days that late summer storm wrecked ships, ruined houses, flooded towns and river estuaries – it killed birds and fish and men. And then the skies dawned pink, and the storm was gone, and we were left to wonder whether it had all been a dream.

But to Xerxes' plans, it was no dream, and ten days later, when an Athenian ore freighter came back in from the mines on Samothrace, he reported to us – and the priests of Poseidon and any other who would listen – that Zeus had broken the chain at the Hellespont, shattering ships and drowning men.

I spent the summer running cargoes. It was a piece with my life in general that I went from hosting royalty to helping a dozen oarsmen muscle sacks of Boeotian barley into the hold of a round ship in just a few weeks, but I'm a poor aristocrat. I can't sit on my hands and watch other men work. I could either drive ships through the water or pound bronze, and I was not man enough to resist the look my sister gave me – or my domesticos. That man – supposedly a slave – had taken over my house and made it all too easy for me to live there. Food appeared as if by magic – wine flowed, or stopped, with more or less water.

When oil jars ran low, more was purchased. Floors were cleaned. No servant or slave approached me for any reason.

Well – I'd been a slave, and I was not a very good master – too involved, I suspect. But my joke to Pen as I paused at her great house to sip wine en route to the Gulf of Corinth was that the house would run best of all if I wasn't there.

I saw Aegypt that summer. Sekla had *Lydia*, so I paid rent to Aristides and took his beautiful *Athena Nike* from where he'd laid her up in Corinth. I got to spend the summer with Demetrios, one of my earliest mentors – one of Aristides' helmsmen. He, too, was rich.

We had a fine voyage. I had learned a great deal of pure navigation in the Western Ocean, and I was no longer cautious about using it. Demetrios was still – like Vasileos and Megakles – a much better dead-reckoning sailor than I, and we challenged each other all summer. I suspect our rented oarsmen loathed us – we spent too much time over the horizon from any land, but we had fun, and we had some very fast passages.

In Aegypt, we found a Corinthian trireme – badly damaged by a storm and abandoned. In fact, locals were starting to pick her apart for firewood. How I wished for Vasileos! But I got her off the beach, towed her into the delta and got some linen patches on her sides – the Aegyptian revolt had cut them off from any source of wood unless Greeks brought it, so that their shipbuilding industry was at a standstill.

We left her there to get new rigging, and we ran a small cargo of perfumes and wines and some finished papyrus to Lebanon – and came back with the whole centreline of the ship burdened with timber. I think that Aristides would have cried to see his magnificent warship, her fine entry to the water ruined by overloading, her beautiful midship catwalk unusable because of fifty great pine logs. We all had to run down the ship's sides with ropes, and it was a dead uncomfortable voyage – rowing all the way, no wind, terrible heat.

But out of it, I got a trireme – a heavy merchant trireme, well built and beautifully rebuilt by men happy to have work. We made a small fortune on the wood – the best cargo in the world is a cargo that your buyer needs desperately and for which you have no competition.

We called her *Astarte* for her new timbers, and we crewed her from rowers stranded in Aegypt by the revolt and loaded her with papyrus and linen, and we used all our profits on the wood to load

Athena Nike's narrow holds with glass – Aegyptian faience, mostly perfume bottles.

Summer was wearing on to autumn. We had our 'home cargo' and we also knew that there was a squadron of Phoenicians preying on Greek merchants – there was the biter bit – off the delta. So we ran out of the eastern mouth of the delta – for the south coast of Crete. I'd done it before when desperate – this was simply good navigation, and I put into Gortyn's port as if I'd had a Pole Star over it all the way. Permit me a little bragging. It was a pretty piece of navigation, given two hard blows and a couple of grey days with no sun sighting.

We'd slipped the pirates – who were, according to the Cretans, the Persian navy enforcing a blockade on Aegypt, which was being punished for revolt. I'll waste a little of your time to say that Aegypt – one of the richest lands in the world – was not in 'revolt'. According to their own way of thinking, they were throwing off the yoke of oppression. To Xerxes, they were rebels.

Old Lord Achilleus was dead – and his son Neoptolymos had died at Lades. But the new King of Gortyn was Scyllus, Achilleus's brother, and his son Brotachus was already a famous soldier. I was feasted in the palace, sold some fancy perfume bottles – wait, I lie. I *gave* the Cretans the perfume bottles of Aegyptian glass, and they *gave* me rich gifts in return. Very aristocratic, the Cretans. Too good for trade.

Bah – none of that matters. What matters is that in the town – the fishing port that supplied the king and his soldiers – I met Troas, the fisherman – still hale, still rude. He crushed me to him, and invited me to dinner.

So I went. Troas no longer lived in a rude shack on the beach. He'd had two boats and a fine son-in-law and some war loot, and from that he'd gone to a dozen fishing boats, nets in a tangle in every direction, a small army of fishermen who worked for him – and a fine stone house.

Gaiana didn't share our dinner – that was not the Cretan way. But her oldest son did. His name was Hipponax, and he was … mine. There was no hiding it – he had my nose, my mouth, my eyes – and her long limbs.

He was overeager to please me, and rude to his mother and his grandfather, and it was quite clear to me that he was a handful.

After dinner, he was sent to the agora on an errand, and we three sat together. Gaiana had aged. She was tall and plump and had lines around her eyes, and probably had a thousand other flaws, but I was older myself and I saw her as ... the same girl I'd bedded in the rain under Hephaestion's porch, fifteen or more years before. She smiled nervously when first I came in, and then she had to find fault with me ...

'I'm sure our manners are too coarse for a great lord like you,' she said.

'Do you ever stop talking to hear yourself think?' she asked, and:

'Do you know any stories that are not about you?'

And a dozen other quips. But after a cup of wine, she looked at her father.

He leaned forward on the kitchen table and held his bronze cup between his hands. 'Would you take your son?' he asked. 'He's going to kill someone. He's set on being a warrior, and fishermen's sons are not warriors on Crete. He fights all the time – with the boys from the warrior societies. He wins, too.' Troas grinned in pleasure. Then shook his head.

'You do not have the best record around here,' Gaiana put in. 'Half the island died at Lades!'

I shrugged. At thirty, I might have launched into some hot-blooded defence of my actions, and Miltiades and the whole Ionian Revolt – a diatribe against the treasons of Samos. But instead I shrugged and smiled at her.

And she smiled back.

'Stop looking at me like that,' she said.

At twenty, I'd have assumed she meant just that, but there and then, I knew she meant the opposite.

'Will you take him?' Troas asked.

'Yes,' I said. I felt good saying it. 'Bless you for raising my son. I'll take him to sea and try to keep him alive.' I looked at Troas. 'You know there is no guarantee.'

Troas raised his chin. 'I lost her husband,' he said gruffly.

'Pater ...' she began, and then paused.

I think we talked more, but eventually old Troas glared at his daughter. 'Shall I leave you two lovebirds alone?' he asked testily.

'Yes,' she said, defiant.

And he did.

Much later, she lay beside me. The gods were smiling – rain was falling on the roof.

'I'm old and fat,' she said.

'No,' I said. I spent some time proving my point.

She laughed and laughed and tickled me. 'Damn you for coming back,' she said. 'I loved my husband. But I'm sick of being in a bed alone.'

And later still, she said, 'Keep him alive. I have two other boys. They'll make good fishermen. But Hipponax is ... something else. When he's not a violent fool, he's ... like a poet.'

Like a poet? I liked the sound of that.

The world is a strange and wonderful place, and one of the ways in which it is strange is this – few women in my life have stirred me as quickly or as deeply as Arwia of Babylon, with her scents and her earthy brilliance and her remarkable body. But while she was an adventure – and a sensual pleasure – Gaiana was ... better. Truer. Better for my soul, anyway.

We laughed a great deal. We talked about ... nothing – but we talked and talked, and then she complained again about her fat, as she called it.

'The answer to weight,' I said, 'is exercise.'

She hit me quite hard.

Hipponax was a trained sailor, and a remarkably sullen and difficult boy. I've known dozens, if not hundreds, of young men, and they have much in common – they do not think, they lie when the truth would have done as well, they think failure is a crime, they think they are the gift of the gods to war, the sea and all of womankind – I'm just getting started, and these views are based mostly on knowing myself.

But even by that standard, Hipponax was difficult. It was as if he was constantly wrestling with some inner daemon, and losing. He said the most astounding things – out loud. He told Demetrios that he – Hipponax – was the best helmsman on the ship.

He came to me our second day at sea and said that he 'wasn't going to take any more crap' from my captain of marines. Siberios was probably not the best warrior on the waves – he was a Corinthian sell-sword I'd found on the beach in Aegypt – but he was a good man in a fight, he had scars to prove it, and he could discipline men.

'He's riding me. Because he knows I'm a better man. I can take him,' Hipponax said.

I looked at him for a moment. 'Are you here on the command deck as my son, or as a marine on my ship?'

He shrugged. 'Whatever,' he said.

'As my son, I'd suggest you learn some humility. As a marine – get the fuck off my deck before I have you bound to an oar, and never approach me again with such whiney crap. Do I make myself clear?' I did think a moment before I shot that out.

He turned red. 'Fuck you,' he said. 'I don't have to take your crap either.'

Demetrios saved me a lot of trouble by knocking him flat – from the side. I think it was better that Demetrios did it.

He bounded to his feet, ready to fight. He really was incredible – fast, brave, strong.

Overweight Demetrios dropped him a second time, and he didn't move.

'I should apologise,' Demetrios said.

'Don't bother,' I said.

But I was wise enough to send Hector to look after him. Hector got him under the awning and kept him cool, and was waiting with water.

I can guess some of the things they said to each other – but they became friends. Hector was younger, but as my right hand, he knew me better. Hipponax craved my good opinion but had all the wrong notions of how to achieve it.

They became ... inseparable. We had a day in port on a tiny island west of Lesvos, and they did something that must have been insanely reckless and stupid, because I still haven't been told.

At any rate, Hipponax became manageable, although, as you will hear, this did not apply to combat.

A day west of Thasos, with all my rowers well rested and a deck full of marines, a pair of pirates came out of the morning haze and were foolish enough to try us – two ships to two, in the open ocean.

I won't bother with the fight. I'll only say that I would have loved to be aboard their lead ship when we turned and attacked them.

See? I still laugh.

They were brutal animals with a dozen women chained to their midships deck and the corpse of a man rotting against a boat sail mast. Neither ship had any recognisable identity – they weren't Samian aristocrats making a little money, or Phoenicians or Carthaginians. These were scum. I'll only relate one incident. I was standing in the bows, waiting to climb on to the rail of the marines' box and leap on to the enemy deck. My marines were all formed behind me, and we

264

were silent with the tension. That heart-grabbing tension that never changes. Every fight.

We bore down, with Demetrios's powerful hand on the tiller, and we made the little leap to the side that Demetrios always makes about fifty feet out from a strike – and my fool son pushed past me and clambered on to the rail.

Even as we struck, he leapt. A full twenty heartbeats before I would have gone – and no one was ready to support him.

No one but Hector.

Hector ran along the side rail – you try that in bronze – and leaped.

It was many, many years since I had been the *third* man on to an enemy deck.

We killed every free man. The slaves caught the last of their marines – he tried to hide among them, and they killed him. I won't describe it, but I'm going to guess he had it coming.

The whole incident reminded me of Dagon. As I have said before, I'm sure you'd like me to have sailed the seas looking for him and for revenge, but by Poseidon and by Herakles, I had better things to do with my time.

But seeing the ruins of the women chained to the deck did something in my chest. I dreamed of Dagon that night, and the next night, and the next. The gods were telling me something.

We were close to Delos. We had a good cargo and time. I put the helm down and took the women we'd saved – if indeed they were saved – to the sanctuary of Delos. I found Dion of Delos, who had helped me with dreams before.

After some time, I decided, with the help of the worthy priest, that I had been commanded to avenge the women – the women who leaped into Poseidon's arms. That's what the priest of Apollo concluded, and I think he had the right of it.

It is one thing to pursue a personal revenge. It is another – I hope – to be told by the Sea God to right a wrong.

But the fight made the bond between the boys as strong as Chalcidian steel. And it confirmed my notion that my ships, despite their lading with luxury goods, were fast enough to run. So I bore away north on a favourable wind for a little spying along the Thracian coast. West of the Dardanelles, it is flat – the delta of the Evros river is rich in birds and fish and mosquitoes. We beached, built hasty stockades to protect our ships against the locals, and stood guard all night, but some of the Thracians traded with us, and we had a good look into the Great King's preparations.

Zeus and Poseidon sent the storm that wrecked the bridges, but the Great King was equal to the challenge. I got close enough to see one span of ships already rebuilt, and another laid out along the Asian coast.

Men say that Xerxes ordered the waters beaten with whips. I think that sounds unlikely, but he was a man not fully in control of his passions, and I suppose he might have given way to a fit of rage.

I also counted almost three hundred and fifty military ships.

I touched at Athens to sell my cargoes and pick up hides and salt for Corinth, but I was in a hurry and all my friends were gone. We were late for the Council, and everyone was already there.

Corinth is a fine city. The magnificent acropolis towers over the town itself, and it is a long climb to the temples, and the pottery workshops aren't what they were in my father's youth, but they have beautiful buildings and superb bronzesmiths. To say the least.

As we beached, a runner came down to invite me to drink wine with Adamenteis. I would not have been suspicious, even though I disliked the man, but the runner would not meet my eye. The whole thing sounded odd, and I read the message tabled several times.

'Please tell our lordly host that I will attend him after I report to Themistocles,' I said.

He cringed. 'No! That is, lord, he needs to see you – immediately.'

Never make a slave improvise.

'Why?' I shot out.

The man's eyes were everywhere. 'I ... lord, I don't know. Perhaps about Persia?' He still didn't look at me, and I smelled a dead rat. Perhaps several dead rats.

I turned to Hipponax. 'Set this man ashore,' I said.

'No!' he said, but he went quietly enough. I sent a runner to Themistocles, and sat tight.

Before the sun set the width of a finger, a small army of magistrates and armed men came down to the beach.

It was all about the ship – the wreck we found in Aegypt. A pair of Corinthians claimed her – and said that I had no doubt attacked her and taken her, as I was a notorious pirate.

Adamenteis supported them. I suppose he'd intended to take me when I went to visit him.

Let me explain that men in Greece do not recognise the laws of other cities, so no man of Plataea cares a fig for the laws of Corinth, least of all me. I told the two magistrates to go about their business or I'd have them thumped by my marines. I was informed that I could not land or sell my cargoes.

This sort of thing happens. I sent Hipponax to Aristides and Hector to Gorgo and got my ships off the beach.

That should have been enough. It should have worked. Adamanteis should have, at the very least, put the interests of the League ahead of his own and let the matter go, but he did not, and by that action revealed himself, at least to me. I still think he took a bribe from the Great King. I know that other men dispute this.

But I say he was a traitor, and he was hosting the conference.

I lost six days in Adamanteis's pettifogging labyrinth of accusations. Among other things, it became apparent – to me – that he had known I had the ship *before* I landed. A priest on Delos, perhaps? But my innate sense of self-preservation said that something was not right, and that this was the long arm of Xerxes reaching across the waves for me.

Neither Aristides nor Cimon would accept a word of it. They saw me as deluded, and while they worked tirelessly to rid me of the burden of accusations, they declined to accept that the Corinthian was an enemy.

So I didn't hear any of the opening orations, and I missed it when the whole delegation of Thebes – a delegation of oligarchs that excluded some of the cities' aristocrats – spoke against resistance. I missed the King of Sparta – Leonidas – giving what Themistocles insisted was the best speech he'd ever heard.

Instead, I took my ships along the isthmus, landed in the Peloponnesus at Hermione, and took a horse back with all my marines trailing away behind me in a cacophony of curses – most of them had never forked a horse before. I lost two more days riding through the Peloponnese – beautiful, but not for riding. We came down out of the mountains and I saw Corinth in the distance, and sent Hector ahead to see whether the way was clear.

Themistocles had bought a Corinthian ally – Diotus, who had had business dealings with me and was the proxenos for little Plataea, and he and Myron had done the best they could – they'd wrapped the accusations in wool, as we like to say in Plataea. So when I arrived, I had to put up almost a third of my profits from the voyage east as a bond, and then I was allowed to go about my business – which was to attend the conference.

One more detail to explain my frame of mind. I went to the great temple of Zeus to swear an oath to answer the charges against me, and there I saw Calisthenes – one of the mighty Alcmaeonidae of Athens. That was like a splash of icy water.

He smiled at me. I know that smile – I've smiled it at other men. He *wanted* me to know that he was involved in the charges against me.

I was concerned, to say the least.

With all that hanging over my head, I was a poor delegate – a week late, and I hadn't made a sacrifice. The conference was actually held in the precinct of the temple complex where they held the games – the Isthmian games, I mean. And even though I'd missed eight days of talk, they were still talking.

The issue was not resistance. Greece had already chosen to resist. Thanks to the gods, men had used their heads and seen that we had to fight.

The issue was command. All were agreed that Sparta should lead the allied army. Why not? The Spartiates were the closest things to professional soldiers that we had. Spartan kings had more experience of planning major campaigns than anyone else. There really wasn't much argument – the only man I could possibly have considered to put up against Leonidas was Aristides, and *he* wanted the Spartans to command.

So Leonidas would lead the field army.

But the naval component was another story. And we all knew that the navy was going to be important. The largest navy belonged to Athens, which, in fifteen years, had gone from a fairly small navy to the largest in the Aegean and perhaps in the whole of the eastern Mediterranean – except Persia, of course. That summer, Athens could put more than a hundred hulls in the water, and Aegina could scarcely muster seventy, and Corinth about fifty. Only Syracusa on Sicily had more.

And no one wanted Athens to have the command.

In vain did Themistocles politic. And let me add – Gorgo and Leonidas were unshakeable in supporting him. Leonidas wanted Themistocles to be the navarchos.

There were other candidates.

Gelon of Syracusa was one. He offered one hundred and twenty ships to the cause if he could be the commander on land and sea.

Adamanteis of Corinth was another, and he scarcely bothered to conceal his loathing of Athens – *That upstart city*, he said in a speech. It was an impious exaggeration – even in myth, Athens pre-dates Corinth, and in fact the evidence of your eyes will show you how long Athens has been a mighty citadel, but other men – our foes – agreed with him. Only a few decades before, Athens had been a minor city-state with a tyrant who could be bought and a small fleet and a small army. The new democracy had flooded her phalanx with new muscle and had made her rowers into citizens, and many of the oligarchs who ruled the cities of mainland Greece felt deeply threatened, no little bit by the growth of the very fleet that Athens swore to use for the common good.

After a day of it, all I could think of was the captains' conferences before Lades. We had supposedly all been on the same side, for the same purposes, and the Samians had betrayed us. Here, we weren't done with the conference and some men – the Corinthians and the men of Argos – were open in saying that they would prefer to see Athens destroyed than to see an Athenian command the allied fleet.

The problem – and it was a problem – was that there were not many compromise candidates. No one was going to accept an Aeginian in command. They had tried to Medise – that is, to support the Great King – at the time of Marathon, and they made no secret of their hatred for Athens. But they were the only other state with a navy large enough to train officers who could direct major sea operations.

Except Corinth. And Adamanteis wanted that command very badly. He fought tooth and nail in the discussions to arrange that a stinging message was sent to Gelon.

For myself, I could have served under Gelon. But the rumour was that the Great King was flinging Carthage at Syracusa to pin the great Syracusan fleet in place, and men worried that Gelon would sacrifice Greece to save Sicily, and of course they were right. I agreed with them – I knew that Artapherenes had gone to Carthage. But I thought that with one mighty fleet, we could probably control the whole of the sea.

At any rate, no one listened to me. Gelon was sent an icy message of refusal, and went back to fighting Carthage.

But Themistocles was no more willing to send the Athenian fleet to sea under a Corinthian than under an Aeginian. So the bickering continued, while the Persians built their second bridge and while their ships and lead elements of their armies moved into Thrace.

I could see it falling apart before my very eyes. The whole alliance – so promising a month before – was going to break up over the issue of the fleet. Half the cities present had *no* fleets and couldn't imagine what it was all about.

About two weeks into the conference, I was sitting on the steps of the shrine of Herakles with two dozen men – really, the whole of the 'Athenian' faction. We were tired, and we sat drinking watered wine, our slaves and hypaspists gathered around us.

We'd come out of the temple still debating the command. Two of the representatives from Megara had come out – we were trying to dissuade them from their pro-Corinthian stance.

'Why does it *matter?*' the elder asked.

And Themistocles stood, and pointed out over the crisp blue water of the great bay before us. 'The war with Persia is all about the sea,' he said. 'Xerxes may come by land, but he cannot maintain his army – or his conquest – without the sea. This war will be won and lost with triremes, not with swords.'

The Megaran sneered. 'You only say that because your political power base is little men who row,' he said. 'Only gentlemen can win battles.'

Themistocles shook his head. 'Persian archers care nothing for the quality of the man in the armour,' he said. 'Arrows are all democrats.'

The Megaran shrugged. 'Only rich men can own the armour to stop the arrows.'

Themistocles shook his head. 'With a fleet, I can prevent the Persians from having arrows,' he said. 'I can prevent them from having bread, or beans, or garlic, or bowstrings.'

The Megarans muttered, and turned to walk away, unswayed.

Stung, the orator shouted after them, 'After the war, there will be an empire! Don't you see it? With a fleet, we can crush the Great King. We can take all Ionia back—'

I put a hand on his arm.

Themistocles sat down and glowered.

That night, I went and drank wine with Leonidas. I was invited. He and his retinue were in a fine country house near the precinct – far finer than his house in Sparta, in fact. The floor mosaics were magnificent. Aristides was there – he didn't attend the meetings of the conference, because of his feeling about Themistocles, but he was in Corinth and attended many private functions. Everyone knew he had been to see the Great King, and since no one could imagine the great Aristides becoming pro-Persian, they trusted him to tell them what the Great King intended, and he told them – right down to the facts of our escape from Mardonius.

At any rate, I lay with him on a kline and listened to Leonidas plan his campaign. He had a straightforward idea – that the Greeks should send their allied army to a forward position so that the Persians would not be in a position to threaten anyone – except perhaps the Thessalians. We needed the Thessalian cavalry to match the brilliant Persian cavalry.

And Leonidas – almost alone, let me add – looked clear eyed at the odds and the campaign. He was the first to propose a series of narrow points – where land and sea were both constrained – as the places where the allied army could face the Great King while the allied fleet contained his fleet. Our spies and our scouts – even my own work – suggested that the Persians would have almost six hundred fighting ships. Even if Xerxes gave us another year, all Greece couldn't match six hundred ships. So the best we could hope for was a series of holding actions, and Leonidas invited me to drink his wine so that I could help Aristides to advise him on naval tactics.

Leonidas was a fine commander and a deep thinker, but he thought sea battles were land battles with water.

But he was very good about the narrow places and he had a much firmer grasp of geography than most men. He *listened* when other men spoke. He was already choosing his battlefields. Perhaps most important, he was almost alone in understanding that we would not be challenging Xerxes to a fair fight on an open field, like Plataea facing Thisbe or Athens facing Thebes.

Oh, no.

Leonidas, the great general, the King of Sparta, the first among equals, the best warrior of Greece, lay on his couch at Corinth and laid out our strategy.

'I'll take the allied army to a narrow place,' he said. 'And we'll fight the Medes the way a cat fights a dog.' He looked around.

Some men flinched.

'With everything we have,' he said. 'And with our flanks defended.'

He chose a dozen sites based on what other men could tell

him, and his own travels and his brother's. Some of them were rendered untenable by distance from the centres at Athens and the Peloponesus. Some were so far 'forward' that they fell immediately to the Persians or even surrendered. But he chose the Vale of Tempe immediately, because it offered almost everything we needed for a forward strategy. He named three places to which he could retreat.

The best of them all was the Hot Gates, and the headland of Artemis, where the north end of Euboea almost meets the coast of southern Thessaly. There, the sea is as constrained as the land.

But Euxenis, the Thessalian, shook his head. 'If you fight there, you will lose Thessaly,' he said. 'And all of our cavalry will be serving the Great King.'

Leonidas smiled. 'Yes,' he said. 'But if I lose Thessaly, I'll have to fight somewhere.'

Sparthius raised a hand. 'Why not just meet them here, at the isthmus?' he asked.

Leonidas shrugged. 'If we fight here, then Athens and Thebes are lost, and Megara and probably Corinth.'

Sparthius looked at me and winked. 'So? None of them has a single Spartan citizen.'

Now, my friends, you may think this is dull – but this is what we faced, in building the alliance. Every state could see how to protect its own interests. And the men of the Peloponnesus were in the most secure position of all.

'If Xerxes' fleet defeats our fleet, he can land an army anywhere,' I said. 'He could take Olympia.'

'Avert!' said a dozen Spartiates. Men glared at me.

'Or Sparta itself,' I said, ignoring them.

Every head turned.

'Not while there was a single Spartiate left alive,' Bulis said.

But Queen Gorgo nodded. 'Yes,' she said quietly. She was only passing through the room – collecting her small weaving bag, or so she claimed, although like many women I've known, she knew how to linger at an all-male party for an hour.

At her one word, all the Spartans fell silent. And she smiled – a carefully dramatised hesitation. 'Yes,' she said. 'You would all die, and then an army of his slaves would take Sparta.'

★

An hour later, with far too much wine in me, I staggered to my feet and clasped hands with Aristides before nodding to the king. Spartans use very little ceremony in private.

I had made it through the doors of the andron when Hector took my arm without a word and led me across the marble-paved court-yard, past a magnificent and ancient olive tree in a basin of marble, and up a set of carved wooden steps to the porch – the exedra – of the women's wing.

Gorgo sat quite decorously with a pair of maidens, enjoying the moonlit air and the scent of olives.

'A Spartan,' she said, as soon as I was at the top of the steps.

I was not at my best. 'What?' I mumbled, or words to that effect.

She waved dismissively. 'Why do men drink so much? Listen, Arimnestos, I need your wits. Let's have a Spartan navarch. A Spartan of unimpeachable nobility and some ability, who can give clear orders – and take them, if necessary. From Themistocles. No – listen! No one in Corinth or Megara or Thebes can imagine that Themistocles the Democrat is really going to ally with Leonidas the great noble. Let us put in a Spartan admiral, and all our troubles are at an end. And we are rid of Adamenteis .'

I leaned against the rail. 'I think Adamenteis is in the pay of the Great King,' I said.

Gorgo shrugged. 'Half the conference have been sent money by Xerxes.' She lowered her peplos from over her head to show her eyes and a bit of her mouth. 'I have myself.'

I was charmed. 'What did you do with the money?' I asked.

'I sent half to the temple of Artemis at Brauron and the other half to Themistocles to build a ship,' she said. 'Do you think we can defeat Xerxes?'

'Yes,' I insisted. 'If you are navarch.'

We laughed together.

The next day, I proposed that Eurybiades of Lacedaemon be chosen as navarchos. I had wandered about – half drunk – and informed Themistocles and Aristides and a dozen of the important men, so that, as soon as I made the proposal in council, a dozen orators rose and supported it.

Adamenteis never had a chance to rally his supporters. We put it to the vote and the thing was done.

Athens chose to trust Sparta with its fleet. Friends – in many ways, it was Athens' finest hour. Someone had to trust a stranger.

And with that trust came the scent of victory. Until Athens conceded that it would give the command to Sparta, we were some sixty odd cities with a common language and a lot of shared hatred. But after the question of the arch-navarchos was settled, the smaller cities began to show signs of fight. And as the last week of the conference rolled along, Themistocles framed a resolution calling for an even division of spoils – as in the Iliad – and the wording suggested strongly that if we won, we would punish those who stood with the Medes.

On the last day, Leonidas walked among the delegates and asked each how many hoplites his city could bring. And when he had counted them all, he nodded, and said – quite loud, so that it carried acorss the temple –

'Sixty thousand.'

Silence fell.

'If every city here does as they have promised, we Greeks can put sixty thousand hoplites in the field.' He looked around, imperious in his scarlet cloak, but he would have been imperious naked.

Adamanteis didn't exactly shrug, but he said – loudly enough to be heard – 'Xerxes will have a million.'

Themistocles laughed. It was a derisive, orator's laugh, but it cut through whatever noble thing Leonidas meant to say.

'We Greeks are poor. We don't have enough wood to build more ships, nor enough food to feed all our people, nor enough bronze to make more armour, nor iron to make weapons.' He raised his hands. 'But thanks to the will of the gods, we will have enough Persians to allow all of us to be heroes.'

We arrived at the conference as factions – as Megarans and Plataeans and Lacedaemonians and Athenians and Thebans and Thesbians.

Most of us left it as Greeks.

The Vale of Tempe – 480 BCE

Tempe, (*plur.*) a valley in Thessaly, between mount Olympus at the north, and Ossa at the south, through which the river Peneus flows into the Ægean. The poets have described it as the most delightful spot on the earth, with continual cooling shades, and verdant walks, which the warbling of birds rendered more pleasant and romantic, and which the gods often honored with their presence. Tempe extended about five miles in length but varied in the dimensions of its breadth so as to be in some places scarce one acre and a half wide. All vallies that are pleasant, either for their situation or the mildness of their climate, are called *Tempe* by the poets.

John Lampriere 'Classical Dictionary' 1788

That winter was one of the most delightful of my life. Perhaps it is only warm and full of light in memory – perhaps I see it that way in contrast to the two years of fear and horror that were to come.

But I had my daughter, and my son. I had Aristides all to myself, except for Jocasta, who has always been one of my ideal women. We were a happy house. Hipponax might have made a great deal of trouble, with his tendency to violence and his angry need for my approval, locked in a house with two old heroes, some women, and a lot of wine. But he didn't. He'd had a strong mother and a strong grandfather – he had good bones, as Plataeans say. And he had Hector.

It was not all ease and light – the two of them stole a sacred bull and drove it through the town; they cut a swathe through the town's unmarried girls and that had consequences; and when they were caught drunkenly spraying urine on a statue of Pan erected by the victors of Marathon, I decided it was time to send them away for a while. I sent them to Idomeneaus on the mountain.

And Euphonia adored them. It could have gone either way, but she chose to follow them around and gaze adoringly at each in turn – and to brag about their exploits to other girls.

As for me, as I say, I was with Aristides. When you are twenty, men of thirty-five seem quite old – and finished, mature, fully developed. But when you come around to that old age, you find yourself young, fit, hale – and still growing, if not in size, then in skill and maturity and some other ways. At thirty-five, I found Aristides to be more the man I wanted to be than any of them – even Leonidas. Oh, he was still a prig. His sense of honesty was so absolute that he would insist on telling his wife where she had gained weight, or how her breasts had looked when she was a maiden.

You may laugh, but I'd like to suggest to the men present that, unless you are Aristides, this is a foolish way to behave with your wife or anyone else's.

Yet despite this failing, and his stubbornness, which could be blind and obstinate or pure and noble, he was in every other way the man I wanted to be. I especially admired his calm. I am a good man in a crisis – none better on a blood-drenched deck. But tell me that the house is out of olive oil and the best maidservant is pregnant and guests are at the door, and I am a very difficult man.

One night, with the winter rains pouring on the fields of Green Plataea and Kitharon lost in the dark and clouds, we lay – promiscuously, let me add. One aspect of change that Aristides had accepted was private dinners with the women in chairs. We had lamb in something saffron and sticky, and a slave had dropped the whole platter, and in a spectacular display of terror – he was new – he'd then collapsed across the as-yet-undamaged food, and then, leaping to his feet, managed to smear saffroned mutton on my second-best chiton.

Really, it was as good as Athenian comedy.

But I shot off my kline and struck him. Then I was in the kitchen, demanding that my butler get the mess cleaned up, when Jocasta brushed past me, shot me a withering glare, and snapped her fingers for attention.

They all ignored me and looked at her.

'That was an accident and nothing to be afraid of,' she said crisply. 'Get Paolis cleaned up and see if we can have those nice large beans from last night – eh?' She smiled at the cook, who had to smile back.

Then she turned on me – the very look that I would give to a helmsman who abused his authority on one of my ships. 'Would you be kind enough to step in here?' she asked, stepping into the cook's tiny office.

I had to bend my head to get in, and I was so close to Jocasta that I could smell the mint on her skin.

'The trouble with men is that, since they feel they are best at crises, they seek to create a crisis at every turn,' she snapped. 'A new slave dropped a platter. The Queen of Sparta was not at your table, and by Aphrodite, sir, even if she had been, there was no cause to strike the boy, who was already terrified. Your anger communicated itself to the servants, and now it will be an hour before we eat.'

Yes, yes.

The nice thing about getting lessoned by Jocasta is that, like a good trierarch, her authority was absolute. I couldn't even manage male indignation. I merely stood, the hero of a dozen battles, and was dressed down – rightfully so – for cowardice and panic in the face of a dropped platter.

I'm sure a dozen other incidents occurred that winter, but that's the one that sticks with me.

The three forges roared, too. They made armour and helmets, and the small phalanx of Plataeans grew better and better armed, until we were a fair show. Women complained that pots were not being repaired, and indeed, Myron called our building the 'Forge of Ares'. Heron the ironsmith took on a pair of journeymen from Thrace – that is, Greeks from the Greek cities of Thrace, not Thracians – and they made magnificent swords, folded and folded again while still white hot so that the breath of the smith god showed on the surface, or that's what they told me. Their swords were as good as the sword I'd brought from Babylon – flexible, sharp and beautiful. I had one hilted up in ivory.

And we made money. Aristides mocked me and said I was now a true aristocrat – my forges made money, my farms made money, and my ships, captained by other men who took the risks – Moire made a winter voyage to Aegypt – made yet more money, so that I sat and learned to be calm and dignified at home while other men worked.

Ah, but I worked too.

I polished the phalanx of Plataea the way Hermogenes was polishing breastplates – the bronze thorakes that keep men safe in the storm of iron. I had my Epilektoi out in the hills after deer, over the fields after a wolf, up the mountain for boar – every week. I organised them into Spartan-style messes, as I'd learned from Brasidas, and I made up three new Pyricche that winter; first I taught them to my elite, and then to the entire phalanx.

There was considerable grumbling. Hilarion objected that he didn't want to be a hero in the Iliad and had a farm to manage. Draco's grandson Andromachos thought that he was too good a warrior to need to drill.

The sons and cousins of Simon stood in a group at drills and glowered.

But they did the dances. And I tried to be fair, but I refused to have faction in my ranks. It is the principal duty of a strategos – or a polemarchos – to choose a place in the phalanx for each man, and to assign the places. A weak leader causes dissent. A strong leader can cause unease. Not every man appointed to the front rank truly wants to be there. The front rank is the place of honour, but it is a terrifying place to endure a battle, even for me.

That said, I had some superb warriors, and a good number of warriors who were 'merely' fine, and veteran. With my marines and sailors added in – all citizens, now, and some had bought property with their profits – I could muster sixteen hundred men, and the front two ranks of eight were *almost* all veterans of a dozen fights.

I concentrated on teaching them a variety of simple manoeuvres and a few complex ones. I was determined that they would be able to form at a run, from a long file of men into a phalanx, and in any direction, because my experience of war said that this one talent was better for the group than that every man present be Achilles come to earth as an individual. I made them march with their aspides on their shoulders or on their arms – everywhere. As often as I could, I made them run.

Draco's sons built us carts, and we hoarded sacks for grain, so that we could march out of Plataea with our food and our weapons and move at a donkey's speed. My understanding was that we'd be marching all the way to Thessaly in the spring, and I was determined to be ready.

Listen – when Greek armies march, they take no food. They expect to fight within a day of home, and so they expect farmers to come to the camp, make a small, rude agora and open stalls to sell food. The small pay a hoplite receives is supposed to buy the food for him and his slave or hypaspitos.

None of us had ever marched a great army of Greeks over the mountains – anywhere, really. But when we lay on our kline and imagined it, or talked it through, we all agreed – all of us being Aristides and me and Leonidas and Adamanteis and a dozen more leaders of military contingents – we all agreed we'd need carts and food and baggage like a Persian army, and this would make us slower and more vulnerable to their cavalry.

Bulis came twice that winter, both times with different Spartans – bringing messages about the allied army assembly points, and collecting information on the Great King. It was from Bulis I learned that Carthage was still trading with Athens, and it was from Bulis that we learned that the Great King's army had marched. And that he had appointed an assembly for his fleet.

That made my heart flutter.

Leonidas was sending the Plataeans with the land army. Bulis reviewed all my phalanx and was complimentary – by which I mean that, after watching two hours of sweating middle-aged men deploying from file to column, column to phalanx and back, sudden movements to the flank, oblique marching, and running charges and step-by-step retreats and closing with a mass dancing of my new, Spartan-style Pyricche, he turned to me and nodded.

'Good,' he said.

The reward for all our efforts was to be sent away from our friends, the Athenians, who, with Corinth and Aegina and Corcyra, were mostly forming the fleet. We would march with the men of the Peloponnesus and Boeotia, to face the Persian land army at Tempe.

I was very much of two minds about this. Like most Greeks, I am equally at home on land or sea, but I owned two fighting ships and had two more 'in my tail', as we say, and I wanted to lead them in person. Further, by sending my best-armed marines and sailors off to Tempe, I was depriving my squadron of their marines and officers.

Almost every contingent had this problem. I solved mine by sending all my marines and sailors to the fleet and filling their places with Athenian exiles led by Aristides.

To add to my troubles, my brother-in-law was one of my best officers, but in this crisis he was with the men of Thespiae – really his home, not Plataea – and suddenly I lost him, forty armoured men and two veteran officers. The Thespians were the better for all those Marathon men, but I was the worse for it, and I cursed a great deal in early spring. Antigonus seemed equally disgruntled, and my sister Penelope cried, worried that without me to protect him – you had to see Antigonus, who was a head taller than me – without me to protect her husband, he'd be lost.

I offer all this wealth of petty detail not because it will truly interest you, but because today, when you young people think of us going to fight the Persians, there is a myth – the myth is that there was a mighty allied army. *There was no allied army.* That spring, as we prepared to march off to Thessaly, we were a hundred contingents, and however good willed we were about being Greek, we had no experience outside our own phalanxes – except a handful of men,

281

like me, who'd served as mercenaries. And the mercenaries became the glue that bound the whole together.

Nor did we march as an army. Indeed, many contingents were transported from the isthmus – my own, for example – by ship to Thessaly, while other contingents marched overland. The allies had failed to nominate an assembly point because, despite our best efforts, most Greeks still thought of this as a fight between two poleis. They imagined that we could assemble our army in the Vale of Tempe, send a herald to the Persians, and fight.

And because we did not march together, we never had a chance to drill together, or form a phalanx together.

So we assembled, one contingent at a time, in Thessaly, at the base of the major pass into Macedon. It was cold – still winter in the passes. Our commander was a Spartan – Euanetus, son of Carenus. The Athenian contingent, which was surprisingly large given the number of ships Athens was manning, was commanded by Themistocles in person. We had, among all of us, almost fourteen thousand hoplites and another six thousand Thessalian cavalry, and we could fill the pass with a phalanx eight men deep and still have the Spartan contingent in reserve and half the cavalry hidden. Leonidas was rallying the main army behind us, but I think we assumed that the great army of forty thousand hoplites would never be needed.

My Plataeans were one of the first contingents to arrive at Tempe, and we used the time to drill. Even my young men hated me after two weeks looking at the mountains of Macedon through the eye-slots of their helmets, and the new Athenian helmets with cheek pieces that raised were suddenly very popular, because no matter how cold the nights and mornings, by midday a man in armour was like a lobster boiled in his shell.

Xerxes, had he been quick enough, could have walked over us any time he liked. The Spartans were late, the Athenians later – in fact, although Aristides and I knew nothing of it, the Athenians were outraged at being required to send sixty ships and a phalanx too, and, as Themistocles said to me the night the Athenians arrived, there were seventy triremes beached in Piraeus for want of marines and officers.

Nor was Euanetus an inspiring commander. He was stuck with an army that had expected godlike Leonidas, and he was himself no god. He had a snappish temper; he was a large man and tended to use force when persuasion might have been better. He savaged

Themistocles for being late, although we had no news of the Persian host, and that was an error, and he compounded it by ordering the Athenians punished, which was a little like punishing a man for being late for a party.

He changed his mind repeatedly about how he intended to cover the pass. First we were close up, and then we retreated six miles, and then we closed up into the pass again. The Thessalian lord Euripides had assumed temporary command when it was only his cavalry and my hoplites on the scene, and he had scouted the pass rigorously, sent two parties off into Macedon and Thrace to find the approaching army, in general had performed the duties of the strategos of an army. Euanetus wanted to be acclaimed and saluted, but he was not an active commander.

My men had been in the pass for three weeks when the Persians struck.

A pair of Persian heralds came to our camp to get safe conducts. They were the first Persians most of our men had ever seen, and we lined the roads like peasants to gawk. Euanetus was anxious to do the right thing and not commit an act of sacrilege, so he allowed the Persian heralds access to Greece and gave them a safe conduct to Delphi, to the oracle, or so they claimed.

The day after they left, a rumour began that the Persian army had marched a month before, and that we were in the wrong pass.

Two days later, while I fed Demetrios and Themistocles and Aeschylus on a deer I'd killed on the mountain, another herald came into our camp, this one from Amyntas, the King of Macedon. Macedon had been among the first kingdoms to submit earth and water to Xerxes, and yet Amyntas always attempted to act as a friend to the Greeks. In this case, he sent his herald to tell us that the Persians were marching by the other pass, near Gonnus.

In vain did the Thessalian lord Euripides complain that his scouts had not returned – that the Persians could not be so close. In a matter of four days, the allied army collapsed. No – there was no great battle. We heard a rumour that Persia was marching, and we scattered.

It was worse than Lades. Almost every contingent ran for home – the Spartans as fast as anyone. Not one contingent wanted to wait with our Thessalian allies and try conclusions with the Persians.

We stayed. I decided that if the rumour was accurate, the army – such as it was – would need a rearguard. And I liked Euripides the

Thessalian and wanted his good opinion, and to be honest, I didn't really think that the Persian army of a million men and another million slaves was going to sneak up on us at Tempe. But by the fourth day after the Persian heralds left our camp, the cause was lost. We stood with three hundred Tegeans where the whole allied army had stood two days before.

Euripides rode to me. 'Do as you please. We can't face the Persians with fifteen hundred infantry, no matter how dedicated we are. We'll surrender. The craven behaviour of this army has convinced us all that we made a mistake. We will submit to Persia.' He shrugged. He was very angry. 'I have little interest in being Greek, just now.'

But he clasped my hand and offered me a last meal, which I accepted.

We marched back across Thessaly, fearing the peasants and the wild animals, and we found our ships waiting, to our enormous relief. I landed my men south of Thespiae, on the stony beach there, and found a messenger from Themistocles ordering me to report to the League at Corinth.

Like every other man in Greece that spring, I truly considered going to my farm. The disaster at Tempe had put it all in perspective. I'd wasted almost two months of my life so an incompetent allied commander and a pair of Persian spies could bury Greek independence. I had many friends in the Great King's camp, and in one sentence, I could have both worldly power *and* the complete protection of my friends and my polis.

I actually imagined going to Artaphernes, giving him the kiss of peace and bowing to the Great King – by Zeus, I'd already done it! And requesting a command. 'I tried fighting alongside the Greeks,' I'd say. 'But they ran for home at the very rumour of your coming, o King.'

I was angry, and young.

Aristides was angry too, and much older. And in no mood to submit to the Great King, and I think he held me steady. I was prepared to grumble my way across Thessaly, and he forbade me to speak my mind in front of the troops. He was right. Had I grumbled what I thought, those men would not have been there for us later.

At any rate, we arrived at Thespiae and I stood on the beach for half an hour – angry, confused and feeling ill done by. Just down the beach, an Illyrian slaver was unloading – his own relatives, it appeared, since the slaves were all blond.

The gods work in the oddest ways.

Aristides came and clasped my arm. 'Will you go to Corinth?' he asked.

Just in that moment I hated him and his calm assurance and his dignified maturity, his stubbornness. I was going to *lose Briseis again.* I could feel it, and the pent-up anger of a decade of frustration – the trauma of Lade, the fear of betrayal – it all boiled up inside me. My refusal was on the tip of my tongue. I drew breath, to give him what I thought of Greeks, the alliance and the gods.

Just off to my left, the Illyrian slavemaster struck a slave woman so hard that he broke her jaw. I heard the crack. Then he kicked her – savagely. Brutally.

She just lay and accepted pain.

The gods flooded me with power – like the onset of love – but suddenly I forgot Aristides and Xerxes and Corinth. I ran, bad leg and all, like Achilles.

The Illyrian saw me coming and reached for his sword.

I killed him with a cut from my scabbard – up into the underside of his arms, rotating my wrist, driving home through his nose in a final thrust. I stepped on his sword-hand to make sure there was no death-thrust, and wrenched my good new sword out of his head.

I had never seen the woman before – she was just another blond slave, and I had four. But I knew what Poseidon was telling me – on a beach, where all kingdoms meet. The Illyrian slaver looked nothing like Dagon, but in that moment, his casual savagery made him the Carthaginian's brother.

I am pious. I worship the gods. I have seen them act among men.

Among the Illyrian slaves was a blond man who did not stoop or cringe. He was beautifully muscled, perhaps twenty or even younger. He caught my eye.

He seemed to glow like solid gold. His mouth moved.

I looked away, because it was hard to look at him – that sounds foolish, but go and look at the most beautiful woman you know – meet her eye. Hold it.

When I looked back, he was gone.

I knew I had seen my lord Apollo in the flesh, on the beach. And although he did not speak, I knew what he said. He said, 'Omen.'

I went and embraced Aristides. 'I'm for Corinth,' I said, or something equally banal. Then I blurted, 'I saw Apollo! Right here on the beach!'

Aristides looked deeply impressed, which was not a look you saw often on the Just Man. 'Ah!' he said. He didn't ruin it by saying more, but embraced me and sent me on my way.

I took one of my own triakonters – thirty-oared ships, good for trade or raiding, too small to lie in the line of battle. I didn't fill her with my best men, either. All my best marines were in Piraeus. There's no room for marines in a triakonter, but usually every man rowing is a fighter, or at least that's how it was in the old days. I had a polyglot collection of professional oarsmen, a former Massalian shepherd, a pair of Africans – but I knew them all well enough, and we passed the isthmus of Corinth like a blade through oil, and I was on the northern beach of Corinth a day later.

Themistocles sent for me as soon as I arrived. He was not in my good graces – despite the various arguments he had been offered, the Athenians were one of the first contingents to march away from the Vale of Tempe and they had caused the break-up of the army.

And Themistocles had made the decision to retreat.

Now he sat on a canvas and iron stool in a tent – a large tent like those the Etruscans use in war. While his slaves served me wine, a herald announced the King of Sparta.

'Do you have my nemesis Aristides with you?' Themistocles asked.

I shook my head. I tried never to discuss the one with the other.

'When you see him, please tell him that I will be sending out an amnesty asking all the exiles to return,' he said.

'He was at Tempe, with the Plataeans,' I said.

Themistocles had the good grace to look away. 'I know,' he said. 'Let me tell you the worst of it, Arimnestos. The Persians have not yet marched. Only their first division is even in Europe. The Great King is still in Asia.' He looked at the ground. 'Amyntas of Macedon thought he was sending good information.'

Leonidas entered and we rose to our feet, but he made a motion that sent us back to our stools. 'Xerxes and Amyntas have done us a favour,' Leonidas said. 'We sent an army to Tempe for a contest of equals. Xerxes has no interest in such a contest. He would have marched around our army – and thus trapped it. To us – this is dishonourable. It solves nothing. We all know that war is about one group of strong men convincing another group of which is in the right. Xerxes does not. As he is a tyrant, so he believes that by manoeuvre and outright murder, he can cow us. And he may be correct.' Leonidas ran his fingers though his beard. 'I will not forget this lesson.'

Silence fell. 'And Euanetus was not the man to command an army.'

'He is an excellent commander for an army of Spartans,' Leonidas said mildly. 'He complained of you, sir. He said you refused to know your place.'

I considered a variety of answers, and elected to smile. 'I'm sure he is correct,' I said.

Not quite the dignity of Aristides, but I *was* learning.

Leonidas either didn't understand my answer or chose to ignore it. 'I will lead the next effort in person.' He glanced at me. 'Gorgo has another mission for you, if you will accept it.'

'Another peace offer for Persia?' I asked.

Themistocles leaned forward. 'We want to try Gelon again,' he said. 'Gelon offered us two hundred ships if we would give him the command, and we spurned him. Gorgo has proof that Xerxes has almost twice the number of ships we have.'

He looked around.

I did a quick count in my head. 'Xerxes has seven hundred ships?' I asked.

Leonidas looked up, and Gorgo entered the tent. She smiled at me, and I rose and bowed, and she raised her odd eyebrow.

'Men bow more deeply to my wife than to me,' Leonidas said, with real humour. In another man, it might have been a bitter statement. Not from the king.

I had a nice piece of flattery ready to deploy, but Gorgo beat me to it and shook her head. 'Men bow to you,' she said. 'They only bow to my beauty.'

He looked at her lovingly. 'Nay, woman,' he said. 'Men bow to the King of Sparta, but they turn and bow to Gorgo.'

She showed her dimples, then.

And turned to me, a little too brusquely. 'Carthage is sending a hundred ships to Tyre,' she said. 'Even as she sends three hundred against Syracusa.'

That was bad news. Mind you, until that moment I hadn't imagined that Carthage had four hundred ships.

'Syracusa is a mighty city,' Gorgo said. 'Go and beg Gelon in my husband's name to bring his fleet here, and we'll give him the command – and when we stop Persia, we will send a Spartan army to Sicily to defeat Carthage.'

Leonidas winced. 'I detest asking a favour of any man,' he admitted. 'But you know this man.'

Themistocles winked. 'He knows everyone,' he said.

'All my ships are at Piraeus,' I said. But I knew I would do it. I knew that this was what Apollo had sent me to do.

I was two weeks sailing from Corinth to Syracusa, laden in wine and Corinthian pottery. The Spartans couldn't believe I was sailing fully laden, but no one was paying me to play Hermes to the tyrant of Sicily, and as far as we could tell when I left, we had a year. We knew a fair amount about the Great King's preparations in Asia, and his ships gathering – indeed, although I didn't know it, Sekla made a similar decision at Piraeus and took a ship all the way to Aegypt and back on the first good winds, because it was obvious that despite the Greek failure at Tempe, Xerxes was not going to march that year. The season was advancing, but Xerxes' army was still near Sardis.

I had a fine voyage, and we ran up the great harbour of Syracusa with the wind at our backs, having scarcely touched an oar all the way. We'd sighted a Carthaginian blockading squadron to the south, but the wind was in their faces and they never had a chance to snap us up. I landed my wares and had Hector and Hipponax – who had now rowed for two solid weeks and looked like Achilles and Patrokles – sell them on the dock. I pinned on a salt-stained cloak, identified myself to the tyrant's bodyguard, and was escorted to the citadel.

It had occurred to me twenty times during my trip that, having extracted Lydia from the tyrant's clutches, I was probably not the right man to flatter him and beg his indulgence. But I stood before him in his magnificent rose garden, high above the city. He looked as hard as rock – he clearly expected to spend the summer in harness, and he had trained hard.

'I thought you would bring me five triremes, and you have come with one triakonter?' he asked.

'Two of my ships are serving Athens against the Medes,' I said. 'Doola should be here with his ship, and Caius with his.'

The tyrant relented and offered me an embrace. 'Dionysus and his contingent have come and gone and come again,' he said. 'Massalia is a loyal ally this summer, and I count your dues as paid. You are here to beg for the Greeks?'

In some ways, it was harder to speak to Gelon than to Xerxes. Gelon looked a bit like my idea of a god, and he was absolutely his own master. He would not ever have ordered the waves lashed. And yet, of all the men who led armies that fateful year, it was Gelon who most likely thought he was a god, himself.

I nodded. 'Lord, I am here to beg for all Greece.'

He nodded. 'The answer is no. Save your breath, my friend. My fleet has sailed – did you see a single galley in the harbour? The dice are thrown. My fleet will try a pre-emptive raid on Carthage which may save us all. I have heard that the Libyphoenicians have sent a hundred ships to Xerxes in exchange for Persian help against me.'

'We hear the same,' I confessed.

He sat back against a marble bench – shoulders still upright, not ever truly relaxed.

'This is the war of the world,' he said. 'Our names will live for ever.'

I didn't roll my eyes, but only from Jocasta's training. 'We will face the Medes without your might, then, lord.'

He shrugged. 'Sparta and Athens wanted my help and didn't want to pay my price,' he said.

'So in the end, you, too, are a huckster,' I said.

He flushed. 'Where is my Lydia?' he asked.

'I do not have her,' I said. 'She is now a wife – probably a mother. I beg you let her go.'

He tapped his marble bench with one hand – the greatest sign of agitation I ever saw from him.

'Confess that you stole her,' he said.

Some sinners never relent.

I stood as straight as I could. 'I confess that I stole her to return her to the life that should have been hers,' I said. 'You had no more right to her than Anarchos, or me. I merely restored her to what she ought to have had.'

He turned to me a bland actor's mask. 'Ah, very well. What's a strumpet more or less? You are forgiven.'

In that moment, I knew that I'd rather die beside Leonidas than defeat Persia with this man. I bowed. 'I must take your answer to the League,' I said.

Gelon shrugged. 'They know my answer, and it is a sign of their desperation that they sent you. Who was it – Gorgo?' He made a moue. 'Gorgo thinks I can be persuaded. But it is now too late, and you might as well remain here. Be one of my captains. Athens and Sparta are done – indeed, Athens may already be afire.'

That blow struck home. 'What?'

He nodded, pleased as a cat. 'An Aegyptian ship came in here yesterday. The captain says that Xerxes marched a month ago, and that the ports of Asia are empty. The Persian fleet is at sea.'

I didn't bow. He wasn't Xerxes. 'I must go,' I said.

He smiled at his guard captain. 'And if I order you held – for your own good?'

My breath came tight, and I felt that power from the gods on my shoulders. I looked back at the mercenary.

Gelon was serious. Or rather, he was prepared to hold me, merely to spite me. Because I'd stolen Lydia. He was not a god, but a petty man with the powers and will of a god.

But I knew there were real gods, and I knew that I was needed. Elsewhere.

Very quietly, and I hope without bluster, I said, 'If you order me held, everyone in this garden will die, starting, my lord, with you.'

I give the tyrant his due – he didn't stiffen, or flush. He met my eye – man to man.

'Perhaps and perhaps not,' he said easily. 'Very well. You may go.'

Artemesium – 480 BCE

The Greeks appointed to serve in the fleet were these: the Athenians furnished a hundred and twenty-seven ships; the Plataeans manned these ships with the Athenians, not that they had any knowledge of seamanship, but because of mere valor and zeal. The Corinthians furnished forty ships and the Megarians twenty; the Chalcidians manned twenty, the Athenians furnishing the ships; the Aeginetans eighteen, the Sicyonians twelve, the Lacedaemonians ten, the Epidaurians eight, the Eretrians seven, the Troezenians five, the Styrians two, and the Ceans two, and two fifty-oared barks; the Opuntian Locrians brought seven fifty-oared barks to their aid. These are the forces which came to Artemisium for battle, and I have now shown how they individually furnished the whole sum. The number of ships mustered at Artemisium was two hundred and seventy-one, besides the fifty-oared barks. The Spartans, however, provided the admiral who had the chief command, Eurybiades, son of Euryclides, for the allies said that if the Laconian were not their leader, they would rather make an end of the fleet that was assembling than be led by the Athenians.

Herodotus, the opening of Book 8, with an English translation by
A. D. Godley. Cambridge. Harvard University Press. 1920.

The Syracusan authorities held us for two horrible days with their pettifogging bureaucracy and foolish made-up taxes, and I thought we'd never leave. But on the morning of the third day we were allowed to go, and we were out of the harbour mouth with dawn – a lucky choice on my part, as it proved. We went south around the heel of Italy and touched at Bari and left the cliffs of the heel behind us. Four days out of Syracusa, as we rowed across the Adriatic from Bari – me all but raging at the helm at every delay, imagining Plataea and Athens afire and Leonidas dead – Hipponax slid down the stubby boat sail mast and picked his way through the benches aft.

'There're a pair of ships on the horizon to the south,' he said. It was a calm day, the sea was like a flat field and the water was warm to the touch. The sky was blue-white with haze and sun, and the rowers were all stripped naked.

I pulled myself up the boat sail mast and had a look.

I had to rest my arms on the narrow trees that we used only when we crossed the yard, and there was no foothold and only the mainstays that braced her. A small ship doesn't need a heavy mast and thus can't support a crow's nest like a hemiola or even a trireme. But a life as a pirate teaches a few tricks.

I watched the spot he indicated. I never saw a ship.

But I did see a rhythmic pulse of light, and I knew it was the sun reflecting on oar backs as they rowed.

'They're in the eye of the sun,' I said. 'On purpose, I think. Two pirates, hunting us.'

I went back and relieved Hector, who was learning to be the helmsman, and after all the admonishments that sailors make to lubbers, I took the oars and cheated us a little farther north.

And so we ran all day, or rather walked, because without a breath of wind, it was a long, long pull, the kind of back-breaking day that makes your oarsmen curse.

All day I wondered who they were and why they were so slow. My gut feeling was that they were both heavy triremes, and thus should have run me down in four hours. I wavered, changing opinion at every rapid beat of my heart – they were after other prey, they were a Syracusan escort, they didn't even know we were here, they were rowing just one bank of oars.

Nothing made sense. A small triakonter with thirty oars is utterly at the mercy of a bigger ship unless there's shallow water in which to hide.

Towards evening, they sprinted at us. At least, that's my guess – they came on, and they had to have known that the movement of the sun across the sky had cost them their hiding. They were ten stades or more south of us and clear as day.

I didn't hasten the stroke. I had to save my rowers, for the moment when ...

when ...

... when Poseidon saved us. It's hard to explain, except that as the lead trireme gained on us, I could see as plain as the nose on my face that it was Dagon's *Spirit of Baal*. The bad rowing was explained.

Gelon had sold me to Dagon. Hence the delay.

I fear death as much as the next man, or perhaps more – I've met the gentleman more often than most. But that day, under the cruel sun, I was sure – *sure* that Poseidon would not let me die at Dagon's hand.

I watched the sea.

Poseidon provided me with a dead tree.

It may seem odd, given the mighty wars I'm describing, but this encounter was all the work of one huge tree trunk, a product of spring storms in the high Alps north of the lagoons at the top of the Adriatic. It was a huge tree, all its branches intact, and mostly submerged. It was almost the size of my ship.

Hector spotted it first, and Hipponax was the first to guess what it was.

We kept our hull between the Carthaginians and the floating tree for as long as we could. Then we went to full speed, so that the waves seemed to part from our bow ...

... and the Carthaginians, of course, had no more to give. Their ships were badly crewed – Dagon always killed his crews.

At full racing speed – still, in fact, slightly slower than my pursuers – I turned north as sharply as I dared, losing a ship's length of my lead and wetting my port-side rowers, but they'd been warned and no one lost the stroke.

How I longed for Ka. How I longed for even one of my archers.

The lead Carthaginian made the turn behind me, closing by another half-ship-length.

'Ready to turn to starboard!' I bellowed. By Poseidon, they were close.

And yet, by Poseidon, I felt the power. I felt that I was the master, and not the slave.

Hector motioned from the bow.

I put the steering oars over, the starboard-side rowers bit deep, the port side raised their oars, and we were around – about an eighth of a circle.

Dagon's ship never saw the log. They started the turn, almost on our stern rail, and they struck at full ramming speed.

The tree had most of its branches intact, and instead of a spectacular collision that broke his bow, instead the first collision checked his way, and then the tree fell off on my enemy's port side, and rowers caught it – oars snapped, and men screamed, and the whole ship turned to starboard. If I had had anything like a real ram, I might have turned and had him. If he'd had anything like a real crew, he could have carried on. If his companion had a captain worth his salt, he'd have manoeuvred, but instead, the following ship fell afoul of Dagon – wood splintered, and oars broke, and we were running free.

I looked at my rowers – near exhausted, and not a man in armour – and put the helm down for Ithaca and kept running.

Behind us – they followed.

I lost Dagon in the islands off Illyria. If it was Dagon, and I'm pretty sure it was. Despite my fears for Athens and Sparta, I had an easy way out of my predicament, and I ran north, not south – to Neoptolymos. A day in his blood-soaked town convinced me that I would never make an Illyrian, but he rented me his trireme – one I'd built for him, really – and put rowers on the benches.

'If I come, I'll have no kingdom when I return,' he said.

I looked at the heads rotting on his gate and the long lines of slaves loading into 'my' trireme.

'You can be king here until someone puts a knife in your belly,' I said. 'Or come with me and be Achilles.'

He chose to treat my words as mere raillery. No light flashed in his eyes, and he looked away when I pressed him.

I rowed away, leaving my triakonter on the beach, with a crew of unwilling slave 'oarsmen' and my own thirty professionals as officers and deck crew and marines, and we wallowed about for three days, scraping wood off her keel at every landing, breaking oars on rocks, catching every crab in the water – this in a dead flat, calm sea – Poseidon, we were pitiful. Worse yet, there was worm in the ship's hull, so that despite all my need for speed and caution, we had to beach for almost a week, barter for timber from barbarous Illyrians and then defend our ship and our slaves.

Really, there are few situations worse than being caught on a hostile coast with the planks off your ship and only thirty trustworthy men to hold your palisade. I cursed my decisions, each of them – to go north to Neoptolymos, to go straight to sea in an untested ship ...

Well, I'm here, so we weren't all taken or killed. Had we been, we'd have missed the greatest days in the history of Greeks, and the worst.

Never mind. After a long and pointless skirmish with the Illyrians – we stared at each other, they screamed challenges, and we sat tight – suddenly a man appeared who offered us good pine pitch and fine, carefully dried pine for repairs in fair Greek. We bought everything he offered, and rowed away the next day short by twenty oarsmen who deserted in the night. A man has to be particularly desperate or a complete fool to desert in Illyria, but there we were.

That night we beached in waters I knew, and I gathered all the slaves and offered them my usual deal – freedom and wages for six months' service.

Of course, they all accepted.

I was a more experienced man than I had been. I had Hector record all their names, and I walked among them. 'You will row for your freedom, every day,' I said. 'No grumbling, no lying on your oars. Six months of work, and you are free men. Six months of bad behaviour, and you will remain slaves.'

A handsome man with a square jaw and a crop of brown-blond hair spat. 'How do we know you'll keep your word?' he asked.

There was muttering from my men, but I raised my hand. 'It's a fair question. I could answer that you'd better hope that I do, because you have no other choice – eh? You are slaves.' I let them think about that. 'But when we reach Piraeus under Athens, I'll be happy to write it in the form of a contract.' I shrugged. 'Until then, trust me or don't.'

I'm not Themistocles or Miltiades or even Aristides. I'm not an orator.

But the rowing improved.

For three weeks we moved like a mouse under the eye of a cat. We rested at day at Corcyra and found that, for all her fair promises, the city was prevaricating – they were sending sixty ships to sea, but only as far as Sphacteria. I heard a great many excuses, but the Corcyrans didn't see any possibility that Persia could ever reach them – whereas they saw it as a certainty that Persia would defeat Athens.

We rowed away south, and my heart was as heavy as iron ore. Corcyra, like Syracusa, had a mighty fleet. But she was a former colony of Corinth, and I could see the long arm of Adamenteis at work. Right or wrong, I held him responsible. Certainly I'd heard his name often enough over wine in Corcyra.

Aside from Corcyra, we hid our camp every night and moved close to the coast by day. I assumed that Dagon was still hunting me – I knew his obsessions, and I knew from bitter experience how well he knew these waters. We never let a campfire show from the shore, and even when we passed the entrance to the Gulf of Patras and left it on our port side, sailing with a fair wind down the west coast of the Peloponnesus, I continued to take all the care I could. We saw a pair of ships well out to sea the day we sighted Mount Olympus, and we took down our sail and crept in with the coast.

Every day, my oarsmen got a little better.

I was lucky in my crew. I was also tested. I had never sailed far without a superb sailor at my side – Leukas, Vasilios, Sekla, Megakles, Demetrios, and their ilk. Professionals, born to the role. I always felt like a fake with them – after all, Plataea doesn't have any ships. I was seventeen before I handled a ship.

But that summer, the best sailor on my ship was me. My son – what a pleasure it is to say that – my son Hipponax was an excellent hand at the steering oar, and he had weather sense, but he couldn't navigate from one side of a public bath to the other. I assume his grandfather had always handled the navigation.

In a way, that was good. I was still a little unsure of my navigation

– I had the pride of a new skill, and I liked to talk about what I was seeing out loud as I took a sighting, or tried to calculate my speed through the water for dead reckoning. Hipponax and I had been entirely distant since the incident when Demetrios knocked him flat. He was correct and polite in my presence, and affected to despise me to Hector while trying very hard to impress me.

You know. Young men.

The day we saw Olympus – and what we thought might be Dagon's ships – I decided to stay out to sea and steal a march on my enemy. I wanted to fight Dagon, but not against desperate odds. The farther I could lead him from his base, and the better worked up my ship was ...

And my gods were not telling me that I had to fight just then. This is hard to explain, so you must believe me. I trusted I would have him. The floating tree had been where I needed it. So would revenge.

At any rate, my rowers grumbled when I said we'd spend the night at sea, but that was all, and we got the sail up again as soon as it was dark, with my veterans rigging the mast by moonlight while the rowers watched us as if we were the Argonauts. And then it was all a navigation problem. I sat in the stern, and it was Hipponax's trick at the helm, and we sailed through the moonlit darkness.

I talk to myself. No, it's true, and sometimes men think I've lost my wits, but navigation, for me, is always a conversation with myself, and with Pythagoras and Heraklitus and sometimes with Harpagos, whether he is there or not. So I stood with a spear shaft braced on the helmsman's rail, taking sightings on stars I knew.

'You can ... find your way with the stars?' Hipponax asked, suddenly. His voice carried the message that it had taken him time and effort to frame this question.

You can almost never go wrong with the young by giving them the full truth.

'Not really,' I admitted. 'With the stars, I could tell you where I was in the most general terms. Which we already know. But that star there will always show me north – see it?'

Hipponax snorted that adolescent boy snort. He knew the North Star. Of course he did.

'Well, it may seem simple to you, but I find it constantly reassuring that I am running south and east, because I've been this way before and that's the way this coast runs. If I make too much way to the east, smack – we'll hit the Peloponnesus.'

We ran on, the silence punctuated by the sound of water on the steering oars, and the ship-noise; creaking, groans from the wood, snapping noises that always sounded a little threatening.

'How else do you navigate at night?' he asked.

'Sound,' I said. 'The look of the waves. The wind. Some stars move less in the wheel of the sky than others and you can use them. Look – right now I'm aimed at the Plough.'

'Sound?' Hipponax asked.

It happened that I knew where I was to within a few stades, so I took the steering oars in my hands and turned the ship – very gradually – to the east, and ran in closer to the long beach. It showed like the edge of a road in the moonlight.

'Listen,' I said, but my son already had the lesson by heart.

He smiled at me.

'Do you want a ship of your own?' I asked.

'Yes!' he said.

I smiled at the darkness. 'Learn to navigate. And to command. That means patience.' Oh – I could see by his moonlit face I was veering off into the kind of lecture boys hate. 'You think you could command a ship for me?' I asked.

He shocked me by looking out over the sea. 'Someday,' he said with a snort. 'Not tomorrow morning.'

Well. We all know where wisdom begins, eh?

The mouth of the Alpheos was once again crowded. Because, of course, it was an Olympic year. I had known this somewhere in my heart – four years had passed since I had sailed here on a bowline from Bari. And it is true that the older you get, the faster time moves. Yet, my visit to Neoptolymos and my sighting of Dagon had made the world of four years before seem very immediate, so that it seemed possible, as I have heard philosophers theorise, that two points in time may not be as far apart as they seem – like wave caps with a trough between.

But there was not a single Athenian ship on the beach, and I could see only Corcyrans and Northerners, and a handful of Peloponnesians. Not a ship from Ionia.

Two from Syracusa.

We ate a very expensive meal on the beach – safe, for one night, from any attempt Dagon might make – and then, loaded to the point that the ship was hard to row, we headed south and stayed at sea for three days and two nights, drinking every amphora in the sand of the hold dry and eating every shred of dried meat, figs, dates and old bread aboard.

We weathered the Hand in fine style, with a beautiful westerly coming under our quarter as we passed the rocks. The seas were as empty as a new-washed bowl, and I worried less about Dagon and more about the Persians.

The seas south of Olympia were *empty*.

I put in at the port of Sparta for water and grain, and traded some of my Sicilian wines. The seas might be empty, but Sparta was not – I gathered from the traders on the beach that the citizenry of Lacedaemon were preparing for their great festivals. Half the citizen population was away at the Olympics, and the rest were preparing for the great Spartan festival – the one where everyone dances naked.

Well, that's what Athenians say. I've never been.

At any rate, there was no sense of crisis. I did learn that Leonidas was already at Corinth, or somewhere east of Corinth.

A fisherman said that a Megaran fisherman had told him that Xerxes had crossed the Hellespont.

The beachside traders were derisive.

'There won't be any fighting this summer,' one said. 'If there were, do you think all the Spartiates would be swanning about butt naked at home?' He made a rude gesture and laughed.

Have I mentioned that the helots and periokoi had no great love for their masters?

We sailed – still cautious, may I add – with the fine west wind at our backs. The fisherman had put a chill into me – I decided to try and navigate directly, Sparta to Athens, without passing up the Gulf of Corinth or touching at Hermione or any of my other favourite ports.

So again we filled the ship with water and food, and I used the profit on my Sicilian wine to buy a small fishing smack. I put Hector and Hipponax and Nicolas – an old oarsman I've mentioned before – and two of the slaves into her with a hold filled with food and wine, and we were away.

I was not the least afraid of finding Dagon out in the Great Blue. I spent too much time at the helm, and I didn't even have Hipponax to teach. Despite which, we made a fine passage for two days, and I liked everything I saw ...

Except a pair of big trireme sails on the horizon.

★

There are so many factors to a chase at sea. In an extreme, a captain can always abandon his course and run with the wind, or land at the first beach, burn his ship and run inland. I've done both.

But my ship was well worked up, my rowers were fresh and healthy and had, from a few good port visits, learned that they were treated like men, given wine and a few coins, and trusted. In return, I felt the first stirrings of a crew becoming ... well, a phalanx. I'd done it so many times by that summer that I could build a crew almost without conscious thought. A storm, or a sea battle – either one would make them mine. They were ready.

And the ship – Neoptolymos called her *Andromeda* – was no *Lydia*, but she was a fine ship and better for our rebuilding. She had a tendency to turn to starboard, like a horse with a bad bridle, and she had no brilliant turn of speed, and we'd had her in the water too long, so that her timbers were heavy with water. She needed a drying.

But I felt in my bones that she was faster and better manned than anything Dagon would have.

And I knew where I was – about five hundred stades west and south of Athens. Unless Dagon had found himself a new trierarch, he'd be worried about fighting here – in the Athenian shipping lanes.

I watched the two sails for enough time for the sun to move across the sky, and then I ordered my sails taken in, the mainmast stowed – what a pleasure a good crew is! Many ships had to land on a beach to stow the mainmast. Hah!

And then I turned the bow south, and went at my enemy.

Well! It wasn't Dagon.

Surprised? So was I. Even two stades away I thought I was watching a pair of Carthaginian triremes, and I had to get quite close – already manoeuvring for a strike – before I caught the flash of a shield from the stern of the nearest galley. It was a Greek aspis, and that gave me a little doubt, so I passed on my oar rake and got upwind of them, passing close.

One of the triremes was badly damaged. The other had a long scar down her paint on the starboard side, and looked familiar, and very Phoenician.

My smaller galley got upwind, and we turned, and the two enemy galleys got their bows around to us – the wounded one took so long I knew she was not any threat at all. But the Greek aspis worried me a little.

301

I let my lads rest on their oars while I drank a little water. We were low on everything, and I wasn't going to fight unless it was Dagon. I had the weather gauged – I could engage or run at my leisure.

Something told me they were Greeks. After laying on our oars for as long as it takes an orator to speak in the assembly, my conviction that they were Greeks was growing, and then Giorgios, one of my old sailors, ran back along the catwalk to tell me that he could hear men shouting in Greek.

We were, as I say, upwind. I summoned Hipponax under my stern.

'Run down and see if they are Greek,' I yelled. 'If they are, raise your aspis over your head. If not, turn to port and run free, and I'll join you, and we'll leave them here.'

Hector raised his hand in casual salute – the two of them were as brown as old walnut by then, and with their burned-blond hair they really did look like gods. The little fishing smack turned on her heel and ran down the wind – wallowed down it, more like. I saw Hipponax stand up in the bow and I saw someone on the stern of the other ship lean far out to shout.

Hipponax's shield came up with a flourish, and I saw the little fishing smack come to under the lee of the heavy trireme, and then we were moving. We rowed downwind, still cautious – I still wished I had my archers.

But my guess was correct. They were Greeks – Ithacans – on their way to join the allied fleet.

And they'd taken Dagon's consort. That took a day to ascertain, but they knew Dagon, and he'd abandoned them when the fight went bad, running due east.

Always a pleasure to have been right. The Ithacans were in an old capture – a heavy Phoenician galley they'd taken ten years before. Possibly in an act of blatant piracy – it takes one to know one. But the other ship they'd taken in a fight, two ships to two, and they were out of water, out of cordage, and desperate – conditions were so bad that the recaptured oarsmen from the Carthaginian had already risen in mutiny once.

Worst of all, they had no idea where they were. They had fought off Ithaca – the irony was that I'd been creeping about for days while Dagon and his consort looked for me in the wrong places, caught the Ithacans, and lost their fight.

At any rate, it took me days of conversations – and interrogations – to discern all this, and to learn that the Carthaginians were not on a voyage of private vendetta. They had indeed been sold information about me – the notorious pirate. But they were en route to join Xerxes with dispatches.

I gave them almost all our remaining water, and exchanged half of my rowers for half of the Carthaginian capture's rowers, and I led them north and east to Piraeus. We saw the Acropolis of Athens in the first light of the new day, and even the sickest rowers came back to life – one of the best pieces of navigation of my life, friends. By the time that girls were doing their dances at Brauron, we were ashore, and a hundred old men were embracing us.

After all, we had at our tail the first capture of the war. The first fruits of Nike.

We might have been feasted like heroes, but all the other news was grim. The worst was the thing I'd feared most – Xerxes was loose, across the Hellespont and marching at speed.

The allied fleet was forming all along the east coast of Attica – we hadn't seen it coming in the dark, but as soon as the sun was well up we could see Athenian ships on all the beaches from Pireaus east to the headland at Sounion. The Spartan navarch was already around Sounion at Marathon, and the fleet already had a squadron of light ships scouting the north coast of Euboea for anchorages.

Themistocles came back from Sounion to see our capture and to embrace us all. I was put in the oddest postion – I hadn't won the sea fight or taken the prize, but everyone treated me as if I had – I finally brought the Ithacan trierarch forward, a middle-aged pirate named Helios, and introduced him.

'This is the man who actually took the Carthaginian,' I said.

He shook his head. 'We'd all be dying of lack of water right about now but for yon,' he claimed.

That evening, over wine at Paramanos' house in Piraeus, Themistocles laid out his plan.

'I'd like you to crew all your own ships and five more from Athens,' he said. 'Can Plataea do it?'

I began to count in my head. 'Not and send a single man with Leonidas,' I said.

Themistocles made a gesture of dismissal. 'Leonidas has eight thousand men to hold a pass less than half a stade wide,' he said. 'He'll have Thebans and Thespians and his own Spartans and thousands of local men. It is at sea we need men.'

I sat back on my kline and sipped wine. 'Where *are* my ships?' I asked.

Themistocles nodded. 'All at Sounion, on the beaches there, and around below Brauron,' he said. 'I will put all of your ships, and all the Plataeans, and Aristides' ship under you.'

I fingered my beard and ate a date. I'd gone three days without food and I was permanently hungry and every old wound and muscle-pull ached or burned. Some ached *and* burned. Lack of food can really hurt.

'I'll send over the mountains,' I said. 'But none of my Plataeans will know how to row.'

He shrugged. 'Half our fleet doesn't know how to row,' he said.

The next week I'll pass over like the blur of exhausted activity that it was.

I sent a professional runner to Plataea for the Phalanx, and told them they'd be serving on ships – the Epilektoi as marines, the rest as oarsmen. I asked Myron to put it to the assembly. Then I took *Andromeda* around the long point of Attica and gathered 'my' ships at Marathon. Why not? It was the site of my greatest day. All of my best men had been there except Moire and a few of the young.

The Plataeans knew how to get there.

We towed five empty hulls, light as cockleshells with nothing aboard but cordage and oars, around. We got them ready for sea.

I took back from the fleet all of the men who were serving elsewhere. Cimon cursed me for taking Giannis back, but I had a place for him better than serving as a marine.

I had *Lydia*. She was five years old, but dry, sound as a nut, and had a crew – like no other crew I've ever had. After I shifted men around I still kept her old crew, so that out of a hundred and eighty rowers, I had only forty new men of Plataea.

Andromeda I gave to Megakles.

Demetrios had Aristides' superb *Athena Nike*. The great man himself was still not allowed 'home' from exile and, stubborn and obedient to the letter of the law, refused even to board an Athenian ship as a marine. But, as you'll see, he went aboard a Plataean ship.

Taciturn Harpagos had *Storm Cutter*.

Moire of Plataea – as he now called himself – had my troublesome Corinthian *Amastis*.

Paramanos – who should have been with Cimon – chose to be

with me. He had *Black Raven*, the third ship of that name. He owned her, too.

Then I stripped my friends of their command elements to captain new ships. As an aside, you will have noticed that the first ships I've mentioned were all privately owned. I owned *Storm Cutter*, although years of careful maintenance (and that costs silver) may have made her Harpagos's ship – in fact, we all behaved as if she belonged to him. *Lydia* was mine, pure and simple, and *Amastis* was mine in law – at least, in Plataean and Athenian law. Paramanos owned his ship and Aristides owned his – he had owned more, once, but they'd been lost.

The five ships I endeavoured to man were 'public' ships, purchased and fitted out by Athens as a state. This was a new arrangement. Demetrios told me that he'd commanded a state galley in the war with Aegina and he admitted that often they were indifferent ships – because there was no rich man to keep watch on the shipwrights. But of the five hulls they sent us, three were excellent and the other two merely average – all a little lighter than I'd have preferred.

Again, I've heard men claim that Athens built her light triremes because of her superior crews. It makes me smile. That summer, half the allied fleet was rowed by men who'd never *seen* an oar before that summer – like Boeotian farmers! Athens built light ships because they'd be easier for untrained men to handle, and because, to crew two hundred ships and send a phalanx, Athens had to skimp on marines. And finally, lightly built ships required less wood, and wood is expensive.

I just want you to get all this.

We were going to fight a fleet that outnumbered us two or three to one. They had professional crews and heavier ships and many, many more marines. They'd been together for almost a year and most of our oarsmen had never been out of sight of land.

I'd like to tell you that our advantage was that we were fighting for freedom, but I'm an old pirate and I'll tell you that men fight wonderfully well for loot. Xerxes had promised his men the rape of Greece.

The morale of the fleet was not good when I joined it. News that the Corcyrans – whose numbers would have been a wonderful addition – were prevaricating off Ithaca came as a blow.

Adamenteis of Corinth said openly that the Peloponnesian League should fall back to the isthmus and leave Athens to its fate. Themistocles made all his usual arguments.

But then, the Plataeans arrived.

They came down the mountain from the direction of Athens, singing the paean, and all the work on the beach of Marathon stopped, even though they were ten stades away.

Did I mention that time doesn't run straight?

The Plataeans' paean rang against the mountainsides, but it also rang through time, and every one of us who had stood in the stubble on that day, ten years before, raised his head like an old dog smelling a much-loved master.

And the Plataean phalanx came down the mountain singing, song after song, as if a march of three hundred stades was nothing to them, as perhaps it was not.

Men went back to work on the beach, but some men smiled. Oh, my friends, no one called us bumpkins and sheep lovers that day, and when the bronze dog caps were close, the Athenians gathered on the edge of the beach and cheered and cheered – ring after ring until my throat ached and my heart was full.

Idomeneaus brought them to the very edge of the beach, where the Persians had had their ships. He halted, and despite being a small army of Boeotian bumpkins, they halted like Spartiates and grounded their spears, all together.

Of course, it was a piece of theatre. If you've been paying attention, you know that Greek armies seldom march in their armour, much less with their aspides on their shoulders. But Idomeneaus, for all that he is mad with violence, is no one's fool.

He halted, as I say, and the men grounded their spears. The cheering Athenians fell silent, and the Corinthians were silent from curiosity, and the Megarans too. Aeginians came and stood.

Idomeneaus saluted me. 'Well!' he said, loud enough to carry to Athens. 'Here we are again. Are the Persians here?' he asked.

Men laughed.

'No,' I said. 'They're over by Thrace.'

His whole face lit up. 'Really?' he said. 'Let's go!'

That story was retold ten times an hour over the next days.

It is easy for any Greek to make great claims for his city. We are all hopelessly partial. Biased. I admit it. I would put Plataea before Athens or Corinth or Syracusa in everything; even while I suspect our temple of Hera is really small and provincial, I will never admit it. So I'm biased.

But I think we transformed the fleet.

Our men came singing. A thousand men who had faced the Persians – and beaten them. Not one Plataean complained about having to row. Men of fifty winters climbed down into the sweltering benches, took up the oars with the same practical interest as they used the spear, the plough or the potter's wheel, and learned.

The second night, when the aches were pounding away – when some of the older hoplites had discovered that I was only putting my youngest, fittest Plataeans in armour, and that meant many older men were going to row – we were gorging on Athenian mutton on the beach of Marathonas, and a young Athenian from Cimon's flagship was complaining about the work – and the dishonour.

Myron – who had come in person – stood up and put a hand on his back like the old man he was. 'Dishonour, is it?' he asked. 'The only dishonour would be to be left behind. In a hundred years, men will no longer claim descent from the gods. They will only say – my grandsire was there when we warred down the Great King.'

All conversation stopped.

'But!' a young man wailed – half in self-mockery, I think – 'But it's hot and it stinks of piss down in the benches! My shoulders hurt and I've no skin on my hands!'

Empedocles, son of Empedocles the Old, laughed. 'I don't disagree, young man,' he said. 'Let's all take an oath, then. After we beat the Medes, we'll never row again!'

The laughter went on for a long time.

Every commander knows that laughter is precious.

Mostly, we rowed up and down.

I confess that I found some irony in the time I'd spent training my phalanx to Spartan-like perfection so that we could use them as oarsmen instead. At least every oarsman understood the basic tactics.

And because they were my phalanx, and not slaves, I got all my people together on the beach every morning, and told them what we'd do – every signal, every manoeuvre. Most of them didn't understand a bit of it, at first, but by the end of the first week, when we had our first rumours of contact with the Persian fleet, most men knew when to reverse their benches and when to rest on their oars before the orders were passed. Citizens can be much better oarsmen than 'professionals', who are too often broken ex-slaves.

And farmers are strong.

Every night, Themistocles hammered home that our tactics must be simple and pure. All the Athenian helmsmen understood the complexity of the diekplous, where you pass through the enemy formation breaking oars and then turn back to envelop their second line. But Themistocles knew better than most men how few of our oarsmen could handle a complex ramming attack.

It will also help explain things if I say that I took eighty veteran oarsmen from each of my other ships – including Demetrios's magnificent long killer, the *Athena Nike*, and I put those, almost one hundred each, into the Athenian public ships and replaced them with Plataeans. In this way, ten of my eleven ships had lower-deck oarsmen who were raw beginners, but upper-deck men and full deck crews of veterans. It also eliminated any possibility of rivalry, and I told them all the first night we were together that we'd share the loot equally – no extra for the officers – a very popular move on my part, let me add. Men love freedom, but loot is ... more immediate. I put ten Plataean Epilektoi on every deck as marines, saving only *Athena Nike* and *Lydia*, which got their own marines back.

Gelon got a ship. As she was a public ship and had only a number, he called her *Nemesis*.

Idomeneaus got a ship. After all, he'd had one before. He called her *Hera*.

Leukas got a ship. After much thought, he called her *Parthenos*, which he claimed was the Greek for a goddess in faraway Alba.

I gave the fastest of my public ships to Giannis. He called her *Sea Horse*. He had, after all, sailed and led and fought his way into the Outer Sea and back. He knew almost everything. And I let him have Alexandros to command his marines.

And of course, I gave the best of the public ships to Sekla. He consulted with a priest of Poseidon and called her *Machaira*.

So as soon as we felt that our oarsmen could manoeuvre from column to line and back, Themistocles had us practise forming close together for defence. He assumed we'd always be on the defensive. The strategy that he and Leonidas had evolved was brutally simple – we'd hold out all summer and force Xerxes to retreat before winter came. None of us could imagine that Xerxes was rich enough to keep his army fed and in the field all winter.

After a few days of practising the most essential single skill of fleet combat – that's rowing backwards all together, if you don't know – Themistocles ordered us to try the 'wheel'.

It was almost the end of the fleet.

The wheel is a complex manoeuvre that depends on perfect timing and brilliant control.

When complete, every ship comes to rest with the stern posts touching and their oars in – you can form as few as fifteen ships like this. It forces your opponents to run in against your bow and to concede the initiative of any boarding action. It allows the force that has formed the wheel to move marines from ship to ship in perfect freedom while every attacking ship has to fight individually. The advantage of the wheel is so great that when a defender forms one, the attacker usually just sails around the outside. There's not much he can do, unless he can somehow attack from every direction all at once – and even then, remember that the wheel's defenders have the advantage of interior lines.

That's the good part.

Here's the bad part. To form the wheel from line ahead, you have to row backwards, get up enough speed to make it to your final resting spot *and no more*, pull your oars in and steer. If you are going too fast astern, you foul another ship and you may even damage each other. If you don't pull hard enough, you come to a complete stop on the water in the face of the enemy and, for a bonus, you may be between two other ships with no room to deploy your oars.

Now throw in untrained oarsmen and hundreds of ships trying to do this all at once.

The first time we tried, we had formed a grand crescent off the point of Marathon, and my squadron was on the left of the line – that's where we'd been at Marathon. Greeks can be creatures of habit.

First we all backed water together – as I said, this is the single most essential tactic of sea warfare, and we did it well enough.

Themistocles blew a trumpet – a Persian trumpet, no less – and we all began to form the wheel.

We were in the most difficult position, because we had to retreat, folding the crescent in the other way and ending on the back side of the wheel – a long pull rowing the wrong way. But on that day, it was entirely to our advantage, as the ships in the centre – and how vociferously they'd demanded that position, the Corinthians, of course – were ruthlessly crushed by the amateur crews of the

309

Athenians and the Aeginians. We backed and backed and heard the screams and oars were splintered. Men died.

A Corinthian trireme rolled and sank, her back broken.

And the nearest Persian was a thousand stades away.

It was like Lades.

The Corinthians and the Megarans were the worst sailors – no, that's not fair. They had the worst *officers*. But they had not suddenly raised a hundred new warships as Athens and Aegina, the real sea powers, had done, and consequently they affected to despise all the other ships. Like the Lesbians before Lade, they said they needed no further practice – that their crews were fully trained.

The Corinthians threatened to go home.

Our Spartan navarch arrived. Eurybiades brought ten ships from the Peloponnesus, and he came almost straight from the Olympics. I have heard him denigrated, and I have heard his leadership derided.

Men are odd animals. Eurybiades, like Leonidas, and like Arisitides and like Themistocles, wanted nothing but the victory of the allies. Because he was willing to listen to Themistocles – because he was ready to *learn* from all of us who had more experience of the sea – men deride him. In fact, I believe that he was the best navarch we could have had. He was cautious. He was mature. He would not hurry a judgement.

He was a Spartan, and would not hear of a contingent refusing to drill, and most importantly, he was a senior officer of the Peloponnesian League. I was present the morning he landed. Themistocles met him on the beach, and Adamenteis hurried across the beach to complain to the Spartans about what he perceived as poor treatment at the hands of Athens.

He came off his ship into the surf and waded ashore. A pair of helots came and stripped his wet armour and began to dry it. He embraced Themistocles and took my hand.

'You appear to have done well,' he said, in his dry way.

Themistocles nodded.

Just then, Adamenteis came up. 'He has not done well, and he and his Athenian cabal will wreck everything. Listen – they've sent the dregs of their oarsmen and kept all their best men home. Look at the Plataeans! Let them drill. We'll sit and laugh.'

The navarch looked at him – a look that I hope no Spartan ever gives me. 'Are you refusing to drill?' he asked.

Adamenteis paused. 'Refusing? No, but—'

Eurybiades nodded. 'Good. We will drill. The king has marched. He depends on this fleet to hold his flank.'

'We're ready now!' Adamenteis insisted.

Spartans do not sneer. I've never seen one do so, because to sneer is to mock, and to mock is to be weak – the Spartans know this. They are too proud to mock anyone.

Eurybiades didn't smile or frown or change facial expression at all. He merely said, 'We will sail when I say. You are ready when I decide.' He paused. 'Yes? Any questions?'

Spartans have many failings, but they are good, reliable commanders. We had been unlucky at the Vale of Tempe, but now we had a simple, plain-spoken man who'd served overseas – in Aegypt and Ionia. He was not a master sailor, but he knew the sea and he'd fought ten battles, and he spoke with absolute assurance.

We spent a third week at drills. Every day. He came aboard each of the squadron flagships and watched our squadrons manoeuvre – usually with Themistocles at his shoulder. Far from ignoring the Athenian democrat, he turned the man into his ... it's hard to name the office. His right hand. Many of the innovations that Themistocles lays claim to – even now, the filthy traitor – came from the Spartan navarch, who did not himself care a whit who got credit for anything, so long as the battles were won and the fleet stayed together.

We had games. After all, we had ten times the men that Leonidas had with the vanguard of the army. The fleet had at least forty thousand men. So, as we did before Lades and before every major military effort, we gave games.

For the first time, I did not participate.

I was thirty-five years old. Men of fully mature age sit in the shade and watch the beautiful youths. We don't compete, and we tell ourselves it is because that would be unfair. I would like to suggest that it is because older men fear to learn that skill and age cannot defeat youth and strength.

Peisander of the Philaedae won our games, a young Athenian of Cimon's family. He ran like a deer, jumped as if he had wings and his javelin flew like a bolt from the hand of Zeus. Or so Phrynicus said.

An Athenian youth – Pericles, an ugly boy with a big head who talked all the time – nonetheless won the two-stade sprint. He was

311

serving as Cimon's hypaspitos, and poor Niceas had to do all the work and was jealous.

And off to the west, other men were at the Olympics as if nothing had happened. As if there was no invasion. No Great King.

At any rate, we all lay in tents on the beach the night after the games – a dinner for all the navarchs commanding the ships and all the victors, crowned in olive. And Eurybiades laid out his strategy.

'We are smaller, and worse trained,' he said. 'But all we have to do is to continue to exist – to retreat after every loss, never allow ourselves to be routed or encircled – and we will not lose.'

It was a long speech for a Spartan.

And Themistocles followed him. 'No matter what the disparity in numbers, Xerxes cannot afford to let us separate one piece of his fleet. As long as we always have a clear retreat and sea room, we can win a string of little victories while we train up our rowers. And never risk a big fight. This is why we must master the wheel.'

No one liked the wheel.

We didn't sink any more ships, but we had some very ugly times – somewhere in the third week, I lost almost a quarter of my oars and Nicolas had his collarbone broken when a ship from the Sicyon contingent popped out of the wheel like a pomegranate seed from between a boy's hands and struck us in the stern – which led to a long series of foulings and a great many curses. Luckily our deck crews were better than our oarsmen, and poled us off before men died – but had the Persians been close, we'd all have died or been made slaves.

At the end of the third week, Eurybiades admitted he was waiting for other contingents. We had two hundred and sixty-nine triremes and a dozen pentekonters as messengers and scouts, as well as a hundred small merchantmen to keep us supplied.

Athens supplied a hundred and twenty-five ships, of which eleven were in my squadron, and technically they were Plataean. I'd prefer to say that Athens supplied one hundred and sixteen including Paramanos, and Plataea supplied nine, but you may count us any way you like.

Corinth promised sixty ships and supplied forty; and two of them slipped away before the fleet sailed and never returned.

Chalcis in Thrace supplied no ships but manned another twenty hulls built by Athens.

Megara supplied twenty triremes.

Aegina, which had sixty ships, supplied eighteen, and those with inferior crews.

We had a dozen good ships from Sicyon and ten ships from Sparta, or at least led by Spartan officers, and another eight from Epidavros in the eastern Peloponnesus. There was one ship from Hermione and two from far-off Ithaca. Troezen, Styra and Ceos all sent ships. Not many, but what they had.

If you count your way through them, you'll find that it was an Athenian fleet with a handful of allies, commanded by a Spartan and full of internal divisions. When Harpagos and I compared it to the Greek fleet at Lades – where we'd had Miltiades and a dozen other first-rate pirates I could name, where we'd had the elite of every Ionian Greek seagoing city – well, we were like to have wept.

But we didn't.

We just talked carefully through what we'd do when the rout began. We worked out where we'd go, and where we'd land. We sent Giorgos back to Piraeus to commandeer one of our merchant tubs, fill it with water and food, and bring it round. Not to share, either. But to give us food and water to outdistance pursuit the first night after the fleet broke up.

We were by no means the only doomsayers. We were merely the most practical.

Well, except the Corinthians, some of whom gave up and sailed for home, and the Corcyrans, who never came.

Practicality, of course, never won anyone their freedom. Caution is seldom the virtue needed *in extremis*.

After three weeks on the beaches south of Euboea, Eurybiades ordered us to sea.

Poseidon, what a mess that was.

I had good officers and willing men. My ships came off the beach quickly and in good order, and my squadron formed as it rowed, so that we reached our place on the left of the line about an hour after we were ordered to sea.

There is a current off the point of Schinias, and my oarsmen were kept busy for the next two hours trying to keep us on-station against the flow of the sea. I pitied them, but it was excellent practice, and I tried not to interfere. Besides, I had a Dionysian comedy of epic proportions playing out to my right, seaward, as the great fleet of the allies crept off the beaches, rammed each other, and slunk to their places in line. It was a wonderful thing that we all spoke Greek, so that the curses, imprecations and rage of the helmsmen could be clearly communicated.

At my elbow, Sittonax fingered his beard and laughed. 'Just imagine, brother, what it is like in the other fleet. Greeks and Persians and Aegyptians and Phoenicians all together, by all accounts!'

Harpagos, who was aboard by virtue of having jumped from his own transom to mine, shook his head in silence. I met his eye.

'We're doomed,' he said, with Laconic brevity.

We ran up the coast of Euboea with a fair wind, but Eurybiades forbade us to sail, which was good officering but bad for his popularity. We rowed. We rowed in various formations, and none of them was very good, but it was our first day moving as a fleet.

Our scouts – Locrians, for the most part, and some Ionians who'd come over from Lesvos and Chios with pentekonters – had chosen us a set of beaches on the western shore of Euboea. Euboea is like a sea-girt extension of my homeland of Boeotia, with beautiful farmland and sandy beaches, too – as close to a paradise as Greece ever gets south of Thessaly. On the western shore, there are broad beaches, but on the eastern shore it is far rockier, and a ship is exposed to the eastern winds and summer storms. The channel between Boeotia and Euboea is so narrow that there's a bridge – you may recall my father died there.

We camped, and the next day we passed the narrows two ships at a time. And camped again.

The Euboeans had been badly handled by the Persians in Marathon year, their two principal cities taken, most of their men of worth killed or sold as slaves, and while there had been talk of recolonising it from Thebes or Athens, no real moves had been made. It is an island half the size of Attica, occupied only by shepherds, and they had done nothing to prepare for the Persians. In fact, before we made our first camp and bought whole herds of sheep, I don't think they were fully aware of the threat.

Immediately their assembly met and started to make demands of the allied fleet – a fleet to which they contributed not a single vessel.

We ate their mutton and prepared for sea. Eurybiades sent Cimon's squadron of Athenians forward, all the way to Chalcis, to find the enemy. He didn't send Themistocles. He and Themistocles sailed side by side, and camped together – a visible symbol of the amity of Athens and Sparta.

We met, from time to time, formally or informally, and the occasion that I remember was of the latter kind – I was having wine with Themistocles when the Spartan navarch was announced, and he came in, wearing a faded scarlet chiton and no sandals – a slave brought a stool, which he looked at with a certain hesitation, and then he sat on it.

'Still nothing from the Medes,' he said.

'Where is Leonidas?' Themistocles asked. He indicated that the Spartan should have wine.

Eurybiades took the cup, poured a libation, and drained it. 'Delphi or close enough. The Thebans are late.' He looked at me. 'I'm sure that comes as a surprise.' He smiled.

The slave poured him another fill of watered wine. Again he rose, poured a libation, and emptied the cup. 'Good wine,' he said to Themistocles.

'I have an idea,' Themistocles began, and Eurybiades smiled.

'Another stratagem?' he asked, with the fondness of a father for a son.

'Without stratagems, what chance have we against the Great King?' Themistocles leaned forward with his fingers steepled.

Eurybiades nodded. 'I will try every trick and every deception that your fertile mind provides,' he said. 'But in the end, for all our planning, we will fight – ship to ship, man to man. There is no trick that will save us then.'

'How will we defeat them, then?' Themistocles asked. He put his face in his hands. 'You saw the formations today!'

'Pray to the immortal gods,' Eurybiades said. 'Every cup of wine I drink, I pray to Poseidon for a storm.'

I held up my cup. When the slave filled it, I rose, and poured a libation to Poseidon, shaker of the earth and master of horses. And then I drained the cup.

Eurybiades nodded. 'Not by the hand of man alone will the Great King be bested,' he said.

Themistocles made a face. But he rose, poured a libation, and drank. 'I do not like to beg the gods.'

'Beg?' asked the Spartan. 'I will fight to the last breath in my body, regardless of what the gods choose. I merely ask.'

Themistocles thought of something – opened his mouth, and

thought better of it. So instead, he smiled his cunning smile. 'Besides,' he said, 'as you say, the wine is good.'

As a fleet, we were the worse for lacking Cimon, whose ships were truly the elite of our force. But by the fourth day, as we brought the northern tip of Euboea into sight, where Cape Artemesium with the temple of Artemis rises as a sea mark for navigators, our fleet could row, all together, in formation. We could form the wheel – not very well, but without disaster. And two hundred and fifty triremes is a very grand sight. I stood on my helmsman's bench and named off the ships to Hector like a rhapsode reciting the ship list from the Iliad, and still my count only reached two hundred and fifty.

'We had more at Lades,' I said.

Nicolas was now my oar-master, and his lover Giorgos was my helmsman, with Hector and Hipponax in training under them as officers. The boys were going to become men. I thought a great deal about Hipponax, my son – because somewhere on the coast of Thrace was an enemy fleet. It not only held Dagon, my enemy. It held Archilogos of Ephesus, and on his ship might well be Briseis' son, who was also mine. Heraklitus would be seventeen, if my maths were good.

I love the gods, but the tragedy of men entertains them all too well – our ironies and injustices spice their feasts. I prayed to Poseidon with a whole heart for a storm, but I prayed to Zeus, father of gods, to spare my sons – and most of all, to spare them the impiety of going helmet to helmet and shield to shield. And despite all this wool-gathering, I was proud of my son, and proud of Hector, who, arrayed in his armour, and two fingers taller and wider than me, looked the part of his name.

The three of us – Hipponax, Hector and I – practised on the deck of the ship. I had had four years to form Hector as a fighting man, and two years with Hipponax, and they were fast, strong and agile. Hipponax was the strongest of the three of us – a blow from his shield rim, perfectly timed, could knock me down. Hector's heavy spear was like a serpent, darting from behind his aspis to strike. He was deceptive in the subtlest ways, showing movement of his legs and then striking down the opposing line.

I put them in the best armour that money could buy. Why not? I wore the best myself – bronze everywhere, for a ship fight. I wasn't going to survive a swim, anyway. I had a bronze Athenian-style helmet with hinged cheek pieces and a magnificent crest in red, black and white. And a fine thorax, a bronze breastplate that mated perfectly to the back and rested on my hips and shoulders, the weight evenly distributed. But I also had armour for each thigh, and greaves of polished bronze, and a full set of armour for my right arm – a vambrace of bronze and a rerebrace of bronze with the raven of my house set on it, as on my greaves. I had a bronze knuckle guard such as the Etruscans wear, which I made myself.

I'd never worn so much armour, but I was getting older, and age slows a man and withers his muscles. And – I had sworn an oath. I shall not dwell on this, but I had determined, as a man sometimes does, not to survive defeat. I laid a trail of supplies and beach havens for the Plataeans in the event of disaster. But I would not be there to lead them.

You see, my friends, I had had a year to learn from Jocasta and Aristides, in much the way I taught my young squires. And what I learned was that life is empty without a companion, home, hearth and children. I wanted what they had, and I would have Briseis, or die. It sounds foolish – she wasn't within a thousand stades of our coming battle.

But I knew in my heart that this was the last gasp of Greece, and if we lost, all was lost. And if all was lost, I planned to perform a deed that would live for ever in the minds of the Persians, so that they would know what the Greeks had been.

Hence, the armour.

I practised in it every day. Some days I wore it from dawn to dusk, preparing my body for the weight of it and the constraints. I danced the Pyrriche in it every night, with all of the marines of my squadron and many of the oarsmen.

The day after we passed the narrows, we danced by firelight on the firm, damp strip of the beach nearest the sea. Hermogenes led the 'reds' and I led the 'whites' and I had Idomeneaus and Stygies on one side of me and Ajax and Peneleos, son of Empedocles and Antimenides, son of Alcaeus of Miletus, on my other side – Hermogenes had Hipponax and Hector, and Teucer, son of Teucer, and Hilarion and Diocles. We all wore our best – all our armour, our plumes and horsehair tails, and we carried our best spears.

Myron stood with the Plataean oarsmen, and old Draco – more than seventy years old, and still rowing for his country – took a spear, and began to tap it on a stone.

There were a dozen musicians – Ka, my archer captain, was quite skilled at the diaulos, and so we had more than just rhythm.

As the music began, men started to come down the beach. The flames licked at our bronze, and men came running. Two hundred triremes fill almost six stades of beach.

We'd danced the Pyricche on other nights, and men had come. But that night we had a curtain of stars and the whisper of the sea, and the air was hushed, and the musicians came.

We had learned my new, Spartan-style Pyricche with new motions and new tactics, but that night, we danced the old Plataean dance. It is not so complicated. At the opening, all the dancers form a small phalanx – or a great one – eight files deep and as wide as there is space and men to fill it. That night we had two groups of sixty-four – eight files by eight ranks. That was all the marines off all eleven ships and most of the officers, so that Moire and Paramanos and Gelon were all in the ranks.

The two groups started at opposite ends of the dance ground. We marched to the beat of Draco's spear, until the lead rank of my whites almost collided with the lead rank of Hermogenes' red, and then we turned – all together – to face the crowd, and all our spears came up together like a flock of steel birds rising into the moonlight, and we gave a great shout.

Many men in the crowd fell back a step.

In that moment, I saw Alexandros smile under his Corinthian, and realised that the Plataean at his shoulder in the second rank was Aristides the Just. I almost lost a step in delight.

Then we turned to the right together, and to the left. We knelt behind our shields and sprang to our feet, thrust low and thrust high.

The diaulos began to play, and four more joined – a wild chant to freeze the blood or make it soar – and we faced the crowd, then turned to face each other, whites against reds, and each small taxis stepped back – once, and again.

And then the dance really began. First the reds swept forward, and collided with the whites, and spears licked out, thrust high, and were turned on white's aspides, and we were pushed back – rotating our front rank as we went, so fresh men could face the next attack, every front-rank man pivoting on his hips to slip between two new men. Then the whites retaliated, dancing forward, their spears held high, and we in turn sent them stumbling back.

We attacked again, this time with spears held low and thrust underarm. Now the whites exchanged their ranks.

Again our blows were turned, and the whites counter-attacked.

By this time, the Greeks on the beach had begun to sing the paean of Apollo. There were forty *thousand* Greeks on that beach.

Then both teams stepped back – one, two – and the whites faced about as the reds danced forward, so once more we were one phalanx, sixteen men deep in files and eight men wide. Older Plataeans had acted to clear the beach to the north of us, so that we could finish in our old, old way – and the former rear rank of the whites – now the front rank of the whole, facing the empty beach – leaped forward two fast steps and threw their spears – turned outward and ran to the rear, drawing their swords. In rapid succession – as fast as I can tell it – every rank hurled their heavy spears – not javelins, but fighting spears, so that the sand grew a forest of spear shafts.

And as the last rank re-formed, the whole stepped forward eight steps.

Hermogenes roared, 'The ravens! Of Plataea!'

And every man pushed forward one step more.

And the dance was done.

I have danced that dance since I was thirteen years old – more than twenty years – but that night in Euboeoa ... that night, we danced for men and gods.

Much later, when other men were asleep, I walked the beach. I found Eurybiades checking his sentries, and offered him wine from my canteen.

He poured a libation. 'It is my greatest fear,' he said, pointing at two young men on the headland, 'to lose all Greece in a moment's inattention – the Phoenicians coming down on us like wolves in the dawn.'

He drank, and handed me my canteen.

'Poseidon watched your dance,' he said. He nodded sharply. 'Goodnight.'

The next day, we left the beaches in much better order and went north. Having secured a whole set of operational beaches at Artemesium, Themistocles wanted to manoeuvre the fleet in the waters where Leonidas wanted us to fight. Simple ideas like this are the very sinews of strategy. It was a brilliant concept – to rehearse the fleet where we intended to fight. We spent two days learning the shoals and the anchorages north and south of the channel, and the narrows and the current and the tides.

The weather was superb – for Persia. Either Poseidon was spurning our prayers, or busy elsewhere. But the habit of praying to Poseidon with every cup of wine had spread to the whole fleet, so that every night when the watches were set and the fires alight, we had forty thousand men pouring their first drops of wine on the sands and shouting Poseidon's name.

We heard that King Leonidas had reached Thermopylae, and Eurybiades sent an Athenian in command of a scout ship, a pentekonter, to Thermopylae to make sure that the fleet and army were in constant contact. The Athenian was Abronichus, son of Lysicles, who was a patron of Phrynicus and a friend of Miltiades. At Artemesium one of our volunteer Ionians, Polyas, kept a pentekonter in constant alert, ready to row for Thermopylae to report any victory or defeat we suffered. He even camped a headland separate from us, to prevent his being taken in the event of a surprise. In this way, the army and fleet of the allies could act in concert, even though they were many stades apart.

The boats went back and forth almost every day, so that we knew that although Leonidas had only three hundred Spartans with him – because of the festival, or so the Spartans would have it – he had another four hundred Thebans; he had the whole phalanx of Thespiae, almost two thousand men, including almost a hundred veterans of Marathon and my brother-in-law Antigonus, and the Phocians – almost two thousand of them, and a further two thousand Locrians.

Leonidas, then, had fewer than six thousand hoplites, where we had almost fifty thousand men with the fleet. But that seemed reasonable to the men who had designed the allied plan of campaign. All of us feared a sudden stroke from the Phoenician element of the Persian fleet – a landing in the Peloponnesus, let us say, or in Attica – that would endanger all of our plans. On the other hand, the rumours of the enormous size of Xerxes' army – most men set the number at a million – caused us to dread it, but not to respect its speed. We knew how slow a Greek army was, and how disorganised. We assumed that with Xerxes marching so late – nearly harvest time – we need only delay him a few months. And we assumed it would take him one or two of those months to reach us. So the Greek states celebrated the Olympic games, and even Athens sent a large contingent. Sparta threw her efforts not into war, but into the Carneia.

The fleet waited to fight the Persian fleet.

And Leonidas settled down to hold the fifty-foot-wide pass of Thermopylae until the main army came up and he could have the battle that all the Spartans wanted, to try the worth of men.

Cimon's squadron returned from their scout along the coast of Thrace. They had not found the Persian fleet, but they had made contact with refugees fleeing the Great King's army, and they had spoken to boats whose crews claimed to have seen the enemy fleet. Cimon feared to be away too long – like the rest of us, he feared the Phoenicians' blue-water navigational powers. He feared that while he scouted the Thracian coast, which he knew so well, they would go to sea, the bowstring to his bow – slip past him and attack us, and we could not spare a dozen crack triremes manned by professional crews with ten years' experience.

Cimon's closest friend was Lycomedes, son of Aeschrydus, who had been one of his father's captains. Lycomedes came in the evening of our fifth day at Artemesium.

I saw him come in, grabbed a spear and ran to Eurybiades' awning. All the navarchs were gathering – we were starved of news.

The young Athenian – younger than me, at any rate – shook his head in answer to a question I hadn't heard. 'We can't be sure. We never saw them. But if the fishermen are to be believed, they sailed from Therma yesterday.'

Themistocles gnawed a fingernail. 'Where are our scouts? We have three ships at Skiathos.'

Lycomedes shrugged. 'The fishermen say that there're Persians and Phoenicians at Skiathos,' he said.

Themistocles looked in a bad way.

Eurybiades didn't panic. But he did turn to one of his Spartan officers and whisper, and the man sprinted away into the gathering darkness.

'And the land army?' Eurybiades asked.

'Marched from Therma in Thrace fourteen days ago,' Lycomedes said. 'A refugee from Thessaly – a gentleman – said the Persians are making a hundred stades a day.'

'Impossible!' shouted Ademanteis.

Eurybiades ran his fingers through his beard. 'That means that Xerxes is – at most – a week away.'

That got a storm of protest.

Eurybiades ignored the murmurs and turned – I'm not sure who he was looking for, but his eye fell on me. 'You Plataeans are always ready for sea,' he said.

Well – we tried. He didn't need to know how long Gelon's ship had taken to get off the beach that morning, or that the two Ithacans had decided to join my squadron – ignoring the navarch's order of battle – and they were always late.

'At your service, sir,' I said.

'I've already sent a dispatch boat to Leonidas today. But he needs to know this immediately.'

I snapped my fingers and Hector appeared at my elbow. At my whisper he pulled out a pair of wax tablets.

Eurybiades nodded in Laconian satisfaction and dictated a rapid message.

Midway through, he turned. 'Is that all?' he asked Lycomedes.

The younger captain raised both eyebrows.

'Cimon is lying at Aphetae tonight,' he said. 'He thinks the weather is about to turn bad.'

'Why Aphetae?' I asked. 'Why not here?'

Lycomedes laughed. 'I promised not to tell,' he said, and grinned wickedly. 'When you are out to the east, the headlands look like one single stretch of land – eh?' He drew them on the sand, and I could see how, if you had too much southing, Artemesium and Aphetae would look like one peninsula.

He put his stick into the sand. 'We missed Artemesium and landed at Aphetae. Cimon was one of the last to come up – he knew the error, and sent me here. We're all still mocking Callisthenes, who led the way to the wrong beach.'

It was, as you'll see, an easy error to make.

We didn't have any Euboean triremes, but for the last five days we'd been fed a great deal of fish by Euboean fishermen, and Eurybiades summoned all those in camp to our impromptu council.

I walked down the beach at sunset. The sky was the warm pink of a beautiful evening. There was nothing that might have piqued my weather sense except the merest flash of white, far off on the eastern horizon, and a cool breeze out of the east. We had olive groves all the way down to the beach on the headland of Artemesium, and suddenly, like the voice of the god, all the leaves moved together.

I walked back to the council.

One of the older fishermen was humming and hawing, clearly

anxious at speaking in front of so many great men. Another tall brute in a Phrygian cap pushed him gently aside.

'Weather might be ugly the next four days, gents.' He shrugged. 'And it might not. Storms come off Africa – sometimes right down the channel.' He looked at me for some reason. 'If you are worried about the anchorage – an' you should be – just slip back to Troezen.'

Themistocles slammed his fist in his palm. 'We can't anchor both flanks at Troezen. We cannot cover Leonidas from Troezen. We must be here!'

Adamenteis shoved his way forward. 'Leonidas can't hold the Gates against a million men! We should go back to the isthmus – now, while we have a fleet.'

Isocles of Aegina, their navarch, shook his head. 'We should do what we should always have done – press forward and strike them when they don't expect us, on the Thracian coast.'

'Are you mad?' said another – one of the Peloponnesian captains. 'They'll slip past us and burn our farms.'

'Four hundred triremes don't slip anywhere, you fool!'

'Back to the isthmus where we can command our own fates!'

Eurybiades didn't seem to straighten up, or fill his lungs. But his voice was like the voice of brazen-lunged Ares. 'Ears!' he shouted.

Men stood silent, stunned.

'Gentlemen,' he said into the silence, in a voice that expected their continued cooperation. 'The allied fleet needs Poseidon's help. If that help is going to take the form of a storm from the north and east, we do *not* want to be caught on a beach facing north and east.' He nodded courteously to Adamenteis. 'Our strategy is set, and will no longer be discussed. In the morning, we will retire to Troezen. We can be back here in six hours. No one is permitted to send dispatches home, or to leave the fleet under any circumstances. Arimnestos of Plataea will take my messages to King Leonidas and meet us at Troezen.' He nodded.

No one offered any protest. Greece was not lost or won in that moment, but it is the moment I think of, when men say that Themistocles defeated the Medes.

His message, which Hector wrote out and I read ten times, said just this.

Xerxes left Therma fourteen day ago and makes good time.

I will retire to Troezen to allow the gods to save us, if they will.

★

Running down a channel at night is never easy. The wind was rising slightly and I didn't care to use the sails, and so my oarsmen got still more practice. I left Paramanos in charge of my squadron, because he had more experience of command than any, even Demetrios, Aristides' helmsman.

At any rate, we rowed down the dog-leg passage. From the open sea and the coast of Thessaly, it runs due west, and then turns south around the island of Euboea and then runs at an angle towards Attica.

There is a deep bay on the western shore of the dog-leg, and the narrow gates of Thermopylae – the so called 'hot gates' where the hot water flows from deep in the earth into shallow bowls – the gates, as I say, were formed by the mountains coming almost to the edge of the sea. Men had walled the pass many times, to stop various invasions from Thessaly and Thrace, with varying degrees of success.

At any rate, we rowed in at first light, and I won't pretend I wasn't very relieved to have made the voyage without touching a rock. There was a light surf running as we turned *Lydia* to land her stern first – the first taste of the easterly blowing down the coast of Thrace from the Hellespont. I am ashamed to admit that I was not at the helm, where I ought to have been, but amidships, shitting away my relief at a successful night navigation with Hermogenes, when we struck a rock.

We weren't moving fast, but we started taking water immediately. The wound was bad enough that I could see where two planks had broken.

We were in no danger of sinking – we were in four feet of water, half a stade off a beautiful beach. It was a simple accident, but it angered me.

We got the ship ashore, rowing like heroes to overcome the weight of water and keep her bottom strakes off the sand, and then my rowers piled over the sides with a will and rolled her dry and carried her up the beach. It wasn't as bad as it might have been, but we had two strakes broken and a third cracked. By the will of the gods – or blessed by Moira – I had not sold my cargo of Illyrian timber and pitch. It had seemed wiser to keep it for emergency repairs, and I had divided the cargo among the ships of my squadron, so that before I went up the beach to find the camp of the Greeks, Hermogenes and Stygies had axes in their hands and splitting wedges and two dozen willing Plataean farmers were giving them advice.

I took both of my boys and walked up the beach, and found the ancient wall, and a very alert sentry from Corinth, in full panoply. This pleased me almost as much as the rock had annoyed me, and I shouted my name and my errand with a will.

The Corinthian sent for a superior. He leaned over the low wall. 'I'm sorry, Plataean. But the king gave orders that we admit no man until daylight.'

I waved at the sky.

The Corinthian shrugged. 'Are you not the notorious pirate?' he asked.

Of course, in Corinth I *was* a notorious pirate.

'I have certainly been a pirate,' I said. 'But that Corinthian ship? I found her high and dry, sold for scrap timber in Aegypt.'

'Really?' he asked, and leaned out over the wall again. 'I hear you killed all the oarsmen and officers and took her south of Cyprus.'

I shrugged. 'Believe as you will. But all my men will back my version, and I could get priests from Aegypt to swear to it as well.'

The Corinthian nodded. 'Of course, all that could be lies and fakery,' he said.

I nodded.

'So it could. What would convince you?' I asked.

Someone came up behind him, and he had a whispered conference. A ladder was lowered.

I climbed it. At the top, the Corinthian peered at me. 'You don't look like a man who would massacre a citizen crew for the sake of a hull,' he said.

The man behind him on the wall was the King of Sparta. He didn't look the worse for sleep, and his hair was long and curly and his beard oiled. He nodded to the Corinthian. 'What is it that engages the two of you so hotly?' he asked.

'A lawsuit in Corinth,' I muttered.

The King of Sparta laughed. 'Truly, you are Greeks,' he said. 'Xerxes marches, and we argue lawsuits.'

'Xerxes is very close,' I said. I handed the king my tablets.

He took them and nodded. 'So I assumed from the moment my sentries reported your ship,' he said. 'No one sends a trireme with good news.'

That day, while the allied fleet retreated from the possibility of a storm, we worked on *Lydia*. We dried her hull upside down in the sun, which was good for her, and Hermogenes led the self-appointed carpenters. We had good tools, but no adze, and the Locrians brought us one, bless them.

While my friends worked, I walked through the camps, and visited. I knew men in many contingents, and I got news of the Olympics, and sat with Antigonus for a cup of wine.

We drank, and talked of farming and lawsuits.

When we'd bored his neighbours into leaving us alone, he leaned close to me – we were lying in the dry grass behind his tent. 'Can the fleet hold?' he asked.

I nodded. 'Every day, we are better. We have good officers and good oarsmen. When the Olympics end, we'll have another fifty ships.' I leaned on my elbow. 'We can hold the Medes for a few days. That's all we need.'

'And the storm?' Antigonus asked. 'Everyone is praying to Poseidon for a storm.'

I remember that I shrugged. Rather impiously, my outswept arm indicated the blue sea and cloudless eastern horizon. 'The fleet is seeking anchorage from Poseidon's wrath,' I said in mockery. 'Tomorrow, no doubt, we'll go back to our station at Artemesium.'

'A sign from the gods would hearten us all,' he said. He drank some neat wine from a canteen and held it out to me. 'But barring the direct involvement of the Olympians, I suppose we'll just have to dig in our heels and fight. Are you any good at mathematics?'

I laughed. 'Fair enough. I can work geometry.'

Antigonus nodded. 'Well – figure this. We have six thousand hoplites and Xerxes has a million. How many do I have to kill?'

'Two hundred, give or take a few,' I said.

He whistled. 'Well,' he said. He looked at me. 'If I fall, tell Penelope that she was ... everything I ever desired in a wife.'

There is something embarrassing about seeing another man's love for your sister, even when you think very highly of him. So I slapped his shoulder and shrugged. 'Tell her yourself,' I said. 'I'd never get it out without mocking her.'

'Fine, then. I'll stay alive to spite you.' He laughed, and I laughed.

We were sharing a third cup of unwatered wine – war is hell – when there was a stir by the forward posts across the wall. There was a party of Tegeans cutting palisades, and they all stopped. There were Spartan helots cutting grass for their master's bedding, out in the wide part of the pass, where there was a low hill and two good broad fields. The helots' heads came up like those of horses scenting danger.

Antigonus and I started walking towards the wall.

There was dust, over to the east.

I remember putting a hand to my eyes to shade them from the sun – Hekatombaion is a cruel month for the eyes. On the beach at my feet, Hermogenes was doing the same.

All the Greeks stopped what they were doing and looked east.

The dust cloud was like a thunderhead. It swam in my vision – shimmered in the heat. My first thought was that Poseidon had sent us a storm after all.

There was a sudden gust of wind from the east with a breath of coolness and all the tents and awnings snapped, like the shields of two armies in the first moments of a battle.

My eyes began to appreciate the *scale* of the dust cloud I was seeing to the east.

The Tegeans were standing to arms, out on the plain, and suddenly the helots broke and ran – carrying, I might add, the forage fodder they'd been sent to fetch.

The wind stirred again, and for a moment the front of the dust cloud vanished, and I saw the flash of bright sun on steel and bronze.

I was not looking at a storm of Poseidon. I was looking at the armed might of the Great King, and it filled the horizon like a thundercloud.

Below me, on the plain, a hundred Persian cavalrymen swept past the Tegeans contemptuously, and began to shoot the fleeing helots with bows. I couldn't tell whether they were Persians, Medes or Saka, but they rode like centaurs and shot like Apollo, and a pair of helots went down – fell face forward, and heartbeats later were speared through the back like new-caught fish.

The Tegeans formed an orb – a tiny island of defence.

The Persian cavalry came all the way down the plain at a gallop, but the helots had vanished into the dust and the brush.

Below me, I saw Ka and six Numidians draw their bows.

They loosed.

It is very difficult to shoot a man over a long range. Arrows – especially the lightest flight arrows that master-archers carry – can fly over two hundred paces, and some over three hundred paces, but such light darts are moved by every breath of wind. Further, it takes long enough for an arrow to fly two hundred paces that a galloping horse has moved ten paces in the interval.

So the lead riders came at us unscathed.

But about midway down the squadron of Persians, two riders fell backwards into the dust, and another horse screamed its trumpet cry of rage and pain and threw its rider on the ground, and the compact Persian troop burst apart like a nest of hornets stoned by boys.

The helots leapt to their feet and dashed for the wall, and the guard – all Mantineans – turned out like heroes, formed under the wall, and covered the helots as they ran.

My sailors and marines were formed and ready to move, with Hermogenes, adze in hand, in his moment of glory.

Ka's archers loosed.

All the armed Greeks on the plain before the walls charged the Persian cavalry at a run, the way we'd done at Marathon. Another Persian fell, and someone waved a sword – and they ran.

Horse archers run all the time. It means nothing. They run so that they can find a better position from which to fill you full of arrows. But that day, when they ran, it was Greece that had carried the day. Two helots lay dead, and three Persians had gone to Hades with them.

If there was irony in that little victory, it might be that all the killing had been done by a handful of Numidian archers, but let us not parse this too carefully. The Tegeans and the Mantineans and the Plataean oarsmen met far out on the plain, slapped each other's backs, and marched into the gates like the heroes of the Iliad. The Persian cavalry ran all the way back to Xerxes.

Xerxes made camp across the plains, at Trachis, where there was room to camp his army.

Antigonus and I had shouted ourselves hoarse like spectators at the Olympics, cheering on our hoplites, too far from the action to even trouble for our armour. But when the Persians ran, we cheered with everyone else.

When the Mantineans returned, we discovered that they had a prisoner. He was the man whose horse had taken so many arrows – he'd been knocked unconscious by a direct hit on his helmet.

I went down to translate. King Leonidas was far too much the gentleman to interrogate a prisoner, but all the Greeks crowded around – the Spartans as much or more than anyone – seeking to touch the Persian. He was quite muddle-headed from the blow, and when we showed him his peaked bronze helmet with a dent three fingers deep, he shuddered.

'Are you Persian?' I asked.

His head turned in shock. 'I am Hyperanthes, son of Hydarnes, friend of the king!' he said bravely. 'You speak Persian brilliantly.'

I nodded. 'I am Arimnestos of Plataea.'

'The ambassador! Mardonius said you were dead!' The young man shook his head and then sank it in his hands.

I gave him water. 'You needn't fear. When you feel better, the king has decreed you will be returned to your host. King Leonidas wishes the Great King to see that Greeks behave according to the laws of the gods.'

The young man brightened up considerably. Perhaps he thought we'd torture him, or kill him and eat him – who knows what lies the Persians told about us? Certainly we told a few about them.

We were standing on the low hill behind the wall, which gave the best view of the enemy. He got to his feet to see.

'Sit!' I said. 'When you feel better – when your army has stopped marching . . .' I pointed at the dust cloud.

He laughed. 'You think that is the army?' he exclaimed. 'That is my father's regiment – the Immortals. They have marched forward to cover the camp while the slaves build it. The army is behind them.'

Leonidas exclaimed in delight, like a man seeing a beautiful treasure. 'Those are the Immortals?' he asked.

The Spartans all crowded to the wall to look. You'd have thought a beautiful woman was walking down the beach to bathe.

The Tegeans and Mantineans and Thespians and Plataeans all looked at each other. And then they looked at the dust cloud that seemed to float all the way back to Asia.

There is a particular arrogance to the humility of some men, and most especially those who claim for themselves the will of the gods. But I will claim that Poseidon favoured me that day – wth the rock under his water, and the damage to my ship.

Because, thanks to the rock, my ship was pulled all the way up the beach of Thermopylae, fifty feet above the waterline, when the storm struck.

Had we been at sea – perhaps we might have weathered the storm. But it blew straight from the east down the first leg of the channel and struck the beach at Thermopylae with gale-force winds and waves as tall as a man. The pass – never very wide – was closed to the width of a wagon in some places by the fierce run of water.

The first night that the storm blew, I walked down to the bow of my ship and watched the waves roll in. The storm hit us with no harbinger but those odd, cool gusts of wind, and I stood in the darkness and blessed the fishermen of Artemesium, and Cimon, who knew these waters better than any of the rest of us.

Hermogenes came and stood with me in the dark.

The wind began first to tug at my chlamys, and then – with the force of a blow – tore my cloak right out of its pin. Hermogenes caught it before it vanished.

A wave broke at our feet, and the water came to within six feet of the ram.

Hermogenes turned and ran. I wondered what madness had seized him, but he came back with a skin of Plataean wine and my fine Persian cup of beaten gold, which I'd had from the Queen Mother. And behind him were my oarsmen, leaning into the wind, with resined torches and the ship's four great oil lanterns, all lit.

We stood on the beach and sang the hymn to Poseidon. We were farmers, not sailors – or most of us were – so we praised him as the creator and breaker of horses, and the shaker of the earth. The rushing monster of the storm drowned most of our song, but I stood there – my chiton soaked by waves and the first lashing of rain, as the lightning forked on the horizon, over and over – and I filled my brave gold cup with the agates and lapis and the largest emerald in Greece to the brim with the wine grown in my own fields in Green Plataea, and then I hurled it as far as I could into the sea.

Let me tell you a thing.

The waters off Thermopylae are as shallow and clear as the waters off any great beach in all of Hellas.

But no man has ever found my cup of gold, or the rock that tore a hole in *Lydia*.

Only fools doubt that the gods walk with men.

For three days, the Hellesponter storm blew like Poseidon's will – and for three days, the Persian army sat opposite us and did nothing. The Spartans champed at the bit like racehorses waiting for the Olympic races, eager and ready, fully exercised. They sat on the wall and combed out their hair, danced their dances, ran races, and waited for their battle.

The Tegeans and Mantineans and the rest were perhaps a little less eager, but Xerxes' hesitation heartened everyone.

Because I had drunk wine with the taxiarchs, I knew that the

Great King's apparent hesitation was created by the weather. Unless the enemy were planning to cross the pass and attack us one at a time – one file – they had to wait for the abnormally high waves to subside.

And unless the Phoenicians had better access to Poseidon than we had, the Great King had to be waiting to see where his fleet was. We all prayed that it had been caught on the sea by the storm, but I suspected otherwise. It had struck us at the edge of darkness. Farther east, it would still have struck after any sane navarch had all his ships on the beach.

All we could do was wait. The same sea that closed the pass made it impossible for us to sail. To make matters worse, we had to guard the ship day and night, because we'd beached her too far along the beach – when we'd landed, it had been Greece, but now it was the no man's land between the hosts.

I wore myself out, walking on the soft sand back and forth between the wall, the army and my ship.

Three times parties of Persian horsemen came along the beach, or along the coast road above it, testing the footing for their horses. They would ride up close to the wall, and the Spartans would wave at them.

The third day, Ka strung his bow. The rain was dying away, but I put a hand on his arm. 'They don't even have their bows,' I said.

'They are still spies,' Ka spat.

I shrugged. 'Plenty of time for killing later,' I said.

Later on that third day, as the sea began to recede, I led a party of Greeks with a herald and the prisoner. We rode all the way to the edge of the Persian camp, and no one challenged us until we left the road for the open ground north of it. Then a party of horsemen appeared, as if by magic. They'd been hidden by a fold of earth and a rock outcropping. I knew they were great horsemen, but it was an excellent reminder.

I knew the troop's commander immediately, and I rode up to the giant, Amu, and saluted him, and he embraced me. This came as a shock to all the Greeks.

'How is your son?' I asked. 'Araxa?'

'Hah! He outranks me!' he shouted with the delight of a father. 'In the Guards, leaving me to outpost duty like this. And who is this lordling?'

I waved him over. 'We took him the first day. He seems to be recovered, and so we send him back. King Leonidas of Sparta wishes the Great King to know that we will abide by the laws of war.'

Amu frowned. He looked around, saw horsemen coming from the camp, and shook his head. 'The word is all of you are to be treated as rebels. No prisoners.' He spat. 'Because Mardonius is a fool. Those are his men coming. Best ride away.' He smiled. 'I'll delay them. Listen, my friend. This will be ugly. Take your women and go somewhere else – eh?'

This disquieted me. I had expected better of the Great King than to have Greeks – win or lose, we were not rebels – treated as criminals.

We rode away.

I left Leonidas that evening, because I thought I could get my ship to sea, and because the Persian outposts were pushing forward as the sea retreated. I didn't want to lose my ship to cavalrymen.

Leonidas did me the honour of clasping my hand.

'Any message for Eurybiades?' I asked.

The king shrugged. 'No – not until we taste their bronze will we know what we have to do.'

I nodded at the sea. 'I have a fast, dry ship and a good crew. I intend to run east and see if I can find the enemy fleet before I go south to Eurybiades.' I smiled. 'Just in case I don't come back.'

He slapped me on the back with Spartan goodwill, and I ran for my ship. Even as I clambered over the stern, there were Persian cavalry and some odd-looking psiloi prowling down the beach.

The Persian camp stretched over forty stades.

The Greek camp covered a little less than two.

The patch held beautifully, and we had minimal stores, a dry hull and a favourable wind. *Lydia* was a trihemiolia, so I raised the yard, hung the mainsail, and we were away. The Greek army cheered.

It is roughly three hundred stades from the coastline at Thermopylae to the headland at Artemesium – perhaps not as the raven flies or the seabird, but as my oarsmen row. We crossed to the Euboean shore before full darkness set in, to be free of the Medes, and made a hasty camp and ate mutton we didn't pay for, and we rose before dawn, had her sternpost wet before the rosy fingers of the most beautiful young goddess danced across the world, and the west wind held and we ran before the wind once we were out in the channel.

We hadn't travelled a parasang before we found the first wreck – a Phoenician turned turtle. Her oars were still in the oar leathers. She'd been rolled while at sea, and there were dead men – bloated, horrible dead men – trapped in her lines and under her deck.

An hour later and we'd seen enough floating wreckage for it to be the whole Persian fleet.

My rowers sang a hymn to Poseidon.

We passed six more floating wrecks, and the last two had no oars in them – they'd been anchored.

That told me a story.

We ran along the south coast of Thessaly, and just north of Artemesium we met up with Cimon, on the same errand but on the opposite tack and headed for the fleet.

'You beach at Artemesium and keep watch!' he called. 'I'm for Malia.'

The end of his shout was lost as his ship swept by at the speed of a galloping horse, but his intent was clear enough.

We beached at Artemesium and put up a tower on the headland.

We were alone, where a few days before there had been two hundred triremes. The northernmost beach was full of driftwood and dead men.

Hermogenes drafted a watch schedule and Hector wrote it all down on the wax, and we pulled *Lydia* clear of the water to keep her dry.

Hermogenes pointed at the tower – an old trick from my time with Miltiades.

'Like old times,' he said.

The next morning, I took *Lydia* to sea as soon as there was enough light to get her off the beach. We ran north and east under the boat sail, keeping well out into the fairway and with two men slung in a small boat from the mainmast, a trick I'd learned on Sicily.

The sea to the north was empty. We found another trireme, turned turtle, all her oars still aboard, some smashed. I hove to, fingered my beard, and then salvaged her.

Imagine our shock to find two Phoenicians alive under the capsized hull. They'd been in the water three days. They were as weak as kittens and out of their wits, but to Greeks, the men Poseidon preserves are sacred. We hauled them aboard and they drank water until I thought they might explode – in fact, Hermogenes took the water from them, afraid they'd die of it. It was hours before they could talk.

In the meantime, with a dozen men to help me, we got ropes on the gunwales of the Phoenician and rolled her upright, and then, with half the oarsmen in her, we baled her dry enough to tow, with two dozen oarsmen aboard just to keep her head up and land her. We only had thirty stades to make, but it took us until nightfall, and we had to row all the way, as our mast was down. The setting sun showed us the allied fleet coming up the channel. Eurybiades had them practising a reverse crescent. They could fill fifteen stades of water and still have a small reserve, and they looked magnificent, and my throat tightened.

I turned to Hermogenes. 'We may yet do this, brother,' I said.

He grinned. 'There are the Plataeans!' he called, and sure enough, on the left of the line, there were ten ships all as neat as a farmer's furrow.

We wallowed our way to the beach and landed before the first ships to the right of the line – Athenians under Cimon – got ashore. I had claimed the spots right by the olive groves – better shade, and a deeper beach. Cimon cursed, but he leaped ashore and we embraced.

'You have a capture!' he said, envious but happy for me.

I shook my head. 'She's Poseidon's capture,' I said. 'The storm got her. I have two men who were alive in the wreck.'

I was gathering a crowd. Cimon took my shoulder and we went along the beach to where I'd had my tent set in the olive grove, and Hector gave Cimon wine. We sent Hipponax for Eurybiades and Sittonax condescended to walk off and find Themistocles – moving slowly, to show that he was above such vulgar considerations as crisis or work.

Themistocles came first. He hugged me close.

'You two!' he said, including Cimon. 'I thought we'd never get the fleet back here. Adamenteis is still threatening to sail for the isthmus. And then Cimon shows up off the beach and says that the Persians are wrecked and Greece is saved, and all our cowardly allies . . . that is to say . . .' He nodded to Eurybiades.

The Spartan nodded and looked at me. 'Prisoners?' he asked.

I saluted. 'Navarch, while they are prisoners, they were rescued after three days' shipwreck. To us, that makes them sacred.'

Cimon nodded. Even pirates have rules.

Themistocles frowned. 'None of that foolishness, now. We need their information.'

Everyone looked at me. This is the price of the great reputation – sometimes men expect you to speak, to make decisions, to be the great man.

I bowed to Themistocles. 'At some point, we define ourselves by what we do. We begged Poseidon for his favour. He answered us with a storm. Is this our thanks?'

Themistocles shot me a glance of scorn mixed with pity – that I was one of *those* men, so easily led, so easily fooled. I hope I shrugged.

Cimon nodded. 'But surely we can ask them questions?'

That seemed suitable to everyone, even Eurybiades, who clearly approved of my answer. When they were brought, they were seated comfortably, and given wine. They sat listlessly.

'Can you tell me what happened to your fleet?' Cimon asked in passable Phoenician.

'It is all wrecked,' the younger said. 'No one could survive such a storm.'

The older man glared at him.

The younger shrugged. 'What is it to me? Listen, then. The beaches were too narrow for the whole fleet, and our admiral ordered the store ships to have the most protected landings. The army had priority over the navy in all things. The ships of Halicarnassus and Ephesus took the inner moorings, which left us to anchor out in rows of forty ships, eight deep in the bay we chose. Eight deep.' He shook his head.

The older man stared off over my shoulder. 'We anchored bow and stern. We are not fools. I had six stones under the bow, and four under the stern – every anchor on my ship. We started to move with the first wind.'

All around my tent, men had begun to babble with relief – with delight.

Poseidon had destroyed the Persian fleet. Or so it appeared.

'How many ships did the Great King muster, when he sailed this summer?' I asked.

The older man rocked his head – as Phoenicians do. 'A thousand? Fifteen hundred?' He shrugged. 'I never counted.'

That made me swallow.

A thousand ships?

But the other captains were delighted with their news. When it

335

was clear that the two captives would say no more – at least, not willingly – Eurybiades summoned his messenger and sent him to Leonidas with what we knew. He was careful, and only stated that Poseidon had inflicted a defeat on Xerxes' fleet.

But the Greek fleet rejoiced.

It was a long night. I heard men – men for whom I had little love and little respect – brag of what they would have done to the Persians had their fleet only endured. I'm an old warrior – I know that no man loves the moment when death is there to look you in the eye, and no man really loves war more than once or twice – that older men have to play the game or be thought cowards, when really they'd like to be at home with their wives. I know this, but the posturing and bragging in the Greek fleet that night was sickening.

Worst of all, I was the hero of the hour. Somehow my salvage of a stricken trireme had become a capture, a conquest, and men would stumble drunkenly to my side to take my hand.

Gah! The fools.

At any rate, Hermogenes was not a fool, nor was Sekla nor any of our captains. Demetrios – the leftmost captain in the line – had commanded the last ship to come in to the beach, and he was insisting he'd seen sails on the eastern horizon.

I had only seen enough wreckage for about forty ships. If they had a thousand ships . . .

I went to sleep to the sound of men working by torchlight on the salvaged ship's hull. The hammers rang hollow, driving pegs into the side.

I awoke to shrieks and desperate cries, as if the Medes were upon us in the dawn.

And they were.

The sun was barely on the horizon, a red ball that threatened further bad weather, and the sea was like a floating forest to the north and east. It filled the channel as far as the eye could see to the right, all the way out into the open ocean.

I clambered up the headland with Hermogenes, to find Sekla and Sittonax already there, Giannis and Alexandros climbing from the other side, and Themistocles standing apart with Eurybiades.

Aristides emerged from behind Alexandros.

My other friends were climbing up – there was Aeschylus, and there, Phrynicus's friend Lycomedes, and Cimon and Gelon and Hilarion, of all men.

It was as if all the friends of my life – every man I'd met since Lades – was gathered on one low headland. Lades killed a generation – worse, it killed a culture, a kind, gentle culture.

All the men around me stared in horror at the Great King's fleet.

However many Poseidon had culled, what was left was three or four times the size of the allied fleet. Perhaps more. It *covered the ocean*. I had been at Lades. I have been told – by Phoenicians – that the Persian fleet at Lades was the greatest fleet of triremes ever assembled.

Perhaps. Certainly, the Great King's fleet had smaller vessels in hordes – pentekonters, triaconters, even Aegyptian lembi. But it also had triremes in numbers that staggered the eye, so that you had to keep looking away and looking back.

Eurybiades couldn't tear his eyes away. It was the doom of Greece.

A thousand ships.

Aristides said, 'Now is Troy avenged.'

At my side, Moire chuckled. 'He has every ship in the Levant here.' He glanced at me. 'Good time to run a cargo to Aegypt.'

I laughed.

As had happened the night before, everyone turned to look at me. Adamenteis of Corinth had just come up the rise from the temple, and he was staggered – as, to be fair, we all were – and he turned as if I'd struck him.

And again I felt the presence of the gods. I had the attention of the commanders.

I'm no orator.

But perhaps Athena whispered into my head, or my ancestor Herakles.

So I finished my laugh by turning to all of them. 'By Poseidon,' I said. 'Did you think it would be easy to defeat the Great King? Did you think that by sailing – unwillingly – a few stades from home, the greatest power under the gods would be defeated?'

I pointed my spear out over the Persian fleet. 'There they are, my friends. Poseidon struck them a mighty blow. Will we do less?'

I'd like to say that they gave me three mighty cheers and we all ran for our ships, but it wasn't like that at all.

Adamenteis of Corinth was visibly resistant to my rhetoric. He stood tall and raised his hand. 'We must abandon this post immediately, before we are all destroyed,' he said. He looked at me with contempt. 'If that is what is left after the storm, then Poseidon has done them no damage at all. Perhaps it is the will of the gods. But there is no combination of luck, guile, bravery and tactics that will allow us to defeat that fleet.'

'I remember men saying the same, at the last war council before Marathon,' I said. 'They were neither fools nor cowards, Adamenteis. They were merely ... wrong. We can defeat that fleet.'

'Silence, puppet of the Athenians. You are a pirate – a rogue and a criminal – and have no right to speak here.' Adamenteis turned. 'He has more friends among the Medes than any man here – he'll fall soft no matter what eventuates. Listen to me! We have lost. The Great King will stamp us under his foot like insects.'

I was considering putting my fist in his face when Eurybiades snapped, 'Silence.'

Every eye went to him.

'Neither Arimnestos nor Adamenteis has been appointed by the League of Allies to command this fleet,' he said simply. 'I have.'

He could not stop glancing at the Persian fleet. Even after ten minutes of looking at it, it was still a shock.

'I will hold a council in my tent after sacrifices have been made,' he said. He turned to Adamenteis. 'Courtesy and dignity are essential tools of good debate,' he said.

Spartans know how to put the knife in, and how to twist it, too.

Our camp was right there. We had been making our sacrifices on the outdoor altar for the temple of Artemis – no man of Plataea has any quarrel with the virgin goddess, and Hermogenes, quite wisely, dedicated our new ship to her, with the name *Huntress*.

So we lingered on the headland. Ever seen the results of a street riot? Or an earthquake? Where men and women lie dead, or mangled, and you can't tear your eyes away?

A thousand ships.

I made a good sacrifice, as did Aristides. I thought of my daughter, who was no doubt dancing for the huntress at that moment far to the south at Brauron. I watched Sekla – who was very much a devotee of the virgin goddess – perform his sacrifice.

Each sacrifice was as nearly perfect as men could make them. The lambs we had purchased from the locals went willingly, heads up, without a bleat.

By the time Ajax, the man who'd served in Persia as a mercenary, made his cut, Aristides was shaking his head.

'I have never seen such a favourable omen,' he said.

Draco came over on his stick – far and away the oldest man of the Plataeans. 'I just killed a lamb with a single blow,' he cackled, wiping the blood from his hands. 'Not a spot on her liver or her kidneys.' He winked at me. 'You hear about these things from old priests, and then you think they're full of shit.' He shrugged.

We all looked out to sea.

The Persian ships were landing at Aphetai. It couldn't really be seen in the haze, so that the vast seaborne forest seemed to slip over the edge of the world and vanish.

But one heavy squadron was coming up from a different angle. I counted sixteen triremes in two columns. They were in a disciplined formation, sails down, and rowing.

Hermogenes was eating olives. He shrugged. 'Scouting?' he asked.

Paramanos shook his head. 'They've mistaken the anchorage. Look – they were flanking the main fleet, out to sea, and they've gone too far south.'

They were thirty stades away. My guess was that the nearest ship was Carian or Aeolian – perhaps even Lesbian. But that was only a gut feeling from years at sea.

'Could they be changing sides?' I asked.

'Would you?' asked Paramanos.

Humour is a useful antidote to fear.

I had all my captains at hand. And my ships were ready.

'Let's get them,' I said.

As the oarsmen poured into the hulls and ran them off the beach, I knelt in the sand and sketched my plan. Listen, friends – when you fight, some men say a good sword is best, and some say a good spear – but I say friends, comrades and dependable officers are the things I most love.

Thanks, Sappho ...

'My intention is to double the head and tail of their line and never let it become a line fight,' I said. 'Paramanos will lead the western squadron against their left, and I'll take the eastern against their right.' I directed them into two groups. I would lead the right hand, with *Lydia*, *Huntress*, *Hera*, *Nemesis*, *Parthanos*, *Sea Horse* and *Machaira*.

Paramanos would lead the left with his own *Black Raven*, and he had *Athena Nike, Andromeda, Storm Cutter* and *Amastis.*

Sekla – who would be at the extreme right of my group – fingered his short, curly beard. 'You don't want us to engage,' he said.

'No – envelop. Sweep wide.' I was watching the ships get off the beach. The battle had already begun, for me. The Persians were fully hull up, now, even in the haze. You could see that the lead ship in the western column was painted a bright blue.

A runner came along the beach – I knew him at a distance to be Cimon's big-headed cousin Pericles, running as if he were racing for laurel. Closer to hand, Eurybiades himself was coming down the low cliff that separated us from the olive groves.

'They will expect a head-to-head fight. We have lighter ships. Our ships are dry and our rowers are at least eager. I want to try them in a running fight.'

I didn't speak my innermost mind, which was this; in a running fight, at worst we'd lose one or two ships, and none would be lost to the sort of amateur errors that our oarsmen might make in their first fight. My greatest fear was friends fouling friends.

My other innermost thought was that the gods were with us, and I was going to give them the opportunity to show us an omen. Why attempt a *small* victory?

Sekla nodded sharply.

Paramanos grinned. 'You are still a mad bastard,' he said. 'You mean, of all these fine ships, only you and I are going beak to beak.'

I smiled. Eurybiades was ten steps away and Pericles was coming in for the finish and all my men were aboard. The marines had their thorakes on.

'That's what I mean,' I said quietly, and clasped his hand.

'Because we won't cock it up,' he said.

'That's right,' I agreed.

Eurybiades came up with a dozen officers. 'You intend to engage?' he asked.

Pericles stood and panted.

'Before you finish singing the hymn to Athena,' I said.

'Gods go with you, Plataean.' He leaned close. '*You must not lose.*'

I looked at Pericles. He nodded with unusual deference. 'Cousin Cimon says he'll have five ships off the beach before the sun sets a finger's breadth,' he said. 'He says to tell you,' the boy had the grace to flush, 'that Athens can't trust a bunch of Boeotian farmers to get this right.'

I laughed. 'Come along, boy, and see how we do.' I saluted the navarch, who stood in his scarlet chiton at the edge of the beach and watched us.

All my ships were afloat. It was the turn of the tide in a light wind, and my oarsmen held *Lydia* just at the edge of the surf so that I was only wet to my crotch getting aboard. Young Pericles soaked his chiton.

I ran for the bow. The enemy squadron were still coming on, four stades away, with bow waves. It struck me as possible that they had not made a navigation error – that rather, they had brave men who held the allied fleet in contempt and had come to show it.

I looked at my own ships. Waved, and Hector raised my bronze-covered shield and gave a signal, and my squadron's oars dipped – all together, or close enough, so that there was a mighty flash, the setting sun on all the blades together.

Nothing for it now.

We were the seventh ship from the right – the centre of the line coming off the beach, with Paramanos three horse-lengths away, but we began to angle east and west immediately.

The enemy squadron was in two columns of eight ships, and just as we came off the beach they began to spread out from their rowing columns into a single line. There was no way of knowing whether they had detected our enmity or whether they were merely preparing to land on the beach.

Sekla was heading north and east aggressively, and the rest of my half of the squadron held station on him, using the light westerly to push our hulls east, which caused us to move faster and farther to the flank than Paramanos, who also had to fight the current.

Three stades. In a sea fight, everything seems to take for ever, and then, suddenly, everything happens at once.

Ka and his archers pushed past me into the bow. Every one of them had two quivers, now, and they hung on pegs that hadn't been there before.

Hipponax and the marines waited on the catwalk. Hector's face was as white as chalk. But he and Hipponax were grinning, all their teeth showing, refusing to let each other see their fears, like young men since the siege of Troy. Behind them stood Siberios, who watched them with an intent, half-amused look.

I ignored the boys. 'When we strike, we're going to *take*. Get aboard and keep her. Take command and make the rowers go for the beach.'

He was watching the enemy over my shoulder. 'You won't have any marines,' he said.

'Let me worry about that. You'll be on your own.' I slapped him on the shoulder, and he laughed.

'Oh, as to that, I'll have Hector *and* Achilles,' he mocked.

I got to the midships platform, where the main deck begins and all the sailors stand. They were armed. We were a rich ship – every deck man had a cuirass and greaves and a sword and spear and helmet.

One stade out, the enemy had formed something like a line, and they had recognised that we were not friends. I could see three ships that looked Phoenician, and the rest looked Ionian or Aeolian – Greeks. The blue ship had Asian decoration under her beak and looked Carian.

The last ship in the leftmost squadron had red sides over dirty white. *Dagon*.

I almost changed course, but it is a pitiful navarch who can't follow his own plan, even for revenge, even for Apollo. But I watched that ship for many beats of my heart, and I didn't think about my son, my daughter, Archilogos, mortality, or even Briseis. I watched the evil Carthaginian.

The squadron facing me began to break up.

You must understand, to understand all that follows – you have only the tactics and signals you have practised in advance. You cannot change a plan at sea. You can't tell all your trierarchs if you suddenly have a better idea. If something unexpected happens, every trierarch has to think for himself. In a line fight, no one has to think.

As they woke up to the fact that we were enemies, we were also forcing them to make decisions. We weren't going to go ram to ram in line.

In another place and time, they might simply have run through our centre – but five stades behind us was a beach full of Greeks, with ships arming and coming off. None of them was actually ready yet except Cimon's pirates, and they, of course, were twenty stades to the south along the beach.

Most of the ships facing me turned outward to fight. Two of the eight turned end for end and ran for it.

Instead of going seven of ours against eight of theirs, now we were seven to six, and not a blow had been struck.

I was going ram to ram against the blue ship with the gold decoration. It was a very heavy ship – pretty, with heavy cat-heads intended to break my oars and kill my rowers.

I ran back to Hermogenes like a mother hen.

'You see those beams?' I asked.

He withered me like Medusa – which I deserved.

Because we had a superb crew, we'd left our ramming speed to very late. And our opponent wasn't superb – he'd practised about as much as the Ionians practised before Lades. You make an opponet ten feet tall in your mind – and then, in reality ...

Ka and his men began to pour arrows over the bow at such a quick pace that it looked as if our ships had a thick black rope connecting the bows.

The enemy helmsman flicked his bow to his right. Helmsmen generally do, just before going bow to bow.

I said, 'Now!' and Nicolas, now the oar-master, slammed his staff on the deck and our ship leaped.

It was a high-risk manoeuvre. Ships generally try to go slightly off line just before contact, but Hermogenes used speed, instead.

The enemy helmsman had to assume he'd turn slightly off line and then turn back at the last moment, but he misjudged our speed, and our ram struck the shoulder of his ship just aft of the cedar beams of his cat-head – a steep angle, and not a quick kill, but our sharp bow swept down his oar-bank even as we got our oars inboard and men were screaming and Ka was standing in the bow shooting down into the enemy oar-deck and then Hipponax and Hector leaped together ...

Ka ran along the catwalk, shooting ...

My armoured deck crew poured grapples into their midships bulwarks and Siberios led the marines over the bow ...

My son and his friend stood back to back on the enemy catwalk and killed men. A tall man in armour covered in gold – who was he, the Great King himself? – flung a javelin and it went through my son's thigh and he fell, and Hector stood over him ...

Hermogenes' hand closed on my arm. 'You aren't in your armour. You are the *navarch*.'

Both were true.

But my son was lying in a pool of his own blood on an enemy deck.

All of my marines were away. To the north and east, Sekla was running free, past the easternmost Phoenician, and all my other ships were engaged. A glance to the west – Paramanos had broken an Aeolian ship in half. He was, after all, the best helmsman in the world. None of the other ships was engaged yet.

'Cut the grapples!' I roared, leaving my son to whatever fate awaited him.

Deck crewmen cut the ropes of the very grapples they'd thrown. Others used pikes to push us off.

Siberios killed the man in gold armour, hammering his teeth into his throat with the pommel of his sword.

Hipponax hamstrung a Carian marine in full panoply from his postion lying on the deck, and Hector stabbed the man in his open-faced helmet with his spear – Hector fought fastidiously, like a cat, his spear flicking out.

I wanted to bandage my son's wound. I wanted to fight.

'Oars out!' roared Hermogenes. Hermogenes, who could not command his way out of a linen sack. He glared at me.

Well he might.

'Arm me,' I snapped at young Pericles.

He didn't bother to protest. He opened my bronze thorakes and got it on me.

Sekla was turning in, and *Machaira* was indeed going to cut like a knife.

The two fleeing ships had their sails up.

Paramanos was turning *Black Raven* to the west, where Harpagos lay oar bank to oar bank with a bigger Phoenician, their marines clearly engaged.

The red and white ship – it had to be Dagon, it had a Phoenician build – turned suddenly away from *Athena Nike*. I had to assume that Dagon had found a good helmsman. Or perhaps it wasn't Dagon at all.

But the red and white ship turned so fast her starboard oars were buried in the water and *Athena Nike* swept by to ram Harpagos's opponent amidships, killing that ship instantly.

I had a moment to regret that we were Greeks killing Greeks.

I turned west, against an unengaged Carian. He was rowing desperately, at full ramming speed, while turning as fast as he could, and all he managed to do was to lose the turning contest to me. We turned in place, our starboard cushions reversed – and again, the quality of *Lydia*'s oarsmen allowed us to leap to ramming speed and catch him just forward of the helmsman's station. We didn't have enough way to break the hull, but our ram caught his gunwale and began to roll his ship over, and Ka's archers cleared the Carian's command deck. We came to a stop – I'd ordered the oars in rather than risk them – and there we lay, our bow against his helm.

I ran down the catwalk and leaped over the marine box – the gate was still open from the first attack – and I stepped down on to our ram rather than leaping.

Ka's arrows flicked over my head.

No marines waited for me, and I put my back to the enemy gunwale and rolled on to their deck at the stern, and everyone there was dead.

The rowers were in shock.

Nicolas – the oar-master – came behind me, with a dozen sailors, but there was no resistance from the oarsmen.

'Greeks!' I roared. 'We are your liberators, not your enemies!'

No one looked relieved, but no one came at me with a sword, either.

'Get her ashore,' I said. I stepped up on to the gunwale amidships and leaped for my own ship – and barely made it, scrambling up the side like a terrified cat.

I used to leap from ship to ship without a qualm for the fate that awaited me if I missed.

I looked west. The red and white ship was running. The blue and gold Carian was now rowing sedately for the allied beach.

Cimon's ships were angling into the flank of Paramanos' melee.

It was over.

Gelon was in the only boarding fight still burning, and Hermogenes put the helm down even while I acted as my own oar-master and we turned, under way again. *Lydia*'s dry, light hull seemed to be powered by the gods.

Gelon had caught a tiger. He'd got the worst of a ramming exchange with a big-hulled Phoenician and had then been flooded with the other ship's desperate marines. Giannis, in the lightest and fastest of the Athenian public ships, had also gone head to head with a Phoenician and couldn't help. Sekla had brought *Machaira* into *Sea Horse*'s adversary.

I went for *Nemesis*. I could see Gelon fighting hand to hand by his helm. He didn't have time for me to manoeuvre.

I pointed to Hermogenes. 'Our bow to his stern,' I said. Then I ran forward and grabbed all the best armed sailors. Armoured like hoplites, they had the most remarkable assortment of weapons – chains, axes, a trident. I had no idea how we'd do against real Phoenician marines.

Hermogenes kissed the stern of *Nemesis* as if he'd been a helmsman all his life and not a farmer. I was ready, standing over the ram. I went sideways, from the top of the marine box into the helmsman's bench ...

Nemesis was almost taken.

The first Tyrian made the simple mistake of thinking he could finish Gelon before I was on him. Gelon got a foot on the man's spear against the deck, and he turned to see my spear take his life, and then I was beside my former slave, and suddenly, everything felt right – my armour, the sun on my back, the deck under my feet.

As if my body said, *Ah! This!*

There was a rush – a press. I punched repeatedly with the rim of my aspis, putting my opponents against the rail, bouncing one man so hard that he stumbled and Giorgos got a chain over his head and put a dagger in his neck, and then we went at them. I rifled my spear at an officer and killed him and then I had my lovely long sword in my hand – thrust, change feet, slip on the blood and cut to cover the loss of balance.

Feint, and see my effort wasted as a long black arrow kills my opponent.

I punch with my aspis, and the spear shaft of his weapon crosses my chest and I get it in my shield hand and my enemy is wide open for my thrust. I have time to watch him watch his death.

I punch with the shield rim and cut with the sword, taking a spearhead cleanly off its shaft, and a spear comes from behind me to finish him. Young Pericles, with no armour on, is fighting as my hypaspist.

What joy.

I go sword to sword with a Phoenician. He is a big man in red, with gold on his armour, and at some point I have moved from *Nemesis* to his ship. He bashes at me with his shield, his shoulder in the top of the rim, and I meet him shield to shield and I flick my long blade up into his eyes. I don't score, but the blow to his helmet rocks his head back and he stumbles. I thrust, passing my right foot forward over my left even as he backs away a step, and he sweeps his sword across his body because his shield is committed – I roll my wrist over the parry, and I can see his eyes as he tries to reverse his parry ...

346

I roll my sword over his again, the double deception I learned in Sicily from Polymarchos, and my thrust goes in just under his ribs, right through his gold-plated bronze scales and into his gut and down into his pelvis – one of the prettiest blows of my life.

Unfortunately, I have to leave my beautiful sword in his body.

Bah – sometimes I relive it. Is it terrible, that ripping a man's life from his body and throwing it through the iron gates to Hades can be such a joy?

I took his spear from his fingers even as he screamed and his entrails loosed and his feet pounded the deck, and stood, but my pirates had cleared the enemy marines and the Phoenician oarsmen had had a long day, a long pull, and had no fight in them.

I stood and panted, and only then noticed that my left leg was covered in blood.

I turned, and blood sprayed. I look desperately at my mid-section, at my armour. There was blood there, too, but no glistening wound, no death blow.

I dropped my sword – my vision was tunnelling – and reached for my neck, and only then did I see it ...

My left hand was cut to the bone and two fingers were severed.

I fell to my knees. Men were running to help me ...

I wasn't in the darkness when we ran up the beach. Hermogenes bound the hand tight while Pericles got my armour off.

The old chiton was turning red.

But I managed to stay upright, as the allied fleet cheered us. I heard later that the Medes could hear our cheers across the straits at Aphetae.

We beached under the eyes of the commander and I watched as Siberios brought the blue ship in – Hector was at the helm. He waved, and I knew from his face my son was alive.

I gave thanks to the gods.

We all went ashore in a great mass, and if the Medes had chosen that moment to attack, they could have had us all. But they had other plans, as you'll hear, and we went up the beach to the altars and made a sacrifice, and Aristides came and embraced me, his right hand as sticky and brown as mine.

'What happened?' he asked.

But what I remember best was Nicolas, who had just had his first command. He rolled up to me with his fisherman's gait and his lopsided grin, and jerked his thumb over his shoulder.

'You'll never guess what I found in that ship,' he said, indicating our last capture.

'Gold?' I guessed.

He barked his odd laugh. The man behind him was Brasidas, the Spartan.

We had a plethora of high-ranking prisoners, but the best report was from Brasidas. For reasons that will become clear later, we covered him with a report that a diver, Scyllias, a native of Sicyone, had swum all the way from Aphetae. In fact, the famous swimmer stole a small boat and sailed to us, and his report was nowhere near as complete as Brasidas'.

What we heard was that the Persians had lost almost two hundred fighting ships in the storm, most of them north of the passage of Artemesium – despite which, their spies had reported us as having abandoned the beaches at the temple, and they had sent a heavy squadron – two hundred ships – to envelop us by rowing all the way around Euboea.

That report might have created consternation. We were about to be attacked from behind.

But we had just gone head to head with sixteen Persian ships and we'd sunk three and taken six of the enemy and lost not a single ship.

Even Adamenteis was silent.

Themistocles had a long discussion with Eurybiades. It is a picture of the two men that sticks in my mind – Themistocles gesturing like a boy, and the Spartan navarch sitting calmly, his hands on his knees.

And then Themistocles came and grabbed my hand like a forward maiden at a party and took me out into the olive trees.

'I'm a little old to kiss strange men in the dark,' I said.

The Athenian laughed. 'No older than I am. Listen, Plataean. The old Spartan will ask you first what course of action we should take. You are the hero of the day, after all.'

I nodded. My son was alive and everything seemed possible. I regretted Dagon, but his flight was an admission of sorts. What can I say? I thought I'd have him in the end.

'What will you tell him?' Themistocles asked.

'What would you like me to say?' I asked. I meant to sound ironical, but Themistocles was a politician, and he took me at my word and leaned forward eagerly. 'You must tell him to attack,' he said.

348

'Attack?' I asked. I had in mind a set of raids, some burned hulls, perhaps a night attack on an outlying camp ...

'If we attack, the Corinthians and Aeginians have to fight,' he said.

I scratched my beard. 'Aren't we outnumbered four to one?'

'Worse when they come behind us. And as you showed today – when one side does something unexpected, the other side can make mistakes. Poseidon, you took a risk today. If you'd lost—'

'I didn't lose,' I said.

But as was often the case between me and Themistocles – I agreed. He was right. An attack with all our ships would commit us, and if Leonidas was winning on land, this was the time. And anyway ...

Morale matters. Ours soared. My little victory was insignificant. Think of the thousand Persian ships. Two hundred lost in a storm. Two hundred sailing to take us in the rear.

We took eight.

We walked back through the grove.

'You really were quite marvellous,' Themistocles said suddenly. And for a moment I saw past his mask. Under the orator, the politician, the democrat, was a man who wanted to be a hero.

These things always surprise me. So instead of making a good answer, I shrugged like a pretty girl given an unwanted compliment and went back to the commanders.

In the end, Eurybiades asked each of a dozen of us what we ought to do. We had two hundred and seventy-one ships plus the captures. Paramanos and Harpagos went among the captives and identified all the Aeolian and Ionians from families we knew, or men we thought we could trust, and Cimon sent a helmsman and four marines, and Demetrios sent four more marines and a cloaked man to be trierarchos, which was how Aristides came to command a ship not his own while pretending to be in exile.

At any rate, Eurybiades came to me with a crown of laurel he'd twisted with his own hands, and settled it on my brow. There it is, on the wall with the fourth aspis.

'So, Plataean?' he asked me, first of all the navarchs.

I looked at Themistocles. I didn't love him, but he was the strategist.

'First let me ask, what news from the army?' I asked.

Eurybiades smiled with satisfaction. 'The Persians and Medes attacked the army all day today,' he said. 'When the packet boat rowed, the king had been engaged twice, and every Greek had fought with honour. There is a pile of Persian corpses by the Hot Gates, and the king says they all saw the Great King in a rage.'

We all cheered.

We were doing it. Saving Greece.

Eurybiades nodded happily and turned back to me. 'Well?'

'I think we should attack,' I said.

It is much harder to fight on the second day.

Every time a man wears his armour, it hurts. The shoulders chafe, and no matter how well made it is, the muscles of the chest are bruised by bronze at the edges of the arms – every cross-body cut, every Harmodius blow, every spear-parry forces your pectoral muscles against the edges of your cuirass. Greaves bite into the in-step. All of this is covered by the spirit of battle, the elation of the moment, fear and fatigue.

But when you fight on a second day, the sores are still raw, the bruises fresh. If you have a wound, as I had, it is raw and red, and you worry still about an arrow from Apollo's fickle bow.

The oarsmen had, every one of them, endured the fear of immi-nent death and had exerted some kind of maximum effort.

Every Plataean marine and all of Cimon's had faced an enemy sword or spear and the horror of drowning in armour.

And some of us had sat up and drunk too much the night before.

There was cursing.

We had the longest pull to our place in the line, but I was con-scious that this was for *everything*. I, who seldom give speeches, had my marines make a small platform for me, like a speakers' rostrum on the Pnyx, and I mounted it, and spoke to all of them – fifteen hundred Plataeans and five hundred former slaves, prisoners and Athenian exiles.

I mentioned the gods, and I talked about Hellas – the idea of being Greek.

It probably wasn't much a speech, but here's the part that I re-member. 'You all hurt,' I said. 'Many of you took a wound yesterday, and we face odds of three ships to one.' I pointed off to the west – towards Thermopylae. 'The King of Sparta is fighting today at odds of ten to one or more, and he's on his third day.'

That got their attention.

'If we lose today, we will be done. The Persians will have us, and our cities will burn, and Leonidas will be forced to retreat.' I looked at them, and they were silent. It was cool and pleasant, despite the time of year – a strong east wind was coming up, and the sun was red, like a big grape on the horizon.

'If we win today, we will win the right to fight again tomorrow!' I said. 'That is all we will win today. And if we win tomorrow ...' I smiled. 'Then we win the right to fight again the next day – and the next and the next until the Great King wearies of the contest or he runs out of slaves or we run out of free men to face him. And if we win? If we defeat the Great King?' I held up my wounded hand.

Some men cheered.

'Then we win the right to fight him again the next time he comes against us. This is what freedom is. The Great King has no idea how poor we are, or what we have in herds or in olive trees. He seeks only to own us.' I smiled to think of Xerxes in his hall in Susa, who was attacking us mostly to satisfy Mardonius.

And for pride.

'We must win today, and tomorrow, and again the day after, and then we must go home and train our sons to win again,' I said.

How they cheered.

I stumbled off my rostrum, and Themistocles took my hand – and hurt me, as it was my left hand he grabbed.

'That was remarkable!' he said. 'You hide your light too much!'

I laughed, uncomfortable, but let's be honest, pleased with his praise, and I saw his eyes harden.

Aristides came up to me.

Themistocles let go of my hand. He didn't glance away, but said, 'By now, the exile must have been lifted.'

'Until the assembly informs me so, I serve only as a Plataean,' Aristides said.

Themistocles nodded. He turned to me, and said one of the few genuine, unposturing things I ever heard from him. He said, 'When Athens exiles me, will I too be welcome in Plataea?'

'How're your farming skills?' I asked.

Aristides laughed and slapped my shoulders. 'I hope you give him shelter, when I have him sent away. He is dangerous – but he may have saved Greece.'

When you think of us – Athenians and Corinthians and Aeginians and Spartans and all – remember this.

We didn't agree about *anything* except that the Great King had to be defeated.

351

We formed well. The oarsmen were tired, but I had us go to ramming speed for about sixty heartbeats, all together, on the way to our station, and then everyone's muscles were loose – like men stretching for the Olympics, really.

By the time Eurybiades raised his shield in the centre of the line, the Persians were coming off their beaches. I have heard since that they were amazed that we were coming to fight with such a small fleet, and came into the water in no great order, each eager to make a kill.

That's what it looked like to us. They had so many ships that I couldn't begin to know, but we think – now that years have passed and all the Ionians are friends again – that there were about six hundred of them facing two hundred and seventy-one of us. But instead of forming a line, they came at us in a long mass, shaped like an egg – the first ships off the beach in the lead. And then they split – every captain for himself – to encircle us.

As soon as we were sure they were coming – and by the gods, my friends, it was hard to swallow! I'm not sure I have ever known such pure fear as that morning, watching that behemoth come for our little fleet – Eurybiades signalled for the wheel.

I had Brasidas with me. He was in a good panoply. Bless rich men – my Cimon had a full spare panoply that fitted our Spartan escapee. Brasidas passed the navarch's signals, and we began to back-water.

The lead Ionian ships went to ramming speed, despite being twenty stades away. They were that eager. Never doubt, my friends, that they wanted to defeat us. I have heard a great deal since Artemesium about how we won because the Ionians fought badly. That's foolishness. No one fights 'badly' in a sea fight where all the losers drown.

We backed faster, and I watched the front face of the wheel form up. The Corinthians were going to face the first rush. And by Poseidon, for all the crap I've said about Adamenteis, that day he was a Greek. Perhaps I'm wrong, and he was never a traitor. Or perhaps, confronted with the choice to fight or die, he fought well.

Either way, we had longer to form the wheel than we'd ever had in practice, because the fool Ionians charged into what had been our centre, instead of going for the edges where the ships weren't in the formation yet – and then flinched away. They turned away rather than face the serried phalanx of the Corinthians, and only then did they begin to circle like sharks – but by then, *Lydia*'s stern was nestled against *Black Raven* on one side and *Nemesis* on the other, and I could see Aristides coasting in beside Cimon's magnificent *Ajax* as we, the outermost arms of the fleet, closed and locked.

We were in.

I'm not sure any Greek fleet – or any fleet anywhere – had ever formed such a big wheel. I suppose it was awesome – Ionians and Phoenicians who were there have told me so – but to us, it seemed very small, and the fleet against us surrounded us, and I, for one, began to doubt the strategy we'd adopted. Because we went after the Persian fleet, we were well across the straight, far from our camp and unable to swim for shore.

Only then, trapped in the wheel, did it occur to me that my captures and my camp and all our spare masts and all of our food were sitting on the beach, and all the Persians needed to do to win the war was to dispatch twenty ships to burn our camp.

War is the strangest of man's endeavours, ruled by the whims of the gods and men's foolishness more than by stratagems and intellect. The Persians never sent a ship to burn our camp. They wanted to fight us ship to ship.

Twice, whole squadrons of them rushed our wheel.

A lone trireme out on the water is barely stable. It has to be balanced. When ten marines cross the deck, the oarsmen curse. Eh? And the ram has to be powered to do damage – at least the speed of a cantering horse.

But tie two hundred ships in a circle, and the decks are steady, moving only up and down with the swell, and the rams – in close series like spears – are steady. They don't move backwards or bounce. The rowers – all free men – *don't need to row.* If every one of them has a spear or a javelin, you have, in effect, two hundred marines in every ship.

Did I mention the swell? The wind was mild, from the east, but the sea was running higher and higher, and the swell was beginning to make it difficult to maintain formation.

At any rate, as I say, they rushed us twice – once the Samians and once Carians.

They retreated and we didn't pursue. But they made no impression whatsoever.

The sun passed the top of the sky. I passed out water and watched Aegyptians watching us.

We were doing it. We were holding the whole might of Persia.

Brasidas had been regaling us – if a nearly silent man who speaks fifteen words an hour can be said to regale – with the Babylonian revolt. He turned and handed young Pericles, who had apparently joined our ship, his water. 'Eurybiades is signalling "attention!"' he said.

'Rowers to your cushions!' I called. 'Marines forward! Ka!'

He held up a thumb and pointed with an arrow.

Hermogenes took a deep breath.

I could see his fear, and he, no doubt, could see mine.

'Everyone ready!' I called.

I knew the plan. After all, Themistocles, for all his failings, was a genius. And Eurybiades, for all his caution, was a Spartan.

The bronze aspis in the centre of the fleet flashed three times.

I thumped my spear's sauter into the deck hard enough to put a small hole in the planking and shouted, 'Row!'

And while I pulled down the cheek plates on my helmet, the allied fleet went over to the attack.

The Persians weren't a Persian fleet. I doubt that there were fifty Persians aboard six hundred ships. There were Carians, and Phrygians, and Ionians and Aeolians and Samians and Paphalogians and Syrians and Phoenicians and Carthaginians and Aegyptians, but they were so very large that they weren't really a fleet. They were really six fleets under six very powerful Persians, and not a one of those powerful men spoke the language of the trierarchs and navarchs under him.

Not a one of them expected us to attack.

And suddenly, on a majestic scale, it was the battle of the day before. No lines, and every trierarch forced to make his own decisions.

Lycomedes made the first kill. He was the first ship out of the circle, his rowers straining like hounds, and he struck a Cypriote, the King of Salamis's ship – shattered the enemy oar bank, and his marines stormed the ship in a hundred beats of a hoplite's heart.

The enemy collapsed in chaos. We took forty ships in as long as it would take for the assembly to vote on something routine – Hermogenes misjudged our little trick, and we sank a Syrian trireme, our bow climbing so high out of the water that I was terrified that we'd capsize, and we lost a marine over the side and he sank away into the depths, armour sparkling. That was grim, but the enemy fled like whitefish from tuna.

And it was more than flight. A Lemnian and a pair of Lesbian ships deserted as soon as we struck – raised their oars. The Lesbians were from Eressos and Mythymna – ancient enemies of Mytilini, and thus willing enough to side with us. The Lemnian attacked a Phoenician to show his true intent.

I knocked my son down and refused to let him board our second engagement. I had ordered him to stay behind, and he had boarded with the oarsmen, and his wound was open, his thigh bleeding on my deck.

'You fool,' I said, but the blood from my hand wound was falling in quick drops on his blood on the deck, and he gave me the mocking glance of the young man who detects the hypocrisy of the old.

Fair enough, my son.

That was a glorious day for Greece. *Lydia* fought four ships and took one, killed one, and the other two fled and my oarsmen were, in truth, too tired to run them down and take them. As the sun began to set, they *broke*.

As they fled from us, they still outnumbered us about four to one.

But they were not cowards. Many of them were skilled sailors, fine marines, and we'd humiliated them without sinking their ships. We were not done.

But we won. And winning is a tonic, in war. We had their measure. Our tactics were good, and though the navarchs all knew that the surprise explosion out of the wheel wouldn't work again, we nonetheless knew we could handle them. In fact, we were not the worse sailors, the worse oarsmen. Victory proved we were better – or made us better.

I never doubted. Oh, I was terrified, fearful, apprehensive – but I'd sunk and taken enough Phoenicians and Aegyptians and Carians over the years to know that Greeks can handle an oar as well as any man.

We went back to the beaches, and Eurybiades proved he was a better man than Miltiades. He gathered all the trierarchs – two hundred and seventy-one, as we had not lost a ship – and got silence despite our restive joy. He crowned Lycomedes for being the first to score a kill, and then he hopped up on the rostrum I'd had built.

'Listen, you fools!' he said. That got our attention.

'They will be back tomorrow, determined to avenge the humiliation of today. They still have a squadron behind us – as big as our own. The last thing I need – that Greece needs – is for you to celebrate victory. By this time tomorrow, a third of you may be dead.' He looked around. We stood in the torchlight, and we knew he spoke the truth.

'A cup of wine per man – a libation for Poseidon and all the gods – and then to your cloaks. That is my command.'

We obeyed the way boys obey a schoolmaster. Even Themistocles.

I confess I had several cups of wine. Every time I saw Brasidas out of the corner of my eye, I had to pound him on the back – I hugged Sekla after the action, and he blushed.

Giannis's fine light trireme had burst its seams, so we replaced it with one of the heavy captures – the blue Carian. So men had to stay up caulking and making her all shipshape.

But when Orestes rose, I went to sleep. I noted as I wedged myself between Hipponax and Hector that Hipponax did not have a fever, his leg wasn't hot, and the east wind was steady.

Morning was leaden grey, and the east wind was steady with fitful gusts that cracked the awning like whips and shot whitecaps over the sea to the north.

Every Plataean groaned. Wounds hurt, and abrasions were raw, and some men had two days of terror to overcome.

I stood in the wind on the headland during the morning sacrifices of the priests and priestesses, and made my decision with the help of the Huntress, and then I groaned my way down the rocks to the beach, gathered my crew, and took *Lydia* to sea.

My oarsmen didn't even groan. That took too much energy.

Forty stades across the strait to Aphetae. I put a small boat up my mainmast with two men in it, but they took too much of the gusting wind, swayed like a tower about to fall and threw the ship off course, so I brought them down. I had all the sails laid to the guards on the hemiola deck, ready to run up the masts.

I tried the boat sail, and it eased the rowing. The gusts could head her, but the main force of the wind came broadside. Triremes do not sail well at the best of times, and we were making so much leeway that we might have ended in Thermopylae, but every so often I'd take in the sails and row.

The Great King's fleet was on the beach. I saw them from six stades out, and not a ship was stirring.

I ran all the way down the beach, east to west, across almost thirty stades of beached ships, and no one offered me a fight.

I remember that, as we passed the headland at Aphetae itself, Brasidas whistled. The Spartan was smiling.

I was smiling too.

We ran a little too far west, because the wind pushed us that way – so my oarsmen, now awake enough to grumble, had to start rowing us back up the channel to Artemesium. I was tempted – sorely tempted – to run down to Thermopylae and see the king, but the Persian camp was under my lee and the wind was strong, and if it kept up for a day, I could be cut off from the fleet. I was like Cimon a week before – I didn't think the fleet could spare me, and besides

... I didn't want to miss the greatest victory since Troy.

From the stern, as we turned, took down our sails and started to row, I could see the fires of the Great King's army – the little student of Heraklitus in my head started trying to calculate the firewood I was seeing burned, because the campfires were like cabbages in a farmer's field, a big field that runs off as far as the eye can see.

As I looked under my hand, I caught a glimpse of sails to the south in the main channel, just exactly between Euboea and the mainland. I was rowing east into the wind, and they were sailing north on a broad reach, so that for the next whole leg, they were gaining on me as fast as a big boy catches a little one.

The Persian squadron.

But a number of factors were against it being the enemy. First, there were not two hundred ships, and Brasidas, of all men, is not prone to exaggerate. Second, I didn't think they could have run all the way down Euboea, weathered the great point there, and come up the main channel without any of our scouts seeing them – without the Ionian packet boat at Thermopylae giving us warning.

It was young Pericles – who had now become a member of our crew – who made the call.

'Those are Athenian ships,' he said.

Now, I've mentioned before that Aegina and Athens both left ships in home waters. Ostensibly, this was to cover Attica if the Persians sent a Phoenician squadron out into the Great Blue and straight in on the coast – I, for one, feared landing at Marathon or Brauron more than anyone. But the sad truth is that neither state trusted the other, and both left heavy squadrons to watch the other's heavy squadron.

Something had changed, then. When we were within a dozen stades, Pericles was sure that the nearest ship belonged to his family.

I thought I saw public ships like the ones Themistocles had built – smaller and lighter that anything in the Persian fleet.

I was the first man off my *Lydia*. Not a ship had moved off the opposite shore.

Cimon's spot on the beach was empty, as were those of half a dozen other enterprising captains, and when I went up the beach, Eurybiades met me hand on hip.

'Next time you wish to scout, ask permission.'

From many other men, that would have earned sharp words or even a blow. But Eurybiades was not one of them, and I was rueful.

'Of course, I want your news,' he said.

There were cries from the main beach.

I raised my hand. 'Ignore them,' I said. 'It's the Athenian reserve squadron. I'm ... almost sure.'

Eurybiades listened to my explanation and shook his head. 'I will not wager Greece on the word of a fifteen-year-old Athenian boy,' he said, and the whole weary fleet was ordered to sea – into the teeth of the rising wind.

We were better men in every way than we had been four weeks before off the beach of Marathon. And Eurybiades was absolutely correct. If we were seeing the two hundred Persian ships of their flanking force, it was our best hope to crush them before they made camp behind us – or even reunited with the main fleet at Aphetae.

But of course, they were Athenians *and* Aeginians. That night, they explained how the storm – a storm we'd scarcely felt – had savaged the Persian flanking manoeuvre and blown the Athenian and Aeginian squadrons ashore by Marathon and the north, all intermingled – and how, when the Persian wreckage began to come ashore, the Aeginian commander had suggested that they run up the channel together.

'They cheered us off Thermopylae!' they said.

Before we got to hear all their news, we had another stroke of luck – or the gods' will – in that a dozen Cilician triremes and another dozen smaller ships – all that was left of the rearguard of the flanking fleet – rounded the coast of Euboea and ran towards Artemesium – the same error again, mistaking the landings. Their rowers were exhausted.

They didn't put up much of a fight.

The Plataeans let the Corinthians do it all. We watched, nearly asleep on our oars. I was rowing, because I was not overtly popular just then, having had my *Lydia* at sea all day – *For nothing and nothing*, as a disgruntled oarsman said from two benches behind me.

But when we landed that night and had the trierarchs' assembly, we had more than three hundred trierarchs.

Themistocles was elated. 'We have more ships by a fifth of our total,' he said, 'and they have fewer by a fifth of theirs.'

It was a pretty piece of sophistry, and we all laughed.

When it was my turn to speak, I said, 'I am happiest that the enemy felt they couldn't come off their beaches today.'

Many of the old salts nodded.

In a fight, when you have the upper hand, you are ruthless, lest the other man discover you are not so very tough.

'I think we must attack again tomorrow,' I said, and Themistocles nodded.

Eurybiades stroked his beard.

'How goes it with the army?' Cimon asked.

'There have been more than twenty attacks on the pass. Each contingent goes forward and fights the Medes by turns. No attack has come to the wall yet,' Eurybiades said, and men cheered. But he held his hand up. 'Leonidas is beginning to lose men. He warns me,' he looked up from a tablet, 'that if the main army does not come in ten days, he will have to retire.'

Themistocles stepped forward to speak, and Eurybiades held up his hand again. 'The king also reports that Xerxes was openly enraged by the defeat of his fleet, and warns us to expect the most desperate measures. The barbarians execute leaders who fail.'

He turned and nodded to the Athenian, who stepped eagerly on to the rostrum. 'Brothers!' he said, a little too brightly and a little too eagerly. We were not a crowd of out-of-work labourers. We were tired men.

'Brothers!' he said again, looking for more effect. 'If we can win again – tomorrow – as we won yesterday ...' He grinned. '... the Ionians will change sides. I promise it. And then,' he was grinning like a boy, 'perhaps we can convince the Great King to retreat without the main army ever reaching King Leonidas!'

A few men cheered, but we were, as I say, weary trierarchs, and I think we all knew what it would take to fight again – a fourth straight day for my oarsmen, at any rate.

I walked down the beach to pray to Herakles and Poseidon, and I threw wine and a fine cup into the sea, and I thought of my son with Archilogos – dead in the storm? Dead in the fighting? Alive, and waiting for the morning?

Where had I acquired all these entanglements?

Aristides came up with me, and we walked the shingle in silence.

I thought of Briseis. I prayed again, this time to Aphrodite.

'Tomorrow,' Aristides said.

I agreed.

The swell was down when I awoke, far too early. My whole body hurt – my shoulder burned, and my hand was infected. It throbbed, and my arm was hot, and I could not get back to sleep.

I opened the bandage, found the red spot, and picked at it with my eating knife until I drained it, and then poured wine on it until the pain was unbearable. And then, again. And then put it in the salt water until the pain was, again, unbearable.

It was to be a fine day.

We sacrificed, and the sacrifices were all confused – some excellent omens and some poor and some merely acceptable. One black ram – a royal animal, to the Spartans – made Eurybiades cringe. When the sun was a third of the way up the sky, the sacrifices grew better, and we were ordered to sea. Eurybiades had given simple orders. We put our rigging aboard the ships so that we didn't have to protect the camp, and then we set sail, offering battle.

Not an oar touched the water. We used our sails to reach across the channel.

And the Persian fleet began to come off the beach. It was not like the first day. They came off and formed their squadrons neatly, even as we manouevred under sail in sloppy, lubberly confusion. Again, this is what Themistocles had designed and Eurybiades ordered.

We used the sails to preserve our rowers. And to slip east, deeper into the channel.

And they followed us.

Where the channel narrows suddenly to twenty-five stades wide, we turned and formed line of battle. We formed in a great crescent with the centre advanced – the Corinthians and other Peloponnesians – and the flanks refused.

The Great King's fleet came out and formed in a great crescent facing us, and they were very great. Even with two full lines of fighting ships, they had reserve squadrons at the tips and behind the centre.

They still had us, two ships to one.

The biggest difference was that while we were still as fearful as ever men are when they face death – still, we were confident. When Eurybiades signalled for us to row backwards, we did. Our centre stretched away first, and gaps opened. But we righted ourselves, and our whole fleet coasted back, and back, into the narrowing channel, forcing the overweighted ends of the enemy crescent to compact on the centre.

I had Phoenicians opposite me – the right of their line. Lucky Plataea, we always face the very best the enemy has to offer. The flanking squadron was second-rate ships – some Lydians and some Carians – and they began to foul the Phoenicians. The coast of Thessaly was getting closer and closer, and it was not beached, but steep, rocky and still dangerous, like an animal gnashing its teeth from the remnants of the swell.

The Carians were good seamen, but the Lydians were not, and they flinched away from the surf and fouled the line.

I could no longer see the other end of our line in the haze. The sun was almost directly overhead, and I was hot, very tired and a little fevered.

But I knew what was coming next, and with the calm acceptance of the fatalist – not my usual role – I could see a certain ship.

I turned to Brasidas and Hermogenes. 'See the dirty red and white ship?' I said.

Pericles, my acting hypaspist, was laying my armour out on the deck. I had a new bandage on my hand and I felt light headed and prickly, but so did every man on the deck.

You can only face the fire so many days in a row, friends.

Pericles got the thorakes around my body and Brasidas closed it with pins.

'When I give the word, go for that ship,' I said.

'So we're going to attack,' Hermogenes said.

I nodded.

He sighed. 'I really want to be old,' he said. 'I have a good life and a good place. But ...' he smiled so sweetly '... I owe it to you. So if this is the price ...' he shrugged '... red and white it is.'

I went around the deck, informing men and shaking hands.

Brasidas turned and waved. 'Signal!' he called.

★

I'd really like to leave this tale here.

But the gods love tragedy, and we'll play this one to the end.

I saw the three flashes.

So, of course, did the enemy.

It was our last ruse. It didn't wreck any ships, but it bought us another hour, as we backed water again, and the Great King's fleet suddenly closed up on the centre to repel our attack. We backed water. They collided and lost spacing – six hundred hulls scattered over forty stades of water. Ships lost oars and fell away behind.

We fed our oarsmen water and some honeyed sesame seeds and garlic sausage.

Again, Eurybiades' ship flashed once.

'Signal!' Brasidas called.

This time, I pulled down my cheek pieces.

This time, men loosed their swords in scabbards and checked their spearheads one more time. Oarsmen spat on their hands.

Aft of me, an old salt looked at the man on the cushion on the other side and winked.

They both grinned.

Men shook hands.

'Ready!' I called. I looked at Hermogenes.

'Red and white,' he said. 'I have him.'

Eurybiades flashed his bronze aspis three times.

We attacked. Let the world remember that when we were outnumbered two to one, we attacked. We waited until the sun was in the west – in their eyes. We tired their rowers all day.

And then we turned like the desperate dogs we were, and went for their throats.

Who knows whether Dagon knew me. He should have known *Lydia*, but it is possible that my fixation on him was not returned.

Bah – I doubt it.

Lydia had the best, fittest rowers, and we leaped ahead of our line and went for the enemy line like an arrow from a string. Nor was the red and white trireme directly opposite us, but a little closer to the enemy centre, so that we ran a little south of east as we started our ramming attack.

You wouldn't think we could have surprised them again. But we'd been retreating for three hours, and we hadn't offered any fight, and then, suddenly ...

The Phoenicians were up to it. Their ships went to ramming speed so fast that their oars beat a froth as if the sea were boiling. And their big ships were fast.

'Show ram,' I said quietly to Hermogenes. 'But go for the oar rake, not the ram. We won't board. We'll sheer off and go through.'

Dagon must have expected me to go for him. To go for the epic fight, the head-to-head ram, the boarding action.

He never had good oarsmen, though, because he ruined his slaves. And I *wanted* that to tell against him. This was not my revenge. This was the revenge of the gods.

A hundred paces out, I saw him and my body moved like a lute string. I *knew* him and, at some level, my body feared him. No man had ever hurt me so. No man had ever made me feel so weak.

But I had planned this moment for a month, and I would not be tempted.

Fifty paces from his ship, Hermogenes suddenly veered hard to the right, and our oarsmen pivoted us brilliantly – right, left, out of the other ship's line completely like a good swordsman. We lost a great deal of speed, but we weren't ramming his ship.

We rammed her oars, and of course his poor slaves and downtrodden thugs couldn't get their sticks in the ports in time. We went by in an orgy of arrow shafts.

I stood by Ka, pointing to Dagon. 'Don't kill him,' I said.

His marines threw grapples, and my men cut them, and we were by, leaving a shambles and blood running over the red and the white, and then our speed picked up as my rowers put their backs into it. Nicolas was shouting, praising them, begging for more speed.

There was a Phrygian pentekonter under Dagon's stern, and he tried to turn, and we went right over him – pressed his whole ship right under the waves. That's why small ships cannot stand in the line of battle.

And just clear of the drowned Phrygian was a Lydian from the reserve squadron in a heavy trireme. He was too close to the first line to do anything to help.

I was with Ka. Hermogenes made the call, and we went ram to ram with the Lydian. He was moving at the pace a man might walk, and we, by then, were a little faster than a cantering horse, and our ram struck somewhere on his bronze.

The bow of the Lydian caved in like a broken nose in a fight, and suddenly we were deep in the enemy fleet and *our ram was stuck.*

'Reverse your cushions!' Nicolas screamed.

Already, our stern was starting to rise. The timbers groaned as the strain of a sinking galley fell on the backbone – the keel.

I thought of Vasileos, thousands of stades away, and all the love and work he'd lavished on this ship.

The first oars bit the water.

Dagon's ship was turning, now. I could see him on the stern, pointing at us.

I could see my ship beginning to torque. I could see deck planks springing out as the immense force of the sinking ship came to bear on the bow and the stern rose another hand's width from the water. The Lydian was sinking with all hands.

I spread my hands to the gods and roared, 'Poseidon!'

The ram seemed to explode straight up out of the enemy galley. All the timbers in her cat-head gave at once, and the marine box on the Lydian flew into the air, and my beautiful *Lydia* righted herself, slapped the water and rocked like a child's toy in a tub of water.

In a big battle, the trierarch has to make ten decisions every heartbeat. I looked aft, where Dagon was turning – my prey, but too far. To my right, towards the centre, a dozen triremes were turning towards me. To my immediate left, Sekla's *Machaira* and the capture *Huntress* burst out of the Phrygian squadron's rear. Even as I watched, a Lydian struck *Huntress* amidships and splintered oars, and Sekla put *Machaira* into the Lydian's side – this in ten heartbeats.

I pointed with my spear at the enemy centre. 'Starboard,' I said.

Nicolas had the port side reverse benches so that we turned in ten paces, and as the turn started, the starboard-side rowers picked up their cushions and turned, so that, as we faced south into the enemy centre, all our rowers were again facing aft, and rowing forward – and the stroke never faltered.

I could tell you stories of the next hour, but they would be lies.

Twice, I was able to rest my rowers. Once, after we were boarded from three ships – Aegyptians, with their fine marines, and I was only saved when Harpagos slew the biggest ship and put his marines into the rear of the men on my deck.

We just lay on our oars or knelt on the deck in the blood of our enemies and breathed.

And the second time was later, when we saw Eurybiades oar bank to oar bank with a ship that appeared to be made of gold – one of the Ionian tyrants. The Spartan thought the man must be the navarch of navarchs and went for him. I led my son on to the enemy deck, boarding on their undefended side, and ran for the back of the enemy marine line.

Two strides from the enemy, my chosen prey turned.

I slipped in the entrails of a dead man, and before I could recover my balance, a dying Spartan, taking me for the enemy, grabbed at my ankle, and down I went.

Hipponax stood over me. He thrust, he cut, he jumped on his wounded leg and danced like a flute girl – and men died.

I got a spear in my crest that wrenched my neck, but I stumbled to my feet, and watched my son kill.

And then, when he made a mistake, I reached over his shoulder and put my spear in a man's eyeholes, and put a hand on his shoulder, and Eurybiades came and smiled at us.

We were almost in the centre of the line.

That time, we rested, watching the battle and helping no one, for almost as long as the oration of a dull man.

In that time, I saw Dagon's ship.

He'd moved rowers about, put oars in empty oarlocks, and he was creeping away. He was not alone – wounded ships on both sides were leaving the fight.

I had had ten minutes to watch. There were huge holes in the allied fleet.

But again, the Great King's fleet had had the worst of it, and was retreating, and Eurybiades and Themistocles were on them – the Peloponnesians and the Athenians and the Aeginians found their second wind, and I limped down the length of my ship to where Hermogenes stood with an arrow in his bicep.

'You have to take the oars,' he said.

Brasidas got him free of the leather harness.

I was back to being a helmsman. My helmet burned my brow, my plume hurt my head every time the wind caught it, my armour weighed like the world on the shoulders of Atlas, my hips had developed a strange new pain and I had a wound somehow *under* my right greave, which was cutting a bloody groove in the top of my foot.

I was better off than many.

'Friends!' I roared. Perhaps I squeaked it, but it was loud in my ears. 'The day is ours. Now – we can rest on our oars, or we can go and help the Athenians finish the Great King's fleet.'

One of the old salts laughed. 'Easy, mate – I'll rest here.'

Other men laughed, too.

'By Poseidon!' I roared, with a little of my old battle lust. 'Then help me get my revenge!'

The old man cackled and flexed his muscles, and in that moment he was like Poseidon himself – old and solid.

'Revenge, is it?' he said. He cracked his hands, spat on his palms, and took his oar.

Men around him shook themselves as if they were coming awake.

Men understand revenge. It is easier than patriotism or love or strategy or tactics or even the rough world of consequence.

And revenge is a universal language.

I left the oars to walk the deck. 'Most of you know I was a slave,' I said. 'The man who made me a slave and tried to break my body lies yonder, and there is nothing between me and him but five stades of water.'

Maybe I should make more speeches.

I got between the steering oars and aimed us astern of Dagon's ship.

And now I had the bit in my teeth.

We passed another Phoenician, wallowing with a bank of dead oarsmen. Easy pickings, and we passed her by. And a Carian full of men who had probably once been my allies – they could scarcely row, and we passed them hand over fist, because of revenge. My oarsmen were heroes, the very Argonauts themselves, and we swept east, the sun under our quarter. I had time to drink some water, to pour more over the wound under my greave, time to take my son's greave strap – his wound had opened. Greave straps are padded rolls of leather you wear on your ankles – fashionable Athenian boys wear them to parties now.

I walked forward, feeling better. Like a man who had fought hand to hand every day for four days. I spared a thought for the allied army, who would be fighting the Persians again in rotation.

Well, we hadn't lost. Again. Even as I turned my head, the Ionians in the centre gave in and bolted, and suddenly the Great King's fleet was running for their beaches.

Only as we closed on Dagon did it strike me that we had won.

But I was not done.

Dagon's ship ran.

We ate her lead. Three stades, then two, then one. Ka and his men were shooting into the wind, but Dagon had no archers at all.

A hundred paces from Dagon's stern, I made them stop shooting. I turned to Brasidas.

'This thing is mine,' I said. 'Do not touch him.'

He shrugged and looked pained. In truth, he was too great a man to understand why I needed to kill one opponent, much less one already beaten. But he nodded.

'And if you fall?' he asked.

'See to my son,' I said. 'Oh, and kill the bastard. He has it coming.'

'Why not let me kill him now, then?' asked Ka.

Hector stood at my shoulder. He smiled.

Hipponax said, 'I want to come,' and we all said 'no' together, and then – then our marine box started to come alongside his helm station.

Ka leaned out and killed the helmsman. Just like that.

Dagon's ship yawed, and we slammed into its side. I fell flat – not ready for the collision – and so did Brasidas.

'Don't kill any more oarsmen,' I said. I got to my feet, put my right foot on our gunwale, and had a moment of sheer fear.

Of Dagon.

Of the leap.

Of old age, and being diminished.

And then I jumped.

Once, I had faced Dagon naked, and another time, with a bucket.

Now, I finally faced him on a steady deck, with a spear and an aspis.

Brasidas landed on the deck behind me, and Hector, and Siberios.

'Ready, Dagon?' I asked.

He was a big man, and his thighs were like a bull's, and his arms were as big as my thighs. His spear was red, and he didn't grunt when he threw it.

He was right behind it, his sword emerging from his scabbard . . .

I threw. He hadn't expected it, and my throw caught him where the crest meets the helmet, and snapped his head back.

I drew, the underhand cut the Spartans had taught me – and I cut to the right, inside his shield, and scored on his naked arm inside his aspis – and I stepped to the left, pivoted, and slammed my aspis at him.

No matter how strong you are, you cannot block an aspis with a sword.

He put his head down, so my following cut – pivoting and stepping

367

again, as Polymarchos taught – didn't kill him, but went into his crest, and half of it fell to the deck, and he shouted and got a cut on my left thigh.

I pushed my right hand home. Herakles, he was strong. But my feet were planted and my footing was good, and my sword was against his helmet, pushing.

He rolled and cut at my feet from behind.

I slammed my aspis into his sword. He rolled from under the blow and got to his feet.

I dropped my aspis. He was bleeding then.

'You!' he said. 'Come and take what I have for you.'

His mad eyes showed no defeat.

His right hand dropped the shards of his broken sword and I could see white where he tried to flex his left.

He attacked me, arms reaching for me despite what must have been blinding pain, and I did what I had wanted from the first. I stepped through his arms, locked his right with my left, the high lock of pankration, and he screamed as I broke his arm – I didn't pause or hesitate, I had done this a hundred times in my sleep, and I pushed my left leg deep behind him and threw him over it – over my leg, over the rail, and into the three decks of slave oarsmen below.

He was alive when he left my hands.

They tore him apart. I would have, if I'd ever had a chance like that.

Then I fell to my knees.

Behind me, Brasidas snapped, 'Boy! Take the helm!'

For a moment, like Miltiades after Marathon, I was out of my body, but Brasidas brought me back.

Many of my old shipmates have asked me whether I killed Dagon, and I am proud to say – no. I merely took him where he could die the way he deserved.

We lost eighty ships on the fourth day of Artemesium. We lost Gelon. We lost Paramanos – swarmed by Aegyptians when I was far away. Cimon lost a son and two cousins and every Plataean lost someone.

Athens lost forty ships.

Aegina lost twenty ships.

We stood on the beach with our captures and our wounded – Hermogenes, white from blood loss, and Sekla, who had an arrow though his foot and a cut across his head, and Giannis, who lost his left hand to a Phrygian axe that went through his aspis.

It was not a victory to celebrate.

Eurybiades gathered the fit trierarchs, and there were about a hundred, and that included a lot of men with bloody rags, like me.

Themistocles looked like a man going to a funeral.

I put a hand on his shoulder. 'We did not lose,' I said.

He turned, and the orator was crying.

Eurybiades stood alone. He was not crying, but his face was closed. He was elsewhere.

I thought perhaps they were in battle shock. So did Cimon. He put a hand on Themistocles' shoulder as I had. 'We are a trifle singed,' he said. 'But the Great King's fleet will not come off their beaches tomorrow. Listen – Arimnestos and I can put to sea ...'

I was going to glare at him, but then I saw Abronichus standing with Phrynicus, and both of them were weeping openly.

I assumed that meant Aeschylus was dead, or some other worthy man, and indeed, as I watched, another Athenian, Lycomedes, pulled his chlamys over his head to hide his tears.

Tired men weep easily.

Eurybiades shook himself like an old dog. 'We must ... retreat,' he said.

Cimon was looking at Lycomedes, as flustered as I was. 'Retreat? We *won*. We lost good men – *great men* – today, so that we would break them and we broke them! Now we must finish the job—'

'Peace,' Themistocles said. 'Be silent, Cimon. We have no choice.'

'No choice?' Cimon asked.

Eurybiades sighed. 'As dawn broke this morning, the Persians seized a pass above Thermopylae,' he said, like a man reporting on a race at the Olympics he had once seen. 'King Leonidas sent the allied army away. Then, with all the Thespians, he formed his phalanx.'

No one moved, or spoke, or groaned. The wind itself stopped.

'The king died this morning. His body was lost twice, and eventually regained.' He shook himself again. 'About the time we engaged the enemy today, the last men died. Thermopylae has fallen.'

I can't remember anything more of that hour except the desolation.

Leonidas was dead. The army was destroyed.

We had fought for four days, for nothing.

We had lost.

Epilogue

No – I'll leave you there. You know what happens next. But it is always darkest before the dawn, and that night, with King Leonidas dead across the straits, his corpse defiled by King Xerxes in a fury of unmanly pettiness, every Greek thought the same.

But when next we meet, I'll tell you more – of Salamis, and Plataea. Of how I met the Great King one more time.

Of what we did, we men of Greece.

But tonight, drink to Leonidas of Sparta, who died for Greece – aye, and Antigonus of Thespiae and all his men, who died with the Spartans. And all the men – Corinthians and Plataeans and Athenians and Aeginians and Spartans and Hermionians and Tegeans and every other man of Greece who fell into Poseidon's waters off Artemesium, fighting for Hellas.

Here is to their shades!

Historical Afterword

As closely as possible, this novel follows the road of history. But history – especially Archaic Greek history – can be more like a track in the forest than a road with a kerb. I have attempted to make sense of Herodotus and his curiously modern tale of nation states, betrayal, terrorism and heroism. I have read most of the secondary sources, and I have found most of them wanting.

But when I come to tell the story of Artemesium and Thermopylae – one virtually unknown to modern readers, and the other perhaps the most famous military event in Classical history – I find that I am locked in a curious dance with supposition, myth, and popular imagination. This book is, I hope, about cultures; about what it meant to be Greek, but also about the differences that divided Greeks. It has my take on Sparta, and I offer no apology for my less than idealized view of that state. Stripped of propaganda, Sparta was not the epitome of military perfection that modern fascists and poor Thucydides imagined. Nor was Athens effeminate or over-full of philosophy, especially in the Persian Wars. I hope that I have done justice to Sparta and her true greatness, and to Leonidas and Gorgo.

Perhaps most complicated of all, I wanted to give the reader an idea of what Persia was like, and what their empire had that was good. It is too easy to play the 'Boy's Own' genre trick of demonizing one race or nation to create orc-like opponents for the hero, but the world has never worked like that; no nation is actually braver or better, unless they work endlessly to accomplish such a thing, and if any nation of the period could be said to have a superb professional army, it was not Sparta, it was Persia.

Most of the bones of my story are taken, as usual, from Herodotus, and from him I hope I have made a convincing set of interwoven plots. I confess that I have no idea if the Greeks used pan-hellenic celebrations like the Olympics as meeting points to debate the coming war, but I've always loved the Olympic Games, ancient and modern, and while watching the games in London, I decided that my book would open with a section on the games at Olympia. I tried to be accurate, but I find that there is as much to know about the ancient Olympics – as and much controversy! – as about trireme tactics, and I doubt I will have pleased every critic.

I'd also like to say a bit on the role of women in the Olympics and indeed in every walk of life in the ancient world. I have tried to use Jocasta and Gorgo to illuminate some very deep divides in Spartan and Athenian attitudes to women. Women were not 'equal' to men in any ancient society and to make them so would be to write anachronism. Yet some women achieved very real power, and current research (*Portrait of a Priestess* by Joan Breton Connelly is especially good) suggests that women were not as thoroughly segregated from public and private life as we were led to imagine – by prudish and misogynistic Victorian historians. I'll add to that a short rant on my favourite subject as an historian – that there is no 'period' called 'Ancient Greece.' Ancient Greek culture was *at least* as malleable and fast-moving as modern culture. In every way from cultural artefacts like military technology to fashion, women's empowerment, and views of homosexuality, the Greek world *changed*. I mention this because even if we believe Roman descriptions of the exclusion of women from the Olympics, they appear to date to the fourth century – a very different time from the period I'm describing.

I pride myself on research and, for want of a better phrase, 'keeping it real.' I spend an inordinate amount of time wearing various historical kits in all weathers – not just armoured like a taxiarch, but sometimes working like a slave. If there is a subject as complex as the Olympics in the ancient world, it would be the ancient mariner. So I wish to hasten to say that I have rowed a heavy boat (sixteen oars) in all weathers; I have sailed, but not as much or as widely as I would like; I have been in all the waters I discuss, but often on the deck of a US Navy warship and not, I fear, in a pentekonter or a trireme. Because of this, I have relied – sometimes heavily – on the words of ancient sailors and their excellent modern reenactors, like Captain Severin and a dozen other authors from the last two centuries. I am deeply indebted to him, to a dozen sailors I'm lucky enough to count as friends, and to the Hakluyt Society, of which I'm now a member. All errors are mine, and any feeling of realism or accuracy in my nautical 'bits' belongs to their efforts. I have at times deliberately used the anachronistic English words of Falconer's Maritime Dictionary (about 1800) because the constant use of Greek nautical terms is, in my opinion, too much of a struggle for the reader's enjoyment.

I also have to note that while working on this book, I am working with friends in Greece to create the re-enactment of the 2505th anniversary of the Battle of Marathon. We hope to double our attendance from the last time, the 2500th. You can find the pictures on our website at www.amphictyonia.org and you really should. It was a deeply moving experience for me, and what I learned there – because every reenactor brings a new dose of expertise and amazing kit – has affected this book and will affect the rest of the series. I have now worn Greek armour for three solid days. Fought in a phalanx that looked like a phalanx. You'll spot the changes in the text. I wish to offer my deep thanks to every reenactor who attended, and all the groups in the Amphictyonia. I literally couldn't write these books without you.

And, of course, if, as you read this, you burn to pick up a xiphos and an aspis – or a bow and a sparabara! Go to the website, find your local group, and join. Or find me on my website or on facebook. We're always recruiting.

I'll close with a return to the politics of the day and the writing of fiction. Neither the Phoenicians nor the Persians were 'bad'. The Greeks were not 'good'. But Arimnestos is a product of his own world, and he would sound curious if he didn't suffer from some of the prejudices and envies we see in his contemporaries.

At the risk of repeating what I said in the afterwords to *Marathon* and *Poseidon's Spear* – the complex webs of human politics that ruled the tin trade and Carthage's attempts to monopolize it – the fledgling efforts of Persia (perhaps?) to win allies in the far west to allow them to defeat the Greeks on multiple fronts – these are modern notions, and yet, to the helmsmen and ship owners of Athens and Tyre and Carthage and Syracuse, these ideas of strategy must have been as obvious as they are to armchair strategists today. Sparta and Athens must have tried for peace – Herodotus suggests it. Some part of the war must have been about trade – again, Herodotus suggests it. If my novels have a particular *point* it is that the past wasn't simple. In Tyre and Athens, at least, the leading pirates were also the leading political decision makers.

In the last two books, I've said that *'it is all in the Iliad.'* I have enormous respect for the modern works of many historians, classical and modern. But they weren't there. Homer and his associates – they were there.

I have seen war at sea– never the war of the oar and ram, but war. And when I read the *Iliad* and the *Odyssey*, they cross the millennia and feel *true*. Not, perhaps, true about Troy. Or Harpies. But true about *war*. Homer did not love war. Achilles is not the best man in the *Iliad*. War is ugly.

Arimnestos of Plataea was a real man. I hope that I've done him justice.

Acknowledgements

On the first of April, 1990, I was in the back right seat of an S-3b Viking, flying a routine anti-submarine warfare flight off the USS Dwight D. Eisenhower. But we were not just anywhere. We were off the coast of Turkey, and in one flight we passed Troy, or rather, Hisarlik, Anatolia. Later that afternoon, we passed down the coast of Lesbos and all along the coast of what Herodotus thought of as Asia. Back in my stateroom, on the top bunk (my bunk, as the most junior officer) was an open copy of the *Iliad*.

I will never forget that day, because there's a picture on my wall of the *Sovremennyy* class destroyer *Okrylennyy* broadside on to the mock harpoon missile I fired on her from well over the horizon using our superb ISAR radar. Of course there was no Homeric deed of arms – the Cold War was dying, or even dead – but there was professional triumph in that hour and the photo of the ship, framed against the distant haze of the same coastline where Mykale and Troy were fought, will decorate my walls until my shade goes down to the underworld.

About the same time – perhaps a few months before, or a few months after – I read Steven Pressfield's superb work *Gates of Fire* which remains, for me, the finest military novel of the Classical World in English. And it is with unaccustomed (you're supposed to chuckle) humility that I set myself to cover the same ground. But from the inception of this idea as a serious book series, I knew that the Plataeans had not been at the Gates of Fire, but rather had been manning Athenian ships. And that idea fired me to research the Battle of Artemesium. And the more I read, the more I was convinced that it was at Artemesium and not at Thermopylae that the real battle happened.

★

The Great King is a different book and I am perhaps a humbler man than when I wrote *Killer of Men*. First, I owe many different debts of gratitude to others for this book; to the Iranian men and women who run a local café and who have been tireless in their willingness to fetch me pictures of monuments, translate passages, and provide quips and quotes in Farsi. Without the folks at R Squared in Toronto, my Persians would be much more wooden!

First and foremost, I have to acknowledge the contribution of Nicolas Cioran, who cheerfully discussed Plataea's odd status every day as we worked out in a gymnasium, and sometimes fought sword to sword. My trainer and constant sparring partner John Beck deserves my thanks – both for a vastly improved physique, and for helping give me a sense of what real training for a life of violence might have been like in the ancient world. And my partner in the re-invention of Ancient Greek xiphos fighting, Aurora Simmons, deserves at least equal thanks, as well as Chris Duffy, perhaps the best modern martial artist I know..

Among professional historians, I was assisted by Paul McDonnell-Staff and Paul Bardunias, by the entire brother and sisterhood of 'Roman Army talk' and the web community there, and by the staff of the *Royal Ontario Museum* (who possess and cheerfully shared the only surviving helmet attributable to the Battle of Marathon) as well as the staff of the *Antikenmuseum Basel und Sammlung Ludwig* who possess the best preserved ancient aspis and provided me with superb photos to use in recreating it. I also received help from the library staff of the University of Toronto, where, when I'm rich enough, I'm a student, and from Toronto's superb Metro Reference Library. I must add to that the University of Rochester Library (my alma mater) and the Art Gallery of Ontario. Every novelist needs to live in a city where universal access to JSTOR is free and on his library card. Finally, the staff of the Walters Art Gallery in Baltimore, Maryland – just across the street from my mother's former apartment, conveniently – were cheerful and helpful, even when I came back to look at the same helmet for the sixth time.

Excellent as professional historians are – and my version of the Persian Wars owes a great deal to many of them, not least Hans Van Wees and Victor Davis Hanson – my greatest praise and thanks have to go to the amateur historians we call reenactors. Giannis Kadoglou of Thessoloniki volunteered to spend two full days driving around the Greek countryside, from Athens to Plataea and back, charming my five-year-old daughter and my wife while translating everything in sight and being as delighted with the ancient town of Plataea as I was myself. I met him on Roman Army talk, and this would be a very different book without his passion for the subject and relentless desire to correct my errors. He and I are now fast friends and I suspect my views on much of the Greek world reflect his views more than any other. Alongside Giannis go my other Greek friends, especially George Kafetsis and his partner Xsenia, who have theorized over wine, beer and ouzo, paced battlefields and shot bows.

But Giannis is hardly alone, and there is – literally – a phalanx of Greek reenactors who helped me. Here in my part of North America, we have a group called the Plataeans – this is, trust me, not a coincidence – and we work hard on recreating the very time period and city-state so prominent in these books, from weapons, armor, and combat to cooking, crafts, and dance. If the reader feels that these books put flesh and blood on the bare bone of history – in as much as I've succeeded in doing that – it is due to the efforts of the men and women who reenact with me and show me every time we're together all the things I haven't thought of – who do their own research, their own kit-building, and their own training. Thanks to all of you, Plataeans. And to all the other Ancient Greek reenactors who helped me find things, make things, or build things. I'd like to mention (especially) Craig and his partner Cherilyn at Manning Imperial in Australia.

Thanks are also due to the people of Lesvos and Athens and Plataea – I can't name all of you, but I was entertained, informed, and supported constantly in three trips to Greece, and the person who I can name is Aliki Hamosfakidou of Dolphin Hellas Travel for her care, interest, and support through many hundreds of emails and some meetings.

Bill Massey, my editor at Orion, has done his usual excellent job and it is a better book for his work. Oh, and he found a lot of other errors, too, but let's not mention them. I have had a few editors. Working with Bill is wonderful. Come on, authors – how many of you get to say that?

My agent, Shelley Power, contributed more directly to this book than to any other – first, as an agent, in all the usual ways, and then later, coming to Greece and taking part in all of the excitement of seeing Lesbos and Athens and taking us to Archaeon Gefsis, a restaurant that attempts to take the customer back to the ancient world.

And then helping to plan and run the 2500th Battle of Marathon, and continuing as a reenactor of Ancient Greece. Thanks for everything, Shelley, and the agenting not the least!

Christine Szego and the staff and management of my local bookstore, Bakka-Phoenix of Toronto also deserve my thanks, as I tend to walk in and spout fifteen minutes worth of plot, character, dialogue, or just news – writing can be lonely work, and it is good to have people to talk to. And they throw a great book launch.

It is odd, isn't it, that authors always save their families for last? Really, it's the done thing. So I'll do it, too, even though my wife should get mentioned at every stage – after all, she's a reenactor, too, she had useful observations on all kinds of things we both read (Athenian textiles is what really comes to mind, though) and in addition, more than even Ms. Szego, Sarah has to listen to the endless enthusiasms I develop about history while writing (the words 'Did you know' probably cause her more horror than anything else you can think of.) My daughter, Beatrice, is also a reenactor, and her ability to portray the life of a real child is amazing. My father, Kenneth Cameron, taught me most of what I know about writing, and continues to provide excellent advice – and to listen to my complaints about the process which may be the greater service.

Having said all that, it's hard to say what exactly I can lay claim to, if you like this book. I had a great deal of help, and I appreciate it. Thanks. And when you find mis-spelled words, sailing directions reversed, and historical errors – why, then you'll know that I, too, had something to add. Because all the errors are solely mine.

Toronto, March, 2013

About the Author

Christian Cameron is a writer and military historian. He is a veteran of the United States Navy, where he served as both an aviator and an intelligence officer. He lives in Toronto where he is currently writing his next novel while working on a Masters in Classics.